He came awake and sat bolt upright. Schroeder was in his mind.

Richard, this is it. I can no longer hold it in. Too weak. What you have known is nothing to what you will know now. I am sorry. Damn these doctors. I thought they were mine, but . . . they have ethics. They will not kill me. And – God help me – I don't know what it will be like in the other place, and I fear it!

Then –

A blinding light in Garrison's mind, an incredible agony in his body. His entire being disrupted by pain!

He tried to cry out but could not. Pain froze the cry in his throat, turned it to a gurgle. He fought to draw air, and his expanding lungs seemed to crush organs already burning in their own hell. His body contorted, twisted, his guts seeming to knot inside him . . .

By the same author

BRIAN LUMLEY

Psychomech

Grafton
An Imprint of HarperCollins*Publishers*

Grafton
An Imprint of HarperCollins*Publishers*
77–85 Fulham Palace Road,
Hammersmith, London W6 8JB

A Grafton Original 1984
9 8 7 6 5 4 3

ISBN 0 586 05787 0

Set in Times

Printed in Great Britain by
HarperCollinsManufacturing Glasgow

This one is for Francesco Cova,
Garrison's Godfather

Prologue

Dark-haired, long-limbed, naked except for a towel wrapped about his middle, Garrison lay sleeping. It had been a hard day, one of many, and he had been exhausted. A couple of brandies with friends in the camp mess had finished him, put him down for what he had hoped would be a restful night. But to make absolutely sure he had also taken a hot shower. Towelling himself dry always wearied him, had a sort of soporific effect which usually blended easily into deep sleep. Tonight had been no exception, but—

—No sooner had he slept than the dream had been there, that same repetitive dream that had bothered him now for some three weeks, almost every night, and which he could never bring back to mind in the world of waking reality, except to say that it was a frightening thing which invariably left him drenched in his own perspiration, and that at its climax he would leap screaming awake. The dream involved a silver car, a black dog (or rather, a bitch), two men (one unseen), a beautiful girl (also unseen), a Machine and a man-God, in the reverse order of importance. And Garrison himself. That much he could always remember quite clearly, but the dream's finer details were always obscure. Except for the sure knowledge that it was a nightmare.

Of those details, forgotten in his waking moments:

He rode the Machine.

It was not a motorcycle, not any sort of vehicle one might imagine, but he rode it. He rode through valleys and over mountains and across oceans, through lands of weird vegetation and weirder, lizard-inhabited rock formations and over primal seas where Leviathan and all his cousins

7

sported and spouted. Behind him, seated upon her haunches with one great paw upon his shoulder, the bitch whined and panted and occasionally nuzzled his neck. She was worried for him. He understood her fear without knowing its source, as is often the way with dreams.

In his mind was the picture of a girl, one he knew intimately even though he had never seen her – which is also the way of dreams. He wanted to find her, save her, kill her – but he did not know where she was, what he must save her from (herself?), or why he must kill her. Indeed he prayed that perhaps he might not have to kill her, for he loved her.

Her face haunted him. It was a face he knew and yet had never seen; but if he closed his eyes she was there, misty in his memory, but with huge dark eyes, small scarlet mouth, flat ears and hair which he painted shiny black without ever having seen it. Or if he *had* seen her, then it had been in a dark room, or through curtains as a silhouette. Yes, he remembered that, the darkness. But his hands knew her!

His fingers remembered her. He had never seen her, but he had touched her. He remembered her body, its feel. His own body remembered it; and he ached with the thought that others – and one other in particular – also remembered her. And the ache turned to anger. Feeling his rage, the black bitch howled where she clung to his shoulder.

Garrison rode his Machine harder, towards distant crags where a lone figure stood beside a silver Mercedes impossibly perched upon a spike of rock. High over a mountain pass, the man and the car. Friends, both of them. The man was large, squat, naked, crewcut and blond, with small hard eyes. But he was a friend and he beckoned Garrison on, pointing the way.

The way to the black lake!

Garrison waved and rode the Machine through the pass, and the man and the car faded into distance behind him . . .

Beyond the mountains a forest of dead, skeletal trees

went down to a shore of pitch washed by a great black oily lake. And in the middle of the lake a black rock loomed, and built upon it a black castle glittered like faceted coal or jet.

Garrison would have flown straight on across the lake, but here the Machine balked. Something – some invisible thing – reached out from the black castle and touched the Machine. He could maintain control only if he drew back from the lake, the castle, the Black Room.

The Black Room!

Somewhere in that castle, a Black Room, and in that room the girl with the face he had never seen. And a man, a tall slender man with a voice that caressed, lulled, lied and cheated! And it was *his* Power that held off Garrison's Machine.

But the castle, the room, the girl, all of these things were the things Garrison sought. The end of his quest. For he suspected that Horror also lurked in the castle, and he had sworn to banish that horror forever. Even if it meant destroying the girl, the man, the Black Room and the very castle itself!

And yet still he prayed that he might somehow save the girl.

He turned the Machine, sent it rushing back over the roof of the bleached brittle forest, turned it again and hurled it at the lake. His mind powered the strange Machine, drove it like a bullet from a gun at the rock that loomed and leered in the oily lake – so that when the Machine came up against the Power from the castle and slammed to a halt, Garrison and the bitch were almost hurled from its glittering back.

How the Machine fought him then. He knew that it would throw him, trample him, kill him if it could. And it could! Except—

As the Machine fought to be rid of him, the man-God came. A face in the sky. Bald, domed head; eyes that loomed bright and huge behind lenses that magnified monstrously; an agonized, pleading voice that cried out to Garrison:

ACCEPT ME, RICHARD! LET ME IN. ACCEPT AND *WIN*!

9

'No!' he shook his head, afraid of the man-God no less than of what he might find in the Black Room. He gritted his teeth and battled with the Machine.

THEN YOU ARE DEAD! the man-God cried. BOTH OF US, DEAD. AND WHAT OF OUR BARGAIN, GARRISON? DON'T YOU REMEMBER? YOU CAN WIN, GARRISON, LIVE. WE BOTH CAN. BELIEVE ME, YOU DON'T WANT TO DIE. AFTER ALL, *I KNOW WHAT IT'S LIKE HERE*!

'*No!*' Garrison screamed.

A cube, small, brown, burning, came hurtling out of the sky from afar. It paused, spinning, between the desperate face of the man-God over the lake and Garrison where he fought the Machine.

The cube expanded, contracted, glowed hot as the heart of a sun – exploded!

White fire and heat and blast and searing agony—

Garrison's eyes!

—And coming awake with a strangled scream, to find an autumn sun shining damply through the drizzle on his windows. And the hands on his alarm clock standing at 6.30 A.M., the calendar telling him it was a Friday in September, 1972, and the nightmare receding.

He clutched at his mattress, damp with his sweat, licked dry lips and desperately tried to conjure the details of the dream. For one instant they stood out clearly in his mind and he could feel again the frantic bucking of the Machine, then swept away, rushing away into distances of mind, they were gone. And only the fading howl of a dog echoed back to him.

And with that howl ringing in his ears Garrison knew that he had dreamed again of a silver car, a black bitch, two men, a man-God, a beautiful girl – and a Machine.

And an unknown Horror.

The known horror was waiting for him in the city. Out in the corridor the night-duty Corporal was hammering out his own hideous version of reveille on an empty fire bucket ...

Chapter One

It was Belfast and the year was 1972, a Friday afternoon in late September.

Thomas Schroeder, German industrialist, sat at a small table in a barroom with a sawdust floor. A brass spittoon lay under the chipped mahogany footrail against the dully stained skirting of the bar. Blinds were drawn at the windows and a single naked electric light bulb high in the centre of the ceiling burned fitfully, its filament almost spent. Its dull gleam was twinned in Schroeder's spectacles.

Beside him, shuffling uncomfortably on a bolted-down wooden bench, sat his friend, his sometime secretary and his constant companion, Willy Koenig. Opposite them sat two other men whose faces were almost obscured beneath thick hair and unkempt beards. What little could be seen of their actual faces seemed largely blank, impassive. They had been speaking to Schroeder, these two Irishmen, in voices which, despite the soft lilt of a naturally roguish brogue, had been coarse and filled with terrible words.

Koenig's hands were nervous on the thick black briefcase that lay before him on the wooden table. An ugly tic jerked the flesh at the corner of his mouth. He sweated profusely, despite the coolness of the room. He had sweated from the moment he and his master had been met by these two alleged members of the IRA, sweated and crouched down into himself and made himself small when in reality he was a large man. By comparison, the tallest of the two seated opposite was only of medium height; but no one watching Koenig sweat and twitch would ever guess his real stature and massive strength.

Schroeder seemed as nervous as his aide, but he at least

was cool and appeared to be keeping a grip on himself. Small, balding and in his late fifties, he could be said to be a typically dapper German, but leaner and paler than might be expected. An additional twenty or thirty pounds of flesh and a cigar in the middle of his face might have turned him into the popular misconception of a successful German businessman, but he neither smoked nor ate to excess.

This was part of a determined effort to live to the fullest extent of his years, of which the best were already flown. He knew this, and also that the rest of his time would not be completely satisfactory; therefore it must be as good as he could make it. Which is one reason why the people he faced should have been more careful. They knew him for what he was now, not for what he had once been. But then, only Schroeder himself knew that. Schroeder and Willy Koenig.

For if the Germans were really the timid, badly frightened men they appeared to be, why had they come? This was a question the Irish terrorists had failed to ask themselves, or had not asked searchingly enough. Was it really to save Schroeder's wife? She was young and beautiful, true, but he was no longer a young man. Could he really love her? They should have seen that this was doubtful, these Irishmen. More likely she was a decoration, icing on Schroeder's cake. And indeed he had come for a different reason. There are some men you can threaten, and there are others you must *never* threaten . . .

Somewhere in a shady corner of the room an old clock ticked the time away monotonously; beyond the locked door, in a passage with leaded lights of red glass, whose outer door opened on the street, two more men talked in lowered tones that filtered into the barroom as mere murmurs.

'You said you wanted to talk to me,' said Schroeder. 'Well, we have talked. You said that my wife would be released, unharmed, if I came to you without informing the police. I have done all you asked. I came to you, we talked.'

His words were precise, perhaps too precise, and sharp with his German accent. 'Has my wife been released?'

Their beards were all that the Irishmen shared in common. Where one was dark-skinned, as if he had spent a lot of time in the sun, the other was pale as a mineshaft cricket. The first was thinner than Schroeder, narrow-hipped, tight-lipped. The second was small and round and smiled a lot, without sincerity, and his teeth were bad. The thin one was pimply, scarred with what might be acid burns across his nose and under his eyes. The scars were white against his tan. He looked into Schroeder's eyes, his gaze seeming to penetrate right through the thick lenses of the industrialist's spectacles. His thin lips opened a fraction:

'That's right, Mr Schroeder,' he softly said. 'Sure enough it is. Indeed it's been done. Your dear wife is free. We're men of our word, you see? She's back at your hotel this very minute, safe and sound. We only wanted to see you, talk to you. Not to harm your pretty Fraulein. Actually, we'd have let her go anyway, for she's nothing to us. But you must admit, she made a fair bit of cheese to bait our trap, eh?'

Schroeder said nothing but Koenig sat up straighter, his small eyes staring into the faces before him. 'Trap? Of what do you speak?'

'Just a manner of speaking,' said the fat man, smiling through his rotten teeth. 'Now calm down, calm down, Mr Koenig. Stay cool, like your boss here. If we'd wanted you dead you'd be dead now. And so would the Fraulein.'

'Frau,' corrected Koenig. 'Fraulein means girl. Frau is a wife.'

'Oh?' said the fat one. 'Is that right, now? And that lovely young German slut's actually married to our Mr Schroeder, is she? Not just a piece of buck-she cunt?'

Koenig looked as if he might respond but Schroeder silenced him with a glance, then turned his eyes back to the two terrorists. 'Men of your word,' he nodded, blinking rapidly. 'I see. Men of . . . of honour. Very well, if that is so will you let me speak to my wife?'

'Of course you can speak to her, sir, of course you can,' the small round one said, grinning. 'For we *are* men of our word, as you'll see. Sure we are.' The grin slipped from his face. 'A pity the same can't be said of you!'

'Herr Schroeder is completely honourable!' snapped Koenig, his blond eyebrows lowering in a frown, sweat rivering his red bull neck.

'Is he now?' said the thin one, nodding his head for a long time, his eyes unwavering where they stared at Koenig. 'Well, it appears you're a very loyal man, Mr Koenig. But do please remember, when we asked him to come alone he brought you with him – you crew cut Kraut sod!' Despite the invective, his tone remained dry and constant.

Willy Koenig half-rose, found his elbow locked in the grip of his employer's hand, sat down again. The sweat dripped even faster.

Schroeder said: 'Herr Koenig goes almost everywhere with me. I do not drive. Without him I could not come. Also, he is my secretary, occasionally my advisor. He advised me to come. That much at least you must thank him for.'

'Oh?' said the fat one, smiling again. 'And can we thank him for the briefcase, too – and what's in it?'

'The briefcase? Ah!—' It was Schroeder's turn to smile, however nervously. 'Well, you see, I thought it might be that you wanted money. In which case—'

'Ah!' they said together, their eyes falling on Koenig's briefcase. After a while they looked up.

'So it's full of money, is it?' said the smiling one. 'Well, that's very reassuring. But it's not just money we're after. See, it's this way. This factory you plan would employ a couple of thousand lads – Protestant lads, that is. It would create, you know – a sort of imbalance. A lot of money in Protestant pockets. Happiness in their black farting hearts.'

The thin one took it from there: 'We only want to restore

the balance, so to speak. I mean, after all's said and done, it is war that we're talking about, Herr Schroeder. Perhaps that's what you don't understand?'

'War?' Schroeder repeated. 'Oh, I understand some things about war. But still I cannot supply you with guns.'

'So you keep saying,' the thin one answered, his voice impatient now, the scar tissue on his cheeks and nose seeming to show that much whiter. 'But we could work something out. You have armaments interests in Germany. You could always give a nod in the right direction, or turn a blind eye on certain losses . . .'

'May I phone my wife now?' Schroeder asked.

The small fat man sighed. 'Oh, please do, please do.' He casually waved his hand at an antiquated pay-telephone on the wall beside the door.

As Schroeder got up and crossed the thinly scattered sawdust floor to the telephone, Koenig gripped the handle of his briefcase but did not pick it up. He remained seated, holding the briefcase on the table before him, the four stubby legs of its bottom pointed towards the two terrorists. One of them, the smiling one, turned to watch Schroeder through droopy eyes. The eyes of the taller, thinner man remained on Koenig, had narrowed slightly and seemed drawn to the awkward position of the German's hand where it gripped the handle of the briefcase.

Schroeder put money in the phone, dialled, waited, suddenly sighed a great sigh. His lungs might have been gathering air for an hour, which they now expelled. His immaculately cut suit seemed to crumple in on him as he uttered that great exhalation. 'Urmgard? Ist alles in ordnung?' he asked, and immediately sighed again. 'Und Heinrich? Gut! Nein, alles gehts gut bei uns. Jah, bis spater.' He blew a tiny, almost silent kiss into the telephone, replaced it in its cradle and turned to face across the room. 'Willy, horst du?'

Koenig nodded.

15

'Men of our word, you see?' said the thin, scarred terrorist, not taking his eyes from Koenig's face, which suddenly had stopped sweating. 'But you – you slimy Kraut dog! – you and your bloody brief—' His hand dipped down into his worn and creased jacket, fastening on something which bulged there.

Koenig turned the briefcase up on its end on the table, lining its bottom up vertically with the thin man's chest. '*Stop!*' he warned, and the tóne of his voice froze the other rigid. The four stubby black legs on the bottom of the case had added substance to Koenig's warning, popping open on tiny hinges to show the mouths of rifle barrels, four gaping, deadly mouths whose short throats disappeared into the body of the case. Those barrels were each at least 15mm in diameter, which might help explain Koenig's rigid grip on the case's handle. The recoil would be enormous.

'Put your gun on the table,' said Koenig. '*Now!*' It was not a command to be denied, not in any way. The thin man did as instructed. His eyes were wide now, his scars zombie white. 'Yours also,' said Koenig, swivelling the case just a fraction to point it at the fat man. The latter was no longer smiling as he took out his gun and put it down very slowly and deliberately.

'Most sensible,' said Schroeder, quietly coming back across the room. On his way he took out a handkerchief, stooped, folded the white square of linen over the rim of the spittoon and picked it up. He took up a half-pint glass of stale Guinness from the bar and poured it into the spittoon.

'You'll not get past the boys in the corridor, you know,' said the thin one harshly. 'Not this way.'

'Oh, we will,' said Koenig. 'But be sure that if we don't, you will not be here to enjoy our predicament.' He pocketed the thin man's gun, tossed the other across the room. Schroeder, carrying the spittoon, caught it in his free right hand. And now the Irishmen were aware of the metamorphosis taken place in the Germans.

Where they had been timid in their actions, now they were sure. Where they had seemed nervous, they were now cool as cubes of ice. Koenig's sweat had dried on him in a matter of moments. His eyes were small, cold and penetrating as he brushed back his short-cropped hair with a blunt hand. He had seemed to grow by at least four or five inches. 'Be very quiet,' he said, 'and I may let you live. If you are noisy or try to attract attention, then—' and he gave an indifferent shrug. 'One missile from the case would kill an elephant outright. Two for each of you and your own mothers – if you had mothers – would not know you.'

Schroeder, smiling through his thick lenses, his lips drawn back in the wide grin of a wolf, came up behind the two and said, 'Put your hands on the table.' Then, when they had obeyed: 'Now put your heads on your hands – and stay quite still.' He swirled the contents of the spittoon until they made a slopping sound.

'Gentlemen,' he finally continued, '—and may the good God, who to my eternal damnation surely exists, at least forgive me for calling you that, if not for my greater crimes – you have made a big mistake. Did you think I would come into this country, and having come here deliver myself into hands such as yours, without taking the greatest precaution? Herr Koenig here is that precaution, or a large part of it. His talent lies in thinking bad thoughts. Never good ones. In this way he has protected me personally for many years, since 1944. He is successful because he thinks his bad thoughts before others think them.' He poured the contents of the deep spittoon over their bowed heads.

The small fat man moaned but remained motionless. The thin one cursed and straightened up. Koenig had taken the man's weapon back out of his pocket. Now he reached over and jammed its barrel hard against his upper lip below his scarred nose. He pressed his hand forward and up until the muzzle of the gun rested squarely in the orbit of an expanded left nostril. The Irishman, because of the bench

17

which pressed against the back of his legs, could not move. He put up his hands before him and they were shaking.

Koenig told him, 'Herr Schroeder ordered you not to move – Paddy.' His accent was thicker now and full of a sort of lust. The terrorist believed he knew the sort, and his hands fluttered like trapped birds. He wished he had not called the Germans names. But then Koenig drew back the gun from his face a little and allowed him to relax. He put down his hands and started to sit, attempting a tight smile through the slop and stale spittle dripping down his face. Koenig had expected some sort of bravado, had planned and prepared for it, had thought his bad thoughts. He had decided to kill this Irishman, if only as a lesson to the other one – and it might as well be now.

He drove the gun forward again, his forearm rigid as a piston. The barrel sheared through lips, teeth and tongue, its foresight slicing along the roof of the Irishman's mouth. He gagged, jerked, reared up again, coughed blood, the barrel still in his mouth. If it had been possible, he would have screamed with the pain.

Koenig withdrew the barrel with a rapid, tearing motion, ripping the man's mouth. At the same time he released his briefcase and grabbed his victim's jacket, then struck him with the gun. Again and again and again. The blows were so fast and deadly that they seemed physically to slice the air; their whistle and *chop* could clearly be heard. The final blow, delivered while the man was still straining up and away, smashed his Adam's apple out of position and killed him. Down he went on to the bench, toppling, his nose torn, his right eye hanging by a thread.

The fat man had seen it all. He had dared to lift his head an inch or two from the table. Now, fainting, he fell back again into the slops. And all of this occurring so rapidly – and in a sort of vacuum, a well of near-silence – that only the blows had made noise.

Something of it had been heard, however – heard and

misunderstood – and a harsh snigger sounded from the corridor. Then the low murmurings continued.

Koenig moved from between bench and table, stooped and ripped the dead man's jacket open. He tore off his shirt and turned to the fat man, roughly towelling his head and face dry and clean before slapping him awake. When the man's eyes opened and his eyeballs rolled back into place Schroeder grabbed his beard and showed him his own gun.

'You are coming with us,' the industrialist told him. 'Oh, and incidentally – you may call me Colonel. Herr Koenig here was the youngest Feldwebel in my rather special corps. You have seen why he was promoted so very young. If you should foolishly attempt to raise an alarm, he will kill you – or I will. I'm sure you understand that, don't you?'

The fat man nodded. He might have been about to smile but at the last moment thought better of it. Instead his lips trembled like jelly. 'Control yourself,' said Schroeder. 'And act naturally. But please do *not* smile. Your teeth offend me. If you do smile I shall have Herr Koenig remove them.'

'*Do* you understand?' Koenig hissed, shoving his square face close and baring his own perfect teeth.

'Yes! Oh, yes, I surely do!' the IRA man cringed.

Koenig nodded. He seemed to shrink down into himself, making himself smaller. The effort forced sweat to his brow. His face began to work again, an insistent tic jerking the corner of his mouth. Schroeder also altered himself, becoming weary in a few moments. He allowed his hands to dangle by his sides as he shuffled to the door. The Irishman followed with Koenig close behind. Schroeder turned the key, stepped into the corridor with the two following on his heels. Koenig took the key, closed the door and locked it, gave the key to the Irishman who automatically pocketed it. If anyone should look into that room before those two Krauts were away, then he, Kevin Connery, was a dead man. And he knew it.

The two men in the corridor tipped their caps respectfully as the three passed them and went out of the second door into the street. It was evening now and an autumn sun was sinking over the hills. It turned the empty street a rich wine colour.

Another man, small as a monkey, sat at the wheel of a big Mercedes where it was parked. He toyed with the controls, making the windows hum up and down, up and down . . .

'Tell him to get out,' Schroeder said as he reached to open a rear door. 'You get in here, with me.'

Connery jerked his head, indicating that the monkey man should get out of the car. As the little man made to do so, Schroeder pushed Connery into the back seat and got in after him. He produced Connery's gun.

Koenig waited until the little man was half out of the car, then grabbed him in one hand and dragged him free. He spun him round, his feet off the ground, once, twice . . . and released him at the two men from the corridor where they now stood in the open door, their curiosity turning to astonishment. The monkey man smashed into them and all three were thrown back into the shadows. Then Koenig was in the driver's seat, gunning the motor, turning a corner on screaming tyres, accelerating down a deserted street. He spun the wheel, turned another corner. And so they were away.

'Well,' said the Colonel to the Irishman. 'We made it, you see? Now you will kindly give directions back to our hotel.' After a moment he added: 'Tell me, Irish, what's your name?'

'Connery, sir – er, Colonel!' said the other.

'Oh?' the Colonel smiled his thin smile. 'Like Sean? And is that how you see yourself? Vie null null sieben?'

'Pardon, sir?' the IRA man gulped as he felt the pressure of his own gun under his heart. He knew the damage it could do.

'As 007?' the Colonel repeated. 'As Mr James Bond?'

20

'Oh, no, sir. Not me. I just do as I'm told, so I do.'

'But it can be bloody work, eh, James?'

'It's Kevin, sir – I mean, Colonel. And actually—'

'Actually, Kevin, you're a damned Irish idiot for telling me your name. What if I pass it on to the police?'

'Oh, they know it well enough already, sir. And anyway, I'll be glad enough just to step down from this car alive.'

'A sensible attitude. But you were saying?'

'Eh? Oh, yes – actually, I'm really a sort of messenger boy. Of the two of us, young Michael is – er, was – the heavy . . .'

'Well, I have my own "heavies", as you see.'

'I do indeed, sir, Colonel. I do that. But I was only doing what I was told to—'

'Shut your fat Paddy face and be glad you are alive, Kevin Connery,' said the Colonel, all banter gone now from his voice. His face had been growing angry, was now white and quite deadly.

Connery could no longer control his trembling. 'I—' he started. And again: 'I—' He gulped, his eyes rolling wildly.

'Oh, I'll let you live,' said the Colonel, 'though I admit I'm not such a man of my word – a man of honour – as you.' His voice was full of scorn. 'So you're a messenger, are you? Very well, you can live to deliver my message. You can tell your superiors they have won. I will not build my factory here. Will that please them?'

'Oh, that it will, sir. Be sure of it. Er, Colonel.'

'But tell them it is not because of their threats, no. Not because of any pressures they might apply. You see, Kevin Connery, I have employed – I still occasionally employ – men who know what terrorism really means. No, you have won for one reason and one reason only. It is this: I would not employ men who breathe the same air as you, who sprang from the same soil, who have lived in the same land. Regardless of their religious or political beliefs, I would not give them work. I would not give them the time of day.'

21

'Sir,' Connery gulped as his own gun stabbed even harder through the fat covering his ribs. 'Colonel, I—'

'Tell your superiors everything I have said,' Schroeder cut him short. 'I am leaving Ireland tonight. Any of you who follow – anyone who attempts revenge on me outside Ireland – will not return to his beloved Emerald Isle. Make sure you tell them that, too.'

They were now deep into the 'safe' area of the city, driving slowly along a quiet street. Koenig stopped the car outside a grocery store. He got out and opened the rear door, dragging Connery out by his hair. The Irishman squealed like a pig and a few passers-by stared for a moment before hurriedly moving on. Koenig grabbed the fat man with both hands and whirled him around and around, as he had done with the monkey man. Finally he lifted and heaved in one movement, releasing the man like a stone from a sling. Connery screamed as he shot headlong through the grocery store window.

Then, before a crowd could gather – before a single voice could be raised in protest – the bulky man got back into the Mercedes and drove it away.

They were staying at the Europa Hotel and had been there through a week of negotiations. Negotiations which were now dead, finished. Urmgard had gone missing just three short hours ago. Then – the telephone call, the threats on her life, the demands. Her life would not have meant a great deal, but – there are some men you must never threaten. The Colonel had made certain demands of his own, which had been agreed; he had made one hurried telephone call to Hamburg; then he and Koenig had gone to meet the men who held his wife.

In their absence Gerda, the nanny, had cared for little Heinrich. She had been told to stay with the boy at the hotel through every moment that her master was away; and the rest of the world had not suspected anything was amiss.

Then there had been the arranged meeting on a certain road just outside the Catholic area; the bearded men getting into the back of the Mercedes and producing their guns; the tortuous route which must surely lose anyone not born to Belfast itself; and finally the destination, a pub in the Old Park district of the city.

But all of that was over now, finished with. Except—

As Koenig turned the big car into Great Victoria Street, so the Colonel sat up straighter in his back seat. No, it was not finished with. Just as the terrorists had underestimated him, so had the Colonel underestimated them. They were not all of the same breed.

Police barriers had been set up, blocking the road and cutting off the hotel. RUC men were everywhere, uniformed, flak-jacketed, SMGs at the ready. Military Policemen and Policewomen searched people on the street, their red hats like splashes of blood in the thin drizzle which now fell from skies turned suddenly sullen.

Koenig's window hummed down and he identified himself to an RUC constable at the barrier. Schroeder leaned forward and said: 'Was ist passiert? What is it? What's happened here?'

'Two men were caught coming out of the hotel, sir. They had guns and shot it out. One's dead and the other's dying. We're talking to him now.'

'Do you know who I am?' Schroeder asked.

'Oh, yes, sir. That I do.'

'I have to get through, get my wife and child out of there. They are in danger. That's who they were after, my wife and child!'

The constable seemed undecided. Schroeder reached out his hand and gave the man a roll of paper money. 'Now really, sir,' the constable stuttered, 'I can't accept—'

'Then give the money to someone who is not so foolish!' Koenig snapped the words directly into the constable's face. 'Only let us through!'

The RUC man checked to ensure no one had seen, stepped out of the way, removed the barrier and waved them through.

Koenig brought the car to a halt at the hotel entrance and the Colonel jumped out. A Military Policeman stood on the hotel steps with his back to the open doors. Inside, a second Redcap was visible, his narrowed eyes scanning the crowded lobby and missing nothing. Twenty yards down the road an ambulance wailed to a halt, its blue lights flashing. A crowd of uniformed RUC men parted and a stretcher was lifted, borne to the rear of the ambulance. The pavement was red with blood. Farther down the road a blanket had been thrown over a crumpled human figure. One foot, the shoe loose, protruded. There was blood there, too. A lot of it.

Schroeder and Koenig ran up the hotel steps and were confronted by the MP. He was very young, perhaps twenty, a Corporal. 'Sorry, sir,' he said, his voice sharp but not nervous. 'They're checking for bombs. You can't go in there.'

'Bombs?' Schroeder's voice climbed the scale. 'Bombs? My child is in there!' He made no mention of his wife.

'Don't worry, sir,' said the Corporal. 'They're starting to evacuate now, and—'

'You don't understand,' said Koenig, stepping forward. 'This gentleman is Herr Thomas Schroeder. Those bombs, if there are any, are meant for him – and for his family! And his wife will stay exactly where she is until he goes to collect her. We have to—'

'Hold it!' the Corporal snapped. 'And don't try to pressure me, friend. I'm just doing my job. Wait a second.' He looked along the street. 'Sergeant!' he yelled. 'Hey, Sarge – give us a second, can you?'

A landrover with Military Police plates and Makralon panels stood parked on the kerb, its blue light soundlessly whirling. The MP Sergeant crouched at its open door, speaking rapidly into the mouthpiece of a radio-telephone. He looked up as the Corporal shouted, spotted the group of three, nodded, finished his conversation and hurried over.

'What's up?' he asked, mounting the steps.

'Sarge, this is Thomas Schroeder,' said the Corporal. 'He thinks all this was for him. He has family in there.'

'Well, we can't help that, my old son,' the Sergeant answered. He looked nervous, his finger lay along the trigger-guard of his SMG. He turned to Schroeder. 'You see, sir—'

'I'll see you demoted to Private if you don't let me through!' Schroeder snarled. 'My baby—' He grabbed at the front of the Sergeant's flak-jacket.

'Sarge,' said the Corporal, staring hard at his superior. 'This is *the* Thomas Schroeder. Look, his wife isn't going to make a move until he goes in for her. I mean him, personally. Let me go with him, eh?'

The Sergeant bit his lip. He glanced at Schroeder, Koenig, back at the Corporal. There was sweat on his forehead under his cap. 'OK, go get them out – but make it snappy. It'll be my neck if anything goes wrong! Go on, move it – I'll get another man on the door here.' He put his fingers to his teeth and whistled, and a Military Police-woman came hurrying from the landrover.

'Thank you!' Schroeder gasped. And again: 'Thank you!' He turned to Koenig. 'Willy, you wait here. We'll send for the luggage later. It's not important.' He ran in through the doors with the Corporal close behind. 'Corporal,' he called back, 'what's your name?'

'Garrison, sir.'

'Garrison? A soldier's name.' He was panting, but not from any real exertion. Garrison guessed his talking was to hide his fear. Fear for his wife and child, not for himself. 'And your first name?'

'Richard, sir.'

'The Lionheart, eh? Well, Richard Garrison, you're a

25

sharp man and I like you for it.' He thumbed impatiently for the lift, then jammed his thumb tight down on the button until the doors hissed open and the cage ejected a crush of white-faced people. 'I'll see to it that your commanding officer hears about the help you gave me.'

'Thank you, sir, but I'd rather you didn't. He'd only charge me with endangering my own life, or some such. That's what's bothering the Sarge, see?'

Schroeder's eyes grew large behind his spectacles. 'Then they really do suspect a bomb?'

'They're searching the upper and lower floors now, sir. Working towards the middle.'

'The middle? My child is on the fifth floor!'

At the fifth they hurried from the lift into a corridor filled with people. A dozen of them immediately crammed themselves into the lift and its doors slid shut. 'My rooms are 504 through 508,' Schroeder said, pushing past hurrying people. 'My wife has 506. That's where she'll be – with Heinrich.'

In front of them the corridor had almost cleared of people. Only a few remained, all looking startled and asking what was happening. As they arrived at 506 the door burst open. Two wide-eyed youths, neither one of them more than eighteen years old, rushed out and collided with the Colonel. He was sent reeling – but not before they had recognized him.

'Who—?' Schroeder gasped, banging into the opposite wall of the corridor.

One of the youths whipped out a gun. The SMG in the Corporal's hands made a harsh *ch-ching* sound as Garrison slammed back the cocking piece, and in the next moment the weapon seemed to burst into a lethal life of its own. It bellowed a staccato message of death that blew the two youths away from the door of 506 and sent them spinning along a white wall which turned red where they touched it.

Then they fell, sprawling in the corridor and dying along with the SMG's booming echoes.

Garrison, down on one knee, had fired upward at them. Those rounds which had gone astray had spent themselves harmlessly in the ceiling. Cleared as if by magic, the corridor was almost empty now; only two elderly ladies remained, clutching at each other as they stumbled along the bloodied wall.

Then Garrison and Schroeder were inside 506, their eyes taking in the scene at a glance.

A toddler in a playsuit was crying, arms reaching, staggering like a mechanical toy across the floor of the room. A woman, young and beautiful, lay on the bed. She was gagged and bound, her eyes wide and pleading. An older woman lay stretched out on the floor, obstructing the toddler's progress. Her bun of dark hair was red with blood, as was the carpet where she lay. A parcel in the shape of a six-inch cube of brown paper sat on the dresser, emitting acrid smoke which curled upward in a deadly spiral. The paper of the upper side was turning crisp and black. A tiny flame appeared, reaching upward through the curling paper.

'*Bomb!*' yelled the Corporal. He grabbed the woman off the bed like a rag doll and tossed her into Schroeder's arms, knocking the industrialist back out into the corridor. Then he stepped over the unconscious or dead woman on the floor and snatched up the screaming child.

'Mein Kind! Mein Sohn!' Schroeder was back in the doorway, having dumped his wife in the corridor. He took a step inside the room.

'Out!' Garrison yelled. 'For Christ's sake, *out!*' He hurled the child across the room into his father's arms, made to dive for the door and tripped on the prone body of the nanny. Flying headlong across the room, he passed between the bomb and the doorway. And even willing

27

himself through the air, as he stretched himself out desperately towards the corridor, his eyes were on the burning parcel.

For this one had his number on it and he knew it. He knew – somehow *knew* – that it was going to explode.

Which, at that precise moment, it did.

Chapter Two

When Schroeder regained consciousness he was in a hospital bed, held together and kept alive by an amazing array of pipes and tubes, wires and stitches, instruments and mechanisms. Koenig was at his bedside. The man was seated, gauze-masked, his head bowed. Tears fell on to his hands which were crossed in his lap. Tears were not characteristic of Willy Koenig.

'Willy,' said Schroeder, his voice a whisper. 'Where am I?' He spoke in German.

Koenig looked up, his mouth opening, a light flickering into life behind the bloodshot orbs of his eyes. 'Colonel! Colonel, I—'

'Wo bin ich?' Schroeder insisted.

'Still in Ireland,' said Koenig. 'You could not be moved. It has been eight days, almost nine. But now – now you will recover!'

'Yes, I will, but—'

'Yes, Herr Colonel?'

Schroeder tried to smile but managed only a grimace. 'Willy, we're alone. Call me Thomas. In fact, from now on you must always call me Thomas.'

The other nodded his blond head.

'Willy,' said Schroeder again, 'I *will* recover, yes. But you should know what I know. That bomb finished me. A year, two if I'm lucky. I feel it.'

Koenig fell to his knees beside the bed. He grasped his Colonel's hand, kneaded it. Schroeder's grip was surprisingly strong. It tightened in a sudden spasm of memory.

'Willy, the bomb! My child! My Heinrich!'

'A miracle,' Koenig quickly told him. 'Not a scratch. Not a mark.'

'You wouldn't lie to me?'

'Of course not, my Colonel – Thomas. The boy is well. His mother, too.'

'And . . . Gerda?'

Koenig looked away.

Schroeder closed his eyes for a second. 'Did she suffer?'

'No, not at all. The bomb blew out part of the hotel's outer wall. Gerda went with it. They found . . . pieces. Probably a mercy.'

Schroeder nodded painfully. 'A lesson,' he whispered. 'Never mix business with pleasure. We were to fly from here straight to Australia. I should not have brought them with me.'

'But you could not know,' Koenig told him.

Schroeder frowned, his entire forehead wrinkling. 'It's so hard to remember. It happened so fast. There was someone else, a young man. Tall. A good-looking boy. Ah, yes! A Redcap. A British Military Policeman. What of him?'

'He lives,' said Koenig. 'He is blind. There were lesser injuries – a few, not many – but his eyes are finished.'

Schroeder considered this, managed another nod of his head, then a slow shake. 'That is very bad,' he said. 'He saved me, my child, my wife. Saved our lives. And he is blind . . .' He lay silently for a moment, then came to a decision. He gripped Koenig's hand. 'Keep tabs on that young man, Willy.' He paused again. 'He . . . told me his name . . . but—'

'Richard Garrison, Thomas.'

'Yes, that was it. Later, when things are better, then I shall want to know all about him.'

Koenig nodded.

'Right now I must sleep, Willy,' Schroeder eventually continued, his voice weakening. 'But first, there are things . . .'

'They have been done, Colonel – er, Thomas,' said Koenig. 'This is a private place. Nine of our best men are here from Germany. You are perfectly safe. Urmgard and Heinrich are in Köln. They, too, are protected. As soon as you are well enough, we fly to Siebert's sanatorium in the Harz. It will be better for you there.'

'And my doctors?' Schroeder's voice was fading away.

Koenig put his lips to the Colonel's ear. 'Their doctors patched you up. Ours were here within hours. They said your internal injuries would have killed any other. Blast is a funny business. It crushed your insides. But it didn't kill you. Not you, Herr Colonel, not you.'

Schroeder's eyes were closed. He was drifting away. 'Garrison,' his whisper was a mere breath. 'Do not forget . . . Richard . . . Garrison . . .'

'I won't,' Koenig whispered. He placed his master's hand on the bed, released it gently and stood up.

Major John Marchant and Corporal Richard Allan Garrison, both of them immaculate in number two dress uniforms, were met at the airport in Hannover as promised. In fact their reception was better than any promise might have foretold. Certainly better than the Major would or could have expected. Mere Majors were not used to metallic silver Mercedes motorcars awaiting their arrival on the landing strips of large international airports. Nor were they accustomed to the ease – the complete waiver of all normal disembarking procedures, including customs – with which certain persons of more influential orbits come and go in the world of affairs, and which they occasionally employ to make the passage of others easier. Quite simply, Marchant and his blind charge were picked up, driven out of the airport and into the city, and all with never so much as a glimpse of the interior of an airport building.

Richard Garrison on the other hand was not surprised, and not especially interested. There were a good many other things he should be doing and this to him was all a great waste of time and money. He could understand this man Schroeder's gratitude, could see how ill at ease the industrialist might feel at his disablement, but what could the man possibly hope to do for him? Did he intend to offer him money? Garrison's pension (the thought brought a wry smile to his lips: 'pension', hah! – to be pensioned off at his age!) and compensation would make him relatively independent. Financially at least. And then there would be supplementary grants from at least three Army funds. No, money would not be a major problem.

Getting to grips with his blindness, however . . . now that would be quite another matter. And he did not want to be – would not allow himself to become – a burden to anyone. People had their own problems and solved them as best they might. Garrison had long ago decided that he must solve his own. So what exactly did this Thomas Schroeder hope to do for him?

'Possibly,' the Major had hazarded aboard the plane, 'he wishes to thank you personally, and in some more or less concrete manner. I believe he's a rich man. Now I understand you're well satisfied with what you've already got out of all this,' (he had silently cursed himself for an unfortunate choice of words) 'but in the event he should offer you money, it would certainly not be in your best interests to refuse him.'

'It would make more sense and be a better deal if he offered me a job,' Garrison had answered. 'One I can handle without eyes.'

'You're a strange man,' the Major had commented, frowning. 'You hardly seem to miss your sight. I mean—' He paused.

'I know what you mean.'

'I don't think you do. I meant simply that I know a lot of much harder men who would have broken up – or broken down – if they'd suffered your loss.'

32

'How do you know they're harder?' Garrison had asked. 'And do you mean hard or hardened? Let me tell you what hard is. Hard is being seven years old and seeing your Mam and Dad falling out of love. It's being brought up by an uncle who strangles your kitten as a punishment for shitting yourself with diarrhoea when you get caught short. It's being fifteen and mad in love for the first time, and finding your girl on the beach with a friend who happens to be screwing her arse off. And it's a hell of a lot of other things in between. These are the things I call, or used to call, hard: things that happen to you when you're not really to blame. Things that hit you out of the blue, when you're least expecting them and can't fight them. And each bit of hard adds a thin layer to your skin, until you've a hide like an elephant.'

'Your life?' the Major had asked.

'Some of it,' a curt nod. 'There were other things, as I've said, but I've killed off the memories. Do you understand that? In my mind, I've killed them off. There's nothing bitter in there any more.' He had shrugged. 'Once you know how to do it it's easy. This blindness is something I'll kill off too. Hell, this has nothing to do with being hard! I knew what I was doing when I joined the Army, and when I volunteered for NI. And when I took Schroeder into the Europa, I . . . I somehow knew – I mean, I really—'

'But—' Marchant had started to speak when Garrison faltered.

'Look,' the Corporal had turned on him then, his face dead white around and behind his dark glasses. 'The only difference between you and me is that you can see. I have to learn to "see" all over again, and without the benefit of eyes. But I'll tell you this: when I *can* see again, I'll see a damn sight straighter than you. For one thing, I won't have the problem of peering round a big fat stiff upper lip!'

'Sir!' Major Marchant had snapped, and immediately wished he could bite his tongue off. He had only recently achieved his majority and enjoyed being called sir. He had been "sir" as a Captain, of course, but somehow it hadn't meant so much. Now, this Corporal – this blind Corporal whose confidential reports had never failed to note the chip on his shoulder, or rather the absence of chinks in his armour – seemed to be trying to make a mockery of the whole thing. The man was an opportunist, without doubt, and he certainly intended making gain out of his disability. His insubordinate attitude was sufficient proof of that. Very well, fair enough to play the game for monetary gain; but to take advantage of a senior officer's natural compassion—

'Sir?' Garrison had slowly answered. 'Listen, *sir*. In a couple of weeks' time the Army is going to boot me out. Pension me off. Send me a card every Christmas and a copy of the Corps Journal four times a year. Hey! And you know something, they'll really *do* that! Some idiot will send Journals – and me blind as a bat! And you want me to call you sir? Now? What'll you do if I refuse? Court martial me?'

After which they had sat in silence. The journey had not been a pleasant one.

Similarly irritating for Major Marchant was the way in which Garrison accepted the idea of a silver Mercedes waiting alongside the runway as the big jet trundled to a halt. He hadn't even smiled at Marchant's exclamation when he and the Major were called forward, first to disembark. Then there had been the curt, typically German handshakes at the foot of the travelling ramp, and Marchant shown into the rear of the car while the uniformed chauffeur took Garrison's white stick and assisted *him* into the front passenger's seat. But then again, it was Garrison this mysterious German industrialist wanted to see. Major Marchant could not then have realized, however, the very small part he himself was to play in the rest of the thing.

He was soon to discover his own insignificance, though; for as the great silent silver Mercedes drove out of the airport and into Hannover itself Koenig half-turned and said: 'Excuse me, Herr Major, but at which hotel have you arranged accommodation?'

'Hotel?' Marchant raised an eyebrow. 'I'm afraid you're mistaken, Herr, er, Koenig? We are to stay as the guests of Thomas Schroeder, at his estate in the Harz.'

'Ah, no, Herr Major. It is you who are mistaken. The Corporal is to stay there. No such arrangements have been made for you. A message was sent, but obviously too late.'

'But, I—'

'The Colonel has instructed me that in this case I am to take you to the Hotel International in Hannover. You shall stay there at no expense to yourself. Whatever you need, take it. If you wish for something, ask for it. If they haven't got it, demand it and it will be provided. Enjoy your stay. The Colonel owns the Hotel International, of course.'

'But—' It was the Major's day for buts.

'Your luggage will arrive at the hotel only a little while after you yourself. I hope all will be to your satisfaction.' Koenig smiled pleasantly over his shoulder.

In the back of the car Marchant sputtered, finally burst out: 'The Provost Marshal himself has ordered me to accompany Corporal Garrison and attend to his best interests. I cannot see how—'

'His best interests are being attended to, I assure you,' Koenig answered.

'You assure me? But you are your master's chauffeur, and—'

'And he has instructed me to speak for him,' Koenig smiled again. 'Anyway, the Colonel has already spoken to your Provost Marshal. Less than an hour ago they talked on the telephone.'

'They did? A Colonel, you say? But what has this Colonel to do with Mr Schroeder?'

'Why, they are one and the same!' said Koenig. 'I thought you knew. Perhaps you weren't briefed too well.'

'Oh,' said Marchant, and he sank back into the deep luxury of his seat. His voice was much calmer now. 'Yes, you're quite right. I don't appear to have been briefed too well. So Herr Schroeder was a Colonel, was he?'

'Was?' Koenig turned, unsmiling, to stare at him. His eyes had turned cold and beady. 'Oh, but he still is, Herr Major. To some of us, he always will be . . .'

After dropping off the Major they stopped again on the autobahn near Hildesheim, where Koenig said: 'I can see you do not like that white stick. Very well, leave it in the car. Here, let me take your arm.' He guided Garrison into a restaurant and to the door marked 'Herren', and while the Corporal answered the call of nature he ordered drinks and Zigeuner-schnitzel.

When Garrison left the toilet Koenig was at the door to meet him. 'Was it difficult?' he asked.

'What, taking a leak?'

'No,' the German grinned. 'Finding your way out of the toilet.'

Garrison shrugged. 'Not really.' He sensed the other's nod of approval.

'Gut!' Koenig took his elbow. 'The Colonel was right, you see? He said these so-called aids – these white sticks and armbands – were merely embarrassments. How do you say it? – "encumbrances"!'

He led Garrison to a table and guided him into a chair. 'What kind of a man is your Colonel?' the Corporal asked when he was comfortable.

'But you met him.'

'Too briefly, I'm afraid. And the circumstances were—' Garrison pulled a wry face, '—difficult.'

'Ah, yes, of course,' said Koenig.

Garrison nodded. 'The events of that day are still a little

blurred. Fuzzy in my mind. I suppose they always will be.'

'I understand,' said Koenig. 'Well, the Colonel is a man to be respected. People who do not know him – complete strangers – when they meet him, obey him. He has a power, a strength. He was a marvellous officer. And he is a marvellous man. No, that is not quite true. According to the letter of the law, he is probably a very bad man. For one thing, he pays not taxes. Or only as much as he wishes to pay. He does not take kindly, you see, to the laws and rules of others.'

Garrison laughed. 'I like him already.'

Koenig also laughed. 'Oh, you will like him. I believe you are much alike.'

'What does he do?' Garrison asked. 'I mean, I know he's an industrialist, but—' He paused, listened to the chink of glasses as the *Kellnerin* delivered their drinks. After she had gone away he leaned across and whispered: 'She's pretty, she's young, and she smiles a lot.'

'How do you know?' Koenig whispered back.

'Only a young, smiling sort of girl could wear that perfume,' Garrison answered. 'Also, her thigh where it pressed against mine was very firm – and very friendly!'

The German laughed and nodded. 'Again the Colonel is right. He says: "Blindness is only a word for having no eyesight." And he also says it is too often used as a synonym of idiot or cretin or vegetable. Well, you may be blind, Corporal Garrison, but you are no vegetable!'

'You must call me Richard, Willy,' Garrison laughed out loud.

'No,' the German shook his blond head. 'That would not be right. I am after all merely a gentleman's gentleman. It would be to demean you. Nor must I call you Corporal, for that also is to belittle you. You see, I was a Feldwebel! No, I shall call you sir – when others are listening, anyway.'

Garrison sighed and shook his head in mock despair. 'Jesus,' he said, 'no more of that shit! I had all that once today with Marchant.'

'Ah?' Koenig's eyebrows went up. 'Yes, I suspected something. Well, the Colonel is not like that.'

'You were telling me about him,' Garrison prompted.

Koenig nodded, just as he would if Garrison had sight. 'I do not think he would mind our discussing him. He was a Colonel at the end of the war. So many young officers were. I was his youngest non-commissioned officer, his batman if you like, though in fact I was more his bodyguard. We were members of—' he paused.

'The SS?'

'Remarkable!' said Koenig. 'Yes, the SS. Does that strike terror into your heart?'

'No, should it?'

'Many people are still foolish about it – especially Germans!'

'Well, I'm a Military Policeman – for a week or two more, anyway. And I've read a great deal about the SS. There were good and bad. There are in all armies, all corps and regiments.'

Koenig grinned, his amusement finding its way into his voice. 'The Royal Military Police and the SS are two very different concepts, I assure you!' he said, his words slow and precise.

'Oh, I know that,' Garrison answered. 'But I've a feeling that you and the Colonel . . . well, that you weren't all jackboots and Mausers.'

'We were excellent soldiers, certainly,' Koenig answered. 'As to whether we were good or bad men, would it sound too – how do you say, trite? – to say that we, the Colonel and I, did not relish our duties? Yet it is true. Fortunately Colonel Schroeder's was an active command. In fact we were permanently in action, on one front or another. It was his punishment, I suppose. You see, he came of very bad stock.'

Garrison's face took on a puzzled look. 'I'm sorry?'

'In the First World War his grandfather was General

Count Max von Zundenberg. And his grandmother was Jewish!'

Garrison grinned again and tasted his drink. 'That might account for his tax-dodging, eh?' Then the grin slipped from his face. He sipped again at his drink. 'That's a very poor brandy,' he said.

'But you like it?'

'Indeed I do. I spent two years in Cyprus as a Lance-Corporal. Could hardly afford to drink anything else. Why, you might say that as a drinking man, which I'm not, I was reared on bad brandy! We Lance-Corporals used to drink two-star Haggipavlu. A gallon of the stuff would only cost a couple of pounds!'

'I know,' Koenig laughed a deep laugh. 'That's why I ordered the worst brandy in the house. Especially for you.'

Garrison tasted his food. Meat in a spicy sauce, with mushroom. He smiled for a moment, then frowned. His handsome brow wrinkled as he turned his black lenses on the German. 'You've done your homework well, Willy Koenig. What else do you know about me?'

'Almost everything. I know you had a fairly rough time as a boy, and that you seem to have come through unscathed. I also know that from now on it won't be nearly so rough.'

'Your Colonel is more than merely grateful, then?'

'Grateful? He owes you his life. *I* owe you his life! And his wife's life. And Heinrich, his son's life. And he owes you your sight. Yes, he is more than merely grateful . . .'

'I want nothing from him.'

'Then you are a fool, for he can give you everything.' Koenig stared for a moment at his own reflection in the dark ovals of Garrison's spectacles. 'Almost everything.'

Their third stop was at a Gasthof on a mountain road, where they both drank a beer and relieved themselves before the final stage of the journey. By then Garrison felt very secure in Koenig's company and he had grown tired. He loosened his tie, his jacket, lay back in his seat and dozed while the big German drove and hummed an accompaniment to soft music from the car's radio.

He was still half asleep when they arrived at their destination. It was early evening and there was a little laughter from somewhere close at hand. A chill breeze was up, carrying piney smells on the sweet mountain air; but there were also splashing sounds, shouts of encouragement, someone urging 'Schwimm, schwimm!' A heated outdoor pool.

But by now Garrison was far too tired to concentrate. When he got out of the car he straightened his tie, did up the buttons of his jacket, gave himself once more into Koenig's care. He was not given his stick back but led into a building, into an elevator, along a corridor and into a room. All of these things and places made impressions, but blurred in his mind and unreal for now. It had been a long day, a long eight months. He remembered Koenig saying goodnight and something about a pleasant day in the morning.

He found the bed and lay down gladly upon it, loosening his tie once again and his uniform. He kicked off his shiny black shoes and wondered if they were as shiny as they used to be. But what difference did it make?

Then, just before he slept—

There was a drink, brought to him by some soft-voiced girl. It made him very drowsy. The girl helped him with his clothes, treated him like a baby, as though she might break him, covered him with cool sheets.

Following which—

'Good morning,' said the same soft voice, the girl's voice. It held the hint of a German accent. Garrison opened his eyes (he always did it, an automatic reaction to waking up) and heard the girl gasp. He at once closed his eyes and groped

40

about for his dark-lensed spectacles: his 'blinkers', as he thought of them. For as if it wasn't enough to be blind, his eyes were now especially hideous, completely white and without pupils. Only in searching for his blinkers did he discover his own nakedness, the fact that in his sleep he had thrown off his bedclothes.

He found his blinkers on a bedside table, put them on, opened his dry mouth to say something sharp . . . and bit the words off unuttered. The girl was still there, had not moved, could only be watching him. He sensed her presence, her – curiosity? – and his anger turned to a curiosity of his own. This was his first experience of anyone taking advantage of him.

Very well, if voyeurism was her scene . . .

He lay back on his pillow and deliberately put his hands behind his head. The very act – of consciously displaying himself, unashamedly lying there naked – gave him a rise. He reached down and gently patted his swelling .hard. 'Good morning,' he answered. 'It's a beauty, isn't it?'

'Why, yes. As a matter of fact, it is.' She moved closer. 'Aren't you going to get up? Or perhaps you would like your breakfast in bed?'

Garrison grinned. 'What's on offer?' he asked. He was ramrod stiff now – half from the need to urinate, the rest from the powerfully erotic presence of this girl. From the very tone of her voice he could tell that she wasn't in the least disturbed either by his nakedness or his hard. But then, why should she be? She had undressed him, hadn't she? He scratched an itchy spot on his belly and wondered just exactly what the girl's duties were.

'Anything you like,' she said, very matter of factly. She came and sat on his bed, within reach. Garrison put out his hand and let it fall on her thigh. His palm touched flesh, his fingers the hem of her shorts. He grinned at her; but after a second, when he made no effort to remove his hand, she took it and placed it on his stomach. Only then did she jerk her own hand away and jump to her feet.

'Oh!' she said, her voice a half-gasp. 'You're naked!'

Now Garrison couldn't stop himself laughing. 'Jesus!' he said. 'Are you telling me you've just noticed?'

'Why, yes,' she answered, plainly indignant. 'Did you think you were the only one in the world who was—'

The truth struck him like a thunderclap. 'Blind!' he finished it for her.

'Yes,' she said, 'I'm blind.'

He reached over the edge of the bed, found his sheets and covered himself. Then he laughed again, and much louder.

'Oh?' she said, her voice stiff. 'And is something funny?'

'Look,' he said, 'I'm sorry. When I thought you could see me I pretended not to mind,' he chuckled again. 'And when I learned you were blind I covered myself up!'

'I don't understand,' she said.

'Neither do I!' he laughed again, then quickly sobered. 'Will you sit down? What's your name?'

'I'm Vicki,' she told him, perching herself on the edge of his bed again. He sat up and took her face in his hands. It was a slim face, elfin. Her ears were small, her hair brushed back and falling over her shoulders. Her eyes had a slight tilt. Smooth skin. High cheekbones. A small nose. A pert little mouth.

'You have a sexy face,' he said. 'Vicki.'

'Oh?' She took his hands and held them. 'Is that supposed to flatter me? Am I supposed to be pleased?'

'It pleases me,' he told her frankly.

She let go his hands and stood up. 'You are to get dressed,' she said, 'and come and have breakfast.'

'OK,' he answered, 'help me dress.' He swung his legs out of bed.

'I will not! Your pyjamas are on the chair by the bed, and there is a robe hanging behind the door. Why should I help you? Can't you dress yourself?'

'Well, I seem to remember it was you *un*dressed me!'

There was a moment of silence, then she giggled. 'I did not. But I do begin to understand. So, you thought I was your own little nymph, eh?'

Garrison began to feel foolish. He should have known it was too good to be true. 'Er, look, I—'

'I brought your drink,' she told him. 'I spoke to you and fluffed out your pillow a little. But Nurse undressed you, not I.'

'Jesus!' said Garrison.

'Willy Koenig warned me about you,' she said, her voice dry. 'He said you must be one of the least handicapped blind men he's ever seen. In fact he's not quite sure you even *know* you're blind yet!'

'Jesus!' Garrison said again. 'Listen, I—'

'Sit still,' she laughed, bending over him. 'My turn.' Her fingers were warm on his face. 'You're a handsome boy,' she finally said, 'but only a boy.'

'Oh? And you're a woman of the world, I suppose? Listen, I'm my own man, twenty-one, an ex-soldier – or soon to be – and if you knew me better you wouldn't call me a boy.'

'I am five years older than you,' she told him. 'I've been blind since I was fifteen and I'm probably far more experienced – in just about everything.'

On impulse he kissed her fingers where they touched his lips. They tasted sweet. 'Your breasts are throwing body heat in my face,' he told her, and at once heard her breathing quicken.

'You are much too forward for my liking, Richard Garrison,' she told him. She stepped away from him and tossed him his pyjamas, which wrapped around his head. 'Now hurry up and I'll show you the bathroom, and when you've washed we'll go down. You can shave and dress later. Life is slow and very pleasant here, as you'll discover. But since staff are few, schedules are important. And you are late for breakfast.'

'One thing,' he said, disentangling himself and pulling on his pyjama trousers. 'Why did you gasp when you woke me up? You said good morning, and then you gasped. That's why I thought you could see. I thought perhaps you had seen my eyes – or perhaps my nakedness.'

She led him to a door and pushed him gently through into a bathroom whose surfaces were soft and rounded, closing the door after him.

'Well?' he called through the door.

'Oh, that,' she said, offhandedly. 'It was just that I tripped over your bedclothes where you had thrown them. I almost fell.'

He thought about it. 'All of my bedclothes?'

'It felt like all of them to me.'

'So you knew I was naked after all?'

For a moment there was silence, then: 'Yes, I suppose I did. But—'

'Yes?'

'Well, you'll find out for yourself soon enough. If you don't know already. You see, it's sort of hard to get embarrassed when you're blind. Little things embarrass you, like bumping into someone or knocking a cup over. But the big things – why, you simply don't see them!'

Garrison grinned, found the taps and ran water into a washbasin. 'Thank God for touch, taste, smell and hearing,' he called.

'Oh, I do!' she answered. 'I thank Him every day.'

He sat down on the toilet to make water. That way he couldn't miss. The rush of water down from the taps covered his own splashing. 'That wasn't exactly what I meant,' he said. 'I meant that although I can't see you, I can at least have the pleasure of knowing how you feel, taste and smell. And the sound of your voice.'

'Oh? And who says you can have those pleasures?'

'Who can stop me?' he asked. 'I've smelled you, touched

44

your face, listened to you talking and tasted your fingers. And—'

'And now you're interested in the entire combination, eh? With perhaps a few variations thrown in for good measure?'

'Oh, something like that.'

'Willy Koenig is right, I think,' she slowly said. 'You hardly seem to understand how badly handicapped you are. And I repeat, you are a very forward boy, Richard Garrison.'

'Not really,' he answered, coming out of the bathroom. 'But it's like you said. When you're blind, it's sort of hard to feel embarrassed. In fact, being blind probably has a lot of compensations.' He found her waist, drew her close and kissed her. Beneath her halter top she wore no brassiere and her breasts were hot and firm against his chest. After a long moment she began to respond to his kiss, then drew breath sharply and pulled away as his hand found her breast. She held him at arm's length.

'Much too forward altogether,' she repeated. But her voice was husky as chaff in a summer farmyard.

He reluctantly let himself be guided to the door and helped into the robe hanging there, and then she took him downstairs.

Breakfast was huge, English (as English breakfasts used to be) and excellently prepared, and it was served in a room where at least one wall was a vast window facing east. Garrison could feel and enjoy the sun's rays on his face and forearms. Moreover, he found himself with a real appetite, something he had missed until now without realizing it. He ploughed through sausages, bacon, eggs and tomatoes, and was following up with coffee, toast and marmalade when Koenig entered the room.

Until then Garrison and Vicki had been on their own, and since they had both come to realize what must

45

inevitably be, neither one of them had found it necessary to say a lot. The space between them was charged, however, as the space between imminent lovers always is.

Koenig's entrance was therefore something of an intrusion. He said nothing, but Garrison had heard the door open and close, and he had recognized the other's sure tread even on the thick pile of the dining room's expensive carpet. When Koenig came to a halt at the table, the blind Corporal sighed and pushed away his plate.

'Good morning, Willy,' he said. 'Why don't you sit? There's more coffee in the pot if you want it.'

'Good morning, sir,' Koenig answered. 'And thanks, but I have already eaten. Actually, sir, I have brought you some new clothes. I am here to help you try them on. They are more suitable to this good weather we are enjoying.'

This was a different Koenig, one Garrison wasn't quite sure he understood. 'Pretty stiff, aren't we, Willy?'

'Not at all, sir. We are merely respectful.' It was strange to hear these so English words spoken in Koenig's so Germanic accents.

Garrison finished his coffee and stood. The electricity had disappeared from the air now and Vicki seemed distant, lost in space and darkness. Garrison turned towards her in something like panic, or as close as he had ever got to panic. 'Vicki, are you there? I mean—'

'I know what you mean. Yes, I'm here. Will you swim with me before lunch?'

He felt reassured. 'I'd like that,' he answered.

Koenig took his elbow but Garrison shrugged him off. On his way out of the room he hit a small table and the door, cursing vividly under his breath both times. Out of earshot of Vicki, Koenig grabbed him and held his arms in a vice-like grip.

'Richard,' the German said. 'This anger is stupid. Is it directed at me because I am stiff? *You* think I am stiff. But I do not feel stiff. You must understand that I am a servant

46

here. Is it not enough that we are friends? Vicki is a friend, too, but I call her madame. One day it may be different between you and me, but for now . . . Besides, your anger caused you to lose co-ordination.'

Garrison gritted his teeth and glared at the darkness where the German's voice sounded. He slowly relaxed, finally nodded. 'You're right, of course. That was rude of me. I got mad for nothing. Jealousy, I suppose.'

'Oh?'

'Yes. You can see her and I can't.'

'You were not really mad,' said Koenig. 'And certainly not jealous. Frustrated, perhaps. A little nervous. That is to be expected. But you'll see – by tonight you'll be completely relaxed and at ease. Now we have to get you shaved—'

'I can manage that myself.'

'—and dressed—'

'I can tackle that, too.'

'—And I have to show you round the place.'

'Show me?' Garrison snorted.

'Bitterness? From you? I can show you by description, can't I? Don't be bitter, Richard. Just believe me: if you'll let them, things *will* get better. Now then, are we to continue to be friends?'

Slowly Garrison's frown lifted. He grinned, however wryly. 'Hell, yes, I suppose so. I mean, you probably haf vays to make me be friendly, eh?'

Then, without further protest, Garrison allowed himself to be led back to his room. Except that this time he committed the way to memory. He would never have to be taken there again . . .

Schroeder was in a wheelchair by the pool. There were no swimmers now but the water was warm. Just a year ago Garrison wouldn't have noticed – would not have been capable of noticing – but now he could feel the warm air rising, could smell the artificial heat of the water. A young woman was with the industrialist, seated beside him taking notes. He spoke to her in lowered tones, but Garrison could have sworn he heard his name mentioned. They broke off whatever they were doing as Koenig and his charge drew closer.

'Mina,' said Schroeder to the woman, 'Would you excuse us, please? We can finish later.'

'Naturlich, Herr Schroeder.' She went, leaving Garrison with an impression of razor-sharp efficiency clad in young flesh of a classic Nordic mould. Schroeder liked efficiency, pretty things, the pleasures of life. What, then, could he want with Garrison?

'Sit, Richard Garrison,' said Schroeder. 'You'll excuse me for not standing. I can stand, but it gives pain sometimes. So I mainly sit. Sometimes Willy pushes me, at others I wheel myself – for exercise.'

Under Koenig's direction, Garrison sat.

'It is good to see you,' Schroeder continued, 'and especially good to see you looking well.' His handshake was firm but his hand felt light in Garrison's grip, and his voice was . . . not as Garrison remembered it. Even afraid (as Schroeder had undoubtedly been at the Europa, though not for himself) still his voice had been strong and had commanded respect. Now . . . he was failing, Garrison could sense it. There was a shortness of breath, a restlessness, an urgency to be done with things while there was still time.

'Herr Schroeder,' Garrison answered, 'thank you for bringing me out here – even though I'm in the dark as to why you brought me.'

'Your being here is my pleasure,' said Schroeder. 'It could well have been the case that you did not wish to see or hear of me again – ever! And I would not have blamed you.'

Garrison offered a little laugh. 'Oh, you may be sure I'd like to see you. Or anyone, or anything.'

Schroeder took his hand again. 'Early days, Richard.

48

Your ears are still too alert and ready to hear things the wrong way. It is a wound, but when it heals you will be the better man. How much does it hurt?'

'That's a new approach,' Garrison told him. 'To ask how much it hurts, I mean. Others just seem to take it for granted that I'm crippled. I mean mentally as well as physically. In actual fact my mind is sharper, clearer. That's only natural, I suppose. But how much does it hurt?' He paused, shrugged. 'Neither God nor the devil himself can put it right, and so I have to get used to the idea. It *did* hurt, yes. I mean, there are so many places, pretty girls, marvels I never had time to see. But now – I have a good clear memory and a good imagination. Also, the rest of my senses are good. I smell things now. I hear things I never heard before. Things taste . . . different. And when I touch something, that is to know it. Like Willy, for instance. Sometimes I feel I've known him for years.'

'So. And Willy has been looking after you, has he?'

'He's been doing a great job. Except—'

'Yes?'

Garrison grinned up at the big man where he stood, shifting his weight from one foot to the other and back. 'Oh, nothing. It's just that he has a certain advantage over me – for now, anyway.'

'Willy, what have you been doing?'

'Nothing, Thomas, I assure you. I think the Corporal means that I am able to see Fraulein Maler while he is not. That is my advantage. They were breakfasting together. Perhaps I interrupted something?'

Garrison and Schroeder laughed together, but the latter's laughter quickly turned to a dry coughing. His grip tightened on Garrison's hand as spasms racked his body. In another moment they passed.

'Willy,' Schroeder's voice was broken. 'You have things to do. You can leave Mr Garrison with me.'

'Yes, Thomas. Thank you.' Koenig turned to Garrison. 'I

hope to see you later, sir.'

When Koenig had gone Schroeder and Garrison sat in silence for a few moments. Finally Garrison said: 'A wheelchair, chest pains, internal damage, general debility. And you ask me how much it hurts? My pain is all in the mind – and fading. Your pains are physical, real – and getting worse.'

'There's more of a difference than that,' Schroeder observed. 'You were innocent. I was not. In a way, I even caused the thing. I probably got what I deserved. You deserved much better. Therefore I am in your debt. It is a debt I intend to settle. Fully.'

'Forget it,' Garrison answered, his tone hardening. 'Let's say we're all squared up.'

'I don't understand.' Schroeder sounded genuinely mystified.

'You can't give me back my eyes,' said Garrison. 'They're gone – for good. I know you're a rich man, but that's a debt you simply can't repay. Don't knock yourself out trying.'

For long moments Schroeder was silent. Then: 'At least you'll accept a drink, eh? Bad brandy, with a coke to sweeten it?'

Garrison grinned, glad that the tone of the conversation had lightened. 'You've been speaking to Willy,' he said. 'And talking about Willy: how come he calls me sir and you Thomas?'

Schroeder gave a dry chuckle. 'I have ordered him to call me Thomas,' he explained. 'I *had* to order it, since that was the only way. As to why he calls you sir: well, he will be calling you that for a good many years to come.'

'I don't follow that. I mean, I'm only here for one week.'

'Oh? We shall have to see. But you should know, Richard, that I have always been a forceful man.'

Garrison nodded thoughtfully. 'I'm sure you have been,' he said. 'I'm quite sure you have . . .'

Chapter Three

'Has Willy shown you over the place?' Schroeder asked.

'Inside only,' Garrison answered. 'He was going to take me through the gardens and into the woods – the pines? – but I was late out of bed and there wasn't time.'

'Ah, yes! Willy is strict on schedules. He always follows instructions or agreed tactics to the letter.'

'Tactics?'

Schroeder chuckled. 'Tactics, strategies – did you think these terms were only used in battle? No, there are business tactics, too, and there are also tactics for entertaining guests. In your case we shall be obliged to mix the two, though as a rule that's a cocktail not much to my taste. But come, you push and I shall steer. You be the engine and I'll be the engineer. We'll talk as we go.'

'Do you trust me?'

Schroeder had a sudden, vivid, dazzling flash of memory. In his mind's eye he saw Garrison in mid-air, stretched out, reaching, limned against a blossoming shock of white fire. And he felt again the senses-shattering, gut-crushing blast of the explosion. He shuddered and the vision passed. 'Trust you? Oh, yes! With my life, Richard Garrison.'

Garrison got to his feet. He nodded and slowly began to push the wheelchair, following the course that Schroeder steered. 'The building you slept in last night is my own private house,' the man in the chair explained. 'At least when I am in this part of the world. And "house" is rather a poor word for it, really; for of course the place in no way resembles a house in the accepted sense of the word. It is more a small, *very* private hotel, I suppose. And it is only one of six such structures. It stands central, with the other five

51

forming a circle about it. Between the buildings are paths, gardens, fountains and three small, heated swimming pools. Maintenance – that is to say the central heating, control of the solar cells and panels, the air conditioning and so forth – is all controlled from beneath the central structure. By the way, did Willy take you up to the roof?'

'Yes, he showed me the whole place.'

'Then you will know that the "attic" is in fact a revolving solarium. Thus the building – my "headquarters", if you like – has a cellar, ground, first and second floors, and a solarium roof. The other buildings are the same, with the exceptions that they have no second floors and no elevators. The roofs of all six structures are domed and half-covered in solar cells. They also have large reflective mirrors which automatically follow the sun, which gives us one third of our power. Seen from above, all glittery and with its central tower, the place looks very futuristic. But I assure you that everything is functional. Nothing is for decoration.'

'Well,' said Garrison, 'so now I know what the place looks like. But what is it for? What's its purpose?'

'Eh? Well for one thing it's my home, or one of them, as I've already explained.'

Garrison was impressed. 'Jesus! *One* of your homes! The place must be worth a million.'

Schroeder chuckled. '*Seven* millions, my young friend. And that was when it was built, five years ago. And not Deutsch Marks but pounds – pounds sterling!'

Garrison whistled. 'But why six buildings? Who do you accommodate?'

'Well, apart from myself, the inner building – the inner sanctum, as it were – accommodates my staff and Willy Koenig. The upper floors are for guests; my staff and I remain on the ground floor. That is the building in which I entertain only the most influential of business friends. You should feel suitably honoured.'

'Oh, I do!'

'As for the outer buildings: two of them are likewise designed as guest accommodation. The other three are rather more special.'

'Special?'

'Oh, yes! One is a small but marvellously equipped hospital. Rather, a surgery. Have you heard of Saul Siebert?'

'The doctor?'

'A surgeon – perhaps the world's greatest. I paid for Saul's studies, his education. It was a favour to his father, one of my junior officers, killed in the war. A favour, yes – but what an investment! Saul is quite brilliant, but he does not forget that he owes everything to me. He has his own sanatorium in the Harz, of course, but occasionally I require him to work here.'

'You "require" him to work here?'

Schroeder ignored Garrison's dry tone. 'So far,' he continued, 'Saul Siebert has saved four lives here. Lives which were important to me. One was that of an oil sheik, another a member of the Soviet Presidium, who now enjoys excellent health. The third was a Greek shipping magnate whose name is a household word, and the last was my own. Saul is not finished with me, however, for there is still much damage. Personally, I do not think he has enough time left to finish the job. Rather, I do not think I have enough time . . .'

As Garrison brought the chair to an abrupt halt Schroeder hastily urged him on. 'No, no, don't stop. And please forgive me for being so morbid. This is poor entertainment indeed! Now then, what were we talking about?'

'Two buildings left to explain,' Garrison reminded him, wheeling the chair forward again.

'Of course,' said Schroeder, 'and once more, forgive me. Two more buildings, yes. One of them is my library.

Nothing but books. I'm a great reader, you see. And the roof is not a solarium but a reading room and observatory. The last building: that is a strictly private place. No one goes in there but me, and very occasionally Willy. And tomorrow – you.'

Garrison felt a sudden chill that had nothing at all to do with the balmy temperature. Curious though he was, he curbed his instinctive desire to know more about Schroeder's 'strictly private place'. Instead he asked: 'Where to now?'

'Carry on straight down this path, slowly. There's a place in the woods where a very special mushroom may be found.'

'Mushrooms, at this time of year?'

'Very special,' Schroeder repeated. 'I had the spawn brought here from the Nan Shan in Tibet. It lay dormant for two years. Then, last year, the first crop. And I am informed that the mushrooms are once again ready to be picked. We shall see . . .'

Garrison pushed the wheelchair and Schroeder down a slight decline for about a hundred yards; after that the way levelled out and quite suddenly the sun's warmth left his face and naked arms. Now he heard the whisper of leaves, smelled the fragrance of the pines.

They came to a gate and Schroeder told Garrison to stop. The industrialist applied his chair's brakes and guided Garrison round to the gate, describing how it could be opened. Working by touch, Garrison managed it easily. Leaving the gate open he went back to the wheelchair, but as he did so there came the rustle of leaves and stealthy footsteps. He heard the sharp *ch-ching* of an automatic weapon being cocked.

'Thomas, *look out*!' Garrison hoarsely yelled, flinging himself face-down in pine needles, leaves and loam.

'Easy, my boy, easy!' Schroeder's voice came to life, as if their previous conversation had been a drugged mumbling. 'There are no enemies here. This is Gunter, one of my men.

There are a good many of them in the woods and on the approach road. They reinforce the warning notices. I value my privacy, you see.'

'Jesus!' Garrison gasped. 'You should have told me.' He climbed shakily to his feet and Schroeder could see that his face was filmed with sweat.

'Your reactions have not slowed down,' the German told him, his eyes narrowing where they peered at Garrison through thick lenses. 'No, indeed. I rather think that Gunter is lucky you don't have your SMG, eh?'

'Damn right!' Garrison growled. 'He'd probably be a dead man.'

'Still,' Schroeder continued, 'it's a pity.' He wheeled his chair over to where Garrison dusted himself down, picked pine needles from the Corporal's shirt and trousers. 'You have come to associate me with danger.'

Garrison turned to the man and frowned. He was trembling a little. 'Yes, I guess I have. But you should know this: I wasn't afraid for myself. Why should anybody want to shoot a blind man?'

'And you asked me if I would trust you,' Schroeder softly reminded. Then, in harsh and stinging tones, he tongue-lashed his watchman for a full three minutes, barely pausing for breath. The man mumbled his excuses, which only brought more fury from his employer, until finally Schroeder was through with him. Then Garrison made out Gunter's gruff 'Entschuldigen sie,' before the bushes rustled and the man was allowed to depart into the trees.

'He is a bloody fool!' Schroeder snarled. 'He frightened me, too, coming upon us like that. But . . . I suppose he was only trying to show me how alert and capable he is. Here, let's have a cigarette as we go. The man's made my nerves jump. The place of the mushrooms is not much farther now. And of course we must be back for your swim with Vicki.'

'Vicki,' said Garrison, his voice giving nothing away. 'So

you've seen her this morning and she spoke of me. Who is she?'

'The daughter of a friend. She has been blind since she was fifteen. Nothing can be done for her.'

'And why is she here?'

'Company for you,' Schroeder was frank. 'I thought you might feel less isolated if there was another blind person here. Also, this is a nice place to holiday. Yes, let us simply say that she is enjoying a holiday with her Uncle Thomas, eh?'

'Listen,' Garrison said, his voice hardening. 'I don't want to seem ungrateful, but I really don't need anyone pimping for me!'

Schroeder was ready with his dry chuckle. 'I said she was "company" for you. I did not say anything about her being your whore! Look, Vicki *is* good company. Whether or not you can take her to bed is your business. But I'll tell you something: she has red hair and brilliant green eyes, and in my experience that's a deadly combination – especially in a German woman! Pimp, did you call me? But you might be safer with a cobra, Richard Garrison, than with Vicki. Yes, and you might stand more chance. But of course I could be wrong . . . Ah! – there are our mushrooms.'

Under Schroeder's guidance Garrison stepped a few paces from the path through grass and clover. He halted at the German's command and went carefully down on one knee. From their feel the mushrooms were more like toadstools: long-stemmed, fully domed and warty. Completely unlike the common field mushrooms of England, they were sticky, irritatingly pungent and they grew tall, at least six inches. Even without Schroeder to direct him, Garrison would have found the things. Once he had their scent he was drawn to them almost magnetically.

'Six will be sufficient,' Schroeder called to him. 'Enough for our purposes. Wrap them in your handkerchief.'

Garrison collected six, returned to the wheelchair and

handed them over. Schroeder sniffed them appreciatively. 'Semen!' he said. 'From their shape and their smell, you could almost picture nymphs of the forest crouching down over them, eh?'

Garrison laughed. 'What are they for?' he asked.

Schroeder reached up and tapped the other's nose twice before he could jerk his face away. 'None of your business. You, who have declared your independence of drugs. But come, turn us about and let's be on our way. You must swim and relax, and I have things to do. And then there's lunch. And this afternoon – the photographers!'

'Photographers?' Garrison was bemused.

'Oh, yes. And my tailor to take your measurements. And your voice to be taped. And a specialist to fit you up. And—'

'Whoa!' said Garrison. 'I'm not getting any of this . . .'

'Ah, but you will! You will!'

Garrison slowly nodded. 'OK,' he said, refusing to be tantalized, 'we'll see what we'll see. But one thing: maybe I'd better cancel my date at the pool with Vicki. I don't have any swim trunks.'

'Trunks?' Schroeder laughed. 'We can find some for you. But what difference does it make? Vicki has no costume either!'

'But—'

'Or perhaps you think that I am not only a pimp but also a peeping-Thomas, eh?' At which they both burst out laughing . . .

At Garrison's insistence, Willy Koenig brought him a pair of swimming trunks. He went to his room to put them on before allowing Koenig to take him out to the pool, by which time Vicki was already whooping and splashing about in the water. She was like a child in her pleasure.

The pool was no more than sixty inches deep, perhaps sixty feet long by thirty wide. It had steps and a slide.

Braving the slide, Garrison seated himself on smooth boards slick with running water, gathered in his breath and was about to take the plunge when Koenig chopped his hand away from the rim and gave him a hefty shove in the middle of his back.

'Bastard!' Garrison expelled his air in a shout, shot down the slide and into the water. The pool's temperature was perfect, so that there was no shock at all to his system as he was fully immersed. Finding his feet, Garrison gasped, 'Willy, are you trying to start World War III?' His question was answered by a receding laugh as the big German walked away. Garrison nodded after him and grinned. 'Oh, ganz komisch!' he said.

Vicki was laughing. 'He pushed you in?'

'Down the slide, yes.' He dog-paddled in the direction of her voice.

'Now you keep away,' she answered, backing off. 'I'm very strong in the water. And I refuse to be ducked!'

'Funny way you Germans pronounce your Fs,' he growled.

'Not only are you forward, you're very vulgar!'

'Who said anything about ducking you?' he laughed. 'And who was it asked me to swim with her anyway?'

'Swim in the same pool with me,' she agreed. 'Not necessarily side by side, or touching. Oh!' He cornered her, drew her close.

'Shit! You're wearing a costume.'

'A couple of hankies, yes. And *you* are wearing trunks. Silly of both of us, really. After all, there's no one else here.'

'There's Willy,' he said, kissing her forehead.

'Oh, Willy is not a peeper.' She splashed water in his face. 'And anyway, there won't be anything worth seeing.' She swam swiftly away from him.

'Vicki,' he said, following the sound of her splashes. 'I was thinking I might have an early night tonight.'

'Oh?' Her tone was casual. 'Are you still tired, then? It

must be the mountain air. Myself, I shall probably stay up very late.'

'Don't take the mickey, you know what I mean.'

'Yes I do. And I should invite you to my room, should I? As simple as that?'

'Well, that would be . . . simple.'

'I may not want it to be simple.'

He trapped her again, drew her close, this time kissed her full on the mouth and moved his body against hers. 'But you do want it,' he said, releasing her.

'There are twenty-four suites in the central building,' she said, her voice at once breathless and husky. 'At midnight, come into my room and get into bed with me.'

'Which is your room?' Garrison, too, had difficulty speaking.

'I won't tell you. Not the room, not even the floor.'

He laughed shakily. 'Hell's teeth! It could be pretty embarrassing if I make a mistake.'

'Then don't make one.'

'No clues?'

'Hmm – possibly. And one rule – you mustn't ask anyone. I don't want it to be common knowledge.' She broke free and swam away. A moment later he heard her feet on the pool's tiled surround. She was moving away, back towards the central building.

'Hey!' he called after her. 'Is that it? Is that our swim?'

'It served its purpose,' she called back.

Garrison stood in silence, the water making tiny wavelets against his chest. A wasp hummed out of the sun and settled on his shoulder. He submerged, came up, swam for a further ten minutes. Time enough for his erection to collapse . . .

Garrison ate only a light lunch. Several things competed to rob him of the morning's appetite, not the least of them being the knowledge that tomorrow would find him entering Schroeder's mysterious building, which apparently contained or explained the reason for Garrison's being here.

But before then there was that army to face, and the cold efficiency with which they invaded and occupied – for however brief a spell – his body. He was photographed a great deal. He was photographed in stills and in motion, dressed and undressed, seated, standing, walking, speaking and shouting; with and without his dark spectacles, in colour and in black and white, with and without sound.

His voice was taped in all its range. Talking, shouting commands in German and in English, swearing. In normal conversation, in excitement, in anger. No slightest inflection, no minor point of dialect (though he was naturally void, or almost void, of dialectal influence), no smallest nuance or vocal idiosyncrasy was left unrecorded.

He was given the most thorough physical check-up of his entire life. The Army's annual PULHEEMS had nothing to compare with this. They measured, weighed, tugged at, listened to, pulled and sampled him. His organs were sounded. His blood and urine were tested. They even dabbled with sweat, saliva and excreta. He expected they might want semen, too, but that was not on their list.

And then he was measured again, but this time by a pair of obviously homosexual tailors, Schroeder's personal tailors from Kassel, come up into the Harz at the industrialist's bidding, to perform his will. Which was to be the manufacture of two uniforms, six suits and a full complement of casual wear, and all in accordance with Schroeder's impeccable taste, designed to his specifications, suggestions and instructions.

And finally there was a specialist of a very different sort. This one, a tiny, dome-headed boffin who could only talk to Garrison through an interpreter, seemed only interested in (strangely) his temples and his wrists. The span of the latter, left and right, the distance between the plates of the former. Finally he made adjustments to instruments taken from a large case and placed a set of earphones on Garrison's head. Another dip into the case brought expanding wrist-bands. These were placed on Garrison's wrists and were then attached to a small battery and push-button which Garrison held in his hand.

The interpreter, Schroeder himself, explained: 'This is purely a demonstration, Richard. The final fitting, perhaps a month from now, will involve a small, painless operation. After that there will be no wires, no visible batteries. The wrist-bands will to all intents and purposes be jewellery – and they will be of pure, solid gold. The spectacles will be a little heavier than the ones you are used to, with silver reflective lenses, and they will perfectly suit your face and swept-back hairstyle. They will never be a substitute for eyes, of course, but—'

The specialist spoke, Schroeder translated. 'Stand up, Richard, please.'

Again a guttural gabble of thick German accents, and again Schroeder's translation: 'One push of the button will bring the wrist-bands into play. They will whistle, the left with a slightly higher note than the right. Try it.'

Garrison obeyed. Two distinct whistles sounded, low and not yet annoying. 'Now I shall wheel my chair in front of you,' Schroeder told him. 'Do not move. Just let your wrists hang normally, thumbs facing forward.'

Garrison waited expectantly, full of a sudden excitement. The tone of the whistles changed, minutely, and almost immediately returned to normal. Garrison was disappointed. 'Nothing,' he said. 'Was I supposed to 'see' you or something?'

'No, no, of course not. You were simply supposed to know that something was there.'

'Useless!' Garrison snapped. The afternoon had frayed at his nerves. He was taking a lot on trust.

'Patience, Richard. Now turn on the spectacles. Another

'push of the button will do it.'

This time there was a sharp stuttering like the chatter of a Geiger counter. The German specialist stepped directly in front of Garrison and the chatter grew more rapid. He backed away and the chattering subsided. Schroeder explained his actions.

Garrison replied: 'I could get more information – distance, location, male/female, friendly/unfriendly – if he were simply to speak to me.'

'But that way you would be dependent upon him, not on yourself.'

The noises suddenly annoyed Garrison intensely. He felt like a dimly flashing light bulb in the guts of some complex, incomprehensible machine. 'The whole thing's a mess!' he snarled. He ripped the wrist-bands off and threw them down, snatched the 'phones from his head and hurled them away. 'How the hell am I to make sense of anything with all this fucking chattering and whistling going on?'

'Richard,' Schroeder's voice attempted to soothe, 'you—'

'Shit!' Garrison shouted. 'I'm sick of the whole bloody game. I thought you were different, Thomas, that I was more than just a freak to you. But Jesus – *this?* Give me back my stick any old day!' He spun about, crashed into a plastic garden chair and sent it flying, picked himself up and ran for the central building. Ran *unerringly* for the central building – and half-way there flew straight into Willy Koenig's arms.

He knew the German's aftershave, knew the strength of the arms that held him. 'Out of my way, Willy,' he snarled. 'I've had this shit up to here. I'll have no more of it!'

'Be quiet!' Koenig growled. 'Listen . . .'

Behind Garrison Schroeder tore into the specialist. He gave him hell. And all in an especially virulent German, so that Garrison would know he was not merely whitewashing. Then there came a crash of hurled instruments – an entire caseful – and finally the hoarse, still guttural protests of the specialist himself:

'Viertzig tausend Marks!' the man was moaning. 'Viertzig tausen—'

'Raus!' Schroeder finally roared, a strength in his voice Garrison would not have believed possible. The specialist gathered up his things and departed.

A few moments later Schroeder came up to Garrison and Koenig on foot. His voice was pained, his breathing erratic. He took Garrison's arm in a trembling hand. 'It was a mistake, Richard. My mistake. I wanted to do too much, too fast. And that idiot – he was like an alien. Mechanical, uncaring. A mind thinking only in terms of money. And today has been – too much. Even a seeing man would have found it . . . too . . .' He started to cough and Koenig immediately went to him. 'Too much.'

Garrison felt idiotic. A small child. Spoiled. He supported Schroeder, said to Koenig: 'Willy, the chair . . .' Koenig ran off.

'I always try to do too much,' Schroeder said. 'And always too fast. It's a mistake. You can burn yourself out. Everything I have, what is it worth? And you – no hangups, no neuroses – and here am I smothering you in hopes, aspirations. Offering you false gods. Except that . . . I *feel* you are extraordinary!' He gripped Garrison's arm and the blind man could feel the strength flowing back into Schroeder's fingers, almost as if drawn from his own body.

'What is it you want from me, Thomas?' he asked.

'I only want to give, pay my debt.'

'No, you want something. I know it.'

The other nodded. 'All right. You are right. But tomorrow will be time enough. For now, all I want is your patience. Then you will understand, and then you will have to be patient again.'

Garrison sighed. 'Very well, I'll be patient.'

'For six months, maybe a little longer?'

'What?' Garrison frowned. 'Why? What happens in six months?'

'Exit one old man,' Schroeder told him. 'A worn out old man with scrambled guts.'

'You? You'll live forever,' Garrison tried to laugh it off.

'Oh? Willy says so too. But tell the grass it must not bend in the wind nor wither in the drought, eh?'

'What is this?' Garrison cried. 'You don't want *my* pity, for God's sake! You're not grass to bend so easily.'

'But I feel the wind blowing, Richard.'

'You'll live forever!' Garrison shouted, angry again.

Schroeder gripped his arm tighter still, digging in his nails. 'It's just possible,' he said. 'Yes, maybe I will. With your help, Richard Garrison, with your help . . .'

What was left of the evening and early night was strangely empty. Koenig helped Garrison change into a grey shirt and crisp new light-blue suit flamboyantly cut. With open collar, handkerchief flopping from breast pocket, his feet clad in blue suedes which were surely out of fashion, Garrison felt better than he had felt for years – and yet at the same time he felt somehow empty, like the night.

At 9.30 after a small late meal, he and Koenig went to the bar. This was in Schroeder's own private suite, where low moody music was carried on a cooling breeze from open windows. There was bad brandy for Garrison and tiny glasses of sweet, sticky Commanderia, another reminder of his Cyprus days.

But still the night was empty and Garrison began to feel depressed. Maybe it was the drink. He drank too much, chatted too much, put on too much of a show. Yes, he was putting on a show – for Schroeder. Anything, just so long as the industrialist (surely much more than any common or garden industrialist) remained calm and did not get overheated or excited.

Mina, Schroeder's cool, efficient secretary, sat with Garrison at the bar, held his hand, talked a pidgin-English that both attracted and repulsed him. He was attracted, too, by her sensuality; and also repulsed by her easy, casual manner. She was simply amusing him, as she had doubtless been ordered to do. Pretending, as he was pretending. It meant nothing, served only to deepen the emptiness.

Vicki, on the other hand, seemed to be avoiding him. She sat with Schroeder at a small table, spoke German all night (in which Garrison was not especially well versed), finally excused herself but without saying goodnight, and did not return. Only Willy Koenig held the thing together at all, until about 11.30 when he suddenly said:

'Herr Garrison, you have had enough!'

'D'you think so, Willy?' Garrison patted Mina's hand. 'Do you think so, Mina?'

'They *both* think so,' said Schroeder, who now sat behind the bar performing Koenig's duties. 'And so do I. Besides, it's well past bar-closing time.'

'Bar-closing time?' Garrison repeated. 'I thought we only did silly things like that in England!'

'Hexen stunden!' said Mina, mysteriously.

'Witching hour? Midnight?' Suddenly Garrison realized how late it was. Suddenly, too, he wondered why he felt the effect of his drinking more than the others felt theirs. When was the last time he'd drunk – or even wanted to drink – to this extent? Damn it, he had *not* had too much – he simply wasn't used to it any more, that's all.

'Is it at all possible,' he chose his words carefully and used them with the deliberate dexterity of a man close to inebriation, 'that I might have a coffee? Or even . . . a pot of coffee?'

Koenig chuckled and went out of the room.

'Well,' said Schroeder. 'Day One, Richard.'

'Eh?'

'Here's to a new life.' There came the chink of glasses

tilted together, but Garrison's glass was empty. He lifted it to his lips anyway, then frowned and asked:

'A new life? What the hell am I drinking to?'

'To tomorrow!' said Schroeder.

'Morgen und Morgen und Morgen!' said Mina, who might also be a little drunk . . .

Garrison drank a great deal of coffee but was still a little unsteady on his feet when he finally got down from his stool. He had committed the layout of the place to memory, however, and no one offered him assistance when he said goodnight and left the bar.

Moments later he was in his room. The first odd thing he noticed was a fresh, pleasing scent of jasmine which he first took to be night-blooming flowers in the gardens. Finding his windows closed, he sniffed the air again and decided that perhaps the fragrance was merely a very expensive air-freshener. It could be a perfume, of course, but not even the most slatternly housemaid would wear *that* much! And anyway, that was not the sort of menial Schroeder would ever employ or even tolerate. On the other hand, his bed had been made and the place tidied up a little . . .

His pillows were laid out in the shape of a V.

Vicki.

She said that maybe there would be clues. OK, so she had been here, fooled with his pillows, left her calling card . . . and a scent for him to follow!

There were nine suites on this floor, and since this seemed the obvious place to start . . .

He left his bedroom and closed the door, cat-footed along the corridor from middle to end and back, then cat-footed in the opposite direction. At the last door he caught a faint whiff of jasmine. When he inclined his head towards the door the smell grew heavy and heady. A tingle of excitement thrilled him, set his scalp acrawl.

He entered quietly, closed the door after him, touched

the light switch and found it in the off position. Hopefully the layout of the room was the same as his own. He made his way to the bed, undressed, piled his clothes haphazardly on the floor, reached to turn back the covers. There was utter silence, not even the ticking of a watch or the sound of his own firmly controlled breathing.

A cool hand touched his thigh and froze him rigid. It traced a path across his front, found and held him. Trembling slightly, he felt lips kiss him there, the merest touch.

'Shower,' she whispered. 'I already have, and so must you.'

'Do I smell?' The words came out clotted and thick as sour cream.

'You smell . . . beautiful,' Vicki's voice husked. 'But wash the alcohol off your skin and the nicotine from your fingers. Men always smoke too much when they drink.' She moved her fingers languidly, back and forth, back and forth, her grip firm for a moment or two before releasing him. 'Go on, now. Do as you're told.'

'Yes, ma'am,' Garrison wanted to say, but nothing came out.

He showered quickly, sober as a judge now, finishing with a burst of icy water which shrank him in a moment, for a moment, and returned to her not quite dry. Getting into bed, he said, 'Vicki, no cliches. If you tell me to be gentle with you I'm sure I'll scream.'

She gave a low laugh, her mouth burning as she kissed his chest, tasting him from nipples to navel. There she paused, with Garrison completely immobilized beneath her hands and mouth. 'Richard, if you even gave a thought to being gentle with me, *I* would scream!'

She turned her body, opened her warm thighs for him. Inverted, they let their pulses pound as they began to feast upon each other . . .

* * *

'You see?' said Thomas Schroeder to Mina. 'I was absolutely right. I guessed it might be like this. No, I was sure. We think alike, Garrison and I.'

He lay on his back, naked and stretched full length on his bed. His abdomen was criss-crossed with new scar-tissue that extended up under his rib-cage, round his left side and was continued on his back. His body was brown, however, and his tan masked the scar-tissue a little, so that his body was not completely unsightly. In fact he might have been ten to fifteen years younger than his actual age; but the suntan and the apparently trim physique could not disguise or compensate for the ravages within. In one respect, however – in one very important respect – Thomas Schroeder had escaped the blast. It had not robbed him of his sex. Not entirely.

Mina was blonde and blue-eyed. Her hair at this moment fell like a golden veil over Schroeder's genitals; but her eyes were fixed like glinting diamonds on a large CCTV wall screen, as were those of her employer. The picture was fairly good but had a reddish blur, an effect of the infra-red camera in Vicki's ceiling.

Mina was naked, too, her body in much the same position as Vicki's against Garrison on the screen; but Schroeder was passive, his hand motionless where it fell on her V of pubic hair. She leaned on one elbow, her free hand lightly on Schroeder, gently mobile, none of her weight resting upon him. She watched Garrison and Vicki for a few more minutes, said: 'You're not concentrating, Thomas.'

'Oh? Well, perhaps I'm not, but what you're doing is good anyway.'

'You'll never get what you want this way.'

'Impatience? I should have thought that was my prerogative.' He sounded surprised. 'Mina, be a sweet and keep quiet. I'm watching Garrison. Oh, and I assure you, this is probably the *only* way I'll get what I want.'

'But you'll not come.'

He sighed and looked at her. 'Mina, I believe you really do think I'm a voyeur.'

'Aren't you? Then why are you watching them?'

'Why are you?'

She shrugged. 'I wanted to.'

'Then you are the voyeur, Mina, not I. You see the sex is incidental; and our simultaneous sex is coincidental. I am simply studying Garrison. Everything he does.'

'Why?'

'My concern, Mina. Yours, at the moment, is to pleasure me.'

Suddenly Schroeder was erect. Mina had been looking at him as they talked but now she glanced at the screen. Vicki was on her knees, legs spread, her face down in her pillows, panting. Garrison kneeled upright between her legs, his hands on her hips, thrusting himself deep into her. His breathing was harsh as he drove to climax, made harsher by the microphone relaying the sound to Schroeder's room.

Mina took what she saw as a golden opportunity, her mouth and hand working expertly as she coaxed Schroeder towards his peak – to no avail. For as Garrison and Vicki disengaged and collapsed in each other's arms, so Schroeder relaxed and his erection slackened. Mina made no complaint (she had probably already said too much) but Schroeder sensed her disappointment anyway and patted her bush of tightly curled hair.

'Have patience, Mina. The night is young – and so are they.' He nodded at the screen, then glanced at his mistress. 'And so are you. Tell me, what do you think of Garrison?'

'Honestly?'

'Of course, honestly.'

'I think – that if you will not concentrate on your own pleasure until he has taken all of his – then we shall be here until 3.30 in the morning!'

Schroeder chuckled. '5.00, I think! Yes, he has a good body. And he's hungry.'

'Vicki, too,' Mina observed. 'See, she wants to eat him again.'

'And he reacts! And now she rides him! They are splendid.'

'She surprises me,' Mina admitted. 'I had thought—'

'A nice girl like her? You are all nice, my dear. But occasionally one of you finds a special man, and then you have to do it. Because it is right and you *must* do it. Yes, and when that happens all taboos collapse. Then of course there are others who do not count the man at all but the zeroes at the end of his bank account.'

'Thomas, that is cruel,' she sounded genuinely hurt. 'Do you mean me? But you know I like you. I'm your mistress.'

'My paid mistress, yes. But—' He shrugged. 'Maybe that's why I don't come – but perhaps not. You see, to concentrate is to strain, and for this damaged body of mine to strain is to hurt, so maybe *that's* why I don't come.'

He stared harder at the screen, its images mirrored in his spectacles. He listened intently to the soft slapping sounds of love approaching another eruption. 'But Garrison . . . he knows none of this. At this moment he knows nothing but his need, his lust. And perhaps something of Vicki's. He is almost automatic. He does not have to concentrate, does not strain, feels no pain. Well, perhaps a little pain – the final sweet agony which is his reward, the incentive to start the sequence all over again.'

While he had talked they both had watched the screen, had seen Vicki collapse on to Garrison, their bodies shuddering in unison. Mina's nipples had hardened along with a return of Schroeder's erection. 'Maybe this time, Thomas,' she said, moving her hand a little faster, more rhythmically, and opening her shapely legs until his hand slid into her moistness.

'Perhaps,' he answered, 'but I don't think so.'

She pouted as only a German girl can. 'You're not even trying!'

'No, I don't think I am. They have me fascinated. See how they cling, drenched in sweat and revelling in it? And Vicki, she—'

'She is surprising even you now, eh?'

'That boy,' said Schroeder, changing the subject in a moment, 'could be an image of myself at his age. He has the vigour.'

'Perhaps he's just been saving it?'

'Oh, yes, I imagine so,' Schroeder nodded. 'Enforced abstinence. His blindness. But the way they *cling* – like real lovers . . .'

'Love at first sight?'

'They can't get enough of each other. They feel they should be able to stretch their skins flat, one on top of the other. She would like to be able to draw him in utterly, his entire being, body and soul. And he desires so to be drawn. They want to explore, to know everything, now.'

'Thomas, I—' She was beginning to sound tired.

'No, no!' he quietened her. 'We must see this out. There's an unusual excitement here. Listen, Mina, you talked about Vicki being a nice girl. Well so she is, but—' He paused. 'Before the night is out, Garrison will enter her by the third route. And it will be a first for both of them.'

'No, you are mistaken,' she told him. 'Only lovers in the fullest—'

'They will!'

'No, by 3.00 it will be over. They'll sleep like babes.'

'5.00 at the earliest,' Schroeder insisted. 'And it will be as I said.'

'Are you wagering?'

'Double your normal cheque if I'm wrong!'

'Ah! You fed him some of your mushrooms, of course!'

'No, *I* had the mushrooms.'

'Then it must soon be over.'

'Mina, you are quite wrong.'

'But how can you be so sure?'

71

'Because I *remember* how it was, Mina! I remember it so well.'

'Double my normal cheque?' she said after a while.

He merely nodded, his eyes glued to the screen. He knew it was money she would never collect . . .

Chapter Four

'Day Two, Richard,' said Schroeder over a very late breakfast. 'And the sun already high, and we haven't even started yet. So much for late nights and demon drink, eh?'

'Yes,' Garrison agreed, his mind dull in a drained body. But the food was good and plenty, and he knew that strength would soon flow back into him. He thought of last night and of Vicki, and begrudged the three and a half hours they had slept (died?) in each other's arms before he had returned to his own room.

Nor had he left her any too soon, for within a half-hour he had been awake again, this time at the insistence of 'nurse', a crusty old Fraulein (Frau?) whose word was apparently law. He remembered wondering what she would have thought if she'd entered his room an hour earlier – or worse, Vicki's room!

'Er,' (he hadn't wanted to seem obvious, but—) 'where is Vicki, by the way?'

'Vicki? She rose, breakfasted, swam, went back to bed. She has no tight schedule like you. Also, she seemed very tired this morning. But don't worry, we'll all have a late lunch and you can talk to her then.'

She must have got up immediately after he had left her, Garrison thought. But was that amusement in Schroeder's voice? He couldn't quite make up his mind.

'Are you ready for today?' Schroeder continued. 'Perhaps you didn't sleep too well? You, too, seem a little tired.'

'Ready?' Garrison answered. 'For the sixth building, the Big Secret – the future? I won't go to sleep on you, promise.'

'First the library,' said Schroeder. 'I want to show you

some books, ask you certain questions.'

Garrison felt a sudden uneasiness. 'This isn't all going to be a pain like yesterday, is it?'

'Oh, no,' Schroeder shook his head. 'If I'm right you'll find it all very interesting.'

They finished their coffees and Garrison pushed Schroeder to the library building. There Schroeder used an electronic key to unlock the library's shatterproof glass doors.

Garrison then guided the chair to the bookshelves lining the walls. Now he found the books – books by the hundreds, the thousands – and let his hands run over their spines.

'The shelves are only two meters high,' Schroeder told him, and went on to explain: 'I hate shelves you need a chair to reach! But they fill all four large rooms on both floors. And they contain more than three hundred and ten thousand books. Hardbacks, softbacks, magazines, periodicals, first editions, rare collector's items, cheap pulps. Yes, and they all have one thing in common. A single theme, you might say.'

'Oh?' Garrison was politely curious.

'The mysterious, the unexplained, the supernatural, the strange, the esoteric . . .'

'Weird stuff? I was never much interested in—'

'That shelf you are touching now,' Schroeder cut in, 'contains books dealing with ESP. About two hundred of them. To your right are some fifty volumes dealing with possession. To your left, about thirty on alchemy. Over here we have astronomy, and right alongside it astrology. A great number of books on the latter.'

Schroeder was on his feet now. He took Garrison's elbow and led him to a shelf standing apart from the rest. Beside it a small table was littered with books. 'This subject, however, is my favourite. You see, I have a table here where I can sit and read without going up to the observatory.'

An odd chill struck Garrison. It was as if a cold wind suddenly blew on him from his host, like the one he had felt in the gardens when they were looking for the mushrooms. Perhaps it had something to do with the man's voice, which had taken on a new (guarded?) intensity. But guarded or otherwise, this preternatural chill told Garrison that whatever Schroeder said or did in the next few minutes, he would be in deadly earnest.

'Do you remember what you said to me yesterday evening when I told you I didn't have a great deal of time left?' Schroeder asked, and quickly continued: 'You said that—'

'You'd live forever,' Garrison finished it for him. As he spoke a word jumped to the front of his mind, formed itself and fell out of his mouth almost unbidden. 'Reincarnation.'

Schroeder gasped but Garrison only smiled. He had always been quick on the uptake. After a moment the industrialist took his elbow and said, 'Sit.' He held a chair for Garrison. They sat at the table and Garrison could hear Schroeder turning the leaves of a book. 'Reincarnation, yes. Metempsychosis. Do you believe?'

Garrison shrugged. 'I suppose I've given it some thought, not much.'

'Men have given it thought since the very first men knew how to think,' the other told him. 'I think, therefore I am – *and will go on being*! I have more than two hundred and forty works on the subject, in all languages, and there is an even greater number which I do not deem worthy of my collection. And I'll tell you something: the older a man gets, the more he thinks about it. It's like believing in God. The closer you get to dying the more inclined you are to believe.'

'And you really do believe,' said Garrison. He made it a statement of fact, not a question.

'I do, yes. Richard, I have a son. Thanks to you he still lives. He is healthy, he will be handsome, intelligent. He will have a full life. If I had twenty years – if I had even ten – perhaps I could find a way to return, to come back in the body of my son.'

Garrison was suddenly prompted to laugh. He did no such thing, however, but merely sat motionless. He could still feel the chill, the tension in Schroeder's voice, the goose-flesh creeping on his arms. No, this was no time for laughter; the man was deadly serious.

Finally Garrison said, 'Come back in the body of your son? Usurp his mind, you mean? Return as Thomas Schroeder?'

He sensed the other's denial, the immediate shaking of his head. 'No, no. That is quite impossible.' (Again the air of absolute sincerity, conviction.) 'No, it would be more a sharing. I would be Heinrich, he would be me. And we would go on together. But . . . I don't have ten years. I don't have ten months. Heinrich is a mere child, a baby. He knows nothing. To come back in him, if it is at all possible, would be to lose myself. *I would not know!* Do you understand?'

'In his untried mind the greater You would overflow, spill out. Only a spark of You would remain. Without even knowing it he would evict You. Your identity would be gone forever.'

'Exactly! Your grasp is amazing.'

The chill was now intense. Garrison could feel Schroeder leaning closer, the man's hot unpleasant breath in his face. He suddenly feared what Schroeder might say next. But when it came it was anticlimax:

'Richard, what of dreams?'

'Dreams? What of them?'

'Are you not a dreamer? Do you dream when you are asleep?'

'Of course. I've had dreams, like anyone else. But not recent—' He froze, the word incomplete. He drew air in a gasp, pictured the industrialist's fear-shiny face as he had seen it at the doors of the Europa in Belfast. Suddenly it fitted perfectly over another face he had thought long banished in realms of nightmare.

A face in the sky – that of the man-God – bald-headed, with a high-domed forehead, eyes made huge through thick lenses—

Garrison shook his head, but to no avail. More of that old dream came flowing back, unbidden except by Schroeder's question, flashing on his mind's eye like stills from some old film.

A man with a crewcut, blond, standing beside a silver Mercedes atop an impossibly steep crag—

Garrison's mind whirled.

'Richard, are you all right?' Schroeder's voice, full of concern, seemed to come from a million miles away. It dragged Garrison back to reality. But though the rest of his dream remained shrouded, those two definite images stayed sharp, mirror-bright on his memory. The man-God's face in the sky – Schroeder's face – and the crewcut man with the Mercedes, who could only be Willy Koenig. Those images and one other: *of a burning brown-paper parcel, a cube of lashing energy and glaring, searing, blinding light and heat!*

Schroeder's fingers dug into his wrist. 'Richard—!'

'I'm . . . all right. You woke something in me, that's all. Something frightening. I had forgotten it, until now.'

'What?' Schroeder did not relax his grip. 'What did I awake in you?'

'A memory. I remembered a dream. A recurrent dream. Parts of it, anyway. A dream of you, and of Willy Koenig.'

Schroeder's fascination was a tangible thing. 'Oh? And when did this occur? When you knew you were coming out here to see me?'

Garrison shook his head. 'No, long before that. It was something that happened to me over a period of about three weeks. A recurrent nightmare that came again and

77

again. A warning. You were in it, and Koenig – and the bomb!'

'The bomb?' Koenig's voice was a whisper.

Garrison nodded. 'And the last time I dreamed it was – the night before the Europa!'

'The night *before* the Eur—' the German repeated, his words fading into a sigh.

For the first time in his life, Richard Garrison was glad he was blind. Glad, at least, that he could not see the other's face. But he could still feel it. That look of amazement slowly turning to—

To what? Disbelief? Hope?

. . . Or triumph?

'A hypnotist? Are you serious?' Garrison had not yet learned that this was a question unworthy of his host. If Schroeder said he would do something, he would do it.

'With your permission, yes.'

'But why? I don't understand.'

They were now in the observatory at the top of Schroeder's library building, seated at a large circular table where the sun struck in at them through curving windows. The table's top was smooth, cool and metallic. Schroeder had come up in a tiny lift only recently fitted, installed specially to accommodate his wheelchair. Garrison had climbed the stairs.

'I wish to know those portions of the dream you can't remember. A good hypnotist could probably draw them out of you. I know some of the very best.'

'But is it so important? I mean, I can't even remember now if the thing was real. Do you know what I mean? I might have confused things. I may have dreamed it after the explosion, while I was still in hospital.'

'I don't think so,' replied Schroeder. 'You were pretty certain a few minutes ago. No, I would prefer to believe that it was precognition. You have that sort of mind, Richard.'

'I do? How could you possibly know that?'

'Powers of observation,' Schroeder answered. 'Your instinctive reactions, for instance. Why, you seem sometimes to act upon a thing before it happens. Take for example Gunter's intrusion upon us in the woods. You sensed, heard, *knew* he was there before I had even suspected it. And I can see perfectly well. And I knew that there were men in the woods.'

'But it's a recognized fact that if you lose one of your senses the other four try to even up the score, become sharper.'

'In time, yes,' Schroeder agreed. 'But your four surviving senses have not yet had time to develop such an edge – or if they have you are even more unusual than I suspect.'

'But what is it about the dream that so interests you?'

'What? Can I believe my own ears? Why, I was part of that dream, before ever you met me!'

Garrison frowned. Shadows seemed to be lifting from his mind. After a moment he said, 'I can remember more of it now.'

'Go on then,' said Schroeder eagerly. 'Go on, by all means.'

'There was a girl, with huge eyes and shiny black hair.'

'Oh? Did she have a name?'

Garrison shook his head. 'I can't remember. But – I had never seen her face. What I knew of her I knew by touch, or perhaps I had heard it from her. I think I knew her body. I'm not sure.'

'Anyone else in the dream who you had never seen?'

'Yes, a man.' Garrison tried to concentrate. 'A man in a castle. No description but—'

'Yes?'

'I think – yes, he's tall, slim, and – a liar. A cheat!'

79

Schroeder frowned, his grip slackening on Garrison's wrist. 'What else about him?'

'Only that I couldn't reach him. I was trying to get to him, but something held me back.'

'And what part did I play in your dream?'

Garrison slowly shook his head. 'I don't know. A face in the sky. Your face. I thought of you as a man-God.'

Schroeder's grip tightened again. 'And Willy?'

'A friend. He ... showed me the way. It's hard to explain. He stood on a tall rock, pointing the way. Beside him, your Mercedes.'

'A Mercedes, yes,' Schroeder nodded. 'My symbol. Here in Germany I own several. All of them are silver in colour. And abroad I always hire one. What else?'

'A ... Machine?'

'Machine? You seem uncertain. And I sensed that you said machine with a capital M.'

'I did, you're right.'

'And what was this machine?'

'That's what I'm uncertain about. I don't know what the Machine was. But I think I rode it ...'

Frustrated, Schroeder shook his head. Garrison sensed that he was eager to know more.

'There are no clear details,' he told the German.

'Again you anticipate me,' Schroeder was quick to note. 'Your perceptions are almost telepathic. But please go on. What more do you remember of this dream?'

'Only one more thing,' Garrison told him. 'A dog, a black bitch.'

Schroeder breathed in sharply and his excitement drove him to his feet. 'A dog? A black dog, you say? A bitch? By *God!*' He slammed a fist into the palm of his hand, then grunted and stumbled, clutching at the table for support. For a moment he swayed before almost falling into his seat. His breathing had gone ragged with pain.

'Easy,' Garrison told him. 'Jesus! Don't go banging

yourself up for the sake of a bloody dream.'

Schroeder snorted, then gave a shaky laugh. 'A bloody dream? My God, a bloody dream! Richard, the more I know of you, the more convinced I am that you – that you . . .'

'Yes?'

'Listen,' said Schroeder, 'that was no ordinary "bloody dream", Richard. It was precognition of the first order. But something puzzles me. If you really did see the bomb in your dream—'

'I saw it. It exploded!'

'—Then why did you go with me into the Europa?'

'The dream was never sufficiently distinct. I failed to relate it to reality. Why should I? I had been dreaming the thing for three weeks. Lots of guys dream of bombs in NI. It just didn't connect. It wasn't until I saw the bomb itself – sitting there in your hotel room – that I *knew* what was going to happen. But the bomb must have blown the whole thing back into my subconscious mind. Jesus, it's only just surfaced again! And even now I can't be sure.'

'But you will let me call in a hypnotist? A very professional one, I assure you.'

'If it will make you happy. But I'm no closer to knowing what all this is about.'

'Very well, I'll try to explain – in a moment. But first – come with me.' Schroeder stood up and led the other to the far side of the table, which in fact formed the platform of a large reflecting telescope. There he placed Garrison's hands on the cylindrical body of the instrument and let his fingers trace something of its outline.

'Telescope,' said Garrison. 'For . . . astrology!'

'Astronomy too,' Schroeder answered. 'But mainly astrology, yes. It is an ancient and quite *exact* science. My personal astrologer is Adam Schenk, who claims direct descendance from Giambattista Porta. In fact he claims he *is* Giambattista Porta! Porta invented photography, wrote the often misquoted *De Furtivis Literarum Notis*, and several volumes on astrology, geometry, astral projection and the power of human thought. He also produced a pamphlet on reincarnation, of which I have a very rare copy. I consider it highly likely that Schenk's claim is genuine, for certainly he seems to have retained and extended many of Porta's facets.

'He came to me here three weeks ago. He worked, ate, slept, studied and came to his conclusions here, at this very table, in almost complete solitude. Part of what he told me prompted me to contact you, to bring you here. I had already decided to provide for you – to repay my debt, as it were – but after what Schenk told me . . .' Garrison sensed the other's fatalistic shrug. 'Now it has gone further than that.'

'Actually,' said Garrison, 'I sort of know I'm tied up with you. I don't know how, or why, but I feel it. It's very frustrating. Lack of understanding can be worse than blindness. Everything is a huge knot. I need it unravelling. Where did it all begin?'

'For me it began in Hitler's Germany,' Schroeder told him. 'There were those high in the Fuehrer's favour who used black arts, dark forces. Oh, yes, they actually did. They interested him in their subject and he was converted. He came to believe in the metapsychic powers of the mind. And he had certain powers, believe me. Or if you doubt me, listen to his oratories. He did not merely rant, Richard.'

'Perhaps he was merely grasping at straws, like us,' Garrison answered. 'I mean, in respect of his war effort.'

'I don't know. He was of course a madman. But if it might help him rule the world, then he must try it. Still, he only dabbled. There were those in his employ, however . . . I was for a time very friendly with one of them, even though I had always considered him a crank. Certain experiments, some of which I myself took part in, helped convince me that there was more to the parapsychological world than mundane science might explain away. You may not sense it in me, but I am highly intuitive.'

'I have noticed,' Garrison wryly answered. 'You often act instinctively, like me.'

Schroeder nodded. 'But I am also a sensitive. That is to say, my hunches work out more often than they fail me. I hope soon to prove that you too are a vessel.'

'Vessel?'

'A receiver for whatever these forces are which we loosely term ESP.'

After a moment Garrison said: 'Go on with what you were telling me.'

'Well, it was then, towards the end of the war, the collapse, that I became interested in the, shall we say, esoteric sciences? And it was an interest which has never flagged. What I have learned has been profitable. I am "instinctive" in business, too, you see? By 1952 I was a millionaire, by '57 a multi-millionaire. Now . . .? Suffice it to say that I am very, very rich.

'However, I do not wish to bore you with the entire story, which would take up far too much of our time. Only believe me when I tell you that I have come to be extremely learned in several obscure fields. Not a master in any of them, no, for I started too late; but I do have contact with the masters.

'Adam Schenk is one such. He is *the* astrologer, a great clairvoyant, an interpreter of dreams. In short, the stuff of ESP is strong in him.

'As to why he came to me: he said I needed him, that the cosmic influences on my life were bending towards a focus, and that the *genius loci* lay in an outsider, a foreigner to whom I owed a great debt.'

'Myself,' said Garrison.

'Who else? And so Schenk came, cast my horoscope and those of my inner circle of friends, and yours—'

'Mine?' Garrison felt a small annoyance.

'Yes, it was necessary. If the idea offends you then I am sorry. But since I had already collected together so many of your, shall we say, "details", it was not a difficult task. And since you were so obviously indicated by my own horoscope, I requested that he do it.'

Garrison's annoyance turned to amusement. Suddenly the whole thing seemed funny to the point of ridiculous. 'I'm listening,' he said, 'and I'm trying to keep an open mind, but—'

'Be quiet!' Schroeder snapped, angry in a moment. 'Open mind, you say? You had better keep an open mind! We are talking about your entire future. We may even be talking about *my* entire future . . .' And again that strange chill struck at Garrison out of nowhere.

'Copies of Schenk's forecasts,' Schroeder continued in a moment, 'are still here on this very table.' There was the rustle of paper. 'Here is yours. There, hold it up for me while I read it. If you don't believe what I tell you is on it, take it to Willy and ask him.'

The strip of card, perhaps three inches wide and nine long, felt heavy as a death warrant in Garrison's hand. He held it up towards Schroeder's voice. 'OK,' he said, 'what's on it?'

Schroeder drew a deep breath. 'Just a series of words. Some bunched together, others by themselves, written in ink to form a column down the left-hand side of the card. There's a time-scale on the right. Are you ready for this, Richard Garrison?'

'Is it as bad as all that?'

'It is . . . remarkable.'

Garrison nodded. 'Let's see if I find it remarkable,' he said.

'"Richard Garrison,"' Schroeder commenced. '"Darkness. Time-scale: now."'

'"Limbo. Time-scale: to six months."'

'"WK and Black Dog, 'S'? Time-scale: to three years."'

'"Girl 'T'. Time-scale: to eight years."

'"Machine. Time-scale: to eight years."

'"RG/TS . . ."

'"Light!"'

Garrison was cold, his flesh creeping. He shuddered, his voice shaky when he asked, 'That means something to you?'

Schroeder had seen his condition, however, and tossed the question right back to him. 'How do you read it?'

'Mumbo-jumbo!'

'Wrong! This is the meaning:

'That you are blind, and for six months your life will be meaningless, suspended in a sort of limbo. Then there will be a decisive change, brought about by WK and a black dog, "S". After three years you will meet a girl, "T", with whom your involvement is to last for four years before—'

'Before the Machine,' said Garrison.

'Yes.'

'And WK? And RG/TS?' Garrison knew the answers but wanted them from Schroeder.

'Willy Koenig, Richard Garrison, Thomas Schroeder,' said the other.

'And light?' Garrison had gone very quiet.

'If darkness means blindness, light can only mean sight,' the industrialist answered.

'I'm to see again, in eight years?'

'So it would appear.'

'But how?'

'New surgical techniques, who can say?'

After a while Garrison said: 'For a man with no real or serious hangups, it comes as a queer sensation to find myself suddenly grasping at straws.'

'I know,' answered Schroeder. 'Oh, I know so well! But grasp at them, Richard, and hang on for dear life. Believe me, you are not alone.'

*　　*　　*

'Who else's horoscope do you have?' asked Garrison after a pause of several minutes.

'Willy Koenig's,' Schroeder answered. 'My son Heinrich's. My wife's, my own and Vick—' He tried to snatch back the last word, but too late.

'Vicki's? What of Vicki?'

'Why, nothing!' Schroeder tried to make light of it. 'She was simply here when Schenk came, that's all. Her horoscope has nothing to do with yours. There's no connection.'

'No connection? Between Vicki and me? There has to be. Read it to me, please.'

'But, Richard, I—'

'You don't know all of it,' said Garrison, never dreaming that in fact Schroeder did know all of it. 'Please . . .'

Schroeder sighed. '"Vicki Maler,"' he began, and at once halted.

Again Garrison said, 'Please!'

'As you wish.' The German's voice was now little more than a dry croak. '"Vicki Maler, darkness. Time-scale: now."'

'"Death. Time-scale: one year!"'

'*No!*' Garrison cried. He reached out and snatched the card from Schroeder's fingers, his instinct deadly accurate. He crumpled the card, threw it down on to the telescope's platform.

Schroeder grabbed his trembling, balled fist. 'Richard, Schenk could be wrong. It's possible. He's only human. He will readily admit that he makes mistakes . . .' He paused. 'But not . . . often.'

Garrison's face was twisted, his teeth gritted. 'Vicki is to die? How? Why?'

'She came here from Siebert's sanatorium where they had been testing her eyes. Saul was hoping that perhaps there was a chance, for partial sight, anyway. While she was there he discovered a disease. Very rare. He knows now that this

86

is what blinded her, and that ever since it has been spreading through her system. A sort of cancer. It is now critical. How critical remains to be seen when the final test results come in tomorrow.'

'And does Vicki know all this?'

'Oh, yes. About the disease, not about the horoscope.'

'And what will these test results tell you?'

'How much time she has.'

'No cure?'

'Out of the question.'

'You told me that the horoscope could be wrong.'

'I . . . lied.'

'This Schenk must be a fraud!' Garrison burst out. 'He must have known she'd been to the sanatorium. Must have known why. He's been in touch with Siebert. He's a con man. If she's to die—' he almost choked on the word, '—she's to die. Why drag this weird bastard in on it?'

'No, no, Richard,' Schroeder tried to calm him. 'Adam is a good friend. I've known him for more than twenty years. He is a very genuine person.'

Garrison snatched up the crumpled card, and his own, and stuffed them into a pocket. 'I'll have Koenig read them to me.'

Schroeder sighed. 'Do you really think I would lie to you about these things?'

'Let's just say I don't want to believe you. But yes, I believe. But I'm blind! Willy's eyes are good. Proof is positive.'

Garrison sensed Schroeder's nod. 'Very well. And I know how you must feel.'

'What of your own horoscope?' Garrison asked. 'And Willy's?'

'This is mine,' Schroeder handed him a card. 'It simply says: "Thomas. Death. Time-scale: six months."'

Garrison gripped the other's hand. 'Jesus! This Schenk's a bloody murderer. No, a witch-doctor. Can't you see he's just a witch-doctor? He's told you you're going to die and you believe him, and you're simply willing yourself to death!'

'No,' Schroeder answered, his voice gentle against Garrison's passion. 'I knew it before Adam told me, before my doctors told me. They only confirmed what I could feel inside. My guts are breaking down.'

Garrison shook his head; and again, wildly. 'But there's no proof yet for any of this. None of it has to be. These are forecasts, that's all. And damned ghoulish ones at that! I still think this Schenk must be a charlatan.'

'And my doctors? Saul Siebert?' Schroeder shook his head. 'No, time will show you how wrong you are.' And once again Garrison felt that unnatural chill.

'What of Willy Koenig?' he asked. 'Is he too to be sacrificed to this supernatural hodge-podge?'

'No, Willy's future seems secure. His card says; "W. Koenig. Time-scale: six months," following which there is only one further entry. Simply your name, "Richard Garrison."'

Again Garrison shook his head. 'You see? None of it makes any sense.'

'Then why does it worry and anger you?'

'I – I don't know. Listen, can we come out in the open, get all of this in a single nutshell?'

'Very well,' said Schroeder, 'tell me – honestly – what you make of it.'

Garrison nodded and licked his lips. 'You believe that in about six months' time you're going to die.'

'I know it.'

'And that after some eight years you will be reborn, reincarnated – in me.'

'It is possible, but not without your help. Not unless you sanction it.'

'How?'

'You must first accept the principle. And then, when I

come to you, you must accept me.'

'Two minds in one body?'

'I've already told you, it won't be like that. More a melding of minds. We won't be aware that there are two of us. My identity will be yours, yours will be mine.'

Garrison frowned, shook his head. 'It's no use. I simply can't grasp reincarnation.'

'That's odd,' said Schroeder. 'An intelligent man like you. And yet, ask any amoeba—'

'An amoeba? More riddles?'

'Consider,' said Schroeder. 'What is the simple amoeba if not a classic case of continuous reincarnation? Why, we might state for a fact that *any* amoeba glimpsed in a microscope *is* the original, primal amoeba from prehistoric oceans. Mitosis has not only assured the extension of the species but also its original identity.'

'We are not single-celled organisms,' Garrison observed.

'I have known several previous existences.' Schroeder ignored him. 'They have been discovered through hypnosis. If you too, under hypnosis, "remember" past lives – that will be another example of our compatibility.'

'You still haven't shown me any proof.'

'Time will provide the proof. But there is perhaps something which will go a little way towards helping convince you.'

'Oh?'

'You mentioned the dog in your dream. A black bitch. And you know how I reacted when you told me about it.'

'Yes. So?'

'Now you have seen the Black Dog, "S", mentioned again in Schenk's forecast.'

'Coincidence,' Garrison shrugged.

'The day before Schenk came here I sent a letter to a man I know in Minden. His name is Heinz Holzer. Heinz and I go back a long way. He used to be a psychiatrist, worked with shell-shocked men from the front line. He is still a psychiatrist of sorts, only now he works on the minds of dogs. Dobermanns. Black bitches. He trains them for blind people, and they are the best, most unusual and expensive blind dogs in the world. I told him I wanted a dog for you – and this was before Schenk, before learning of the dog in your dream. Wait—' He got up, went to a telephone, dialled and after a moment said: 'Mina. I want the first letter to Holzer, about three weeks ago. That's right, my original instructions. The dog for Richard Garrison. Have someone bring my copy to the door of the library, please. Thank you . . .' He put the phone down, turned to Garrison:

'That letter, too, you may keep for Willy to read to you.'

'OK,' said Garrison. 'Let's just say I believe you. I may be going mad, but I believe you anyway. But tell me, what makes you so sure I'll accept this blind dog?'

He sensed Schroeder's smile. 'But you will, obviously!'

The German's faith in the occult order of things was getting to be unnerving. Suddenly Garrison had had enough of the library and observatory. He stood up. 'Are we finished here?'

'We are finished here, yes. Finished for this morning. But look, the sun is so warm. Why don't we swim, eh? Vicki is bound to be in the pool again by now. She loves the water. Lunch will be late, and this afternoon—'

'The other building?'

'Yes. For that is where you shall learn that there really is substance to all of this, that it is not simply a matter of complex coincidences. Oh, and incidentally, when I asked you about dreams, that was no coincidence either.'

'I didn't for a moment suppose that it was.'

'Since the bomb, during this long convalescence of mine – useless, wasted effort that it is – I too have dreamed. The dream is always the same: a light shining in darkness. And when I get to the light I find that it's a mirror.'

'A mirror?'

'Indeed, Richard. A polished glass. And when I look in it – why, it's not my face I see at all but yours! And you are not blind, Richard, for you see me, and you smile.' Schroeder suddenly shivered. 'A very strange smile indeed . . .'

Chapter Five

As they left the library building Willy Koenig met them with the letter to Heinz Holzer. 'Give it to Richard, Willy,' said Schroeder. 'Later he will ask you to read it to him. Right now, however, we are going to swim. It's very warm and the water will give us an appetite.'

Later, as they sat in the sunlight at the pool's edge, Schroeder said to Vicki: 'My dear, you must be more careful. For the first time I have noticed your bruises! Goodness, how you must bump into things! I had thought you overcame that problem years ago.'

'Strange surroundings,' she answered at once. 'And I bruise so easily. And anyway, I refuse to accept that it's all my fault. It seems to me that I don't so much bump into things as things bump into me!' She laughed, and Schroeder too.

Garrison also laughed, more inwardly than outwardly; but only Schroeder knew that they all shared the same joke.

Lunch came and went and later, after long cool drinks in the bar (non-alcoholic drinks, Garrison noted) he and Schroeder went to the sixth building. Here there was a difference in the atmosphere: the other place had reeked of paper and print, of old words in old books. This one smelled – different. It was like entering the lair of some unknown, unknowable beast.

'Well,' said Schroeder, once they were inside and the doors were closed behind them, 'and what does your ESP faculty tell you about this place, my young friend?'

ESP, yes. The question contained the clue.

'A laboratory,' Garrison replied, almost without conscious thought. He inclined his head upward, sniffed the air, listened to the silence. 'A test centre.' He sensed that Schroeder was impressed.

'To test what?'

'Why, ESP, of course! A place to measure the unknown, to sound the unfathomable.'

'That is very profound,' said Schroeder. 'Like many of the things you say, it belies your youth. I'm sure that you have lived before, Richard Garrison.'

'Where do we start?' Garrison asked. 'And what will we be doing?'

'Measuring the unknown,' Schroeder answered at once. 'And we start right now.'

'You mean I'm right? One hundred per cent? This is an ESP laboratory?' Even Garrison sounded surprised.

'You are right, one hundred per cent, yes. It is a complex of machines – you might even say one big machine, creating the perfect environment – for testing ESP abilities.'

'You mean the whole building? One big—'

'Ah! I can see the question written on your face,' said Schroeder. 'You wonder if this complex could possibly be the "Machine" of your dreams, eh? Well, I too have wondered about that. Could it be that I shall come to you eventually through the medium of just such a machine as this?' His gesture encompassed the room, the entire building.

'Did you hold up your arms just then?' Garrison asked.

'Yes.'

'I knew you had. Maybe there's something to all of this after all. But no, I don't know anything else about the Machine in my dream.'

'Hitler dreamed of a Machine too, you know,' Schroeder told him.

'His war machine? The might of Der Vaterland? Ten million jackboots on the march? Yes, I know that.'

'No, a different sort of machine. An ESP machine. A

device to unlock man's latent, superhuman psychic powers. He even started to build one.'

'You were on it? That's where you got the idea for all of this?'

'No, it was completely different to this. All of these things are toys by comparison. Hitler's machine was not designed to read or measure the psyche but to alter it, to increase it beyond all known levels of awareness and capability. Literally to create supermen! I wasn't in on it, but I knew many of the people who were. It was called the Berlin Project. Top Secret. And oddly enough, one of the top members of the team was Heinz Holzer.'

'The man who trains blind dogs?'

'Yes. His job was the definition of the working of the mind, or the psyche. His qualifications, you understand, were not confined to a purely psychiatric level. He was skilled in every area of mental science and knowledge and had a prodigious medical background. His own father was a pathfinder amongst neurologists, his mother a surgeon, and Holzer himself one of the first really effective neuropsychiatrists.'

Garrison put it more succinctly. 'No ordinary shrink,' he said.

Schroeder snorted. 'Not ordinary in any way, no.'

'And he trains blind dogs? Isn't that a hell of a waste?'

'He is a good man, you understand,' said Schroeder. 'But he is also a wanted man. At the end of the war the Allies knew about the Berlin Project, and they wanted to know more. It would not do for him to return to his old work, brilliant though he was. They would sooner or later trace him through that work. And of course his real name is no more Holzer than mine is Schroeder. As for training blind dogs: that is as close as he dares come to using his skills as they were given him to be used.'

'I don't get that,' Garrison shook his head.

'Oh? Well, dogs have minds too, you know. They are

highly intelligent creatures. And minds can be – directed?'

'He brainwashes dogs?'

'In a manner of speaking. But to my knowledge his methods are far and away superior to conventional training systems. In most animal training the principles of fear, punishment and reward still apply. Not in Holzer's. How he does it *exactly* I don't know – but his methods speak for themselves. Have you not wondered what has become of your old clothes and uniforms? Or why we required all of those specimens of . . . well, of you? And the photographs and films, and voice-tapes? Now you begin to appreciate why one of Holzer's dogs costs so much, eh? She will not be simply a dog, Richard. She will be a marvel!'

'So he brainwashes dogs with a machine, does he? A scaled-down model of the one Hitler would have used to produce supermen. And he produces superdogs.'

'Ah!' Schroeder's denial was immediate. 'No, I didn't say that. Oh, it's possible Heinz has built less complex devices, I suppose, but nothing on the scale of that machine envisioned by Der Fehurer. Even if he had the money it would still be out of the question. To my knowledge there was only one man in the entire world who had the technological skill to build such a machine, and he died when the Russians swarmed into East Berlin. There were rumours that he had escaped, and until recently the Israelis had men in Brazil following false trails, but I think he must be dead. His name was Otto Krippner. He was a real Nazi and, I think, a madman . . . Anyway, *these* machines—' again the encompassing gesture, '—are not of that order. They are, as you had it, machines to measure the unknown, to sound the unfathomable.'

Garrison stared blindly in the direction of Schroeder's voice and slowly the frown lifted from his forehead. 'OK,' he finally said, 'I'm hooked. You want to test me, I want to be tested. Perhaps I am – an Esper? – I don't know. But yes, I've sometimes – often – felt that I've lived before. Déjà vu, yes. I've looked it up. The sceptics call it paramnesia. And I've perhaps been more interested in parallel phenomena than I've admitted. But—'

'I understand your apprehensions.'

Garrison nodded. 'First you'd better tell me exactly what you've got here. I mean, I know you have machines – but what *sort* of machines? What are they exactly?'

'Machines without engines!' Schroeder answered at once. 'They are designed to harness the hidden powers of the human mind – if the subject has the required talent. Also, I have the equipment to test remote viewing. Do you know what that is?'

'Seeing afar – without telescope or binoculars but by using the mind's eye.'

'The mind's eye . . .' Schroeder repeated him. 'Excellent!'

'What else?'

'We also have a Ganzfeld state room, to induce maximum ESP receptivity; and devices to assist in self-hypnosis, so that we may attempt a little precognitive clairvoyance. As for more mundane tests, we have a rather sophisticated Zener cards machine, and other similar devices based broadly on the work of J. B. Rhine. Rhine "invented" ESP, you know. And there are dice, thrown mechanically and in a sealed chamber, for assessing psychokinesis; cubicles for TET – telepathic exchange tests; de-magnetized rooms for teleportation and levitation . . . And many more. Where would you like to begin?'

Garrison shrugged. 'I'm in your hands.'

'And how do you feel about it? I mean, if your approach is negative—'

'No, I feel receptive. Responsive.'

'Good!'

That was at 2.45 P.M. It was 10.30 when they left the laboratory. By then Garrison was feeling shaken, Schroeder was jubilant, and both of them were exhausted.

And they had made a pact.

*   *   *

An hour later Garrison made his way to the bar. Late as the hour was, he felt he needed a drink. And Schroeder had told him to use the bar whenever he felt inclined. Willy Koenig was there, mixing a drink for Vicki. She had already had several but was very sober. She sat at the bar on a stool; Garrison located her as soon as he entered the room – her perfume. Two of Schroeder's guards were seated at a small table in one corner, playing cards and sharing a bottle of Schnapps. Of Schroeder himself there was no sign.

Garrison found a stool beside Vicki's and seated himself. He took her hand. 'Hi,' he quietly said. 'I'm glad you're here.' He wanted to add: *I couldn't sleep and wasn't ready for bed, and I was half-afraid you might already be asleep. I wouldn't have wanted to disturb you*... But he merely repeated, 'I'm glad you're here.'

Perhaps she understood, for she squeezed his hand and he felt her smile warm him. 'It was heads an early night, tails a drink. The coin came down heads.'

'So why are you here?'

'I had to make it the best of five! No, seriously, I thought you might come for a drink before . . . well, before.' Over in the corner one of the guards guffawed and slapped the table. The other muttered a gruff curse. Germans are voluble about their card-playing.

Koenig had already sensed an atmosphere between the two at the bar. He knew nothing of their affair, but sensed something. There was a sadness, an aching. But not a needful aching. It was a time for privacy. He snapped his fingers in the direction of the corner table.

'Raus!' he said, his voice rough as sandpaper. 'Es ist spät.'

Grumbling, the two got to their feet, came over to the bar. 'If you don't mind,' one of them said in German, 'we'll take a bottle with us.'

'I do mind,' said Willy quietly. 'Get out of here!'

'Now wait a moment—' the second guard began.

Koenig growled and started to come out from behind the bar.

'Let them have a bottle,' said Vicki quickly. 'It's on me.'

Koenig paused, shrugged, said: 'As you wish, Fraulein.' He passed a bottle from the back of the bar and the two men went out. They were very quiet now and seemed relieved.

'Well,' Koenig nodded, managed a good-natured smile, 'I was just about to leave. Will you excuse me? I have things to do. I'll be back later to tidy up.'

'Willy, don't go just yet,' said Garrison. 'Actually, I was hoping to find you here. There are some things I'd like to ask you.'

This seemed to unsettle Koenig. 'About the ESP building? I don't know a great deal about that place.'

'Willy, you have to understand, I'm blind. Really blind. I only have Thomas's word for what happened in there . . .'

'Richard—' The other had dropped the 'sir' and his voice was tense. 'We can't talk about that building, not in front of . . . not *even* in front of—'

'I'm going upstairs now,' Vicki discreetly said. 'I've had my drink. It wasn't my intention to get merry or maudlin.' She placed a hand on Garrison's knee, squeezed gently, got down from her stool and left.

'Listen,' Garrison continued when she had gone, 'I know you love your Colonel. I've only known him a little while but I can understand that. And I don't blame you. I envy you all the years you've known him. He's a very strange, very wonderful man. But – I couldn't *see* the results of what we did in there. I sensed that what he told me was the truth, but—'

'If Thomas said something was so, then it was so,' Koenig interrupted. 'He has tested me, too – though with middling results. He scrupulously records all such tests. The machines themselves record the results. What good to cheat oneself when the machines give the lie?'

'Yes, well I'm sure you're right – but I wasn't so much worried about him cheating himself as cheating me.'

'But don't you see? Why, that would amount to the same thing! He sees his future as being tied up in you. I saw him briefly tonight. He told me he had made a pact with you. In matters such as this, as in all business matters, he is absolutely straight. Why should he rig a deal of this sort? And why rig it in your favour?'

'You know all about this reincarnation thing?'

'Of course. He confides in me.'

'And you believe—'

'I believe he will do it, yes. That is why, when he dies, I must come to you.'

'But according to our horoscopes by this chap Schenk—'

'I know about that, too. Eight years, yes. And who is to care for you through those eight years, eh?'

'Jesus!' Garrison's face turned pale and angry. 'I have to learn to care for myself!'

'Oh, you have much more to learn than that, Richard. A great many things. And who is to teach you? Let me assure you, Thomas Schroeder does not intend to come back as a poor man, nor as a weak one. And anyway, what have you to lose? If he fails you will not lose. And if he succeeds—' Garrison sensed his shrug. 'Whichever, you can only win. Anyway, the pact is made . . .'

They drank together in silence then for a while. Finally Garrison said, 'Those tests, they're weird!'

'I thought so too,' said Koenig. 'But then, I was no good at it. Thomas, on the other hand—'

'Is exceptional,' Garrison finished it. 'And yet he said I made him look like a beginner.'

Koenig was impressed. 'But that is very good! What tests did you undergo?'

'Almost everything.'

'In one afternoon? That really is fantastic. Tell me about them.'

'I caused an exact kilogram of lead to weigh one tenth of a gram less for a period of three-quarters of a second. I levitated or teleported three droplets of water from a full glass to an empty one. I caused a tiny propeller to spin in an airless container. All useless things. Using my hands, I could have performed these same tasks and fifty others in minutes, and almost without conscious thought. I mean, what did I achieve? I change things more effectively simply by lifting this glass to my lips and drinking! And what did I get out of it? A headache! I could have got that, too, from drinking, but far more enjoyably.'

'No,' said Koenig, 'you are not telling it all. You astounded Thomas, and that is no easy task. You can't fool me, Richard. Thomas has given you something to believe in, and the belief is spreading through your system like wildfire.'

Garrison looked as if he might deny it, then sighed and nodded. 'According to Schenk's forecast, I shall see again. Isn't that something to believe in?'

'Oh, yes! That would be a wonderful thing. But come on – what other tests did you perform?'

Again Garrison sighed. 'Of all of them, one in particular stays in my mind,' he eventually said. 'I sat in one soundproof cubicle, Thomas in another. I had a board with four buttons marked with symbols. The symbols were a circle, a square, a triangle and a wavy line, in that order. The game was this: I chose a symbol, passed it through my mind to Thomas, and after a few seconds pressed its button. In the Colonel's cubicle a red light would come on each time I pressed a button, when he must try to guess and press the same symbol. We were testing our telepathic abilities, you see? And the machine logged my choices and the Colonel's responses. The odds against him getting any correct answers were three to one every time. But . . . he did very well. Better than forty-five per cent, which he says is far and away the best he ever did. Then it was my turn . . .'

'Yes?'

'Thomas became the sender and I the receiver. And—'

'Go on.'

'My results were almost one hundred per cent. It was only later we realized I hadn't even been able to see the red light!'

Koenig gripped his shoulder. 'But that is amazing! No wonder Thomas is exhausted. The excitement—'

'If . . . *if* I can believe him about all the things we did in there,' Garrison continued, 'then I must at least concede the possibility of the rest.' He remembered again the horoscopes, the fact that he still had two of the cards in his pocket. He took them out, smoothed them flat on the top of the bar.

'Willy, will you read these for me? Honestly, mind you?'

'Of course I will.' Koenig picked up the cards. 'And honestly, you may be sure.'

'Wait,' said Garrison. 'Have you seen these before?'

'No, I was only told the result of my own reading.'

'OK,' said Garrison, 'read them to me.'

'The first one is – Vicki Maler,' said Koenig.

Garrison nodded. 'Go on,' he said.

'"Vicki Maler, darkness. Time-scale: now."'

'"Death. Time-scale: one year!"'

Garrison nodded again. He felt sick, as if Koenig's words had somehow increased the probability of Vicki's death. He took a deep breath. 'Yes, that's what—'

'There's something else,' Koenig interrupted.

'What?'

'At the bottom of the card. A question mark. And in the time-scale column, the figure eight.'

Garrison took back the card. 'I didn't know about that. I don't know what it means. Thomas didn't mention it.'

'An afterthought, perhaps, on Schenk's part? A doodle?'

Garrison sat stiffly on his stool, frowning. He licked his lips. 'My card,' he said. 'Read that one to me.'

'"Richard Garrison,"' Koenig began. '"Darkness—"'

'No, from "Machine", near the bottom.'

'Ah, yes. I have it. "Machine. Time-scale: to eight years. RG/TS . . . Light!"'

'That's all?'

'No,' the other gave a half-shrug. 'Another doodle. A sort of scrawl, crossed out, and another question mark.'

'Can't you make out what it is?' Garrison was eager.

'Initials, maybe. Let me see. A "V" perhaps? And . . . one other letter. Also obliterated. Something Schenk must have known was an error.'

'An "M" maybe?'

'Possibly. Yes, it looks like an "M".'

Garrison took back the card. 'One more thing. This letter.' He took out Schroeder's letter to Heinz Holzer and passed it over.

'Do you want me to read everything?'

'Just the text.'

'As you wish.' He cleared his throat. 'Moment mal. A moment, please. I have to translate . . .

'"Dear Heinz, a long time since we corresponded. We must get together sometime.

'"Meanwhile, I have a job for you. A young man is blind and I am heavily in his debt. I want one of your dogs for him. A young one. I know you specialize in black bitches bred in your own kennels. She will need to be of the very best. Tell me what you require for the training. I remember you need many things and would like a comprehensive list.

'"As to the fee: name it and I will pay half as much again.

'"Also, rely on me for any support, moral or financial, now and in the future. Not only in this present matter but in any eventuality. If you do have needs, let me know them now. I suspect I may not have too long. That bloody bomb! But for the moment I am only a phone call away.

'"Your dear old friend . . ."'

Slowly, thoughtfully, Garrison took back the letter. They drank in silence for a while, until Garrison asked:

'Why doesn't Vicki have one of these dogs?'

'Holzer's techniques – his training methods – have only been perfected over the last six or seven years. Fraulein Maler had long since overcome her disability.'

'Overcome blindness?'

'She has grown accustomed. Also – let us be realistic – the Colonel's interest in her is that of a friend. It is not the same interest he has in you.'

Suddenly there was an urgency in Garrison. He was like a man waking from a sort of trance or spell. Awareness came as a white flash bursting upon his consciousness. Time was passing. Vicki's time. He got down clumsily from his stool, faced Koenig, searched for words to explain what he felt must look like an attack of blind panic.

Koenig understood and needed no words. It was as he had supposed: belief *was* spreading through Garrison's system like wildfire.

'Goodnight, Richard,' said the bulky man behind the bar.

'Yes. Goodnight,' Garrison answered and left.

'Richard,' Vicki whispered in his ear as they lay in each other's arms. 'I'm frightened.'

'Me too,' he said.

'I'm frightened because you were so gentle,' she confessed. 'I wonder if that means you know something?'

'Everything except—' he held her more tightly, fiercely, '—except the answers.'

'For me the answer comes tomorrow,' she said. 'At first light.'

'I know,' said Garrison. 'And I have my fingers crossed, just to be on the safe side.' *You are going to die!* said a voice in his mind.

'Richard, you're trembling!'

'A cold coming on.'

'Warm yourself in me.'

103

Don't die, Vicki! he silently cried. *I can make love to you, yes, but I daren't fall in love with you. Not if you're going to die.*

'The Little Death,' she said, and felt the short hairs stiffen at the back of his neck.

'What?' His voice was a croak.

'My, but you are getting a cold, aren't you? You've gone quite feverish.'

'What did you say just then?'

'Oh, that. An old French saying, I think. They call love – specifically the moment you come – the Little Death. I want to feel you die a little in me.'

Her hand reached for him and he prayed for an erection. Amazingly, as she found him, he stirred into life. She let him grow, snuggled her head to his chest and kissed his left nipple. Then she curled her body in towards him and deftly fed him into her.

The Little Death . . .

In Schroeder's room Mina asked, 'Thomas, won't you watch them tonight?' Her hand wavered over the wall-screen's switch.

'No, leave them in peace. Tonight we concentrate on *my* satisfaction!' he answered.

'You think they would be a distraction rather than an inspiration?'

'I thought I told you,' he answered roughly. 'I'm no voyeur. Also, they deserve some privacy.'

'Privacy? Am I listening to Thomas Schroeder?'

'*What?*' He turned on her in anger. 'Mina you . . . you take too much on yourself! Soon we must see about finding you a new employer.'

Her hand flew to her mouth. Tears stood in her eyes in a moment. Schroeder saw them and softened. 'Mina, I'm tired, and when I'm tired I snap like a log on a fire. Also, I have only a little time left. Your love-making has been good for me, but I don't want you around at my deathbed. That's all I meant. You should not be working for a dying man. Tonight must be the last.'

'But—'

'No buts. Oh, don't worry. I've made provision for you. You need only work if you wish it.'

She was angry with herself for all his reassurances. 'My mouth always runs away with me. I had no desire to hurt or anger you.'

'I know that. It was just your suggestion that we spy on Garrison, that's all.'

'Spy on him? But didn't we watch them together last night, Thomas?'

'That was last night,' he snapped, the anger back in his voice.

She hung her head and tears fell on him. The sight of her nakedness, her bowed head and her tears worked on him. She saw it and sought him with her mouth.

'Yes,' he huskily approved, 'tonight I can concentrate. But as for watching Garrison – I can do that no more. Why, one might just as well spy on oneself!'

Garrison dreamed.

He dreamed of ice. A glacier. He climbed a glacier. Clad in rags, bloodied and cold to the marrow, he trod steep and treacherous snows until he reached a glassy peak. He stood at the top of the world, conqueror! Then—

He remembered why he had come, his quest.

A great block of ice stood upon the peak. It was blue, white-streaked and opaque with rime, its square foot bedded in crisp snow with an icy crust. He went to it, cleared away the frost from its surface. He gazed upon a face. A slim face, elfin, with small ears and red hair brushed back. Her slightly slanted eyes were closed, but Garrison knew they would be green. No breath of life moved her breast.

He beat on the ice with his fists and the block flew apart, burst like a grenade. Unsupported, she swayed and would have fallen but he caught her, kissed her, breathed on her. He kissed her eyes and they opened.

And they were green as emeralds—

—And utterly lifeless!

Her stomach and breasts burst open in rotten tatters and great leprous tentacles sprang out, like the guts of a ruptured golf ball. She was dead but the cancerous thing in her was alive! Before his eyes it began to devour her shell . . .

He came awake screaming, sensed, felt and smelled Vicki's room around him and shudderingly reached for her.

She was not beside him.

Beyond the windows the sun was high, its beams slanting into the room. He had overslept.

He dressed quickly, omitted to wash and shave, took the elevator to the ground floor. The results of Vicki's tests were in. She had left half an hour ago. Schroeder did not know where she had gone. One of his men had taken her away, possibly to Hildesheim. Or she might be in St Andreasberg. She had friends in both places, and a companion in the latter. And now . . . now she could go anywhere. Anywhere in the whole wide world. There would probably be a great deal she wanted to do. Things she had always wanted to do.

'It was the very least I could do for her, Richard,' Schroeder explained. 'She is not without means, but – for the rest of her time her bills come to me. I want her to do what she wants to do. You, surely, would want that also?'

'Meeting you,' Garrison finally ground the words out, 'has been a nonstop curse! You've turned my life upside-down and me inside-out.'

'I did not make her go, Richard. She wanted to leave. You may follow her if you wish, but—' He took the other's shoulders. 'It would be slow torture for both of you. Vicki obviously understands this. Why can't you?'

Garrison had no answer. He made fists until his nails dug into his palms, then slowly turned away . . .

*   *   *

106

The rest of the week seemed to pass almost as a day, so that later he would have difficulty recalling much of it. He did remember his session with Schroeder's hypnotist, however – if not its middle, when he was 'under', certainly its beginning and its end – and its result: that quickening of Schroeder's already intense interest, his seemingly *proprietary* interest, in the blind Corporal. For indeed it appeared that Garrison had lived before, if the hypnotist's probing could be trusted and his findings credited. These previous lives were not distinct, no, but deep in his subconscious there was an awareness of them.

One other thing Garrison specially remembered of those last few days in the mountains was his request, right at the end of his stay, that Schroeder do his best to ensure that Vicki's body, when and if she died (he still had hopes that she would not), be placed in cryogenic suspension.

Schroeder asked no questions but said it would be done, he would obtain Vicki's permission if it were at all possible, and that of her guardian, and he would make all other arrangements and lay aside a sum to cover recurrent fees. There was a place in Switzerland, a shrine built into the side of a moutain, where she could rest through the years in deep-frozen repose. Schroeder himself had little faith in such methods, but—

'I dreamed I saw her locked in ice,' Garrison had told him.

'Ah! Then it shall be done . . .'

At the Hotel International Major Marchant was waiting, immaculate, as usual, in number two dress uniform. He had been contacted earlier and told to prepare for the journey back to England. It was 9.30 in the morning when Koenig drove up in the silver Mercedes, Garrison seated beside him.

'What the devil's going on?' the Major wanted to know. He stuck his head in through Koenig's window as the car halted at the kerb before the hotel.

'Why,' answered Koenig, 'we are going to the airport, of course!'

'Of course? Man, if you'd only check the flight schedules you'd know that our flight to Gatwick doesn't leave until 3.30!' He waved his own and Garrison's air tickets in Koenig's face. 'And whose idea was it to phone me and tell me – no, damn it, *order me* – to be ready inside an hour? Do you have any idea what sort of a rush I—'

Koenig lifted the tickets from the Major's hand with a deceptively casual movement and calmly tore them up. He stuffed the fragments into the car's ashtray. 'Please, Major, do not wave things at me. And do not shout at me. My nerves, you know. Please get into the car.'

'I will not! And the tickets! Who the hell do you—?'

Garrison leaned across, his dark lenses glinting. 'Either get in or go and arrange another flight for yourself. Thomas Schroeder's private jet leaves in half an hour, and I'll be on it with or without you!'

'Corporal Garrison, I—'

'Call me mister, Major Marchant,' said Garrison. 'I was discharged, *in absentia*, first thing this morning.'

'What? How—?'

'Thomas Schroeder requested it, that's how.' Garrison sat back and said to Koenig. 'If he's not in the car on a count of ten, leave the bastard.'

Marchant heard him, hesitated for a single moment, got in. A hotel porter dumped his luggage in the boot. The Major sat stiffly in the back as Koenig pulled away from the hotel, then leaned forward and tapped Garrison brusquely on the shoulder. 'And is that the uniform you'll be handing in now that you're discharged, "Mr" Garrison?'

Garrison turned and grinned. 'Right, two of them. Not quite regulation issue, I know, but pretty good stuff, eh?'

'Don't be too cocky, Garrison,' Marchant growled. 'The quartermaster would be perfectly entitled to make you pay for the originals.'

'The quartermaster can "require" whatever he likes,' said Garrison. 'But just think about it: some lucky sod will probably draw this lot up. He'll be the best dressed Corporal in the whole British Army!'

'But where did you get these . . . clothes?' Marchant demanded to know. 'What on earth has been going on?'

Garrison's grin left his face. He frowned and turned away. 'You know,' he said over his shoulder, 'I was going to sit and talk to you on the way back to Blighty. Put you partly in the picture. Tell you my good fortune. Let bygones be bygones, sort of thing. But you've just decided me not to. That stiff upper lip of yours keeps getting in the way. Actually, you rather piss me off.'

Maddened almost beyond caution, Marchant sharply drew breath and raised his short cane above Garrison's shoulder. In all likelihood he never would have struck the threatened blow. Reason would have prevailed. But Willy Koenig was taking no chances. Having foreseen the outcome of Garrison's deliberate impertinence, the bulky German had pressed a button on the dash to send a thick pane of plate glass hissing up from behind the front seats, snapping the thin bamboo neatly in half and sliding firmly into a slot in the ceiling. Behind the glass Marchant roared and raged, but the two in the front seats heard only their own laughter.

By the time they reached the airport, Marchant had calmed down. Garrison allowed him to sit in the rear of the small executive jet; but when drinks were served by the pretty hostess he made sure that the tray went no further than Willy Koenig and himself where they sat in luxurious comfort at the front. The trip was a very short one, and for Major Marchant very dry.

At Gatwick Garrison was taken out of Koenig's care by the Provost Marshal's own driver while the Major was left to fend for himself. Garrison tried but couldn't feel sorry for the man. And what the hell? – he had his stiff upper lip, didn't he?

Chapter Six

There are centres across the land where soldiers, sailors and airmen may rest, recuperate and rehabilitate following illness, accident or injurious acts of war. The same is mainly true of establishments catering for the civilian population, but military rehabilitation centres are generally acknowledged as being amongst the best. The place where Garrison went was no exception. Spacious in its own grounds and only a stone's throw from the sea, the Hayling Island Recovery (as the inmates knew it) was a haven, or would have been without its strict routine and dedicated adherence to military method and regimentation.

Matron (or 'the RSM', as Garrison designated her) was a lady of some forty-five years whose prior service in the QARANC had endowed her personality with just such qualities as the ex-Corporal had always detested. Not that he was completely rebellious; he never had been, for he understood the elements of discipline; but he did believe that the 'born leader' bit and bullshit and parade-ground vulgarity and harsh, barking voices had their own place and time. For which reason, whenever Matron encroached too closely upon his privacy in supposedly 'private' hours, he would take every opportunity to remind her that while he was making use of the centre he was nevertheless a 'civvy'; that he was merely blind, not deaf; that she could pin as many Dymotape name tags to his clothes as she liked but he would always find and remove them; and (which annoyed her most of all) that while she could legitimately 'order' him to attend Braille classes she could never compel him to study or learn the damned thing, for it was not his intention to spend the rest of his life fumbling about with printed Morse code when he could always find himself a pretty girl to read things to him.

For these and several other reasons, Garrison was not Matron's favourite.

He was not to be deflated, however, and certainly not to be defeated. In attempting, by whichever method, to knock him down, Matron merely succeeded in getting his back even further up – which happened to be exactly what she wanted! For perceptive as he was, Garrison had quite failed to recognize that Matron was just as important to the centre's operation and well-being as the doctors, psychiatrists, physiotherapists, nurses, teachers, cooks and dishwashers. She formed, in fact, a high percentage of the incentive to 'get the fuck out of here' which all of her charges shared as a man. And for all her bluster she was highly intelligent, compassionate, and extremely perceptive in her own right.

For example, she had not failed to note Garrison's involvement with one of the prettiest and youngest nurses, Judy, an affair which started in his second week and carried on into the sixth. Even then it might not have finished if Matron had not inadvertently let the nurse know that she knew of the thing; this by reminding her one morning that she had forgotten to take her pill. There was also the matter of an impending posting and imminent promotion which, together with Matron's sure knowledge of her affair and not knowing which way the old bird would jump, convinced Judy that the fire must now be allowed to burn itself out. She and Garrison did not, after all, love each other; they had merely been attracted to and delighted in each other's bodies.

With or without Matron's assistance the affair was destined to end abruptly. For as Garrison's sixth week came to a close the centre's Commandant, Doctor Barwell, sent for him and had him brought to his office in an ocean-facing wing of the complex. Garrison feared that he might be in for the Big Ticking Off, for he had certain other things moving as well as his running battle with Matron, but his fears proved groundless. It was simply that he had an appointment in Harley Street, where one of Britain's finest surgeons wished to see him.

Completely in the dark (Garrison was quite up to that sort of pun now) he let himself be taken to London and delivered to the clinic in question, and there discovered that he was to undergo surgery. Something of panic had set in then – until Thomas Schroeder's name was mentioned in connection with a German firm specializing in optical instruments, and Garrison found himself introduced once again to a man he had met once before. In the Harz.

It was the same tiny dome-headed boffin who could only talk through an interpreter, and on this occasion he had brought one with him. Garrison was surprised, for he had thought that episode conclusively killed off by his own (and by Schroeder's) tantrums that day; but no, Herr Killig was here at Schroeder's request, and now it was up to Garrison to say whether or not the operation went ahead.

It would be a simple matter: the positioning of tiny silver discs under the skin of Garrison's temples just above the cheek bones and immediately in front of his ears, one to each side. It was a small thing and there would be no scars to mention. Killig would direct the surgery, which itself would be performed by the British specialist. Since that specialist was Sir Ralph Howe, with more letters after his name than Garrison could ever hope to remember or even identify, everything seemed very much in order. When it was over Killig would return to Paderborn where final adjustments would be made to Garrison's 'instruments', which the ex-Corporal would receive at a later date. All concerned were very persuasive and Garrison knew why. This must be costing Thomas Schroeder a small fortune.

When he got back to Hayling Island five days later Judy had been promoted and moved to a centre in the Midlands, which move Garrison immediately assumed to be foul play on the part of Matron. Still, he held no grudge. Life, like every other physical thing, must move on; when it becomes static it stagnates. And so with a shrug of his shoulders he settled once more to his life of (Matron's phraseology) 'near-criminal activities'.

There was, for instance, the matter of his keeping an especially vile brand of alleged cognac in his tiny room, and of inveigling others of the patients in to sample it, with occasionally uproarious and now and then near-catastrophic results. And it would not be the first time that centre staff had been called out to a local seafront pub where patients (who by all rights should be safely tucked up in their beds) were drunk, disorderly and refusing to leave the premises despite the fact that time had been called; and where invariably Garrison was discovered to be the ringleader. A case of the blind leading the lame and sometimes maimed . . .

. . . And the fact that Garrison had drawn to himself a small core of his fellows, a circle of close friends – one might almost say disciples – with whom he would spend a great deal of time in the discussion of subjects or experiences or beliefs as far removed from his apparent character as chalk from cheese. Matron would not be at all surprised to find them one night in the middle of a seance or other esoteric experiment; but usually it was just drink and talk. The warm evenings would find them down on the beach where (this time characteristically) Garrison had already been warned about his reckless attitude towards swimming alone, in the night, with no possible hope for survival in the event of a failure of his sense of direction.

These then were some of the traits (Matron might balk at the word 'qualities') which set the ex-MP aside from the majority, the run of the mill sick and disabled servicemen; but there were others which were less obvious and far more puzzling. Of these there was the fact that he seemed unaccountably well off for a Corporal in the Military Police (his bank statement showed a monthly interest of amounts well into the four-figure bracket), and also that he numbered among his friends and acquaintances an important German industrialist and a world-wandering heiress – or at least a lady of considerable wealth – whose cards were invariably postmarked in impossibly exotic and, to Matron's way of thinking, incredibly expensive places. Garrison got cards from Istanbul, Tokyo, Melba, Niagara, Johannesburg, the Troodos Mountains of Cyprus, Berlin and Hong Kong; and they were not merely 'get well soon' cards but thoughtful little reminders from someone who had obviously been a lover. Never wordy, always full of meaning, they would say: 'I loved the way you loved me.' Or: 'You were *very* forward – thank goodness!' And by Garrison's expression whenever such as these were read out to him by one of his circle, Matron knew that if ever one of the cards said 'Come' – simply that – then Garrison would discharge himself and go. It must have been a very strange affair, that love could linger and hurt, and both parties feel it, and yet remain apart.

There were, too, letters from Germany (of a business nature, Matron suspected) but she never got to see or learn of the contents of these. And eventually there was the parcel . . .

That was towards the end of September, in the third month of Garrison's sojourn. The parcel arrived out of the blue, special delivery. It was taken to him where he sat in a quiet room enjoying the autumn sunshine falling on him through great bay windows. Opening it (no easy task for the thing was extraordinarily well-wrapped and padded), Garrison took out a pair of wide gold bracelets and built-up, gold-plated spectacles with fixed, wide sides and 'blind' lenses in a reflective silver. There was no accompanying note, no instructions, no batteries or wires.

Under Matron's eagle eye he put on the bracelets and the headpiece (he would never think of the device as a pair of spectacles; 'spectacles' as a word had quite lost its meaning for him personally). Tiny claws, on the inside of the headpiece arms where they fitted exactly to his temples in front of his ears, gripped and irritated a little, but not much. The claws were of course a necessity, for through them he 'heard' the sound-pictures which would take the place of his sight. And then for a week he did nothing but practice, so that soon he even had to be reminded about meals.

Now he knew what Schroeder meant when he told him that those other instruments had been merely 'for demonstration'. In less than a month his new possessions had made him almost totally independent.

Near the end of Garrison's fifth month at the centre (he must be out of the place and fending for himself before Christmas) he was called to the telephone. He knew it would be bad. His sleep had been poor for days, full of a tossing and turning, which had left him with an erratic temper. He had suffered a good many 'phantom' pains, originating in his guts and causing nauseous headaches and even vomiting; and yet he knew somehow that his physical health had never been better. He was suffering, in fact, someone else's symptoms, and he knew who that someone must be. So that even as he picked up the telephone the name 'Thomas?' came automatically to his lips.

'Richard,' came the ragged whisper over the wire. 'Yes, it is Thomas. I called to say many things – but chiefly to say that it won't be long now.'

Garrison caught his breath. 'Now listen,' he answered, his throat treacherously dry, 'I won't—'

'*Please!*' whispered Schroeder. 'Even speaking is painful. Just hear me out. Then you can talk and I'll listen . . .

'My place in the Harz, it's yours. You are always to allow Saul Siebert access to the surgery, and Adam Schenk into the library and observatory, but apart from that the place is yours to do with as you will – except you must not dispose of it. It will run itself. It is funded separately. Willy Koenig

115

knows all of the ins and outs. Now listen carefully, Richard. Quite apart from the three hundred thousand pounds I settled on you after our meeting, I have deposited eleven and a half million Deutsch Marks in a numbered Swiss account. Again, Willy is the key. This is basically "working money" and should be very fruitful; that is to say, profitable. I foresee the annual interest to be somewhere in the region of three to three and a half hundred thousand pounds. You are extremely rich, my boy.'

'Thomas, I – don't know what to say.'

'Say nothing. We made a pact and I have kept my side of the bargain.'

'I'm still half inclined to believe you're a crazy man. All that money!'

Schroeder's chuckled was a rasp over the wire. 'What good is money to me now, Richard? Anyway, it will all wait for me – for us! And Richard – if only you knew how *much* there is, salted away in so many places, all growing as the years pass. One day – oh, yes, it will happen – we will be among the richest men in . . . the . . . world!' He began to cough.

'Thomas! For God's sake don't!' Garrison clutched the telephone and doubled over. 'Thomas, I can feel something of it, inside me. *Your pain!*'

'*Ah!*' the voice on the line gasped. 'That was not intended. I must . . . try to make sure it does not . . . happen again. But in any case, it won't be long.'

'Thomas,' Garrison felt the pain ebbing slowly away, 'why must you always—'

'I know, my boy, and I'm sorry, but . . . Listen, Richard. I have to go now. But when the time comes I won't be able to control it. I'll try, but . . . I hope it won't be too bad. Well—'

'No, wait!' Garrison cried. 'Listen, we'll share it. The pain – the *final* pain, I mean. I'm strong, I can take it. Don't

116

hold it in, Thomas. When the time comes, I'll take my share.'

'Richard, oh Richard—' the whisper was a sad small thing, and Garrison had a vivid mental picture of the other shaking his head. 'Ah, you're a fool! Do you know what dying is?'

'No, I don't. But I do know that I don't want you to suffer it all.'

After a long pause Schroeder said, 'I made a good choice in you, Richard Garrison – if, indeed, I had anything at all to do with it . . .' And after another pause: 'One more thing. Do not attend the cremation. There will be nothing there for you. It could even be dangerous. Well, I won't say goodbye, Richard. Let's simply make it auf wiedersehen, eh?'

Then there came the click of a handset replaced . . . and after a moment, the continuous and staccato stutter of a disconnected line. In Garrison's ears, much more than a telephone's death rattle . . .

The pain came in the night four days later. It was a Tuesday late in November, a date which would burn itself into Garrison's mind forever. For now at last he was to learn what dying was like, or at least what Thomas Schroeder's death was like.

It had been working up in him over the preceding Sunday and Monday, a burning in his chest, guts and loins, like some virulent poison or acid eating away internally. And he knew that these were not pains he could dispel with pill or hypodermic. What use to drug his body when it was not *his* body that produced the pains? For the pains were Thomas Schroeder's.

Up until that Tuesday night they had been bearable, coming and going in regular spasms which Garrison guessed must coincide with the pain-killers Schroeder's

117

doctors were giving him, but on Tuesday night . . .

He had looked so ill towards nightfall that Matron, who knew he had been sleeping poorly, prescribed sleeping pills and an early night in bed. Garrison, weakened by his attacks and desiring only a break from them, succumbed easily enough. By 10.00 P.M. he was asleep – and by midnight he was suffering agonies. Only half-conscious as a result of Matron's draught, half-awake through the steadily increasing pains, he was too weak and confused to cry out but could only lie there, clutching at himself and sweating until his bed seemed awash.

Then, about 1.00 A.M., he came awake and sat bolt upright. Schroeder was in his mind.

Richard, this is it. I can no longer hold it in. Too weak. What you have known is nothing to what you will know now. I am sorry. Damn these doctors. I thought they were mine, but . . . they have ethics. They will not kill me. And – God help me – I don't know what it will be like in the other place, and I fear it!

Then—

A blinding light in Garrison's mind, an incredible agony in his body. His entire being disrupted by pain!

He tried to cry out but could not. Pain froze the cry in his throat, turning it to a gurgle. He fought to draw air, and his expanding lungs seemed to crush organs already burning in their own hell. His body contorted, twisted, his guts seeming to knot inside him. He writhed, thrashed, banged his head against the wall in a wash of searing agony. He clawed at his belly and chest, felt blood flow and mingle with the sweat that coursed from his every pore in a hot, sticky tide.

He could not scream for gasping at air, could not gasp at air for the pain it brought, could not subdue agonies which were not his but those of another, flooding in on him from Thomas Schroeder's mind amok.

By 2.00 A.M. Garrison knew that he too would die. Twice he had blacked out, only to recover, swept aloft on fresh waves of agony. Bile steamed where he had thrown up, over himself and on to the floor. There was blood in it. Blood seeped from his nostrils, his bitten-through lips, the raw grooves he had torn in his chest and stomach.

Thomas! he cried in silent agony. *Thomas, you're killing me, too!*

No answer but a fresh flood of torment, a rolling, rippling swell of nerve-endings dissolving in vitriol, a mental scream that echoed and echoed in his mind. Bent almost double, Garrison's spasms grew so violent that he crashed from his bed, his body throbbing on the floor like a pinned worm.

Die, you bastard, die! he screamed into the telepathic void between minds. *Die, for Christ's whoring, screwing, fucking sake! Die, Thomas, die!*

Acid dripped in his eyes, ears, brain. Fire licked his lungs, heart, his very soul. The core and spirit of Garrison threatened to leave him. Blood spurted from his nose, dripped from his convulsed mouth.

Damn you, Thomas. If you won't die, then I will! He banged his head on the floor, again and again. Jesus, he didn't have the strength to brain himself! He found a bottle, knocked from his bedside table and smashed in its fall. The broken neck's razor edge cut his hand as he lifted it spastically to his throat. One lunge with that glass dagger, one quick slash that he wouldn't even feel in the torrent of tortures already racking him . . .

. . . The door burst open and a young physiotherapist, the night duty intern, rushed in. He had spent the last couple of hours chatting up a nurse in the centre's grounds, had actually got to the point of seducing her, entering her on the grass in the cool shade of a shrub, when the loud crash had come from Garrison's room. There had been noises from that same source all night, but Garrison was a bit of a lad and probably had a nurse of his own in there. That had been the thought in the intern's mind, but the crash convinced him otherwise. That and Garrison's choked, frenzied screaming: 'Die – die – die – *die!*'

The intern kicked the broken bottle from his jerking hand, threw himself on top of him and pinned his thrashing body to the coarse-carpeted floor. Garrison had no strength left. He could not fight the intern off. His writhing was not conscious but born of the pain within. He threw up again, violently, and started to black out.

Alerted by the intern's nurse friend, others of the staff were now on the scene. Even Doctor Barwell, who had been working late on reports in preparation for an administrative inspection. On the doctor's orders Garrison was carried out of his room to emergency, gurgling and spewing all the way. He emptied his bowels into his pyjamas, clawed open the face of one of the interns. He bit his tongue through and arched his back until they thought it must break. And finally, as they stretched him on a padded table—

He went limp . . . life seemed to rush out of him.

Doctor Barwell immediately put his ear to Garrison's chest. 'Cardiac arrest—' he began, but in another moment contradicted himself. '—No, there's a spark, a flutter! A beat, stronger now but erratic. Strengthening. That's better.' He glanced up at a sea of damp faces, not really seeing any of them.

'What was it?' the duty intern asked, pale and trembling.

'A fit – epilepsy – I don't know,' the doctor shook his head. 'Someone get on the phone to St Mary's. I want an ambulance right now. Two of you get dressed, quickly. You'll go with him. I'll speak to some people I know in Portsmouth. I want him under strict observation for a week. Whatever that was, it nearly killed him.'

But as it happened, Garrison would only stay in St Mary's for three days . . .

On Thursday he was back to normal, or as normal as his

bruised and battered body would permit. He had broken two fingers, was fortunate not to have fractured his skull, and the left side of his face was one massive bruise. His tongue and lips were twice their normal size. He kept choking on his tongue and couldn't eat; and his throat was raw from choking and vomiting. Bruises on his arms, body and legs gave him a sort of Dalmatian appearance, but worse by far was the look of his eyes. Where before they had been smooth and uniformly white, like the rolled-up eyes of a dead fish, they were now quite scarlet, as if filmed over with blood. The doctors at St Mary's said something about ruptured blood vessels and that the effect would wear off, but it never did.

Mid-afternoon Friday he was well enough to discharge himself and return to Hayling Island. He spoke on the telephone, haltingly and with some difficulty, to Doctor Barwell, who protested at first but finally gave in and sent a nurse to collect him; and he had been back at the centre less than an hour when he was once again called to the phone. A call from Germany. It was Willy Koenig.

'Richard, Thomas has gone.' His voice was flat but showed no trace of its customary harshness. Koenig sounded drained.

'I know,' Garrison answered, a shudder in his words. His tongue was still badly swollen, but the shudder had come from deep inside his body.

'He said you would know. I phoned to say I'm coming soon.'

'When?'

'A week to ten days, as soon as possible. I have one or two things to do . . .'

'I'm sorry about Thomas, Willy.'

'He was in a lot of pain. I'm sure he was glad to go in the end.'

'Willy, you should know something. He wasn't glad to go. He wasn't glad to go at all! He fought it. Fought hard.

121

Jesus, Willy, no man *ever* went like that before. I was with him . . .'

'Oh?' There was wonder now in Koenig's voice. 'I . . . I didn't know. He didn't want me to be there.'

Again Garrison shuddered. 'Well I *was* there. It's hard to explain – and anyway I don't want to remember.' He paused, then said: 'It will be good to see you, Willy.'

'To see me? So you've slipped back into the phraseology of the sighted, have you?' A new note had crept into Koenig's voice. A note of interest.

Garrison managed to grin, however painfully, and his amusement carried right down the line. 'I suppose I have. And I do believe your English has improved. You seem to have less of an accent.'

'Well, I have been practising. For six months!' There was life now, animation. 'It seemed prudent, since English is to be my Sprache for the foreseeable future.'

'And how do you view the foreseeable future, Willy? Personally, I think we both deserve a long holiday.'

'An excellent idea,' Koenig answered with enthusiasm, '—but work to be done first. Affairs to be put in order. One week, perhaps, to straighten things out, and then . . . Where will we go?'

'Oh, I don't know. The Greek Islands. The Americas. The Seychelles. Hawaii. Somewhere I've never been. Or maybe all of those places.'

'Well, why not?'

'Could we?' Garrison felt a rising excitement, like fresh air after a long session in a smoky barroom.

'Of course we can. Before that, though, we must come back to Germany, to the Harz. It's yours now, you know, this place.'

Garrison's excitement ebbed. 'Yes, I know. But why must we go there first, and for how long? The place will seem—' (he almost said 'dead') '—empty – now.'

'But there is someone you must meet.'

122

Garrison's heart gave a little lurch. 'Someone I know?' Impossibly, he was thinking of Vicki.

'No, no – a total stranger. Well, no, that's not true. She, at least, knows you.'

Garrison frowned. He never really had been able to fathom Willy's mind. The rapport was there, but hidden, deep. 'What are you talking about?'

'I'm talking about Suzy, the "S" on your horoscope.'

'The "S" on my . . . the black dog? Suzy's a dog?'

'Indeed she is. A beautiful black Dobermann pinscher bitch. Just one year old, and in love with her master, and pining desperately for him.'

'Her master?' Koenig didn't seem to be making sense.

'You, Richard, you!'

Garrison shook his head. 'I don't think I follow.'

'Then you have forgotten what Thomas told you. Suzy was trained on your scent, your clothes, the samples taken from you, your body. She knows and loves the smell of your blood, sweat, even your urine. She longs to hear your voice. Her heart is bursting to hear you laugh, shout, command.'

Now Garrison understood. 'A brainwashed bitch,' he said. He somehow felt let down, disappointed.

'If you wish. But wait until you see her.'

'I'm still not sure I want a blind dog. Isn't it a bit like carrying a white stick, or those shitty armbands they make you wear in Germany?'

'No, not like that at all. Just take my word for it. With Suzy, it will be a whole new world.'

Garrison said: 'I seem to spend an awful lot of time just taking people's words. But we'll see. One thing's certain – I'll be glad to see you again. It will be just like old times.'

After a slight pause, Koenig asked, 'What old times?'

Garrison was caught short. That was a damned good question. 'Just . . . old times,' he finally answered. He could somehow picture Koenig nodding his crewcut head in understanding.

'Just a week to ten days, then,' the German said.

'Yes. I'll be looking for you. But Willy—'

'Yes?'

'Tell me, what's in this for you?'

'Oh, my payment is good, be sure of it. And anyway, the Colonel wished it. In fact, those were his last words to me.'

Garrison felt a sudden chill, that same alien cold he had known when speaking to Schroeder himself. 'What were his last words to you, Willy?'

'Why, that I let nothing happen to you, of course. "Guard him well, Willy Koenig, with your own life," he said. "Let no harm come to Richard Garrison."'

Garrison's flesh had turned to ice. After a little while he shook himself and said: 'He really did believe, then?'

'Did?' Koenig's voice came back, a little tinny now with static and distance. 'Oh, but he still does believe, Richard, and so do I. Yes, and so do you . . .'

The next morning Garrison was left to sleep it out. He was finally brought awake by a dream, a nightmare. He remembered a little of it. Fire and smoke and a dreadful roaring, and a smell like something cooking in the devil's own kitchen. And somewhere a voice intoning and others singing, and the strains of an organ mournful in a dirge. Fire consumed him but he felt nothing, and in the end he knew his body was a pile of hot ashes.

That was when he came awake.

Laved in sweat, it took several moments to realize where he was. Then he put out his hand and touched the naked hands of his alarm clock. 9.00 A.M. – in Germany 10.00 A.M. – and Thomas Schroeder had been cremated . . .

Chapter Seven

When Koenig arrived at the Hayling Island centre with his silver Mercedes, Garrison introduced him to staff and friends alike as 'Herr Koenig, my man,' which is exactly what the crewcut German was. Immaculate in a sort of semi-uniform, Koenig looked every bit a combination of chauffeur, gentleman's gentleman, confidant and companion, and he conducted himself accordingly. Garrison was 'sir', he was 'Willy', and when the initial astonishment wore off, then the staff of the centre – particularly Matron – began to realize and understand how very different the ex-Corporal really was. It perhaps explained something of his earlier rebelliousness, though Garrison had never seen himself as a rebel.

As for Matron: her role at the centre had at last dawned on Garrison, and he had come to respect her more than any other member of the staff. Which was why, on that cold Monday morning in December when his discharge became official (that is to say, when he had been 'rehabilitated') and he was his own man at last, Garrison hugged her to him and in a James Cagney voice said: 'Listen, Boss Lady, I've got your number. You ain't so tough, sister!'

'Matron, to you, Mr Garrison,' she answered, but there was an unaccustomed warmth behind the gruffness. Then she leaned forward and whispered in his ear, 'Listen, I don't know how you do it – in fact I'm beginning to wonder if I even know who you are – but you *are* a damned disruptive influence. So for the last time, Richard, will you take your damned Kraut and your whole bag of tricks and kindly get your arse out of my rehabilitation centre?'

'Shit!' Garrison answered, in that same confidential tone.

'Just when I was getting to like the place . . .'

And that was that. Handshakes all round and a wave from the rolled-down window of the big car, and Koenig drove Garrison away. It was only as they crossed the Hayling Island causeway and turned right on the A27 towards Chichester that Garrison thought to ask: 'Willy, where the hell are we going?'

'Ah!' Koenig answered. 'I thought you would never ask. Well, sir, you have acquired a property in Sussex. We are now on our way to take possession and inspect the staff. Then, tonight, London. You have a little business there – some investments to make – which should take a few days. Unfortunately we'll have to stay at a hotel; the Savoy, I think, if only for convenience. Being wealthy, you see, has its drawbacks. For one, you have to be sure you can trust the people who are handling your money. The Colonel never trusted anyone with his money, which is why he spread it out. And after London, back to the house – it stands in seven acres – where a top interior designer and decorator will await your instructions.'

'Phew!' said Garrison, and after a moment: 'Hey, do you think I might one day get a chance to organize my own life?'

'All you want,' Koenig shrugged. 'But you will discover in the end, sir, that big men only dream up the acts while smaller men perform. Running your own life simply means commanding others to run it for you, smoothly.'

'Oh? Well, I've always been a bit of a performer myself, you know. And anyway, you're not my idea of a small man. And you have your own life.'

'All wrapped up in you, sir.'

'And this "sir" business. That has to go.'

'Very well, Richard – but never in public. You have an image – or will have.'

Garrison turned his head and stared at the man beside him through silver lenses that conveyed a sound-picture of not quite subsonic blips and beeps. It was a picture which would soon become as recognizable and as trusted as the palm of his own hand. But for now he said: 'There's more than money in this for you, Willy Koenig.'

Koenig glanced at him and smiled. 'Indeed there is, Richard. My old master has determined to make himself eternal, immortal, and you with him. I believe he will do it. Together you will be . . . very powerful. Myself, I have never been able to picture a world in which I do not exist. I can't imagine myself dead. How better to preserve my life, then, than to place it in the hands of men who know how to prolong it indefinitely?'

Ten more days saw them in the Harz Mountains, where the snows were already crisp and vehicles chewed along the black, icy roads on chained wheels. They stayed over Christmas, which was not Garrison's intention but a decision forced upon him by Suzy. For he fell head over heels for Suzy from the moment they met, and he wanted to get to know her better before setting out with Koenig upon their as yet unplanned 'holiday'.

That first meeting with Suzy was almost magical, and it formed another turning point in Garrison's life. He would never forget it; it would always rank among his fondest memories.

Mid-December and the big Mercedes had hissed through shallow, crusted snow into the grounds of Schroeder's retreat. (Garrison now owned cars and houses in both England and Germany.) For reasons of Schroeder's own, the industrialist had never given his place in the Harz a name, but Garrison intended to change that. From now on it would have a real name. There would be a stone archway at the entrance to the grounds, and iron letters nine inches tall would curve with the brickwork of the arch, proclaiming the place 'Garrison's Retreat'. The name might never find its way on to a map but at least it would be better than being simply 'here', or 'in the Harz'.

Garrison finished describing what he wanted done – the archway and legend – as Koenig brought the car to a halt. The staff had been warned that they were coming and were there to meet them. So was Suzy, and Garrison sensed the presence of the big dog before ever he 'saw' her.

She was on a chain, obedient but restless at the feet of one of the 'groundsmen'.

'Release the dog,' Koenig ordered as he helped Garrison out of the car. Garrison heard the rattle of a chain and a low, measured panting. He smelled a sharp, clean dog smell on the frozen air. With the fur collar of his coat turned up against the back of his head, he waited.

'She suspects you are here but will not let herself believe it,' Koenig whispered. 'She smells the air, looks at you. Ah! Her attention is riveted! Call her name – no, whisper it – just her name.'

'Suzy.' Garrison barely breathed the word.

The low panting grew deeper, quickened, became a whine.

'She comes!' said Koenig. 'All trembling – but *now* she believes. She has found her Master, the God that Heinz Holzer promised her!'

The black bitch came to Garrison, sniffed at a dangling hand, dared tentatively to tug at his glove. He removed the glove, let her smell his hand. 'Suzy, girl, Suzy!' he said.

She whined again, high-pitched and joyous, then laid back her head and howled long and loud. In another moment she had taken his sleeve, was half-dragging, half-leading him forward into the entrance and through the glass doors. Now he led her, talking to her as they walked the remembered way to the bar – his bar, now – where he ordered drinks for everyone present.

Nurse was there, and Cook, and one or two others Garrison remembered, even Gunter. And all of them approaching him in their turn and introducing themselves, and Garrison politely acknowledging their welcome as he assumed his new role of master. And Suzy at his feet, quiet now but watchful, and quick to show her teeth as each member of the staff drew close to her God. For it was an agony to her that they should be allowed to touch him, and Garrison sensed her jealousy.

Later he would fondle and pet her, and never fear spoiling or weakening her character. For her character was steel and moulded into a rigid, unbreakable shield. Her loyalty, her life, belonged to Garrison. And in his mind's eye as he fondled her he saw Suzy exactly as she was – as she had been in that old, almost forgotten dream of his. And so another link was forged in that strange and inexplicable chain, and from that time on Garrison and Suzy were inseparable . . .

The next few weeks were the busiest Garrison had known since his previous visit to the Harz. First of all there was his own familiarization with the running of Garrison's Retreat; as the new master he insisted on knowing every last detail. Then there were extensive holiday arrangements and preparations to be made; and finally the business of Suzy's shipping to England and her quarantining, whose supervision Garrison himself attended to. In respect of the latter: it was his intention to return to England at least three times during the next four or five months, simply to go and see Suzy at the kennels. After that, during the final month of her quarantine, Garrison would have returned to England following his holiday and he would go to Suzy at least once a week. And during her last week until he collected her he would stay close and see her every day.

His rapidly growing affection for the dog might be most easily explained by an incident which occurred on his fifth night at Garrison's Retreat. It was this:

Towards morning he dreamed his dream of the Machine again, that dream which had forewarned of the bomb blast that blinded him; but this time the thing was far more real and vivid than any dream or nightmare he ever knew before.

Once more he rode the Machine across a weird world, a dreamworld of lizard-rocks and primal oceans, of strange valleys and mountains and hideous vegetation. Suzy sat behind him on the Machine, one great paw upon his shoulder. She whined and nuzzled his neck, pressing her black, sinuous body against his back.

He rode the Machine towards crags where the figure of Willy Koenig stood at the open door of a silver Mercedes, perched impossibly atop a spike of rock high over a mountain pass. Koenig beckoned him on, pointing the way to the black lake. Garrison could see that the German frowned, that his face was full of worry, concern for the Machine's rider.

Then he was through the pass and Koenig and the Mercedes faded into distance behind him as the Machine raced on. In another moment he passed over the forest of skeletal trees and down to the black lake where it lapped greasily upon its shore of pitch. And there in the lake the black rock, with its black castle glittering like some awful crown of shattered coal.

Garrison knew what must happen next: how he would have to fight the Power from the castle, hurling himself against that invisible force again and again, to no avail. He knew too that the man-God Schroeder would come to him in the shape of a face in the sky, demanding that he let him in, that he accept him. And then of course there would be the bomb.

These things were fixed certainties in his mind, utterly inescapable, except—

—It was not to be, for here the dream was different. Something had changed it.

Garrison had actually commenced the old sequence – had begun to hurl himself and the Machine time and again against the wall of Power from the castle – before the changes in the dream made themselves apparent. They were these:

One: that Koenig, driving the Mercedes, came crashing through the bleached forest, splintering a path through its trees and ploughing to a halt in the sticky pitch of the shore. Koenig leapt from the car and shouted: 'Richard, that's not the way. Don't ride the Machine, Richard. Get off it – *get off the Machine!*'

Two: that Suzy suddenly sank her teeth into his sleeve and tried to drag him from the back of the Machine. He hung on desperately and at last the dog's weight tore his sleeve so that she fell to the tarry shore where the oily lake lapped.

Only then did the man-God Shroeder appear, that great face in the sky crying, 'ACCEPT ME, RICHARD! ACCEPT ME AND WIN. LET ME IN . . .'

'Accept him, Richard!' Koenig cried from where he dragged his feet in tar. 'Remember your pact—'

'*No!*' Garrison screamed, and he turned the Machine until it once more faced the invisible wall of energy, the Power from the castle. He must make one final assault on that barrier, must break through and cross the lake and enter the castle and find the Black Room. That was where the Horror lurked, in the Black Room, and he must banish the Horror forever.

'Richard! *Richard!*' Koenig cried, his voice full of distress. Garrison, suffering agonies as he heard that cry, turned his head and looked back. The silver Mercedes was sinking into the tar, going down fast, its bonnet already disappearing as black bubbles rose all about, bursting into sticky tatters.

As yet Koenig came on, his feet sinking in the black ooze but still moving fast enough to keep its hideous suction at bay; like a man running on ice which crumbles beneath his feet, so that he must keep running or sink.

'BELIEVE ME, RICHARD,' boomed the man-God, 'YOU DON'T WANT TO DIE. YOU *MUST* BELIEVE ME. AFTER ALL, I KNOW WHAT IT'S LIKE HERE!'

And then the bomb, the burning, brown-paper cube, spinning out of the sky and hovering over Willy Koenig where he struggled in tar up to his knees. 'Willy, look out!' Garrison cried. He turned the Machine towards the spinning bomb and rammed it where it flared and sputtered over Koenig's head. Even knowing the thing must soon blow him to hell, he rammed it again, knocking it away from Koenig and placing himself and the Machine between bomb and mired man.

'ACCEPT ME, RICHARD!' the man-God Schroeder thundered again. 'ACCEPT ME NOW!'

And a moment before the bomb exploded Suzy made an improbable leap and slammed into Garrison where he gritted his teeth and clung like a leech to the bucking Machine. Angry with him that he should deliberately endanger his own life, the Dobermann snarled in his face as her weight unseated him.

Then, caught in the bomb-blast, they fell . . . fell . . . Fell.

—And Suzy was licking his face, whining where she crouched over him.

He lay in a tangle of sheets beside his bed, Suzy pawing at him, whining and licking his face. For a moment still dreaming, he cried out: 'Willy! – Willy, the bomb! I'm blind again! Willy, are you all right?'

'Richard, Richard,' came Koenig's calming voice. 'Of course I'm all right. We are all fine. It was a nightmare, Richard, only a bad dream.'

'But the bomb . . . and Thomas. The Machine—'

'A dream, Richard.'

Garrison allowed himself to be helped up. He sat shakily upon his bed. Fully awake now, he shook his head.

A dream, yes. But why was Suzy here? And Koenig? So

quick off the mark. Garrison found his voice. 'Was I shouting or something?' He put on his headset and bracelets.

'No,' Koenig slowly answered, 'you didn't yell until just now.' His voice told Garrison that he was frowning. 'It was strange, really. I was up early and went out with Suzy. She was nervous and irritable this morning, didn't seem to want to stray too far from the house. Then – well, she began tugging at her lead, trying to drag me back here. I shouted at her to behave herself, and – she turned on me.'

'Suzy turned on you? But next to me, you're the one she trusts!'

'Well, she did not exactly turn on me. She – threatened me. She bared her teeth at me. Then – she was sorry. She whined and licked my hand, but she kept right on tugging at her lead. Obviously she wanted to be free. I argued no further but loosened her lead – and she sped straight back to the house.'

'But she has rules,' Garrison protested. 'She knows she's not allowed in the bedrooms.'

He sensed Koenig's shrug. 'This time she broke the rules. She came straight to your room, was pawing at the door in a frenzy when I got here. By then I had an idea you were in trouble. I had also been on edge, you see? That's why I was up and about so early in the day. And when I saw Suzy at your door I knew why. That was when you started calling my name, and something about the bomb . . .'

Garrison waited for him to continue.

'Anyway, I opened the door and Suzy sprang in and jumped at you. Actually she cushioned your fall, for you were on the point of tumbling out of bed. And—' Koenig shrugged again, 'the rest you know.'

Garrison nodded. 'So Suzy knew I was in trouble – even though my trouble was only a nightmare.'

'So it would appear.'

'And you too.'

Again the puzzled shrug. 'It would seem so. But Suzy's instincts were surer – and much swifter – than mine.'

Garrison got up and began to dress himself. He was once more in control. 'It would also seem,' he quietly said, 'that I can't ever afford to be parted from you two.'

He sensed Koenig's grin, the half-amusement in the other's voice. 'But it was only a dream, Richard. Do you remember what it was about?'

'Yes,' Garrison nodded. He tucked his shirt into his trousers and turned to face the German. 'I remember it clearly. I'll tell you about it later. But right now I'll tell you this much: it was much more than just another dream . . .'

January was Australia; it was a country Garrison had always wanted to visit. Australia had not been one of Schroeder's favourite places, however, and so was strange to Koenig; but both of them enjoyed it to the full.

In Sydney Garrison purchased a large Mercedes and then, because he had not been able to find a silver model, had it sprayed. Willy Koenig was delighted. Mid-February they sold the car and returned to England. They stayed for a week, each day visiting Suzy in the quarantine kennels at Midhurst not far from Garrison's new Sussex home.

By the end of February, over and above Koenig's obvious duties, the blind Englishman and his German aide had become inseparable. They were now, in all respects, friends; but despite all Garrison's protests he was still 'sir' to Koenig whenever the German thought the occasion warranted it. Their three weeks' cruise in the South Pacific was just such an occasion, when Koenig's complete subservience towards his master left no one in any doubt but that Garrison was a man of great substance indeed. So much so that he became a permanent guest at the Captain's table.

The cruise was especially good for Garrison's ego in that (and quite apart from the dawning in his mind of knowledge of his own importance) he soon became firmly committed to a shipboard romance, which was a fantasy he had often entertained as a Corporal in the Royal Military Police. They were heady days, romantic evenings and – not to stress too heavily a point – lustful nights.

And such was Garrison's expertise – his ever-growing skill in the use of his 'seeing' devices – that it took him several days to convince his lady of his total blindness. When the cruise ended the romance also came to a close, by which time both he and the girl knew it must be that way. They parted the best of friends with the usual promises that they would 'look each other up', both perfectly well aware that they never would. By mid-March he could not even remember her second name.

By then, too, they were back in England; Garrison had developed a keen interest in the financial side of his affairs and soon would show an acumen away and beyond any expectations Schroeder might have had for him; and of course there was Suzy's welfare to be borne in mind, though on that score Garrison need not have worried. The love of the great black bitch seemed to grow apace with his absence from her, and, strangely, his for her was similarly enhanced.

About this time a novel idea occurred to Garrison. What prompted it he could never say with any certainty, except that perhaps the thing he chiefly missed in his blindness was the sheer pleasure of driving. Or perhaps it was the fact that Koenig, driving one day along the North Circular behind a large, articulated lorry, was surprised by his master's observation that if he dropped a gear he should now have little difficulty in overtaking despite the heavy traffic. Garrison's road-sense – his sense of speed, direction and timing – had grown out of all proportion to compensate for his blindness; so that Koenig was prompted to remark:

'You know, Richard, I honestly believe that if there was a second steering wheel on your side, you would be quite capable of taking over and driving the car yourself!'

April found the pair in Paris (whose atmosphere particularly appealed to Garrison, seeming to him full of fragrant poignancy), and the Mercedes in a specialist London garage being fitted with a second steering wheel. The job was still not complete when they returned for four days in mid-May, but it was not inconvenient. They had only come home, of course, to see Suzy.

Then, in Crete at the end of the month, another strange event.

They had hired a small car in which to explore the island. Koenig knew Crete well for he had been there several times with Thomas Schroeder. To Garrison's mind the atmosphere was much the same as Cyprus, and he liked nothing better than to sit of an evening outside some seafront cafe and eat kebabs in unleavened bread envelopes, washing the food down with sips of mediocre brandy-sour.

They were staying in Kastellion and on their first day had visited the Knossos palace. That had been quite sufficient of tourism for Garrison. He insisted that he was *not* here as a tourist and could not bear the droning guides and crowds of shuffling people. Also, though he had never been here in his life, he somewhere at some time or other must have read extensively of the place, for there seemed very little that was new or strange to him. Perhaps this was an effect of his years spent in Cyprus, perhaps something else entirely. Whichever, he felt that it would be better by far simply to drive, avoiding all places of public interest and visit instead those out-of-the-way towns and villages which the majority of tourists seldom found.

In the afternoon of the third day, eating dark olives and drinking ouzo at a tiny restaurant under the northern foothills of Idhi, Koenig suddenly said: 'Thomas had a very good friend here. But that must have been, oh, ten years ago. Strange, it does not seem ten years since I was last here.' He shrugged. 'He is probably dead now. He was old even then.'

Garrison looked up and seemed to stare at him through those reflective, often enigmatic lenses of his, and said: 'Oh, no, I shouldn't think so. Why don't we simply go to Rethimnon and find out?' He could not, of course, see the expression of Koenig's face when he spoke these words, but he did detect something of the wonder in the other's voice:

'Rethimnon, yes. In the Bay of Armiros. But Richard – how could you know that?'

Garrison frowned. 'No mystery,' he answered after a moment's hesitation. 'Thomas must have mentioned it to me . . .'

'I really fail to see that, Richard,' said Koenig slowly.

'But I'm certain of it!' Garrison replied too hastily. 'Gerhard Keltner. Yes, certainly.'

Koenig took his elbow and gripped it hard. His voice was cold and very low when he said: 'Be careful, Richard! Yes, you are correct, Keltner was his name – and it is a name which, rightly or wrongly, may be found high on the wanted lists of all the world's Nazi hunters! If we are to see him it must be as another man entirely.'

Garrison stroked his forehead, aware of a sudden headache. Puzzled lines furrowed his brow. 'Yes, of . . .of course,' he stammered. 'Nichos Charalambou . . .' And as the pain in his head increased, so he sensed the other's growing astonishment.

'Richard,' Koenig whispered, 'there is no possible way that Thomas would have mentioned *both* of this man's names – not in the same breath. I—'

'My memory really is—' Garrison cut him short, only to gasp and clutch at his temples for a moment before he could continue, '—amazing, eh?'

'Amazing, yes – if it really is *your* memory! But your head hurts. Forget about Charalambou for the moment.

137

Perhaps we should stay here tonight, or maybe we can find a better place at Margarites, and go on to Rethimnon tomorrow?'

'No,' Garrison answered, shaking off Koenig's now solicitous hand. 'No, I'll be all right. Let's get on to Rethimnon today, right now. I have to know if—'

'If?'

'—If this Nichos Charalambou is really the man I seem to remember.' He turned his pale face seemingly to stare at Koenig again. 'And if so, where I remember him from!'

It was the same face, but that hardly answered Garrison's question. In any case, the peculiar phase of pseudo-memories had worn off him by then, by the time he came face to face with this stranger he had thought he knew, whose names he remembered without ever having known them.

It was early evening when Garrison and Koenig arrived in Rethimnon, and knowing the way the big German drove straight along the shore road to the west side of town, turning down a track to the beach where the Sea of Crete washed blue (and just a little oily) on the gritty sands. Quarter of a mile along the beach stood Charalambou's house, a fairly modern affair in the flat-roofed island style, in a walled garden of citrus and pomegranates. Not a particularly rich house, but one with charm and a deliberately contrived Cretan beauty, so that it would be perfectly obvious to any outsider that the owner must indeed be a Cretan, or certainly a mainland Greek come here to spend his retirement.

Koenig parked the car and led his friend and master into the garden through a carelessly constructed, vine-draped arch of brick and trellis. Seated there in the fast-fading sunlight, a tanned, shrivelled little man turned the embers of a raised charcoal fire under sizzling, spitted cubes of lamb. Beside him on the seat of a cane chair were side plates of sliced tomatoes, diced cucumber, shredded cress and other greens, and a large freshly halved lemon.

As Koenig and Garrison approached he looked up, smiled and called into the house:

'Alexia, we have guests for supper – I think. A little more meat, if you please.' He stood up and extended a shaky hand towards Koenig. 'I believe I know you gentlemen . . . but perhaps I am wrong. In any case, what can I do for you?'

'Gerhard,' said Koenig, his voice very low. 'I've brought a friend to see you.'

The old man's jaw at once dropped. 'Willy Koenig!' he breathed. 'And—' he turned to Garrison, 'Thomas? – but why are you so silent, my old friend?'

'I am not Thomas, Herr Keltner,' Garrison answered, his voice quiet as Koenig's. He shivered despite the warmth of the evening. 'My name is Garrison, Richard Garrison. Thomas was my friend.' He turned to stare blindly, accusingly at Koenig. 'Willy is also my friend – but he didn't tell me that you, too, were blind.'

'A little blind, yes, for many years now, coming on me slowly, and now more quickly. I can see now that you are not Thomas, but – here, let me take your hand.' The hand that grasped Garrison's was dry as old leather, but he felt a tremor of – what? Recognition? – in the fragile fingers. 'Ah! Not Thomas Schroeder, no – but you *are* the one! No wonder I thought you were he . . .' He paused. 'You said Thomas was your friend. Was. Does that mean that he—'

'Yes,' Garrison answered. 'He's dead. But what did you mean by saying that I am the one? You . . . know about that?'

'Certainly. I was with Thomas in the old days. I knew of the growing interest in these matters. He often spoke to me about it – his faith in reincarnation. Thomas could never be described as eccentric, and anyway I knew too much about their work. He intended to have a son, come back in his son. Apparently that did not work out . . .'

'No, it didn't.'

'And so you came to an agreement with him – and it appears he was wrong after all. You have a certain aura – but you are not Thomas.'

'Do not be too sure, Gerhard,' Koenig joined the conversation.

'Please!' Keltner whispered. 'It's better that you call me Nichos. Alexia will be distressed if you use that other name. It is one we have almost managed to forget. And after all, Nichos was my father's name.' He turned almost blinded, faded green eyes towards the house. 'Alexia, come – come meet our guests. An old friend, yes – and a new one.'

He turned quickly back to the pair. 'About Thomas: when was it?'

'Six months ago,' Garrison told him.

'Ah!' The word was a sigh. 'I knew he had been hurt – the bomb – it was in the news. But somehow I seem to have missed his . . . his passing.'

Garrison gently squeezed his forearm, felt the trembling in the old man's bones. 'Don't distress yourself. There has been enough of pain. It hurt all of us, and no one more than me. But it was also a mercy. His body was finished.'

'So,' the other nodded. 'And poor Thomas, wrong after all, eh? He did not return. And yet—' Dim eyes burned into Garrison's face until he could feel them as an almost physical heat. 'And yet—'

'There is time,' said Koenig.

'Time, yes!' Garrison was suddenly angry. 'Oh, yes! My good friend Willy here can't wait until Thomas joins me in this blind shell of mine – if I decide to let him in!'

Koenig, taken aback, made no answer; but the old man shoved his face close and whispered, 'Ah! But you did not know Thomas Schroeder as I knew him. If he *can* come back he will, Richard – and what power could deny him then, eh?'

* * *

Three days later they were home. It was June now and the summer promised to be a good one. All the decorations and alterations in the rambling house had been completed and were much to Garrison's satisfaction – not so the recently arrived mail. Koenig suspected that the latter was probably the cause of Garrison's recent fits of depression; as his psychic powers increased, so his awareness of tragedy became more acute. And there had been a tragedy.

There were two cards from Vicki, both of them lucid and bright in their simplicity. Signed at Saul Siebert's clinic in the Harz, the earliest said: 'Richard, I know now that I left because I loved you. I believe that it was because you loved me that you did not follow. I thank you for that. I do not fear death. I *did* fear it greatly, until my body began to waste. That is the only thing that hurts: that this body you loved so well should now have grown so unlovable . . .'

The other said: 'Be happy. I don't ever recall seeing you truly happy, and I can't bear the thought of your being sad for my sake. And who knows? Maybe the Big Death is just like the Little Death, but lasting so much longer . . .'

And there was a letter, arrived that very morning, to say that Thomas Schroeder's wishes (Garrison's wishes, of course) had been carried out to the letter. Vicki Maler's diseased body was now in cryogenic suspension at Schloss Zonigen in the Swiss Alps. There it would remain, presumably preserved forever, or at least for all the foreseeable future.

Chapter Eight

Three months later, in the middle of a gorgeous Indian summer, another link was forged in the chain – a link that neither Garrison nor Koenig, nor even Thomas Schroeder himself, had he been alive, could possibly have recognized as such. And yet its source was right there in Sussex, not many miles east of Garrison's English residence.

It began with the discovery of a tramp asleep in a garden shed at the edge of a country property owned by Dr Gareth Wyatt, the once-famous neuropsychiatrist. The discovery was made by one Hans Maas, formerly Otto Krippner, returning to his rooms in what was once a gatehouse of the Wyatt estate following his nightly constitutional.

Maas was attracted to the shed, which leaned against one wall of the old gatehouse, by the tramp's snoring. The reek of cheap booze as Maas pushed open the creaking door was an almost physical force striking him in the face. There lay the tramp in one corner, a sack of half-spilled, sprouting potatoes serving as his pillow. An empty bottle hung from limp fingers, and grime was thick on him. He had put down some empty sacks for his bed, but the evenings were still warm and so he had not bothered to cover himself.

At first Maas tried to wake him, but when he was unable to do so he uttered a low curse in German, then left the shed and let himself into the gatehouse. There he took off his coat and hung it on a rack in the tiny hallway before reaching for the telephone. With the phone in his hand he paused and stared at himself in a full-length wall mirror. Wiry, sixty-seven inches in height and still smooth-skinned in the main, the years had not changed him much. Indeed, he could wish they had been less kind to him. He looked closely at his small, square-cut beard, once more registering surprise (as he invariably did) at the way it had altered his face. Yes, it still surprised him. And how long had it been now? Thirty years? And him still not used to his disguise! Still, not much of a disguise really.

Perhaps it was that his cheeks were a little hollower. Well, and wasn't he an old man now? And his iron-grey hair, which had once been shiny-black. But these were the only real changes. And all external. Inside he had not changed at all. He shook his head and looked away from the mirror, stared for a moment at the telephone in his hand. Then he dialled Gareth Wyatt's number in the house at the head of the drive.

While the number rang he thought back on the years flown since the end of the war. Thirty years in hiding, and for what? War crimes? Otto Krippner had committed no crimes. No more than a gardener who clears scum from the surface of a pool – or attempts to grow the perfect rose. Oh, yes, Krippner had cleared away scum, lots of it. And he had tried to grow a rose, too – though there were those who would see it as a monstrous, hybrid orchid. The master-race! Yes, he had once thought it possible, but now . . .

Gareth Wyatt answered the phone, his cultured voice not yet betraying his naturally scandalous and unscrupulous nature. 'Wyatt here. Who is it?'

'Maas,' the ex-Nazi answered.

'Oh, it's you, Hans. Can't it wait? I have . . . a guest.'

A guest, yes. One of Wyatt's endless line-up of girls, no doubt. Attracted by his good looks, intelligence, charm – only to be seduced and dumped in short order. If the man would only pay as much attention to his business as he did to his womanizing . . .

'It could wait, yes,' Maas answered, 'but on the other hand—'

'Well, then, what is it, Hans?' Impatience in the sharpness of his tone.

The German lowered his voice. An idea, vague at first but forming rapidly now, shaped itself in his head. 'We needed a subject, Gareth. And right now he lies sleeping off a drunk in your garden shed. A tramp, unconscious on a pile of sacks, so drunk I could not wake him up.'

Wyatt's voice grew quiet to match that of Maas. 'A tramp? Are you crazy? What sort of subject would a tramp—'

'The *perfect* subject!' Maas cut him short, his German accent thickening as his excitement grew. 'Think, Gareth. A tramp. If anything should go wrong this time—'

'You assured me nothing would go wrong.' Accusation.

'I adjusted the machine as you ordered,' Maas answered quietly, '—but cheaply. When one cannibalizes components, one takes a chance on being let down. More money would have bought better parts. But . . . I repeat, nothing should go wrong, not this time. If it did, however – well, would the world miss a tramp? I doubt it.'

'This tramp of yours,' Wyatt chuckled drily over the wire, 'he's not a Jew, is he? My God! All these years and you still think and talk like a true Nazi. But I admit there's some value in what you say.' He paused, then: 'Very well, but keep him out of sight. Let him sleep it off. If he's still there in the morning we'll talk some more about it. Right now I'm . . . engaged.'

'Of course, Gareth, I understand,' Maas answered. 'But you shouldn't go tossing that word Nazi about too freely. You helped me, yes, and you were well paid for your help. And you learned more from me than you ever did from your college professors. But always remember: if ever I am discovered then so are you. And there are punishments for traitors no less than for Nazis.' His words were greeted with black silence. 'Until the morning, then . . .'

Maas gently put down the telephone's handset and went to the window. At the top of the drive there were lights in the big house. Some in the downstairs servants' quarters and others in Wyatt's study and adjoining bedroom upstairs.

And so to bed, Gareth, Maas thought, *with your new whore. Ah well, men have their passions, their ambitions. Yours would seem to be money and women. The amassing of the first and the ruining of the second. Mine? Mine is a dream I've nurtured these thirty years. A race of supermen. A Fourth Reich!*

In his darkened bedroom in the large and sumptuous house, in his bed with its black silk sheets, Wyatt's mind turned over just such thoughts and ambitions as Maas had recently ascribed to him. Satyrish, he must have his women, and more often than not these days that meant money. Not for common little sluts like the one who shared his bed tonight, no, but for those rarer treasures whose positions often demanded long pursuits and secretive courtships. But then, surely that was the pleasure of it: the chase before the kill.

Wyatt sighed. The girl was asleep now, her blonde hair spread like a fan on her pillow, her flesh white against the black sheets – but soon he would wake her. Needs such as his were not satisfied easily. Nor were they satisfied cheaply. Again he thought of money, of steadily dwindling reserves. A certain debutante was demanding money he could ill afford; a recent female client demanded the expensive attentions and clandestine meetings he had once foolishly promised; even his servants were demanding higher wages. The first he would bluff his way around; the second he must politely delay, perhaps with more lies and spurious promises; and the third he would simply dismiss, not only from his mind but from his service. Labour was cheap. If they did not like the wages he paid, let them look elsewhere for employment. Others could be found to replace them.

As for Maas: something might have to be done about him, too. The man was forever issuing these veiled threats. Or if not threats, warnings. And what if the hunters should eventually track him down? It would doubtless be as the ex-Nazi said: Wyatt, too, would be made to pay the price.

But what of this tramp? A subject for Psychomech? The perfect subject? Possibly. What drives a man to the road in the first place? What reduces a man to that position of penury, seemingly satisfied merely to exist, but outside of society? *Something* must have driven this man out, had set his feet to wandering, to escaping. And if that something could be found . . . would that give him back the spark? Would it return him whole to the world of men?

That was what Psychomech was all about: a mechanical psychoanalyst, designed to seek out the fear in a man's mind and crush it – but the fear, not the mind! And that was where Psychomech had so far failed. Wyatt blamed the machine's designer and operator, Hans Maas, or Otto Krippner as he had been when his master was Hitler; but within himself Wyatt knew that this was an injustice, that without Maas his fortune would have failed long ago. For more than twenty-five years they had been together; and Wyatt's reputation (if somewhat jaded or tarnished now) had been built on the Nazi's knowledge. Why, Maas had forgotten more of psychoanalysis and the allied sciences than Wyatt could ever hope to learn.

If only the man's damned machine could be made to function! But even in that respect Wyatt knew that he must blame himself. He had not allowed the German the money he had needed to build the thing. Maas had worked quite literally to a shoe string budget. And like all projects built on shaky foundations, the machine had let them down. That had been six months ago, since when Maas had made several adjustments and alterations, but—

Still Wyatt shuddered when he thought about it.

The subject (Wyatt knew his name but could no longer think of him as having a name, or of needing one) had been middle-aged, middle-income, middling in every respect – except for one. His rampant, runaway, and rapidly accelerating neuroses. The man had been riddled with minor mental disorders, complexes, neurotic imaginings and fancies and fears of all sorts and natures. Frightened of his own wife, his very children, even afraid of Wyatt's treatment (and as it happened with good cause), he had been a wreck.

At first it appeared that there was hope, a certain slow response to Wyatt's orthodox psychiatry. The subject had seemed to improve. Then—

Maas had suggested that they use Psychomech, that they task the machine with its first real problem. And again there was a positive response, an improvement in the subject. Of course he had been sworn to secrecy: Wyatt had impressed upon his all too receptive mind the machine's experimental nature and the fact that its use was vastly expensive – which in fact it was not. Their agreement had been simple: the subject would be, to all intents and purposes, a guinea pig, and his treatment would be the substance of his reward. Mental stability in return for lending his mind to Psychomech. That was how it was supposed to have been . . .

And at first it had seemed to work. One by one Psychomech had discovered and destroyed the subject's innermost terrors, functioning perfectly and rapidly as it ferreted out his fears and gave him mastery over them. Wyatt and Maas grew over-confident; the profits to be made through Psychomech were enormous; the pair could no longer afford to waste such potential on people like the subject. Moreover, Maas now desired to test the machine to its full capacity.

Condensing what should have been a long course of visits into one last weekend, they had strapped the subject into Psychomech for the last time and Maas had set the controls. Then, leaving the anaesthetized man and humming machine alone together, they had gone about their normal business, confident that within two short days the machine would make of the subject a new, better man. Instead—

Inside six hours Psychomech had turned him into a gibbering, raving idiot!

Something had failed within the machine. A fuse blown, a wire snapped, a valve filament shorted, something as simple as that. And Psychomech, its function reversed, had pumped the subject so full of fear as to crack his mind wide open.

Wyatt had managed to get away with it, had somehow managed to keep it quiet (the subject had been half-mad already, and something outside the psychiatrist's sphere of knowledge had finally driven him over the brink), but it was a close thing. And somehow Psychomech escaped detection; no mention was ever made of any mechanical device or aid as used in the subject's treatment.

Maas had not even suffered an investigation, of course, for what was he but Wyatt's gardener and handyman? No more than a dozen or so people even knew that he existed, and less cared. And if he suddenly ceased to exist . . . who would miss him?

Just like the tramp. Who would miss a tramp?

For now Wyatt put everything from his mind and turned to the girl. He touched her, and again, insistently, and her blue eyes sluggishly opened. 'Darling,' she whispered, her white arms twining round his neck. She made to cradle him between her legs but he drew back, roughly turning her over on to her face.

'No, not that way,' he told her, his cultured voice guttural with lust. 'That was last time. This time we do it this way . . .'

And in a nearby room whose door was triple-padlocked, Psychomech stood in idle silence, dead, inert, switched off. Psychomech: a mechanical mishmash, a potential God-maker . . .

*   *   *

'Oh, I know what did it,' the tramp told them. 'What does it every time. Rape!'

'Rape?' Wyatt half-filled the tramp's glass with sherry. 'I'm not sure I follow you.'

'Rape, yes – my wife was raped. Since then, well, it just went from bad to worse. I can't keep it from my mind, d'you see? Booze is the only solution. The soft blackness deep in the heart of a bottle.'

Maas and Wyatt looked meaningfully at each other as the tramp reached out for the decanter and filled his glass to its brim. The German glanced at the ragged, seated figure out of the corner of his eye, saw that he was staring into his glass and took the opportunity to nod a slow affirmative at Wyatt. In return, the psychiatrist pursed his lips for a moment, and finally nodded his agreement. George Hammond Esq, of no fixed abode, was to be the new subject, test material for the rebuilt Psychomech.

With or without Wyatt's agreement, Maas had already decided as much. That is to say, he had set his black heart on it. He needed the machine tested, and not for Wyatt's purely selfish or avaricious reasons. Wyatt was no technician, no engineer; he understood only half of Psychomech's components. The rest of the machine was a mystery; meant nothing to him. But it meant everything to Maas, its builder. For when at last that secret part of the machine was brought into play, then there would be a wonder. Wyatt saw Psychomech as some sort of panacea for mental maladies and morbid imaginings – which in part it was or could be – but Maas had built it for an entirely different purpose. Psychomech was the booster which might multiply Man's latent psychic powers to the very limits of the ESP Universe!

Last night, after speaking to Wyatt, Maas had gone out and quietly dropped the latch on the garden shed. 'If he's still there in the morning,' Wyatt had said, and so Maas had ensured that he would be. And early this morning, when he had heard the girl's tiny car start up and saw it coming down the drive from the big house, turning out past the gatehouse and away towards London, he had waited no longer but unlatched the shed and shaken the tramp awake. Then, with promises of food and strong drink, he had led him to the house.

Strangely, the man had seemed normal in almost every respect – with the one exception that he was a tramp. And finally the questioning and the drink had produced the desired result, and now Wyatt had his answer: rape. Rape had driven this man from society, had reduced him to his present condition. The rape of his wife.

'And before that you were, well—' the psychiatrist shrugged offhandedly, as if in casual conversation, '—you were a perfectly ordinary member of society.' He stated it simply, skilfully avoiding making it a different question.

'Society? Ordinary? Normal, d'you mean? Huh! Stuff your society!' George Hammond retorted vehemently. 'You know what society is? A zoo, that's what. An open zoo with wild animals on the loose.' He looked up, his mouth slack behind beard and stained moustache, slitted his eyes and winked half-stupidly. But his voice was clear and his words direct: 'Listen, Boss, whoever you are. You want to know something? Last night, within twenty, twenty-five miles of this very house, there were two rapes and two more attempted rapes! And of the actual rapes, one was a gang-bang. You know what a gang-bang is? Well, that's what happened to my wife. Turned her into a cabbage and me into . . . into this. And you talk about "society" to me?'

'Two rapes and two attempted?' Wyatt's eyebrows lifted. 'Are you quoting statistics? Is that the average for an English county?'

'Shit, statistics – I state facts!' the tramp answered. 'Check your morning papers. You'll find I'm right.'

'You've read the papers, then?' Maas asked.

'Eh? Come on, Chief! You know as well as I do that I've been locked up fast asleep in your shed all night. I mean, it was you came and let me out! I heard you lift the latch.'

Wyatt sighed. 'Then how do you know what's in the papers?'

'I *always* know, that's how!' The tramp turned his red-rimmed, suddenly wild eyes on Wyatt and Maas. 'Christ, I see it, don't I?'

'You see it?' Maas's interest matched Wyatt's scepticism.

'Right. I see it in my dreams. All the rape in the world. All those vile bastards sticking those poor girls. Oh, some of 'em ask for it, right enough – but what of the poor little innocents who don't, eh? And what of me, who suffers it all?'

In answer to which, Maas and Wyatt could only shake their heads . . .

Then there was more probing to be done: questions about family, friends, the police; people who might know or want to know where George Hammond was; all seemingly innocent, casual, and all answered in an encouraging negative. Only George himself knew where George was, and as for family and friends: they no longer existed. The police? Oh, no – he'd always steered clear and had never had any trouble with them. No, George was no trouble to anyone – except himself. It was the dreams, you see? The dreams of rape. Which could only ever be drowned out in a bottle of decent booze.

By which time he had all but finished off an entire decanter of good sherry!

The sherry did for him, however, and he went down for the day; which was all to the good. It allowed Wyatt and Maas time to prepare for the night. Neither one of them had thought to check the morning papers, where they might easily have verified what Hammond had related to them about certain events of last night. Or to be more exact, Maas *had* considered checking – only to put the idea from

151

his mind. It would be too much of a coincidence, too much to hope for. Later he would remember and check out of sheer curiosity – but by then it would be too late and Hammond already on the machine.

For scattered throughout the newsprint were the usual brutalities, of which not a few dealt with sexual attacks on lone females. Seven miles away in Chichester an elderly spinster had been raped by a burglar. In Winchester a girl had been threatened obscenely but had managed to frighten off her attacker. In Bognor Regis two girls had been dragged into a van, driven away and attacked in nearby woods. One of them had escaped but the other had been raped repeatedly by three drunken bullies, until police officers had caught them in the woods, still taking their terrible pleasures of the by then unconscious girl. And all within twenty-five miles of Wyatt's house . . .

For all Psychomech's electronic and mechanical intricacy, the theory behind the machine was simplicity itself. The majority of human minds harbour certain fears, each of them specific to the individual. When these are common-place they are easily recognized and named – such as claustrophobia and agoraphobia, to name two of the commonest. But fear is a much more complicated thing than that, and its sources are far more diverse than enclosed or wide-open spaces.

Psychomech's purpose (as explained by Maas to Wyatt long ago when first he started to build the machine) was this: first of all to excite the subconscious fear areas of the subject's psyche, then to feed both body and mind with the strength necessary to overcome the fear, the while gradually removing the fear stimulus. A dream would be the result, induced and controlled, a dream in which the subject would come face to face with his own worst nightmares – those things he most feared, the demons of his mind – which he would then overcome and destroy. Which was in effect the entire foundation of psychiatric theory and practice: to make a mind face up to and gain mastery over its own deep-seated fears. And all to be performed through the magic of Psychomech.

But Wyatt knew nothing of the machine's principal function, which could only come into play after these initial exorcisms had taken place; knew nothing of the theory that an entirely liberated fear-free mind would realize its full ESP potential, would in fact turn man into superman. Maas, however – Maas could read the machine's charts and graphs and so learn the full scope of its success or failure – he did know. And whereas Wyatt had agreed that George Hammond should become a guinea pig, only Maas knew how far the experiment would go. Last time there had been failure, true, when the subject's fear-centres had been overstimulated without back-up or relief from the machine; but this time . . . And what if Hammond really did have this ESP power he had mentioned, this mental apparatus for remote viewing, which allowed him to see distant occurrences 'in his dreams', as he had it?

. . . In the evening Hammond came briefly awake, and was immediately subdued with a little food and several large glasses of brandy; which saw him safely out of the way until around 10.30 that night. When next he started to recover but before he could fully rouse himself, Maas gave him a mild general anaesthetic and with Wyatt's help wheeled him into the machine room where they attached him to Psychomech. And there at last, with the many monitors taped securely into place on Hammond's head and body and with the machine fully programmed, the experiment was ready to begin.

It was 11.10 P.M. when Maas administered the required drug, an opium derivative, and switched the machine on. The preliminary phase of dream-inducement, fear stimulation, confrontation, battle and victory would take between two and two and a half hours to complete, but

Maas had told Wyatt that it would take six. He required the extra time to check Pschomech's secret but primary function: to supply Hammond's mind with an extra-sensory boost which Maas should be able to monitor on his screens and graphs. In this way he hoped to develop a finer measure of control over the input calibration.

With Hammond strapped down and sinking rapidly into his own subconscious world – which would soon become peopled by the most hideous nightmares he would ever experience, dreams of brutalized women, red rape and mindless perversions, where only the dream-Hammond himself might intervene and so destroy the cancer of his psychosis – Maas left Wyatt to keep watch and went downstairs to make sandwiches. Wyatt's servants, a living-out cook and cleaner and an odd-job man, had been given today and all of tomorrow off. Maas himself was, ostensibly, the estate's gardener; but in fact professional help had to be called in quarterly to keep the gardens up to scratch.

The German made sandwiches for himself and Wyatt, gathered up the morning's newspapers (already sixteen hours out of date), and retraced his steps upstairs. He delivered Wyatt's food to him in the machine room, then went into the psychiatrist's study to eat and read the papers. As he ate and read, so the lines of a frown slowly began to crease his forehead. In minutes his sandwiches were forgotten as he tore through the newsprint, pausing briefly here and there and then hurrying on. And by midnight he had pieced together the whole thing, a complete corroboration of what Hammond said he had 'seen'.

And it was now plain to Maas that Hammond had, *must* have, second sight. Oh, yes, for he had seen just such men before, when long ago he had tried to build Psychomech for Hitler! The man was a remote viewer, beyond any reasonable doubt. And Maas believed he knew how it had

154

come about. His wife's experience at the hands of her rapists – or rather, his mind's constant *preying* upon by that horror – had developed into something away and beyond any ordinary psychosis. In some inexplicable way latent ESP powers had been awakened, a clairvoyance concerning itself solely with sexual attacks upon women. And so sensitive had his remote viewing become that Hammond had almost \been driven insane. He must have been an extremely strong man, for instead of succumbing he had gone 'on the road', where only his incessant wandering and the occasional bottle were able to ease the nightmarish empathy he felt for the victims of those brutal crimes his mind detected in their enactment and showed to him in ESP visions.

Maas was jubilant. Normal ESP patterns, even boosted one thousand per cent, might be difficult to detect on the cheap calibrators Wyatt's tightwad money had provided – but Hammond's ESP patterns should be quite abnormal. Why, he should be able to detect them right now, before ever Psychomech supercharged the tramp's mind.

He deliberately forced himself to a semblance of calm and finished his sandwiches, even though they now tasted like straw. Then he went through into the machine room where Wyatt was checking Hammond's functions. On the bed of the machine – not really a bed so much as a padded platform complete with straps and manacles – Hammond was sweating freely and twitching spasmodically. Dwarfed by Psychomech's electrical and mechanical bulk, his grimy, naked tramp's body seemed very tiny and insignificant; but when Maas tuned in the additional monitoring system he could see at once that this was not so. No, Hammond was in no way insignificant. On the contrary, he was a very extraordinary man.

'Hans,' Wyatt mumbled round a mouthful of food, 'what are you doing?' Without waiting for an answer he continued: 'Are you sure he's OK? I mean, heartbeat, respiration, blood pressure, temperature, adrenalin – everything is up. Up and rising.'

'I see it,' Maas answered calmly. 'It's only to be expected.' He turned down the power to those screens he had been watching, faced Wyatt. 'Look at him. The anaesthetic has long since worn off and Psychomech the hypnotist has taken over. His worst fears are realized as he comes face to face with them. He wades thigh-deep through violent, vicious scenes of rape run rampant while the machine prepares him for battle, feeds him those impulses which will turn him into a psychotic killer – but only in his dreams. When he is through, Rape will be banished. Aided by Psychomech he will have destroyed Rape. He will no longer fear but despise Rape. It will no longer ride him through life like some morbid hag clinging to his back.'

Together they gazed at the beleaguered man . . .

Hammond reeled across the shallow, misted depression of a moonlit valley of scabrous trees and jutting, weathered rock formations, like the ruins of some vast and ancient fortress long fallen into decay. His eyes were tight-shut and he held his hands to his ears, vainly trying to insulate himself against the horror spawning all about in the night. Mist eddied about his calves, swirled where he stepped, a warm mist rising from hideous hollows of depravity and lust. But even with his hands clamped over his ears he could not shut out the bestial grunting, the screams of ravished women and girls; and through the soles of his staggering feet he felt the shuddering of the earth to the incessant, frenzied pounding of naked flesh.

The entire valley, whose expanse stretched away to black, low-domed hills, seemed full of heaving, fighting, writhing bodies; where with each passing moment women would come running, screaming, panting, fleeing before leering gangs of pursuers, only to be caught, stripped naked and hurled down into the mist. White limbs would kick spastically upward, straining violently before falling back exhausted; and brutish backs and buttocks would work in a frenzy of near-mechanical lust while gangling beast-creatures stood about waiting their turns. All about Hammond as he stumbled through his nightmare, the shallow valley was alive with an unending orgy of rape!

He tripped over an extended, shuddering female leg and fell to his knees, his eyes popping open automatically as he threw out his arms to break his fall. Agonized eyes gazed into his through tendrils of mist – his wife's eyes! She lay there in her rags, soiled and broken. Hammond sobbed and reached for her but a hairy fist crashed into his temple. He flew over on to his back, got to his knees, gazed through dripping blood that mercifully obscured his vision. But not enough. Slavering mouths descended upon his wife's breasts, biting deep and drawing blood; dirt-clogged fingers clutched her thighs as a grunting, hunched figure drew her on to himself as if she were an old garment.

Hammond screamed and surged to his feet, crashing against a gnarled black tree where a bloodied figure flopped spread-eagled, bound to the rough bark, her dark head lolling. He knew her ravished figure, her black hair, the voice now choked and sobbing that mumbled its terror into the rotten glow of the night. Again his wife! Rough hands pushed him aside, sent him staggering into the rising mists as squat, naked figures converged on the tree, scrambling to be first with this tortured creature whose body had already suffered a hundred rapes.

Hammond could take no more of it. All of them – all of these tortured souls – were one and the same woman. They were his wife, suffering again and again that horrific rape which had robbed her of her very humanity.

He fell on a white thing that laughed like a hyena as its buttocks contorted in the foul, swirling whiteness. He dragged it upright, a man-beast spurting semen as it came to its feet from bleeding, violated flesh. Hammond's knee smashed into the creature's throbbing groin, his hurled fist broke through its teeth, his forking fingers stabbed deep into eyes already glazing as the creature toppled. Then—

A dozen of them converging on him, all hair, swollen genitals and grinning yellow teeth, leaving the crushed bodies of their female victims for the moment to give their attention to this new diversion. Hammond whirled, saw the ring of inhuman faces closing, the bestial half-animal things that crowded to drag him down . . .

Hammond was not winning his battle, that was plain. Psychomech's controls were now set to give him maximum aid, to ensure his victory over whatever terrors beset him in his nightmare – but he was not winning. The horror was too great, his psychosis too deeply rooted. On the bed of the machine he writhed and thrashed, his sweat a river that washed him and ran grimy over the bed's padding. His straining flesh was cut by the straps, his wrists and ankles chafed where the manacles – for all that they were padded – gripped him. His choking, terrified scream rang in the soundproofed room, sending Wyatt staggering back in naked fear. A physically weak man, the psychiatrist could not bear to watch the torture Psychomech inflicted upon its subject.

'Hans, for God's sake – the machine's killing him! We have to stop this.'

'No, no!' Maas shook off the other's trembling hands. 'This is the peak. From now on it goes in his favour. Look—' And while Wyatt's eyes went back to the shrieking, pitiful man on the machine's bed, Maas flicked the switch which brought Psychomech's surge into play. The surge: that ESP boost to the man's already massive psychic powers.

In this action Maas knew he took a chance, but he had no choice. For once Wyatt was right: Psychomech was killing Hammond. Even with the defence input at maximum, still the mental disease eating at the man's mind was winning the subconscious battle. To apply the surge now was a pure

158

gamble, but there was something Maas *must* know béfore Hammond succumbed and died. And after all, if he did die, who would miss a tramp . . . ?

Weighed down by a mass of revolting, lusting flesh, Hammond knew now the terror of a woman tormented by sex fiends. The beast-men were sunken to such levels of depravity that all flesh had become one to them. Their vile bodies worked even against each other as they fought to violate Hammond where he writhed, pinned face-down in mist and mire. Exhausted, on the brink of the pit itself – that dark chasm named Death – he searched desperately for reserves of strength which he knew were already drained . . . and found them not drained but brimming, overflowing!

   Strength!

   The awesome, miraculous powers of God and the devil combined, filling Hammond in an instant. A surge of power impossible! He rose from the mist in slow grandeur, unhurried in his newborn, as yet untested might. He rose up, Behemoth hurling off his foes, with burning eyes that tore the mist and steamed it away, revealing the rottenness that gasped and heaved beneath. And those monsters of his dream too slow to release him were the first to know his wrath. In easy, effortless ecstasy he drew their scabby arms from torn sockets, and with fists like swinging scythes he disembowelled them and sent their tatters flying in red ruin.

   His fiery eyes sought out the demon hordes that endlessly coupled with the stark, screaming innocents of this realm of horror, shredding the mist and sending aloft clouds of steam like exhalations from hell. And wherever he found the foully jerking flesh of Rape he struck, striding like a death-dealing avenger through the steaming valley, his hands scarlet with the slimy blood of those he slew.

   And fast? – he had the flickering speed of a snake's forked tongue, though to him it seemed his pace was measured and

*that of his enemies dull and sluggish. And sharp? – his hands
and feet and knees and elbows – even his jutting jaw and his
very teeth – were razor edges to the stunned and suddenly
quivering flesh of his enemies. He cut, crushed, tore,
dismembered, destroyed them, his fury such that not a beast
of them survived his onslaught; and when it was done a sun
rose slowly over that valley of horror, and the ragged women
– those poor ravished females – covered themselves as best
they could and crawled away, scarred but free now of the
night's menace.*

*And Hammond, the world's greatest weapon against the
mindless flesh-lust of Man, could at last lie down and sleep on
earth where green grass pushed upward to the light through
the dust of crumbling toadstools. And he feared no more the
monster Rape, banished for the moment, at least – from his
dreams . . .*

The time was 3.30 A.M. and the sweat had dried now and
grown chill on the faces of Maas and Wyatt. Their shirts
stuck to them clammily.

Wyatt's face was grey with worry, lined with fear not yet
fully subsided – but Maas was triumphant. His play,
however dangerous, had paid dividends. Following the
surge, Hammond had drawn on Psychomech's backup
systems like a human leech, his body seeming to gulp at the
intravenous nozzles supplying it with adrenalin, plasma,
oxygen and sugars. So vast his intake that he seemed to
swell on his platform, his hands knotting and relaxing,
knotting and relaxing. And when he had opened his
eyes . . . !

That was what had frightened Wyatt the most: Hammond's
scarlet eyes opening like bleeding pits, and the lunatic *smile*
that had remained frozen on his face while all of
Psychomech's screens and printouts recorded tremendous
brain activity. Maas had been obliged to shout at the
psychiatrist then, to restrain him from switching off the

machine completely. But now it was over and Hammond slept a true sleep, his eyes closed, his breathing regular, a normal smile on his face. He seemed clean somehow, bathed not only in his own sweat but in some inner stream. Like an innocent child sleeping and pleasantly dreaming.

And where Wyatt had been left drained by the experiment, Maas felt only a soaring sensation of complete success. For on those screens which only he understood he had read Hammond's psychometries, had seen what the ESP surge had done to the tramp, how his perceptions had expanded far beyond all previously known levels of metaphysical or parapsychological activity. The Superman was no longer a dream: Psychomech had solved the final question. Now it was only a matter of time and further experimentation, and the machine was not only the answer but the key. There could now be – *would be* – a Fourth Reich, with Maas the superhuman leader, Der Neuerer Grossfuehrer!

The connection between Richard Garrison and the foregoing occurrences at the home of Gareth Wyatt was not nearly so tenuous as might be imagined at first glance. Indeed Garrison – his entire household – became very much involved with those occurrences through a horror which struck in the garden of his Sussex house, though the origin and true nature of that horror would always remain unknown to him.

It happened this way:

At that very moment when Maas fed Psychomech's surge into Hammond's mind and body, a man and a girl were walking in the lane at the edge of Garrison's property. The time was 2.15; the Indian summer night was warm; the man was from out of town and had picked the girl up in a disco at Wickham. She was much younger than he, had had a little too much to drink and had foolishly agreed that he could drive her home to Amsworth, some four miles away down the country lane that ran by Garrison's house.

His plan for her was simple though not without certain dangers, but these would not deter him. The plan had worked before and he was sure it would work again; and providing she did not scream all would be well. He was in short a rapist and murderer, having raped several women and murdered one. The latter, his most recent victim, had screamed. Despite all his warnings she had screamed into the night, and he had sliced her throat. And as she had spilled out her life, so he had spilled his lust into her. That had been some six weeks ago, since when he had lain low.

Tonight, however, the need was once more upon him. His car (complete with false number plates) was parked behind a hedge in a field one mile away down the road, where it had 'broken down'. And so he and the girl went on foot. She was nervous now and resentful of his arm around her waist – and aware of his bulk against her and the strength in the fingers pressing her side and almost cupping her breast. Sobering, she knew how silly she had been in accepting his abortive lift home. For some minutes she had felt a tension building in him and dared not even guess what it meant. Then, as they passed a gap in the high brick wall that marked the boundary of Garrison's property—

In a moment his hand was over her mouth as he dragged her through the gaping brickwork and into the dry, dark shrubbery. Thrown down on a bed of dead leaves, she gasped – until once more his hand fell heavy on her mouth, splitting her upper lip. Moonlight silvered the sharp blade he now held to her throbbing neck.'

'All right, little Alice,' he rasped, all gentleness gone now from his voice. 'One peep out of you and it's all over. I'll stick this right through your windpipe, got it?' Her eyes went wide and she lay frozen. '*Got it?*' he insisted, shaking her like a rag doll.

She nodded frenziedly, shrinking from him in a paroxysm of fear.

162

He tore open her coat, used his knife to cut her dress down the front, buttons flying from sliced threads. Beneath the dress she was soft and white, the sight of her body drawing a sob from his quivering lips. He tore away her underwear and fumbled for a second with his own clothing.

Alice was a virgin. She saw him throbbing and huge and forgot his threat. Her scream, slicing the night air, was sharper than his knife – but not nearly so deadly.

'*Bitch!* – I warned you!' he hissed. He jerked the knife to her neck – and something caught at his arm, dragging it up and away from her throat, holding it like a vice. His hair stood on end as he jerked his head round to stare wildly about in the darkness. All was silent, no one there – but his arm was caught up on something.

Waiting for the glistening blade to descend, the girl drew breath and screamed again. Through the shrubs, lights came on in the lower windows of a large house. A dog barked. The rapist sobbed and strained to bring his arm sweeping down. The sleeve of his coat must be caught on something – barbed wire or a tough vine – but he could see nothing. He dropped the knife and grabbed at the girl's throat with his free hand, forcing himself between her legs and trying to enter her any way he could. But the grip on his inexplicably trapped arm tightened, drawing him to his feet and away from her. And still there was no one there.

No, there was something – some*thing*!

Above him in the night, gigantic – two glaring red eyes gazed mercilessly down. And as the grip on his arm increased tenfold, suddenly it was the rapist's turn to scream . . .

When Koenig got back to the house he was white and drawn. Even Suzy, who had accompanied him into the grounds when the screaming started, came back trembling and cowed. For Suzy to suffer from any sort of real shock or fear was a rare thing, but for Koenig it was unheard of.

'Richard,' he said, 'I have to phone for the police. There was a girl in the garden, stripped and knocked about a little. Also, a man – I think.' He quickly telephoned the local police station and spoke briefly to the constable on duty, then put down the handset. During his short telephone conversation, Garrison heard the words 'rape' and 'murder'. They set his scalp tingling, bringing him more fully awake.

The entire household – Garrison, Koenig, Cook, Joe the gardener and handyman, Fay the maid, and of course Suzy – had heard and been awakened by the screams. High-pitched at first and obviously female, they had roused the house from slumber. But then they had turned hoarse and mannish, rising to a crescendo of utter terror before gurgling into an abrupt silence. By then Koenig had thrown an overcoat over his pyjamas and gone out with Suzy and a powerful electric torch into the darkness. Moments later he had called for help from Joe and Fay, and he had bundled a crumpled, ragged figure into the house and on to a bed in a spare downstairs bedroom. Then, while they attempted to revive the girl, Koenig had gone back into the garden. Suzy had gone with him, but reluctantly.

By this time Garrison was dressed and downstairs, waiting for Koenig's report when he returned, and there he now stood stroking the trembling Dobermann while Koenig got a grip on himself. Finally, taking his friend's elbow, Garrison led him through into the library and closed the door behind them. A moment later, before he could repeat his question, Joe knocked and entered. He stuttered as he spoke to Koenig:

'She's come to, Mr Koenig, sir. Bruises on her throat, poor lass, and her mouth's bleeding a bit – and shocked rigid, no doubt about that – but she'll be OK. Fay's giving her a hot drink right this minute. Name's Alice Green, from Amsworth. And you were right, it was rape – attempted, anyway. She didn't know the chap – met him in Wickham at a disco. That's all I know at the moment.'

'Did she say what . . . what *happened* to him?' Koenig asked.

'No she didn't. Just something about him being snatched up – and about his screams. But we all heard them, I'm sure.' Garrison sensed Joe's shudder. 'Actually, I'd say it was – I dunno,' he shrugged helplessly, '—a pack of dogs?'

'Thank you, Joe,' Garrison told him. 'The police will be here soon. Please let us know when they arrive, will you?' As Joe left he turned to Koenig. 'Willy, what the hell has been going on? I've got some of it, but—' His hands made a bewildered gesture.

The German was more or less in control of himself now. He poured brandy into two glasses, something he would not normally do without first asking, and they both sat down. 'I gather there was an attempted rape,' Garrison started the other off. 'Take it from there, eh?'

Koenig knocked back his drink in one and answered, 'That is correct, Richard, an attempted rape. He – whoever he was – cut off the girl's clothes with a knife. I saw the knife lying where Suzy and I found the girl. I left it there for the police. Anyway, the girl was scared witless and she passed out before I could get much out of her. She did say she had seen something big and black.'

'Wait,' Garrison held up a hand. 'Willy, you've so far avoided mentioning him, the rapist. And what was all this about murder?'

Koenig nodded and cleared his throat. 'Yes,' he answered, 'murder – *his* murder! Actually, I was glad to get back into the house. Whatever killed him *was* big. It must have been . . .'

'Go on.'

'Well – of course it was dark out there and I can't be sure, and my torch was not very good in the shrubbery – but I think there are bits of him scattered about all over the garden!'

'*What?*'

Koenig gave a nervous shrug. 'That's right, Richard. A hellish mess. You heard the screams . . .'

'They woke me up, but—'

'They would have roused the dead,' Koenig shuddered. 'The bushes where the girl was lying are – well, they're red. I saw an arm. And a leg. And part of a face – I think.'

'Jesus!'

'Jesus?' Koenig's voice was very quiet and still a little trembly. 'Even if I were a believer, still I could not see Jesus – or any son of any sane God – having anything to do with what has happened out there tonight!'

For Gareth Wyatt the night had been nerve-wracking; for Otto Krippner alias Hans Maas it had been wildly successful; for George Hammond it had effected a cure, in that he was later able to adjust himself once more into society and become, as he had been before, a solid citizen; but all over the central south of England it had been, to lift a leader direct from a local newspaper in the Portsmouth area, 'A Very Bad Night for Rapists!' That is to say the very least.

Wyatt failed once again to read the papers, however, and so made no connection; even if he had read them it is doubtful he would have noticed anything out of the ordinary. Or at the most he would have termed it a coincidence. After all, sensationalist reporting is commonplace. Maas *did* read the papers and noticed everything, which only served to reinforce his will and spur him on towards his crazed ambition.

What the newspapers said was this:

That over an area of some six hundred square miles a series of amazing accidents or occurrences of a weird nature had seemingly conspired to defeat the activities of at least four would-be rapists. A freak whirlwind, coming up from nowhere out of the still night, had snatched an attacker

166

from his victim in a railway siding on the outskirts of Barnham, hurling him under the wheels of a passing train. Another sex-fiend had lured a girl into his car in Havant, had then parked in a dark alley on an industrial estate, and had been on the point of assaulting his frightened captive when a large vehicle had struck his car, decapitating and thus killing him outright. The girl, miraculously, had not been harmed, though firemen had been obliged to cut her from the wreckage. Only a very large vehicle could have delivered the tremendous punch, and police were still seeking assistance from an as yet unknown driver of an articulated truck. Then there was the attempted rape in Garrison's garden, where the authorities had been unable to supply a better answer to the riddle than to echo Joe's statement and report that a man had been 'killed by a pack of dogs'; and finally, a middle-aged night cleaner in Southsea had been attacked while preparing rooms on the top floor of the Bonnington Hotel. She had struck out at the man with her bucket but had not thought she actually hit him, which was why she had been astonished when he 'flew away' from her, taking an entire window and frame with him and falling six floors to his death on the street below.

And all of these things occurring in that hour following immediately upon Maas feeding Hammond with Psycho-mech's surge.

A very bad night for rapists indeed . . .

Chapter Nine

Time passed swiftly for the new Richard Garrison. Thirty months gone by like leaves blown from an autumn tree, utterly beyond recovery. But not wasted like dead leaves. Filled with activity.

In fact there had been almost too much for him to do, especially since the news of Vicki's death. For Garrison had deliberately buried himself in work, knowing that in this way he could avoid the brooding sorrow which must otherwise fester within him.

His prime concern had been to put Thomas Schroeder's more than substantial legacy to work, as a result of which his assets had grown in direct proportion to his expanding business acumen – and Garrison's name had rapidly become synonymous in the city for shrewdness in all business matters. Well on his way to making his first half-million (other, that is, than the money Schroeder had left for him), his judgement was always sound, his thinking unmarred by sentiment or sense of duty. Duty had been for the Army; Garrison was all for Garrison. In short, his lack of ethics – or rather, his ignorance of the niceties or dictates of ethics – worked as a protective cloak against the powerful business counter-forces which must otherwise crush him. So that despite the fact that he was a relative newcomer, a mere entrepreneur on the wheeling-and-dealing scene, he was nevertheless one whose talent and naked vitality left little doubt but that he should be played very carefully. Even the most powerful forces were wary of Richard Garrison.

Lady Luck had played her part in his success, certainly; but the Lady loves a gambler, and Garrison had always been that. It had not all been luck, however, for as well as Koenig's invaluable assistance (the 'chauffeur' had picked up a good many tips from his old master) Garrison had also employed the skills of one other. Skills, that is, if one might accept the rulings of the very stars themselves! For Garrison, ever a searcher after knowledge, had early decided to take a leaf from Schroeder's own book and employ talents – or invoke powers – others might all too readily scorn. In this way he soon came to heed the advice of one whose work he had earlier seen as trickery and sheer charlatanry, namely Adam Schenk, Thomas Schroeder's astrologer.

As to how they came to meet: that was due to Schenk's need to use Garrison's Retreat, to which facility Schroeder had said Schenk must always be allowed access. Garrison grudgingly bowed to his ex-mentor's wishes, but at the same time he remembered and resented the fact that Schenk was the man whose horoscopes had foretold the deaths of two people he had come to love. But for all that, even Garrison had to admit that his resentment was tempered by the knowledge that to date Schenk's horoscopes had worked out 100 per cent correct right down the line.

Out of curiosity then, he had contrived with Koenig to be at the Retreat at the same time as the astrologer. This occurred in the winter, shortly before Christmas, some eight or nine weeks after the attempted rape in Garrison's garden, which had terminated so terribly and inexplicably.

And for once Garrison was quite wrong. Adam Schenk turned out to be just the opposite of what he had expected. A youngish forty, with wild blond hair, watery blue eyes and gangling frame, Schenk was hardly the suave occultist, the devil-worshipper, the Black Magician and necromancer type that Garrison had pictured. But he was everything Thomas Schroeder had said he was.

He and Garrison had become friends almost from their first meeting, and with the passage of time their friendship and correspondence grew hand in hand with Garrison's dependence. For having met Garrison and gained a greater insight into the man, Schenk's interest in him and concern for his future (and doubtless for Schroeder's future, for of course Schenk knew of Schroeder's aim: to return from the dead into Garrison's body) prompted him to offer what assistance he could, which meant that his forecasts were soon to become a regular feature of Garrison's life.

And again those forecasts proved accurate, not once but repeatedly; so that with his advent into Garrison's life those seeds first sown by Thomas Schroeder took root and grew in the blind man, until his own interest in esoteric matters became all-consuming. From that time onward, during his not infrequent trips to the Retreat, Garrison would spend much of his time in the library and observatory, and especially in the ESP-test building, ever broadening his knowledge and experimenting with the powers he now believed lay within himself; until, within two short years of Schroeder's death, he had become something of an expert in his own right in the so-called 'fringe-sciences' of parapsychology.

In this respect, too, there had developed a special link between himself and Suzy; for example:

He no longer had to call Suzy to him; the merest thought would bring her padding silently to his side, the slightest glance would be transformed into a command. Even out of sight, Suzy would respond to Garrison's mental instructions. She had been taught the basic commands, of course (indeed Heinz Holzer had taught Suzy much more than that; for as a blind dog she was totally alone in a class of her own, unclassifiable by common terms of reference), such as 'down', 'sit', 'stay', 'come', 'watch', 'heel' and even 'attack!' – but it was remarkable to see her performing her repertoire in one corner of the garden while Garrison sat in another fifty yards away, his eyes closed, directing Suzy with his mind alone! Only Willy Koenig was aware of their rapport, however, and though he never once voiced his opinion aloud, Garrison guessed that the German believed this to be another sure sign of Thomas Schroeder's disembodied encroachment, his drawing closer to the soul and being of the man he had chosen as his host to be.

As for Koenig himself: rapidly approaching fifty years of age, he looked no more than forty and kept himself – and Garrison – in perfect trim with regular workouts in the small gymnasium which now occupied a ground-floor room of the Sussex house. Firmer friends than ever, he and his employer enjoyed a relationship beyond that of mere friendship; and only Suzy's love of Garrison was greater than that of the former SS Feldwebel's. They were like brothers; for Koenig, like Garrison himself, was a man in every sense of the word.

Infrequently, when Garrison did not need him, Koenig would take himself off to London where several ladies enjoyed his attentions, and twice yearly he would spend a week in Hamburg (his home-town in the old days) in pursuits that Garrison could well imagine but about which he enquired not at all. And for all that Garrison insisted Koenig should have these breaks from his duties, still he was invariably pleased and relieved to have his friend home again when such R & R excursions, as he termed them, were at an end.

One incident taken at random from several of a like nature may best serve to illustrate the way the rapport between Garrison and Koenig had expanded:

They were driving in London one day in the summer of 1975, with Koenig at the wheel of the Mercedes proper and Garrison relaxed and comfortable in the front passenger seat. Garrison himself had 'driven' for a little while – on the motorway and along the better roads, where traffic was no great problem – but now he sat back and enjoyed a cigarette, letting Willy get on with the job.

As they approached a level crossing in the suburbs of the

city, suddenly Garrison became aware of a cold tingling at the nape of his neck. The short hairs there were reacting to something as yet unseen, and his palms had gone clammy in an instant. Into his mind there flashed a vivid premonition of disaster. He 'saw' an accident!

'Willy – *hit the brakes!*' he yelled.

Cursing in his mother tongue, Koenig reacted with incredible speed – almost as if he had heard Garrison's command in the instant before it was given. At the same time Garrison snatched himself upright in his seat and grasped his own wheel, wrenching it savagely to the right – and Koenig, still braking, offered no resistance to the other's play. Instead he instinctively released the main steering wheel, letting Garrison skid the car sideways–on to where it rocked shudderingly to a halt and stalled in the middle of the road. From somewhere close behind came the shriek of hastily applied brakes and the angry honking of horns.

In that same moment several things happened together. An oncoming car screeched to a halt at the far side of the crossing; the crossing's warning system began to clang; and most important and frightening by far, the vast bulk of an inter-city train blasted by in a rush and a roar, its many carriages a blur that seemed to flicker in time to the clatter of its wheels. If Garrison had put his arm out of the window he could have touched the charging metal giant, whose nearness was such that the Mercedes rocked to the blast and suction of its passing.

All of this was as clear as sight itself in the eye of Garrison's mind; but he could not see what Koenig now saw: the white-faced figure in the window of the crossing's elevated control room, his hands to his head and his eyes and mouth straining wide in horror. And the red and white barriers jerking and twitching fitfully but refusing to come down, locked in their raised position by some mechanical failure. But in another moment the train had rushed off into the distance and the track was clear once more. And – miraculously! – no harm done . . .

Starting the car's stalled engine, Koenig straightened her up and drove slowly across the tracks, his eyes staring to left and right as he went, peering along those still vibrant but now vacant parallels of bright metal. Safely on the other side he picked up a little speed and turned to Garrison.

'A failure in the barriers,' he said. 'We were lucky.' His voice had a nervous edge to it.

'Lucky?' Garrison repeated, his own voice revealing how shaken he was. He shook his head. 'No, not lucky. And the way we worked together . . . that was sort of fantastic.'

Koenig forced a chuckle. 'Yes, you do very well for a blind man, Richard.'

'I was thinking something similar of you,' Garrison came back. 'Namely, that *you* do pretty well for someone who has no ESP talent! That's what you once told me, remember? The test room? How Thomas tested you, and how poor your results were?'

Koenig nodded. 'Oh, I remember all right. And it's true enough, my ESP ability is a big zero.'

'Balls!' Garrison snorted. 'You snatched my thoughts right out of my head back there. Your foot hit the brake in the same moment – even before! – I started shouting.'

Koenig chuckled again, but drily. 'It was often the same with the Colonel,' he reflected. 'But I still insist that I have no talent. It was your talent, Richard, yours. Can't you see that? Even a weak receiver will pick up a strong signal. And your signal was loud and clear that time, believe me! And what of the precognition which set the whole thing in motion? You *knew* there was danger ahead. No, the power is yours, Richard, not mine. I deserve no credit. It is a wonderful power, without which we'd both be dead.'

Garrison nodded, then said: 'It wasn't all my work. I was warned.'

'Warned?'

'By Schenk. We spoke this morning, about today's business. During our conversation he had a premonition, asked how we were travelling into London. I said by car. He told me that should be all right, but whatever I did I should not go by train. "Beware of trains today, Richard," he told me. "Steer clear of them." Those were his very words: "steer clear of trains" . . .'

One year later – the closing week of May 1976.

It was the beginning of what was to be one of England's hottest, longest summers in living memory. Three years since Garrison's first visit to the Harz, and he was now rich beyond his wildest dreams. Not yet twenty-five, he owned homes and properties in England and Germany, controlled large amounts of money in various banks and businesses (chiefly in Zurich), and lived a life which was the envy of his few contemporaries. He had his women – elegant ladies all, but none of them given any serious consideration – a few friends, though of these only Koenig was really close to him, and complete freedom to be and do exactly as he wished. And yet . . .

There were streaks of premature grey in the hair over Garrison's temples which, while they served to enhance his good looks, were still a sure sign that he was not an easy man. Not easy in his mind. For the one thing which escaped him, escaped him utterly, was happiness. This was due in part, of course, to his blindness; though amongst those who thought they knew him were some who suspected he merely affected the guise of a blind man, for only sight itself could be better than the pseudo-vision he had now learned to control so marvellously.

As for those few souls who were closest to him:

Willy Koenig had changed little, indeed seemed almost unchangeable, though Garrison had recently noted a sort of increased wariness or watchfulness in the man, who was

174

no longer quite so willing to spend more than three or four days away from him at any one time. Suzy was now four years and four months old, big, black and beautiful, and her unwavering love for her master burned as fierce as ever. The staff and servants of both the house in Sussex and Garrison's Retreat in the Harz remained unchanged, and not a man or woman of them would exchange their master for any other employer. And yet for all this there remained a large gap, one which could never be filled. Adam Schenk was no longer there to guide Garrison's feet along those paths of the future which only he had read so well.

It had happened with shocking suddenness, and Garrison had been stunned. He had not known of Schenk's problem. The astrologer had been dead these past three months, and still Garrison brooded over it. It was becoming harder for him to kill things off in his mind. With most of life's hardships removed, the need to maintain his defences had decreased. Things hurt him more now. And Schenk's death had certainly done that. The man had burned himself out by his increasing use of those drugs which helped him penetrate the mysterious veil of future times and events; and the one event he had not been able – or perhaps had been unwilling – to forecast, had been his own end. Garrison missed him, and being a realist missed his predictions. The astrologer had been invaluable to him.

But he still had those horoscopes Schenk had drawn up three years earlier, though they had lain long forgotten in an envelope, locked in his desk in the study of his Sussex home. And it was there, at the desk, that Willy Koenig found him one warm May morning, rummaging through the drawers. Garrison's cursing and banging about had brought Koenig starting awake, and donning his dressing gown he had hurried to the study.

'Willy,' Garrison's voice was tense, 'come and help me find Adam's horoscopes. They're here somewhere, in an envelope.'

Garrison's ability to know instinctively who was there no longer astonished Koenig. Very little about Garrison surprised him any more. He stepped to the desk, stopped the other's hands from their useless and unaccustomed fluttering and immediately found the manila envelope pressed flat to one side of the drawer, trapped there by a fat bundle of old documents. 'Here it is,' he said. 'But what is your hurry? Has something happened?'

'Hurry?' Garrison took the envelope, glanced up, smiled nervously. 'Yes, I am in a rush, I suppose. But . . . I dreamed again.'

Koenig knew from the almost unnoticeable emphasis on the word dreamed that this must have been one of Garrison's rarer dreams, one of premonition or clairvoyance. 'About Adam?' he said.

'No, about a girl. Terri . . .'

'Terri?' Koenig repeated him – then inhaled sharply. He understood. Terri: the 'T' on Garrison's horoscope.

Now Garrison had the envelope open, shook out the strips of card on to the desk. 'My card,' he said tersely, his voice shaky. 'Find it and read it.' Normally he would have added 'please', but right now he had no time for niceties. 'Read it from the entry "WK and Black Dog",' he ordered.

Koenig nodded, picked up Garrison's horoscope and stared at it, licked his dry lips. He found himself caught up in the other's strange excitement, felt his nerves tightening. 'WK and Black Dog, "S"?' he began. 'Time-scale: to three years.'

'Stop!' Garrison held up a hand. 'And it's now three years since he wrote that. And you and Suzy have been with me most of that time.' As he spoke Suzy herself appeared at the door, tongue lolling, padding across the floor to flop at Garrison's feet. 'What's the next line?'

'Girl "T",' Koenig dutifully continued. 'Time-scale: to eight years.'

'That's far enough,' Garrison stopped him again. He

176

frowned. 'Girl "T" – Terri!'

'Terri,' Koenig repeated the word, musing. 'She was in your dream? But who is she?'

Garrison looked full into the other's face – and once again, as so often before, the German wondered exactly what the blind man saw. It was almost as if those lenses looked right into a man's soul. 'I don't know who she is,' Garrison finally answered. 'But I do know *where* she is. At least, I can describe the place. And one thing is certain: I've never been there.'

'Describe it, then,' Koenig invited.

'Let me think, get it out while it's still clear in my mind.' Koenig waited, and eventually Garrison continued. 'There was a bay. Blue ocean, with hills climbing away behind a town – no, a village. With boats in the harbour. Orange houses, some white, and some with flat roofs. And flowering trees. Some palms. Oh, and trellises with grapes – and masses of purple climbing flowers. And at night, fireflies like tiny aeroplanes, their lights winking as they—'

'Italy!' Koenig exclaimed with certainty. 'I *have* been there, and your description says it all. But let's make absolutely certain, if we can. Is there more to go on?'

'Small bars with tables on the pavements, gazing out to sea,' Garrison quickly went on, as if afraid of losing the vision. 'And open-air restaurants with waiters serving—' He paused, gasped, gripped Koenig's arm where it rested on the top of the desk. 'For a moment there it came back to me, vivid in my mind. Dark-haired people at wooden-topped tables, eating with forks which they twined!'

'Pasta!' Koenig nodded. 'I was right, it is Italy.'

'But *green* pasta?' Garrison's frown deepened more yet.

Koenig chuckled. 'Ah! But your education is incomplete, Richard. Your geography is lacking. Obviously you have totally omitted Italy – and Italian cuisine! Green pasta, you say? Well, that narrows it down a little – I hope. I would say that is a basil pasta, and furthermore that it is a north

177

Italian dish, where basil is a speciality.'

Garrison was unimpressed. 'Narrows it down, did you say? Northern Italy is one hell of a lot of land, Willy.'

'But we are talking of a place on the sea, in a bay,' the German reminded him. 'And did this place have a name?'

'A name?' Garrison pressed his knuckles to his forehead. 'A name – yes! But—' he smiled tiredly and brushed his brow. 'No, that's crazy.'

'Perhaps not,' said Koenig.

Garrison snorted. 'Arizona?'

'Ah, well that *is* crazy, yes.' Now it was Koenig's turn to frown. 'But not so crazy if it was spelled Arizano! That would sound much more—' And again Garrison gripped his arm.

'But that's *it!*' he whispered. 'Or nearly it. It begins with an 'A' and ends in 'zano' – I think.'

Koenig stood up, crossed to a bookshelf and took down a world atlas. He brought the large book back to the desk and opened it to the map of Italy. Then turning the page and turning to the index, he read out:

'Arezzo, Ariano Irfino, Ascoli Piceno—'

'*No!*' Garrison cut him off, frustration sharpening his tone. 'The first one was close, but . . . I told you, Willy, it ends in "zano".'

The other sighed and closed the atlas. 'A place on the coast,' he nodded. 'Probably in the north. Very well, it's high time we had a holiday, you and I – especially you. Two years now, and you've travelled no farther than Zurich and the Harz. And if this Terri is in Italy—'

'A holiday?' Garrison was at once interested. 'What do you suggest?'

Koenig stroked his chin for a moment, thought about it, then smiled. 'I suggest we fly to Italy,' he said, 'hire a yacht and crew in Naples, and then—' he shrugged, 'we simply follow our noses – or your nose.'

Garrison nodded. 'I could of course have a list of coastal

Italian towns and villages drawn up, and take my pick of those that sound right. But – your idea sounds far more interesting. And you're right, it would be good to get away for a week or two. Whichever, it's a problem we won't solve sitting here. So – when can we go?'

Koenig spread his arms. 'As soon as you like.'

'Today!'

And the German knew that there would be little point in arguing.

On the 2 June they set out from Naples and headed north along the coast. Their hired motor-yacht, a rather cramped eight-berther, had herself supplied Garrison with his first bearings; for her name was *La Ligurienne.* And so they forged for the Ligurian Sea, that incredibly beautiful expanse of ocean between Corsica and the Gulf of Genoa. Also, north had smelled right to Garrison; and of course he had Koenig's knowledge of Italian foods!

To anyone who did not know Garrison, following up a dream in this crazy fashion must seem the very epitome of all wild-goose chases; but Garrison knew enough of himself now to realize that this was no folly. And as for Koenig: he was equally eager to see Garrison's dream realized. To his way of thinking it would take him that much closer to reunion with his *first* master, who was not really dead but merely . . . waiting.

The evening of the 6th, however, found their spirits dampened more than a little. They now sailed south-westward, following the coastline round towards Monaco and Nice, and it would not be long before the waters they sailed were no longer Italian but French. Considering this, Garrison's mood was gradually turning to one of despair. Which was just the perfect time for things to take a turn for the better.

Genoa's lights were beginning to come on, gleaming distantly astern and mirrored in a perfectly flat sea, when

Garrison sat up straighter in his chair on the narrow deck and called Koenig to his side.

His hushed voice was almost drowned by the leisurely throb and burble of the engine; he hardly dared voice his thoughts as he said, 'Willy – we're nearly there!'

'Are you sure?'

'Oh, yes, I'm sure. Get one of the crew, will you?'

Koenig immediately brought the captain, a light-skinned Roman named Francesco Lovi, from his position at the wheel. 'Francesco,' said Garrison, 'can we get up a little more speed?'

'But certainly, Mr Garrison. Shall we put in tonight?'

'I think so, yes.'

Lovi gave an exaggerated sigh. 'And perhaps this time it will be the place you seek, eh? We have been to many places, but they were not what you sought.'

'I'll know it when I find it,' said Garrison. 'In fact, I believe I have found it. Tell me, what ports do you have on your charts?'

'Oh, Savona, perhaps?'

'Is there nothing closer than that?'

Lovi wrinkled his nose. 'A small port,' he said. 'We should be standing directly off her right now. Ah, yes!' He pointed to starboard. 'You see the lights?'

Koenig answered him, 'Yes, I see them.'

'Good,' said Garrison. 'What's the town called?'

Lovi shrugged. 'I have never put in there. A tourist trap, I think. A holiday place. But Marcello will know. He was born in these parts.' He put a hand to his mouth and bellowed, 'Hey, Marcello!'

A huge bearded man came out from the cabin, spoke briefly to Lovi, turned to Garrison and nodded in a friendly fashion. His hairy face split in a smile.

'She holiday town,' Marcello rumbled. 'Little place. Not good for rich man. Savona better.'

'I'll decide that,' Garrison answered, his patience wearing thin. 'Now please, what's the name of the place?'

Marcello scratched his chin, shrugged, said, 'Oh, she called Arenzano.'

Garrison felt his blood cool in a moment, forcing an involuntary shiver down his spine. Koenig, too. They looked at each other, unsmiling. Finally Garrison turned his lenses on the captain. 'This is it, Francesco,' he said. 'This is the place. Tonight we put into Arenzano.'

When the captain went back to his duties and they were alone again, Garrison asked Koenig to sit beside him and said, 'Willy, there's something I still have to tell you.'

'About your dream?' The other looked at him sideways. 'I thought there might be.'

'When we find Terri,' Garrison began, 'it may well be that—'

'—We also find trouble,' Koenig finished it for him. 'She's in danger, eh?'

For once Garrison was astonished. 'Now how in hell . . . ?'

'Richard,' Koenig patted his hand in an almost fatherly manner, 'did Thomas never explain why he employed me? I have this knack, you see – no, not an ESP facility that I'm aware of, just a knack – of sensing trouble before it strikes. Sometimes it lets me down, but not often. Thomas used to say that my prime function was to think bad thoughts before others thought them. Well, since first you told me about your dream I have been thinking bad thoughts. I am prepared—'

'You're a remarkable and valuable man, Willy Koenig,' said Garrison slowly. 'And you're right – there was violence in my dream.'

'How much violence?'

'Four men, a knife – I'm not sure. But your walking stick was in it, too. And I notice that you brought it with you.' The stick he mentioned was one that Koenig had used ever since Garrison first knew him. An ordinary stick with a crook, the German walked with it in the country and when exercising Suzy, flicked leaves with it, used it to gesture and to point things out. A casual, comfortable sort of stick, time and use had polished it black. But Garrison knew that his friend never left it lying around where idle hands might pick it up.

'My stick, yes,' the other quietly answered. 'And did I use it, in your dream?'

'Again, I'm not sure,' said Garrison, the frown back on his face. 'But I don't think I should want you to use it . . . fully.'

Koenig nodded. 'Then we must hope that the violence was not – will not be – too excessive. But did your dream tell you nothing of the timing of this . . . trouble? Like where or when it will take place for instance?'

'My dream, no,' Garrison replied thoughtfully. 'It's a feeling from inside that tells me that. The place is . . . there,' he pointed uncertainly towards the shore lights. 'Is that the right direction?'

'Yes,' Koenig nodded, 'Arenzano. And the time?'

Garrison shrugged, the gesture uncomfortable, his shoulders hardly moving at all. 'Oh, soon.'

'Tonight, do you mean?'

Garrison turned his head to stare directly at the other, his lenses silver now in the twilight on the sea. 'Yes, I think so,' he finally said. 'Tonight . . .'

Chapter Ten

Lovi berthed *La Ligurienne* at the end of a jutting concrete quay, and with Garrison's permission he and the four members of his crew went ashore. Left to their own devices, Garrison and Koenig prepared for the night's business and half an hour later, clad in open-necked, lightweight evening suits, made their way from the motor-yacht to the seafront.

To anyone who watched them it might seem that Koenig was the blind one, or a partial cripple at least, for he was a bit slow and leaned heavily on his stick. Also, he had seemed to age by at least ten years. Garrison, to the contrary, went with the unerring certainty of a man with all his senses intact, 'remembering' something of the way from his dream and knowing a tingling sensation of déjà vu which at once alarmed and excited him.

It was still quite early, not yet 9.30, but already the lights of the town were a riot of colour. The place must recently have known some festive occasion, for bunting was still in evidence across the streets and looped between the palms along the promenade. Even though the tourist season was not yet fully into its swing, the warm weather had brought people out to enjoy the balmy evening. The open-air restaurants and cafes were busy; the bars thronged with people. German, Swiss and French accents – even a few British ones – mingled strangely with the native Italian; which, together with the hooting of car and scooter horns from the road, and juke box music from the cafes, painted a picture in Garrison's mind of some great polyglot fairground. In other circumstances it was a picture he might have paused to absorb and enjoy, but not tonight. Tonight it only served to disorientate him.

Finding a vantage point, a hastily erected bandstand or speaker's platform standing on the seaward side of the road that ran parallel with the curve of the small bay, the two climbed rough plank steps to where they could stand and survey the scene. 'Describe it to me,' Garrison eagerly instructed.

Koenig commenced a brief description of the promenade's main features, but as soon as he mentioned an open-sided, canopied restaurant that spanned the width of an old, disused stone wharf, Garrison stopped him.

'That last place,' said the blind man, his voice hushed. 'Describe it again, but in greater detail. What does it look like, this place with the canopy?'

The wharf was no more than thirty or forty yards away, its canvas-roofed dining area bordered by fragile-looking white rails which were intended to prevent unwary or drunken customers falling into the somewhat oily waters of the bay. At the back of the covered area a brick building, probably a landing stage in the old days, had been converted into a huge kitchen and wine store. Derelict stone steps went down from a bricked-up door in the now blank wall of the kitchen to the idly washing sea. There were people seated beneath the canopy, but not many. With its commanding view of the bay, the place would be an expensive spot to eat. Quiet though business was right now, trade would doubtless pick up later in the season when more tourist money was available.

'What of the canopy?' asked Garrison. 'Its colour? Is it red and yellow, with scalloped edges that flutter a little? And is there a central pole that gives the whole affair a tent shape?'

. 'Yes,' Koenig answered. 'That's it exactly! Is this the place?'

Garrison's mouth was dry. He nodded.

They descended the wooden steps of the bandstand and walked along an aisle of palms to a narrow plank pier that led to the jetty proper. Seeing Garrison's blindness, strolling people made way for him. Koenig thanked them in Italian as they passed. At the entrance to the pier a canopied archway bore the legend 'Marios'. With Koenig taking the lead, they went through the archway and on to the pier. Because of the uneven planking underfoot, Garrison was obliged to use the iron handrail.

A second archway formed the entrance to the eating area where, beneath the huge red and yellow canopy, six great wooden tables were decorated with beermats, baskets of bread, bowls of nuts and squat bottles with coloured candles whose flames flickered a little in the slightest trace of a breeze off the sea. The place would have seemed atmospheric to anyone – to Garrison it was electric!

His sensors swept the enclosed space, forming indistinct silhouettes which his mind enhanced into 3-D images. There were a dozen people in the place: a table of five, one of four and another of three. The rest of the tables were quite empty. The group of four, two couples, were just leaving. They brushed by Garrison and Koenig, tossing back the customary 'ciao' over their shoulders, to no one in particular, as they went. But the two women were also speaking to each other in lowered, outraged tones; and while Garrison's Italian was negligible, still he found himself interested in their muttered conversation.

When the couples had ducked out through the covered archway he turned to Koenig. 'Did you catch what they were saying?'

'A little of it,' the other answered. 'And it seems your ESP talent is working overtime tonight, for they were talking about the girl – the English girl – and they were feeling sorry for her. It's a great pity, they said, and her so young and all. And the Borcinis such an inbred and boorish pack of dogs.' He nodded towards the table of five. 'That must be your Terri. And the four men with her – they can only be the Borcinis.'

185

Now Garrison's radar gaze settled on the table at the far edge of the wharf's platform. Seated with their backs to the white rail, beyond and beneath which the bay glittered with reflected lights, were three men and a girl. Two of the men sat on her left, the third on her right. At the head of the table, also on her right, sat the fourth man. So far the party had not seemed to notice the newcomers; but even as Garrison stared the girl laughed, then clapped her hands and called out to the waiter that he should bring her another drink. She seemed in high spirits – or perhaps in strong spirits. Her laughter had been edged with the semi-hysteria of too much hard drink, and for all her excellent Italian, still her voice had been more than a little slurred.

They made their way between the tables and across the floor, and Koenig spoke to the oldest Borcini, the one seated at the head of the table. The German's Italian was fair when he asked if he and Garrison might be permitted to sit. Narrow-eyed and swarthy, the man looked them over. Before he could answer, one of his younger brothers asked:

'Hey, German! Aren't there enough empty tables, then?'

'Aha!' said Koenig. 'Well, you see, my English friend here is blind, and—'

Garrison touched his arm, silencing him. He could not speak a word of Italian, but he had detected the harshness in the young Borcini brother's tone and correctly deduced the meaning of his words. 'I'm sorry,' he spoke in English. 'It's just that I thought I heard a girl's voice. She spoke Italian but sounded English to me, and—'

'Of course!' the eldest of the four finally spoke up, also in English, however coarse and guttural his voice and use of the language. 'Of course, and not needing to explain. It is nice in the strange places to be speaking to your own kind. Unfortunately,' he cocked his head to one side and shrugged, 'we leaving soon. The girl too. Quite. But until then,' he waved one hand laconically, 'please sit.'

Koenig took a seat directly opposite the girl, and

Garrison sat on his left facing the two men. Still under the guise of a semi-invalid, the German nodded politely and smiled at each of the Italians in turn. The oldest of the brothers, and the youngest who was seated on the girl's far left, nodded grudgingly in return, but the two seated closest to her only scowled. There was an urgency about all four brothers that Koenig did not like at all, a greasy eagerness. They were like vultures waiting for some injured creature to die. He laid his walking stick along the edge of the table, directly in front of him, his fingers resting lightly upon its polished stock.

Meanwhile, the girl had finished her drink. She called out again to the lone waiter, swaying a little in her seat as she beckoned to him with a rather limp hand. Koenig, smiling at her, knew beyond a doubt that this was Garrison's Terri. She was quite lovely – or would be if she were sober. Her eyes were large and dark, her mouth small and red, her ears neat and flat and her long hair black as a raven's shiny wing. Exactly as the blind man had described her. Terri: the 'T' on Garrison's horoscope, the girl in the Black Room of the black castle on the black, oily lake. He also knew that she had been pumped full of booze – which explained the tension in the Borcinis. They were the sort who would cut cards to be first.

'Borcini,' said Koenig musingly. 'That's your family name? A coincidence! There's a hotel along the seafront called Borcini.'

'My hotel, yes,' said the swarthy man. 'My brothers help me to running it. But how are you knowing we are the Borcinis?'

'Possibly I saw you earlier – at the hotel,' Koenig shrugged. 'And the girl, Terri, she is staying there?' He smiled again, his enquiry innocent.

'Tonight she is, anyway!' One of the younger brothers put his arm around the girl's shoulders. 'With us. She owes us, you see?' He spoke in Italian, a snigger threatening to

187

break through his words.

By now the girl's head was lolling and the men beside her sat closer, propping her up. She blurted something unintelligible and rolled her eyes. The drink had caught up with her – as doubtless it had been intended to.

Koenig said, 'Oh, dear!' the English words sounding strange as his German accent began to thicken out. 'I do hope the poor creature isn't going to be ill. Do you think perhaps she has had too much to drink?'

'She's tired, that's all. Needs to get to bed!' The sniggering man cupped her chin, grinned at the girl through bad teeth. She smiled back at him lopsidedly, a little desperately, her eyes slowly closing.

'Well,' said the older brother, making as if to stand up. 'So you are seeing me earlier at the hotel, eh? And you are also knowing the girl's name. All very interesting. And now it really is time that we were on our way.' He nodded, his eyelids drooping to make slits of his eyes. 'Quite!'

'Does she owe you money?' Garrison's voice was quiet but tight.

'Not that it is your business, Mr Englishman,' answered the older Borcini, 'but yes, she does. In your currency, sixty pounds.'

'Willy,' said Garrison, his lenses burning into the faces of the four, 'pay the man.'

Koenig stood, took out his wallet and counted out three twenty pound notes. Placing the money carefully on the table, he said: 'Her debt is now paid and you will release her into our care.' His voice turned cold to match his small eyes. Before they could answer or even move, he leaned forward over the table, caught up the girl by her wrist and waist and dragged her forward and up. He lifted her as if she were a small child. Garrison had meanwhile stood up and pushed his chair to one side. He took the girl out of Koenig's arms and set her on her own feet, steadying her as she mumblingly shook herself awake.

Caught completely off guard, the brothers on the far side of the table began to curse and snarl, reaching viciously across to grab at Koenig – but too late. The German had already thought his bad thoughts. In a lightning-fast movement he rammed the table forward, crushing the two against the white wooden rails until they snapped. With cries of outrage and astonishment the two toppled over the edge of the wharf and splashed down into the sea.

The third of the younger brothers had managed to squeeze out from behind the table and now stood with the older man. Crouching, they closed on Koenig menacingly, both of them producing wicked-looking switchblades.

As the sharply pointed blades clicked into view, Koenig went into action. He snatched up his stick and held it in both hands, parallel before him. Seeing his defensive stance – and noting for the first time that he was no invalid, that in fact he was squat and massive and suddenly quite deadly – the brothers paused. That was a serious error, but at the same time it probably saved them from far greater injury.

As they crouched undecided, Koenig lashed out with his stick, catching the younger one under his chin with the crook and sending him sprawling. Then, when the older brother lunged with his knife, Koenig reversed the stick and gripped it with both hands, pointing it at Borcini's chest. From the brass ferrule a needle blade slid soundlessly, almost magically into view, eight inches long and glittering like ice.

Borcini's eyes went wide, for Koenig's weapon was nothing less than a sword! He dropped his knife and backed off, shaking his head and making horizontal waving motions with his hands. 'No, no!' he gurgled. Stumbling, he backed up against the broken, dangling rail.

'Jump,' said Koenig. He made as if to stab – and Borcini gave a little shriek and jumped. The younger brother was still on all fours, dazedly shaking his head. Koenig turned to him, showed him the stick with its murderous tip.

189

'Jump,' he said again – and the last of the Borcinis gave a despairing cry and toppled from the edge of the quay.

'A pity it isn't a cliff,' the German muttered. He stooped and picked up the three notes from where they had fallen, turned and handed them to the astonished and not a little frightened waiter. Curses floated up from the water below the wharf, along with sounds of frantic splashing and gasping. 'The money is for the damage,' said Koenig in Italian, his stick a normal walking stick once more. 'It is more than enough, I'm sure.'

In English, on impulse, Garrison added: 'And our compliments to the chef!'

Marios' last patrons, three Italian girls seated together at a table close to the wide doors of the kitchen, laughed their delight out loud and spontaneously clapped their pleasure and approval.

Playing up to them, Garrison bowed, then turned to Terri. She was still barely able to stand unsupported. 'You're safe now,' he told her, 'and you're coming with us. But we have to go quickly or the Borcinis will be back.'

'Eh?' She made an effort to get him into focus. 'You're English? Thank goodness for that!'

She offered no resistance but with their assistance went with them, and they hurriedly made their way back to the motor-yacht. Strangely they were not stopped or questioned or even followed – or perhaps not so strangely. Later they decided it must simply be that the Borcinis were not much loved, as witness the attitudes of the two couples, and, later, those of the three Italian girls. The brothers probably had not even dared to report the affair.

But just to be on the safe side, when morning came they paid the Hotel Borcini a surprise visit – after first going to the police station. Having listened to their tale, the local Sheriff wanted Garrison to prefer charges (the Borcinis were very bad for business) but the blind man had declined the offer. He wanted to be on his way as soon as possible.

They did take with them to the hotel a large member of the constabulary, however, a man who quite obviously hated the Borcinis and was delighted to be of assistance.

All four brothers were at the hotel, all looking sullen and sheepish; and more so when they saw Garrison, Koenig and the constable. They made no fuss but handed over Terri's single large suitcase, and no mention at all was made of the girl's supposed indebtedness.

Then, their business in Arenzano finished, the two returned at once to *La Ligurienne*. By 10.30 A.M. the motor-yacht was on her way again, bound for Naples, and she now carried a young, very shapely and highly hung-over extra passenger . . .

When finally Terri staggered out on to the deck she was a mixture of gratitude, alarm, self-pity and shame, not necessarily in that order.

But in the end she was quick to accept Garrison's assurance that she was no longer in any sort of danger. Especially after he had described for her – vividly and leaving no room for doubt – the fix she had been in with the loathsome Italian hotelier and his brothers. Her shame sprang from the fact that she had been stupid enough to walk right into a situation which had smelled decidedly fishy almost from the start, and her self-pity from the dreadful hang-over she was suffering, coupled now with early symptoms of seasickness and a general feeling of disorientation. As for her gratitude: her escape from the Borcinis had been a close thing, and she shuddered at thoughts of the sort of ordeal they might have put her through in her drunken or drugged condition.

Now they sat together on the deck, Garrison with a long Italian drink, Terri drawing deeply on an English cigarette. He had given her sickness pills, had poured black coffee down her until she could hold no more, and, when she had begun to shiver, he finally wrapped her in a fluffy blanket against the fine spray which an unseasonal westerly was whipping up off the small wavecrests.

Beneath the blanket she still wore the red dress (a rather revealing evening-gown perfectly cut to compliment her figure) she had worn last night; but Garrison did not have the equipment to appreciate her looks. In any case, those looks this morning would not have seemed much to appreciate.

'What a little fool I was,' she said for what must have been the tenth time. 'No wonder the Borcinis thought I was easy meat.' Her tone was sour and Garrison guessed correctly that she scorned herself.

'You *were* easy meat,' he told her mercilessly. 'And that's how they would have used you – as meat! A pretty piece of unresisting flesh.'

She shuddered again, and he relented. 'There must be a story behind all of this?'

'A story?' She sat up a little straighter in her chair. 'Oh, yes, there's a story. But it would probably bore you to tears.'

'Try me.'

She shrugged. 'All right. Here goes:

'My father is Harry Miller, a nobody who became a somebody when his small electronics firm made him a million pounds in nine years. He's also a sweetheart and broke again, or very nearly so. And he lost his money in only a quarter of the time it took him to make it.'

'How?' Garrison cut in.

'Oh, I don't understand business. Too much expansion too fast, maybe? Personally, I think the big companies ganged up on him. His line is micro-electronics. Is that important?'

Garrison shook his head. 'No. Go on.'

'My mother is Italian, the daughter of a count. Not that that means anything these days. Members of the so-called Italian nobility are ten-a-penny. But daddy likes the idea, and she is a beautiful woman. Perhaps too beautiful. Her name before they married was Maria Torino. To my way of thinking, a cow from a long line of cows!'

Garrison wrinkled his nose, unsure that he liked her manner of expression. 'I take it you don't much like your mother,' he said.

'I used to,' she was quick to answer, 'but . . . she demands too much, spends too much – cheats too much! Everything she does, she goes overboard. Her lovers . . . I suspect there have been too many of them, too. The last one – a greasy dog not fit to shine my father's shoes—' she paused, '—well, he found them together. There was a row, a hellish fight. With everyone accusing everyone else of everything. And she was going to run off with her horrible friend. That would have broken daddy's heart, so . . .'

'Yes?' Garrison prompted her when she paused.

'So I told her that her lover had also tried it on with me! He was nothing but a fortune-hunter, after daddy's money – or the money he thought daddy had. I told her that if she told him the facts, how close daddy was to bankruptcy, he'd simply disappear overnight.' Again she paused. 'So she did, and he did.'

'And you were telling the truth? About this boyfriend of your mother's trying it on with you, I mean?'

'Oh, yes! His name is Wyatt. Dr Gareth Wyatt, so-called psychoanalyst – or neuropsychiatrist, whatever that's supposed to be. What daddy would call a "trick-cyclist", anyway – and a bigger fraud you've yet to discover, I promise you! Wyatt – *hah*!' She was vehement. 'Wyatt as in Earp. A real pistol!'

Garrison nodded. Terri was still feeling sorry for herself and he could feel that she was close to tears. 'But none of it did any good,' he guessed. 'Your father and mother split up anyway, right?'

She gulped and nodded, turning her face away.

'No need for that,' he gently reminded her. 'I'm blind,

remember? I can't see your tears.'

She turned back again. 'You have to be the most seeing blind man I've ever met,' she said after a little while, the catch still there in her voice. 'Just how blind are you?'

'Totally,' he answered. 'This headgear of mine, and these,' he shot his cuffs to show her the gold bracelets on his wrists, '—they give me tiny electronic sounds which I turn into pictures – but the pictures are only silhouettes, really. Some depth but not much. Everyone is a cardboard cut-out, if you see what I mean. As for my physical co-ordination: that's mainly use and instinct.'

She stared at his face, at the silver lenses.

'Go on with your story, Theresa Miller,' he told her.

'Why are you so interested?' she suddenly wanted to know. 'And just why did you pull me out of that mess anyway? It wasn't your business – and it might all have been perfectly innocent.'

'I've always tilted at windmills,' said Garrison. 'Anyway, it seemed to me that you needed help. And as it happens you did. Also, you're English. And you're a lovely girl. How old are you, Terri?'

'I'm twenty-two – and don't change the subject! I mean, I would be interested to hear just how you came to be—' She paused and Garrison could almost feel her frown turning into a smile. After a moment she continued: 'Yes, let's change the subject. Flattery gets you everywhere. And maybe I can kill two birds with one stone. You said I'm lovely – but how would you know that? Also, how did you just happen to turn up at exactly the right time last night?'

Garrison grinned. He was tempted to tell her all of it but decided against it. A little knowledge could do no harm, no, but not the whole story. 'If I tell you the truth will you believe me?' he asked.

'Try me,' she echoed his own words of a few minutes earlier.

'Well, you see, I've dreamed of you – twice. And in my

dreams you were lovely. It's as simple as that. Are you telling me now that I was wrong, that in fact you're just a plain Jane?'

'Oh, people say I'm good-looking,' she said. 'But—' And now he heard a sharp intake of breath. She took his right hand in both of hers and leaned closer. 'Richard, did you really dream of me?'

'Didn't I say so?'

'But that's quite . . . amazing!'

'What is? Clairvoyance?'

'No,' she shook her head, 'more than that. You see, I've dreamed of you, too! The night before last . . .'

'Oh? Two-way clairvoyance!' He was flippant, but mainly to hide his sudden intense interest. 'What did you dream?'

'I'm trying to remember,' she said. 'It came back to me a moment ago but now it's gone again. It was at the hotel. One of the younger Borcinis, Alfredo, had been paying me too much attention. When I went to bed I locked my door and just lay there wishing I was out of the place. Finally I dropped off to sleep . . . and dreamed.'

'About me?'

'About you, yes – or a blind man, anyway – and about . . .' She came to an abrupt halt.

'Yes?'

'Oh, nothing. And . . . the blind man couldn't have been you. No, it wasn't you. I'm sorry.'

Garrison was disappointed. 'You're sorry it wasn't me? Can you be sure of that? A blind man is a blind man after all. And though there are plenty of us, I'm sure we're not just everyday occurrences – in or out of dreams. Is there something you don't want to tell me?'

'Yes . . . no! . . . Well, if you must know, I also dreamed about this Gareth Wyatt creature.' She paused. 'I don't suppose you know him?'

'Never heard of him. Where did he fit into your dream?'

She sat back and shook her head. 'No, it doesn't matter. And this really is a silly conversation. I mean, my blind man was a *real* blind man. Not like you at all. And I was . . . frightened of him.' She squeezed his hand. 'And you don't frighten me a bit.'

Garrison let it drop – for the moment. Better not to push things. 'OK, so go on with your story. How come you're in Italy?'

She shook her head, patted his hand, said, 'First tell me about your dreams – if you really did dream. I mean, I know it's silly but I'm interested anyway.'

'There's nothing much to tell, really,' Garrison lied. 'I just dreamed of this lovely girl, that's all.'

'And what makes you think it was me?'

He shrugged. 'Black hair, small flat ears, lips that are naturally red, large dark eyes – who else could it be?'

'A thousand and one girls!' she cried. 'I mean, a description as general as that?'

'No, it was you. And you were right here in Italy. And you were in trouble.'

'Precognition!' She clapped her hands.

Garrison was pleased. He could tell that she was feeling a lot better. 'Possibly,' he eventually answered. 'Are you interested in ESP?'

'Not at all.' She drew back from him a little and cocked her head on one side. 'Are you sure you're not just pulling my leg?'

'Ah!' He grinned. 'But that was my *second* dream!'

'You *are* pulling my leg!'

'No,' he said, more soberly. 'Actually I did dream that I had known you . . . rather well.'

'How well?' She was wary.

'Very well.' He was frank.

'This sounds like a new kind of line to me.'

'Terri, there are a thousand and one girls who look just like you, you said so yourself just a second ago. If I was simply a dirty young man I could easily have found myself one of the others. Or ten of them.'

'Oh?' There was a pseudo-haughty edge to her voice. 'You're pretty damn sure of yourself, Mr Garrison.'

'Call me Richard. And I am sure of myself, yes. I know what money can buy.'

She looked about, as if noticing her surroundings for the first time. 'This very swish little motor-yacht is yours?'

'No,' he shook his head. 'I'm hiring it. And the crew. For as long as I want them.'

'And that gentleman?' She inclined her head in Koenig's direction, where he sat apparently asleep in a chair some little distance away. 'German, isn't he? He's not one of the crew, and I seem to remember that he was with you last night.'

'That's Willy Koenig, who you might call my gentleman's gentleman – and he's my friend, too.'

'Your gentleman's gentleman . . .' she mused.

'Yes, except he's sometimes very *un*gentle.'

She looked at him curiously for a moment, then asked: 'Are you really quite rich?'

'Extremely.' (A departure for Garrison, who was normally evasive on this point.)

'Then I was simply an adventure? As you yourself said: a girl you decided to help out of a fix?'

He shrugged, smiling.

'And you didn't really dream about me at all. You were just making amusing conversation.'

Again he shrugged, this time without smiling. The conversation was beginning to irritate him. He had been telling her too much too fast – or she had been drawing it from him. Whichever, it now appeared that Terri was deeper than he had supposed. But if the stars and Adam Schenk were to be believed, and if this really was 'T', things should soon begin to work themselves out. Why attempt to hurry (or to delay) the inevitable?

Abruptly, breaking his thoughts, she dropped his hand. 'I don't think I'm amused any more,' she said.

A vivid picture formed in Garrison's mind and a feeling etched itself invisibly on his fingertips. Mind and fingers seemed one as they traced a familiar, albeit mental, pattern. His hand jerked as if from a mild electric shock. He seized upon these impressions, voicing his thoughts almost without conscious volition. 'You have a tiny moon-shaped scar just under your navel. A childhood accident.'

She gasped, stood up . . . flopped down again into her chair. 'Dirty young man indeed!' She sounded disgusted. 'I hadn't realized I was *that* oblivious last night!'

'No one touched you last night, Terri,' he said. 'I find the suggestion revolting – no, degrading! Christ, you weren't worth touching!' He let this sink in for a moment, then lowered his voice. 'I sat up and watched you. I was afraid you might be sick and choke in it. That's the closest anyone got to you.'

'But how could you know about . . . about—' She was close to tears again.

'Just believe me. I've been blind for some time. Blind people are often gifted with a different sort of sight.'

'You're a very strange man,' she said after a while. 'But I think I do believe you. What are you doing here in Italy? Apart from rescuing me, I mean?'

He smiled, his anger ebbing as quickly as it had advanced. 'I asked you first – but I'll tell you anyway. We're here on holiday, Willy and I.'

She nodded and bit her lip. 'I see. And blind and all you saw and—'

'—Recognized you as a girl from my dreams, yes. That's more or less the truth.'

She shook her head, her intense gaze attempting to penetrate the reflective surfaces of his lenses. Then: 'Can I have more coffee?'

'Of course.' He could have sighed his relief that at last

198

she seemed to have dropped it. 'And a little food? I'll join you.' He called out to Koenig who immediately came awake, asking him to arrange coffee and sandwiches.

'Richard—' She caught up his hand again as he turned back to her. 'You *are* very strange, you know?'

'But you're not frightened of me?'

'No, not at all. You're not like the blind man in my dream.'

'You never told me what he was like?'

'Oh, I can't remember what he looked like. But he was angry – and *powerful*! Don't ask me how. Actually, I don't think it was him I was frightened of so much as his dog.'

Garrison's heart went cold inside him. 'His dog?' His throat was so dry he could not be sure he had spoken the words.

'Yes,' she confirmed it, 'a great black Dobermann. A guide-dog, obviously. But I told you. He was a *real* blind man. Not like you at all . . .'

After that . . . Garrison conversed with Terri for a little longer. She had come to Italy for two reasons; to try to get her mother to return to England and their home in Winchester, and to have a short holiday and so put herself out of the way in the event that her parents became reconciled.

Having seen her mother in Milan, however – and realizing that at the moment the gap between them was too recent and too deep a wound, but having at least satisfied herself that at present there was no plan for divorce – she had journeyed to Arenzano where she had friends. Except that her friends had moved out of the district some months earlier to an address unknown.

Determined to give herself some sort of rest from travelling, not to mention respite from her emotional upsets, she had then booked into the Hotel Borcini. That had been eight days ago. Two days later, while shopping for gifts and souvenirs in the tiny town, her bag was stolen. With it went her money, traveller's cheques and one or two small valuables. Fortunately her return air ticket and passport were safe back at the hotel; unfortunately her passage was booked from Milan and she had not purchased a return ticket. Also, she now owed two days' board at the hotel.

From then on things went from bad to worse. She was unable to contact her father in England and use of the telephone was expensive, adding considerably to her bill. The Borcini brothers were only too obliging, not only allowing her to bill all her requirements but actually seeming to encourage it; and while Terri had no drink problem, still her nerves were so badly frayed that the only way she could rest at all was to get herself half drunk. This, too, the Borcinis encouraged, inviting her to the bar whenever she appeared on the scene and generally pushing the booze at her; but by then they had also begun to pester her, however obliquely, so that she determined to sneak out of the hotel and hitchhike, if necessary, back to Milan.

Before that, however, she tried to contact her mother, who by then was also unavailable. On the fifth morning Terri woke up to discover her passport and flight ticket missing. The Borcinis told her that she had had them during the course of the previous evening, in the bar. But . . . well, she had gone to bed a little under the weather, and there had been several strangers . . . out-of-towners, possibly undesirables – in the bar, and . . . And they had shrugged. They were sorry, they said.

The only undesirables to Terri's mind were the Borcinis themselves! – but what could she do? She tried to contact the British consul, tried for hours on end, to no avail. Only later did it dawn on her that the switchboard at the hotel was operated by one of the Borcinis.

Finally she had broken down and begged Carlo Borcini, the senior brother, for his help. The next day, after more abortive, expensive telephone calls and a sleepless, tearful night, he came to her with her passport and ticket. He had traced them (he said) to one of the local troublemakers, a youth he had briefly seen in the bar on the night they were stolen. As punishment, he had warned this person never to enter his hotel again, but he had not reported him, no. The boy's parents were too important. And to make amends for the various troubles she had experienced while staying at his hotel, Carlo Borcini himself would arrange transport for her back to Milan the very next morning. As for her bill; she could send the money on later.

Her relief was so great that it washed over her like a flood, making her feel sick and weak. She slept most of that day and got up in the evening when Borcini came to her room to enquire if she was quite well, and to tell her that her transport to Milan had been arranged for midday tomorrow. Her gratitude then was boundless; so that when the hotelier politely and apparently innocently asked her if she would care to join him and his brothers that night in a meal and drink at Marios' (they were celebrating a birthday) she had readily agreed.

Nightmare followed fast on the heels of nightmare.

Her first drink at Marios' had tasted . . . not quite right; everything after that had seemed addled; she had vaguely known she was in trouble but had been too far gone to do anything about it. The Borcinis had seemed like vultures closing in on her, and there had been nowhere to run.

Now, having heard her out, Garrison remarked, 'I've a mind to go back and let Willy and Francesco and his boys work those bastards over!'

'No,' she answered, 'I'd rather you didn't. It was all my own silly fault.'

'You were unlucky,' he told her. 'You just happened to fall among animals. And maybe I will go back there one day, just to see what damage I can do them.'

The way he said it left little doubt in her mind that Richard Garrison, if ever he set himself to the task, would

201

be very capable of an awful lot of damage. 'Well, anyway,' she finally broke the brooding silence conjured by his suddenly grim mood, 'I'm very grateful for what you've done already, except—'

'Yes?'

'There is one more thing. My plane leaves Milan for London in three days' time. If you can put me on a train in Naples, I—'

'Forget it,' said Garrison.

'Oh?' She raised her eyebrows.

'Yes, for you're coming home with Willy and me. We leave as soon as *La Ligurienne* puts into Naples.'

'But my ticket!'

'Forget that, too. Or I can try to get you a refund. You see, I have my own plane and pilot waiting for me. Occasionally – but not very often, only when I'm in a real hurry – I hire one.'

'You hire planes?' Boats and planes. She looked at him in the dawning of a new light. He had said he was extremely rich. 'Really? And there's one waiting to take us home to England?'

He nodded. 'To take us home, yes. To *my* home, in Sussex.'

Her voice went very quiet and became slightly speculative. 'Am I to spend some little time with you then, Richard?'

He thought of Schenk's horoscope, smiled and said, 'It certainly looks that way, Terri. Unless you decide otherwise. I'd say four or five years at the very least . . .'

Later, when she had retired to her bunk to catch up on a lot of lost sleep, Garrison spoke to Koenig. 'You weren't sleeping, Willy. How much did you hear?'

'All of it.'

'And?'

Koenig shrugged, answering carefully: 'She seems – at first glance, you understand – to have a lot of faults.'

'Oh?'

'If she isn't an alcoholic already, she turns to drink very quickly in a crisis, I mean.'

'No need to hide your meaning with me, Willy,' Garrison said. 'I know what you mean, and yes, it's a fault – maybe. But after all, her fix was pretty bloody. And she has suffered emotionally.'

'So she says,' Koenig nodded. 'But isn't that simply another fault? Hangups? Emotional instability? Also, she's a quitter. She could have tried harder. But for our intervention—'

'OK,' Garrison growled, 'I get the point.' He frowned. 'What about her dream?'

'That's difficult to say, but—' He paused. 'I've given it a little thought. You have to remember, though, that I am not expert in these matters.'

'Go on.'

'Well, you remember the crossing barrier that got stuck? How you were sending your mental warning signals so thick and fast that I acted before you actually spoke?'

'Yes, I remember,' Garrison nodded. He saw the point Willy was making. 'So you think that perhaps she picked her dream out of *my* mind, eh?'

'It could be. You were concentrating so hard on finding her that she sort of picked up a telepathic echo. Perhaps that's how you *did* find her, how you knew with certainty that Arenzano was the right place.'

'And the dog? Where does Suzy come into it?'

Again Koenig shrugged. 'Why, obviously Suzy has been on your mind. Terri picked that up too.'

'And this bloke Gareth Wyatt?'

'Ah! Well, he came out of her own mind. According to what she told you, and if she's been hating him as much as she says, it was only natural that he would crop up in her dreams.'

'That all seems to make sense,' Garrison said after a moment, 'but there's still something that bothers me. Her fear – of the blind man, I mean.'

'She was afraid, yes,' the other answered, 'but not

necessarily afraid of the blind man. Maybe it was Wyatt she feared – certainly she was afraid of the Borcinis. But the blind man was the stranger in her dream – the unknown factor – and so her fear attached itself to him and his dog. After all, an angry, powerful blind man must form a pretty frightening and enigmatic dream-image. Don't you agree?'

'No,' Garrison shook his head, 'I'm not sure I do. I mean, why should anyone fear – or even think they fear – a blind man?' He puzzled over it a moment longer, then said: 'Anyway, forget it. I've got her now.'

'You've got her? There is no doubt in your mind, then? She's definitely "T"?'

'She's the one, yes. And from now on in we play it according to the stars. All the way down the line.'

'And just what is in the stars, do you think? For you and Terri?'

'I'll marry her,' Garrison immediately answered.

Koenig raised his eyebrows. 'Just like that?'

'More or less.' Garrison felt a momentary panic. 'Willy, she is lovely, isn't she?'

'Very.'

'The thing is,' Garrison said, 'I can hardly wait to get my hands on her!'

Koenig was mildly surprised. 'You are very open.'

'Why not? If I can't talk to you, who can I talk to?'

'Of course.' Koenig was flattered.

'You see, Willy, I already know every curve and hollow of that girl's body. I see it – feel it, I should say – in vivid flashes. Christ, I already half love her! I've known her ever since that first dream of mine, the one that started everything, back in Belfast. It seems strange, I know, but I can still *remember* how she feels!'

'Strange, yes,' Koenig agreed, 'for of course you are remembering how she *will* feel!'

And the sun burned on them and the sea breeze blew in their faces as *La Ligurienne* throbbed southwards on the blue, blue sea . . .

Chapter Eleven

For the better part of a fortnight Hans Maas had lived with terror. Terror had walked with him through every waking moment, had slept with him – when he slept at all – in his tumbled bed, had peered over his shoulder, one bony hand clutching his black heart, whenever he opened a newspaper or Gareth Wyatt's mailbox. Terror born of three apparently unconnected incidents and bred of the ever-present knowledge that sooner or later the past must catch up with him. Or if not with Hans Maas, with Otto Krippner.

The first of the three occurrences had been a brief mention in the press of the demise by suicide of one Nichos Charalambou at his home in Crete. Charalambou, an ex-Nazi no less than Maas, one-time Commandant of the 'Advanced Medical Unit' at Saarenlager, had finally been tracked down by Amira Hannes and her squad of Israeli bloodhounds. Before the Israelis had begun any sort of interrogation, however, the old man had shot himself – at least, so it was reported. Certain documents, including a will, discovered in the house at Rethimnon had proved conclusively that Charalambou was in fact Gerhard Keltner, a frightened puppet of a man whose wartime activities had been somewhat more cowardly than criminal. He had been a Nazi, yes, but scorned by the hardliners of the party. Which was why that dirtiest of all jobs, Commandant of the Saarenlager 'butcher's shop', had been given to him. He simply had not dared refuse it!

The prime concern of the Jewish Organization had not been to have Keltner executed (what could be gained from the death of one frail old man?), neither that nor even his humiliation or extradition, they had simply wanted to examine him: to draw upon his memory of names, dates, faces and places. To fill in some of the blanks in the world-spanning jigsaw of their never-ending search. Keltner as a man was small-fry, but he might know the whereabouts of some of the bigger fish.

And the Jews might not have told all. Who could say what they had or had not squeezed from Keltner before he killed himself? This single thought had been the start of the terror for Hans Maas, and it had been reinforced by the arrival of an envelope, German stamped and franked, from one Ernst Grunewald, his cousin in Osnabruck. For he did not have a cousin in Osnabruck and knew no one by the name of Ernst Grunewald. In the fine paper of the letter had been a special watermark, however, which had told him that the real sender was a member of Exodus.

Exodus: one of the most successful of all Nazi escape routes, and named with all the irony and the malice of a smiling skull!

The letter, hand-written, had said simply this:

'Dear Hans,
    I can tell from your last letter how hard you have been working. Isn't it time you had a holiday? At your age it is dangerous to work too hard. So many of our old friends are gone now (G.K. quite recently, I hear) and I would hate to lose another. There seems to be a creeping sickness about that seeks us out and drags us down. So do give yourself a break, I implore you, and be sure to look after yourself.
    I spoke to an old friend of yours in Detmold last week, and he—'
    Etc, etc . . .

But Maas had not concerned himself to read the etceteras. He knew that only the first paragraph was significant, that the rest of it would be meaningless padding. It was only the third such letter he had received in thirty years (the first had been congratulatory, following his successful flight from Germany; likewise the second, upon his initial liaison with Wyatt), and he knew it would never have been sent if the danger were not very real and imminent.

206

The third and by far the most terrifying manifestation had been the arrival in London of a Jewish delegation for talks on the Middle East problem, and Maas had carefully watched the maddeningly few TV screenings concerning these visitors. The negotiators came of course with their own personal bodyguards, nameless figures who stayed as far as possible in the background – but not beyond the trembling scrutiny of Hans Maas. Mere glimpses, exposures of seconds only – but sufficient to confirm his worst suspicions. The diplomats were here to talk, yes, but what of the sharp-eyed hunters who had come with them? Maas had definitely recognized at least two of them; and now he understood the urgency in the letter from Exodus.

He knew that the circle was closing. What he did not know was that Wyatt was also aware of the net's closure – and no less terrified!

For some little time, when Wyatt's limited funds had allowed, Maas had been replacing Psychomech's older and riskier components; for Wyatt, having long since realized that the machine was a potential goldmine, had determined to sink most of his now almost vanished savings into the project. He had also taken a greater interest in the machine's mechanics, and he had grown aware that there were facets of its operation about which Maas had deliberately kept him in the dark; but recently, however covertly, he had been studying the monster. And he was growing especially interested in those areas of Psychomech's hardware which seemed to him superfluous to its prime function. He was of course unaware that these were the components which actually governed that function, and that the function itself was other than he believed it to be.

There were several reasons for Wyatt's unaccustomed curiosity, not the least of them being strictly commercial. He knew that Maas, when he had perfected the thing, would expect a large slice of any takings; possibly to set himself up in business elsewhere – in South America, for example, where the natives were far less suspicious of foreigners and not much given to keeping records. And of course Exodus would expect Wyatt to give Maas every assistance in the realization of any such ambition. Well, Wyatt could hardly complain about that; over the years he had received substantially from Exodus, though recently there had been nothing. Nothing, that is to say, with the exception of a letter delivered just a week ago. It had come from a doubtless fictitious address in Stuttgart, and its message had been quite as simple as that of the letter to Hans Maas. Namely: Wyatt should waste no time in seeing Maas on his way, and even less in covering the German's tracks.

But here Wyatt had known he was at a disadvantage, which was this:

Any investigator assiduous enough to trace Maas this far would have precious little difficulty in tracking him one stage further. If Maas was going to be found out, he would be found out no matter where he went. And Wyatt with him. Now Wyatt was not a Nazi and never had been, but he had studied psychiatry in Köln in 1955–58, where and when his sympathies had been noted; such sympathies that he had been contacted and recruited by Exodus as a future friend and agent in England. He had been very short of money at the time, and so his seduction had been made that much easier by a considerable payment 'on account'. Which had seemed to him a very worthwhile transaction considering that his connection with Exodus was to be, initially at least, on a strictly passive basis. Then, in late 1958 he had come to England, and shortly after that his passivity had been abruptly terminated when Maas was ferried across to him.

It was then Wyatt discovered that Maas knew more of every aspect of psychiatry than he could ever hope to learn, and from the very beginning he had leaned upon and drawn from the German's superior knowledge. Maas, not Wyatt, had written those papers which were now credited to the Englishman, those brilliant if unorthodox theses which had given him a transient (but very profitable) claim to fame. And later . . . Wyatt's clients had been amongst the richest men and women in the country, and not one of them had ever suspected that in fact his or her treatment was being directed by one of the cruellest monsters Hitler's regime had ever spawned.

But . . . the German's usefulness was now at an end. He had no money – or very little – no friends, nowhere to run. All he had was Psychomech, and Psychomech was not something he could simply pack up and take with him. Besides, he wasn't going anywhere. Wyatt had already decided upon that. If and when the pack closed in, it would only be to discover that the ex-Nazi's trail ended right here . . . Period.

There was a pool in the grounds of Wyatt's house, deep and dark and green with waterlilies gone wild; the kind of pool in which things rot and disappear very quickly. Like a body, for instance. A drugged drink one night; a visit to the pool under cover of darkness; lead weights in a belt about the German's waist. Wyatt would wait until the effect of the drug was beginning to wear off – then topple him gently into the black water. Any struggling would only serve to make the end that much quicker . . .

—Oh, Hans had been the gardener, that's all. Not very good at it but . . . well, hired help was hired help these days. One managed with what one could get. Yes, Hans had been his name. Hans Maas. A German gentleman, yes – not that you'd ever suspect it – spoke perfect English. Who? Otto Krippner? No, no, his name was Maas, be sure of it. Oh, he had saved a little over the years and now had desired to return to Germany for a visit. Well, yes, he *had* allowed his holiday to run over a little, but he was sure to be back soon. A pretty reliable man really. If only he were a better gardener! Yes, it had been rather sudden, this desire of his for the old country. Doubtless a whim, a spur-of-the-moment decision. A funny sort of chap, really, come to think of it . . . Interested in psychiatry? Well, oddly enough he had shown some small initial interest in one's practice, yes – but that had all been twenty years ago. And when one had been curious about him, about his knowledge of psychiatric matters, why, his interest had quite faded away! What? A *war-criminal*? A *mass-murderer*? Incredible! Incredible! Who, Hans? That quiet, likeable little chap? Really? Were they absolutely certain they had the right man . . . ?

Wyatt's chance came a week later on the 26th of the month. It had been a week of frantic activity on the part of Maas, when from morning till night he had worked unceasingly on Psychomech, preparing the machine for . . . for what? Wyatt, feigning a mildly bored curiosity, had nevertheless kept a keen eye on the German's activities, and he had not failed to notice that the bulk of the ex-Nazi's time was consumed in the re-wiring of those previously mentioned 'superfluous' circuits and components. Moreover, there had been an addition to the Psychomech's bulk in the shape of a controlling computer; the machine could now be programmed to the subject's specific physical and mental requirements.

Finally, time pressing and his actual curiosity getting the better of him, Wyatt had asked what it all meant, what new experiment did Maas intend to conduct? For there had been several so-called experiments since that night when Hammond had sweated and writhed out his nightmares strapped to Psychomech's bed, and all of them had seemed successful enough to Wyatt; but always Maas had insisted that there were bugs in the machine which must be ironed out before it could be put into commercial use, before its existence could be announced to a sick world in general. Understanding so little of the working of the machine,

Wyatt had had no choice but to agree; since when he had determined to master Psychomech's intricacies.

At first Maas was evasive, but when Wyatt pressed him, finally he answered: 'I think Psychomech is ready for one last test. And if this one is successful, then we can put the machine into full-time use.'

'A test run?' Wyatt repeated him. 'When? And who have you in mind for a subject?'

'Tonight,' Maas answered, 'as soon as I finish here. As for a subject – who better than myself? It will give me first-hand knowledge of the machine's effect.'

'You? But you know I don't fully understand the damned thing! How am I to—'

'Wait.' Maas held up a hand. 'It is precisely because you do not understand the machine that I have now incorporated a programmer. I merely require you to administer the drug and to strap me down. And of course, in the event of any unforeseen mechanical failure, to shut Psychomech down before the critical stage is reached. Surely you are capable of that?'

And Wyatt at once saw and seized upon his chance. 'Of course. But why use yourself as a subject? We could use someone else. I still have patients. Are you really so sure that the machine is ready?'

Maas nodded. 'And surely the supreme proof – proof positive – of the machine's efficacy, would be for it to effect my own cure.'

'You?' Wyatt was astonished. 'Neurotic? I had thought you almost completely emotionless, nerveless! – until recently, anyway.' He smiled caustically. 'The great Hans Maas – or should I say Otto Krippner? – himself a case for psychiatric treatment? What is it you fear, Otto? What is it torments you enough to make you risk your own neck on Psychomech, a machine which could so easily kill you? And you the one who has for so long held me back from exploiting the machine.'

211

'The machine was not ready!' Maas protested. 'Not until now. As for my own fears,' he shrugged unconvincingly, 'there are certain nightmares I would exorcise, yes.'

Wyatt moved closer and stared into the German's hard, unblinking eyes. 'The screams of a thousand dying Jews, perhaps?'

Maas slowly grinned, his teeth unusually healthy in glistening pink gums. The grin of a shark. 'Ah, no, my friend. Those are not nightmares but my favourite dreams!'

Wyatt turned away half in disgust, half in fear. 'Have it your own way.' He shuddered. 'Call me when you're ready. I'll be downstairs.'

And the experiment commenced at 11.45 that night . . .

He was no longer Hans Maas but Otto Krippner, pride of the Third Reich's Experimental Science and Psychology Division. Herr Doktor Krippner, who had most successfully murdered more than a thousand Jews and personally driven mad two hundred more.

But . . . his days of dubious glory were over and now he walked in a valley of bones. Something gnawed at him inside, a task uncompleted, something left undone. The bones crumbled and crunched beneath his booted feet, causing him to stumble. He paused, brushed the white dust of the dead from his immaculate uniform and adjusted the monocle in his right eye. The monocle was pure affectation, Krippner knew that – but he also knew it inspired terror in the hearts of his enemies. Rather, in those passive, sheeplike enemies of the Third Reich.

Slowly his surroundings impressed themselves upon his mind. The valley was not a valley but a huge trench whose sides were steep, white with burning salts, brown with earth and rust red with blood. The smell was that of a charnel house, or perhaps an abattoir. On the horizon square black towers smoked, sending up concentric rings of stinking steam, their reek drifting like vile mist across the vast trench, cloying to the nostrils and sickening to the taste. It was an odour a man might actually taste; but Krippner was used to such smells. He had been the cause of them . . .

The gnawing inside grew stronger, became acid eating at his guts. Work incomplete. Things still to be done.

Gold gleamed in the white fragments beneath his shiny leather boots. A skull stared at him blindly, mouth agape. A tooth, full of gold, seemed to leer singly at him. A ring glinted, loose on its bony finger. Krippner stooped, broke the tooth from the skull, reached for the skeletal hand with the ring—

—And it reached for him!

Krippner gagged, jerked away from the twitching skeleton, stumbled and staggered in osseous debris. His monocle fell out of an astonished orbit, his hands went down to cushion his fall. Fleshless jaws clamped shut on his wrists; clattering arms encircled his thighs; bony feet tripped him as he tried to rise, his throat convulsing in a useless attempt to scream.

The bones – the heaped bones beneath him – gave way, pitching him down into white caves of more fretted bones. And even as he landed in shards that powdered under his weight, so he saw that the walls were closing in on him, that they too were formed of bone – the fleshless skulls of the miserable dead!

Except that now flames seemed to flicker in those hollow orbits, deathly blue balefires of hell; and as he began to scream in earnest and stumble along bone-dusty rib-cage and thigh bone corridors, so the pallidly lambent eyes of the dead seemed to follow him in his flailing panic flight . . .

Wyatt stood and sweated and watched Maas-Krippner writhe on the machine's bed. The psychiatrist's almost effeminate hands fluttered no less than the limbs of the German, the flesh of his handsome face twitching with each tremor that passed through his victim's body. His victim? No, Maas was not that yet – not just yet. But soon.

With each creak of the old house's timbers, with each

muffled crackle of electrical discharge or *beep* of the monitoring systems, Wyatt would tremble afresh and wipe at his clammy brow. Oh, he must murder Maas and he knew it; but as the time drew closer to the moment of the act so he sweated more freely, his mind skittery about the actual contemplation of the thing.

Half-a-dozen times in the last thirty minutes he had told himself what he must do, had even rehearsed the action, but when the time came . . . would he be able to do it? But he must, he *must*!

Maas moaned, causing Wyatt to start, his eyes jerking round to stare at the manacled man, his hair rising on his head as the German's eyes bulged open and foam began to fleck the corners of his mouth. Psychomech had commenced feeding him now, trickling the impulses and energies which he needed to overcome his nightmares, those monsters of his id released by the stimulation of his brain's fear-centres. But Wyatt must not act until the trickle became a flood.

His eyes went again, as they had done so often in the last half-hour, to the switches which activated – or de-activated – Psychomech's feeders. With those switches depressed, Maas would have no back-up, no assistance or sustenance from Psychomech. Naked and alone and trapped in his own personal hell, he would be at the mercy of its denizens. And Wyatt was absolutely certain that those denizens would be far stronger than the mind which spawned them . . .

It had grown darker and the walls of bone seemed to press in on Otto Krippner that much closer. Dangling skeleton fingers had brushed his peaked SS cap from his head, sharp edges of bone had cut his uniform to ribbons. Now he ran in tatters, blood flowing down his calves from the gashes of a hundred jawbones which had sprung into life as he passed, attacking him in his nightmare careering down the calcium corridor.

But now the whiteness was a more grey uniformity and the

shadows were acreep, and the floor as its crackling components shattered beneath his ragged no longer shiny boots seemed soft as snow and yet thick as mud, dragging him inexorably to a halt. If that happened he knew that the tunnel would collapse upon him, would bury him under tons of bone, and that then he too would soon be chalk and bone and choking dust.

Then—

—A light ahead! A pinpoint of light gleaming in the surrounding darkness. Krippner fell to all fours, crawling through his own blood, his knees and elbows torn by brittle, broken bones and bitten by jagged stumps of teeth in vacantly chomping jaws. The walls, ceiling and floor all seemed to converge, driving him along an ever-narrowing funnel of bone towards the light, the blessed light.

The light – bright-shining, beckoning him on – a glowing star, silvery dazzling – six-pointed . . .

Six-pointed?

The Star of David!

Its brightness was a fire that burned his torn flesh. He recoiled from it, cried out, burst upwards, clawed through bones, bones, bones, fought for air in the fall of carrion dust, the crumbling of once-living calcium, death's powdery disintegration.

He emerged, his bleeding head and shoulders coming out upon a plain of bleached white. His horizon was the wall of the pit. On all four sides the walls rose, like the dry lips of a toothless square mouth – and him the morsel being sucked in. Beneath him the bones shifted like quicksand. He would go down again, down into darkness, and this time there would be no fight left in him. He must struggle on!

As the bones heaved and shuddered and settled like sieved bits of broken porcelain, Otto Krippner dragged himself away from the quake's epicentre, crawled like a limp and bloody rag towards the side of the pit closest to him. He reached it, managed to stand upright, stretched up his arms and sank his *fingers deep in bloody soil and hauled himself up until his head drew level with the pit's rim. With his last ounce of strength he drew his aching, bleeding, ragged body up and out of the great grave, collapsing on the rim—*

—Where THEY *were waiting for him!*

Wyatt saw the sudden wild fluctuations in the dials and graphs of the monitors, saw them and knew their meaning. Maas was approaching his climax of terror. He was face to face now with his own wildest nightmares, the terrors inside his skull. The moment of truth was fast approaching.

As for the physical man: he whined now like a rabid dog, whined and keened like a thin wind blowing through a crack in a wall, his teeth bared and grating together like rasps, his eyes bulging in his thrashing head. Saliva frothed from the distended corners of his mouth and ran down his straining jaws like so much shaving cream.

Pretty soon now the whining would become screaming, and when that moment came Wyatt knew what he must do. For the screams – or rather the mental torment producing them – would trigger Psychomech's back-up systems to greater productivity and Maas would wax stronger than his nightmare. Unless, as had happened once before (by accident on that occasion) unless there was no back-up. The rest would be simply: hyper-stimulation of the fear-centres, producing insanity and eventually death.

Wyatt's hand trembled over the switches of Psycho-mech's feeder system, and the sweat ran almost as freely from him as from Maas . . .

THEY *were waiting for him.*

THEM: *the Patient Trackers, with long thin noses that sniffed – the Singleminded Bloodhounds whose red tongues lolled – the Accusers whose trembling fingers twitched and pointed, twitched and pointed as they came closer, with hands like divining rods and fingers like hazel twigs scenting water.*

216

Except that they did not scent water but blood. Nazi blood!

From the holster on the now scuffed black leather belt at his ragged waist Krippner drew out his luger. The pistol gave him strength, a capacity for anger. He grew taller as his anger swelled into rage. He aimed the pistol, pulled the trigger. He emptied it into them – and watched them fall, their sniffing noses deflating, their lolling tongues stilled, their pointing fingers flopping limply on suddenly flaccid hands and arms – and watched others step up to take their places! He couldn't kill them all! His pistol fell from nerveless fingers.

Krippner found his voice, screamed into their horrified, wide-eyed accusing faces. 'Why me? What of Gerber, who's now a banker in the Germany we loved?'

But they only shook their heads and kept right on pointing, and all the time they shuffled closer. No, for Gerber had never been a butcher. He had followed orders, but even his worst enemies knew he had resisted wherever he could, and that he had never enjoyed it. Otto Krippner had exceeded his orders, and he had always enjoyed it.

'What of Fledermann?' *he screamed.* 'He's a chemist in Paderborn! And Stock, the Steel Man of the Ruhr? What of them?'

But still they shook their heads, and still their fingers pointed. Until one of them – a small man, a little Jew with a wrinkled face and hollow cheeks – stepped forward, reached out and touched Otto Krippner. Touched him as if he touched ordure or dabbled his hand in sulphuric acid. As if he touched the devil himself. And Krippner remembered him. Oh, yes, the others he might have forgotten, but this one he remembered. Not his name – neither that nor his number, no – for what is one more name or number amongst many? But his haunted face, his agony, which must surely have gone with him from this world into the next – these things Krippner remembered. For of course he had murdered him, personally and in the cruellest way imaginable.

By now the ring of Accusers had closed in on Krippner and

their shuddering fingers were touching him; and now he saw that those fingers were not true fingers at all and that their shuddering was produced through vibration. They were rotating half-inch drill bits – and where they touched they bored into him. His blood turned to ice – which immediately commenced to spurt out of his body as the finger-drills entered his flesh.

Screaming as no man ever screamed before, Otto Krippner crumpled to his knees . . .

When Maas stopped whining and began screaming Wyatt clapped his hands to his ears and almost ran from the room. Then he heard the hum of Psychomech's back-up systems as they stepped up their aid to Maas, feeding him the psychic and physical strength he required to fight back and win over all odds, and he remembered his real purpose in being here. But even as he reached for the cut-out switches he was aware of a subtle difference. It was not that the machine was malfunctioning in any way, rather that it functioned *in excess* of the requirement. Lights suddenly glowed on panels where Wyatt had never before noticed them, and the spinning tapes of Maas's newly installed automatic systems had commenced to whir and click behind their clear plastic covers. Pre-programmed for this precise moment, the machine was delivering its surge, flooding the ESP areas of Maas's mind with the powers of a God!

Without understanding what was happening, and yet shudderingly aware that something outside his experience – some utterly abnormal thing – *was* happening, Wyatt's trembling fingers found the cut-out switches . . .

Renewed, swollen, bloated, Otto Krippner stood within the circle of Accusers and glared. Glared? His eyes, so recently bright with fear, were now almost glassy with power! He glared, yes – a glare of pure malevolence – and the Accusers fell back from him like leaves blown in a gale, melting as icicles in the withering blast of a furnace. In a moment they were gone, banished back to his id, the black vaults of their spawning.

And now his uniform was whole once more, replete with jackboots, swastika armband, SS cap and badge, Sam Browne belt, cross-strap and pistol holder. Otto Krippner in full regalia, completely in command – and commanding more sheer power than any fifty Nazis before him!

And now let them beware, the ones who sought him. Now let them fear his wrath, where he for years had feared theirs.

With enhanced clairvoyance he searched for them, found them; with remote viewing he spied upon them, saw what they were about; and telepathically, telekinetically he visited them, briefly, simultaneously, and let them feel his presence, his power . . .

Felix Goldstein was at a dance in the American Embassy, enjoying himself as best he could and perhaps drinking a little too much to disguise the sour taste of defeat. Defeat, yes, for yet again a hot lead on Herr Colonel Doktor Otto Krippner had proved to be nothing more than a wild-goose chase. It was sickening, physically sickening! The trail had looked so good, and then – nothing. If Krippner had come to England, then he had died here quietly and in obscurity; or he had acquired a new identity which, through the accruement of years, must by now afford him complete protection.

Yet even as these thoughts played in Goldstein's mind he remembered Charalambou–Keltner's dying words: how Krippner had come to England, and the name he had used, Hans Maas. With that thought came another – so hard it was almost a physical blow – and Goldstein reeled with the force of it: a vivid mental picture, clearer than any photograph, of the man he sought. Krippner, smiling hideously, large and larger than life, in uniform befitting the Nazi's rank and suiting perfectly his clinical, cold-blooded (or was it hot-blooded?) evil. In another moment the vision had disappeared and Goldstein steadied himself and shook his head. He must have been working too hard. Unsteadily, he walked out on to the balcony to get a breath of fresh air. He wondered how the others were progressing, and guessed that they would not be making any headway. But . . . it was their last chance: immigration for the years 1957, 1958 and 1959. A man calling himself Maas, if Keltner had been right and the Nazi really had come over to England under that name . . .

In the private library of the Golders Green home of a prominent British Jew, Gerry Hochstern and Ira Levi wearily sat at a desk and pored over the foolscap photostats of near microscopic print. A stack of discarded sheets, all void of the one name they sought, cluttered one end of the desk. They worked in silence through the night, as they had worked for hours, in the yellow glow of a desk lamp, almost without hope – until suddenly Levi drew breath sharply and stabbed with an extended forefinger. 'There!' The word was a whisper. 'There. Hans Maas – July '58 . . .'

'Where?' Hochstern leaned across the desk, shrugging off his weariness and coming to life in a moment, placing a magnifier over the spot where Levi's finger pointed. 'Maas,' he breathed. 'Hans Maas, alive – at least in 1958. Hans Maas – alias Otto Krippner!'

It was like an invocation.

The desk light grew dim, blinked out in a moment, and in that same instant the temperature of the room plummeted. Their breath plumed in suddenly freezing air. '*What the hell*—?' Levi hissed.

A bluish radiance glowed into life in one corner of the room. Frozen, the two men sat in the eerie illumination, their hackles rising as they gazed wide-eyed and awestruck at the apparition – or was it an apparition? – forming out of the blueness. Otto Krippner, uniformed, malignant, bloated tall as the ceiling and glowing with the blue rottenness of loathsome, poisonous fungi.

But his huge hands, reaching out, were not apparitions; those great hands, big as meat platters, the left closing over Levi's head and the right over Hochstern's. And beginning slowly to squeeze, while the burning eyes of Otto Krippner glared and glared, and the room was filled with all the eerie energy born in a madman's mind and now released in a massive psychic attack . . .

Gareth Wyatt's fingers depressed the cut-out switches and the fortified, expanded ESP centres of Hans Maas's mind were instantly denied Psychomech's assistance. A moment more and the figure of the man on the machine seemed to crumple. He began to scream. But there are screams and there are screams, and these were different to any that Maas had ever heard. They were such that he could not bear to listen to them. Nor could he bear to look at Maas on the bed of the machine; a single glance was sufficient to send him flying from the room. With hands that shook uncontrollably, he locked the door behind him, then hurried downstairs and sat alone, sweating and shuddering in a quiet room in the most unquiet house in the world . . .

Miles McCauley, American diplomat, went out on to the large balcony of the embassy high over central London's streets. He had seen an old friend of his, Felix Goldstein, wander out there with a drink in his hand. Goldstein had looked a bit down in the mouth, had seemed pensive and worried, and perhaps this would be a good time to talk to him. Maybe seeing McCauley would cheer him up a little. McCauley wondered what sort of work he was doing these days. Still tracking down war-criminals, he supposed.

And he supposed correctly, except that this time a very special war-criminal had tracked down Goldstein.

Later, McCauley would not be able to remember exactly

what he saw out there on the balcony. He would never be quite sure. But there was Goldstein on his knees, gasping, his face contorted in agony and his arms held up at strange, strained angles. And McCauley *heard* those arms snap, heard it quite clearly, as the other screamed and his arms began to flap about like snakes with their backs broken.

Then the Jew dragged himself – or *was* dragged, by something invisible – towards the balcony's low stone wall, lurched upright – or was snatched upright – and bent backwards against the parapet. Impossibly, in that bent over backwards position, he began to slide *upwards*, over the parapet, his feet lifting clear off the floor.

Leaping across the space between, McCauley sensed a malevolent presence. He felt it even as he grabbed at Goldstein's legs, felt it effortlessly dragging the Jew from his grasp – until suddenly the shrieking man fainted and fell back into McCauley's arms, at which very moment the force withdrew. One second it was there, this feeling of a hateful, destructive force, and the next . . . gone.

In Golders Green also those same weird energies, that malefic Power, had been shut off, leaving Hochstern and Levi crumpled over the desk of the now scattered photostats. They, too, were alive, but it had been a close thing.

Finally Levi was able to lift his bruised and bloodied, sweat-soaked head from what had been a green desk blotter, now stained uniformly brown. Hochstern stayed where he was, bleeding a little from his ears and feeling as if his head had been in a vice. Opening his bloodshot eyes, he blinked until his vision cleared and looked at Levi. The desk light burned as steadily as before and all seemed back to normal – with the exception that the two men knew their heads had been very nearly crushed.

But by what?

'What the hell was *that*?' Levi croaked.

'Krippner!' the other answered at once, his voice a groan.

Hochstern was a member of an Israeli metaphysical society and was generally recognized as having some clairvoyant ability. 'It was him, I'm sure.'

'But how—'

'How did he do it? I don't know – but when we can move, I think one of us should contact Felix. I've a feeling he may also have been . . . visited! Whether he has or hasn't, one thing is now certain. Otto Krippner was still alive, and he was here somewhere in England.'

'Was? But you just said—'

'He's dead now,' Hochstern said with certainty. 'He died doing – that. Maybe it killed him, maybe not, but be sure he is dead. If he wasn't dead – then we surely would be!'

It was more than an hour before Gareth Wyatt dared return to the room of the machine. And when he saw what lay upon Psychomech's bed he had to go away again and be sick – very sick indeed – before his nerves were steady enough for what must be done next. Then he thanked whichever lucky stars shone down upon him that the house was empty, that he had fired his servants some four months ago when it became clear that he could no longer afford to keep them. That made very easy work of what must otherwise be impossible, or at the very least extremely dangerous.

But in fact it was simpler than he ever could have imagined. Hans Maas had not been a heavy man before, and now he was little more than a bag of bones. That was something which would frequently return to haunt Wyatt for the rest of his life: the awful *depletion* taken place in the body of the ex-Nazi. It was as if Psychomech had completely drained him of his body's fluids; had sucked the entire essence of Maas into itself, like some gigantic mechanical vampire . . .

After the thing which had been Maas had disappeared into the deep waters of the pool, Wyatt returned to the house. Tomorrow there would be much to do. He must search the old gatehouse thoroughly, from top to bottom, removing and destroying anything which would incriminate him or Maas.

But tonight – tonight Wyatt would do nothing. He would not even sleep, for sleep was out of the question. No, he would simply sit downstairs, with all the lights of the house ablaze, and he would drink coffee. A lot of coffee. And upstairs, silent now and utterly inactive, Psychomech would crouch on its metal and plastic haunches, a great glutted bat in hibernation.

And it would be a long time before Wyatt ever unlocked the door and entered that room again . . .

Chapter Twelve

Three and a half years later; the end of February 1980 . . .

Full years for Garrison, they were nevertheless gone in a twinkling. His wife Terri (she had married him only three months after their first meeting) had also found them full; of newness, excitement, some strangeness, even sorrow. The latter had been occasioned by the death of her father – dead, she had used to claim, of a broken heart, though the doctors had diagnosed a brain tumour – but its pain was largely over now; and this only a short while after Garrison had stepped in and bought up a majority of supposedly worthless shares in Miller's company, which now gave him the controlling interest. Moreover, under his guidance the company had recovered and prospered; he had made and was still making a great deal of money from it, as well as from his other ever-expanding business ventures.

Koenig, of course, was bound to see Garrison's success in so many fields as increasing evidence of his beloved Colonel's continued presence and influence over Garrison, and in this respect he was happy with a situation which so far agreed precisely with Schroeder's (or rather with Adam Schenk's) forecasts. If only Schenk were still alive to throw some light, as it were, upon the events of the immediate future. For as time passed both Koenig and Garrison were ever aware of the approach of that deadline, that last enigmatic entry on Garrison's horoscope:

'Machine. Time-scale: to eight years. RG/TS . . . Light!'

Eight years from the early summer of 1973; in other words the summer of 1981; which in turn was only fifteen or so months away.

'Light!' – which Garrison could only take to mean the

return, by some miraculous event or other, of his sight.

And 'RG/TS'. Richard Garrison – Thomas Schroeder. Schroeder's return, his reincarnation from beyond the grave, into Garrison's body. A metempsychosis, a sort of sharing: which transition Koenig obviously believed was already well underway . . .

Three and a half years. Full years but far from easy ones and, quite apart from the death of Terri's father, not even completely happy ones. She had disliked Koenig from the start; or rather, from the moment she had recognized the strength of his influence with the man she had supposed to be his master.

At first, perhaps not unreasonably, she had tried to oust the German from Garrison's affections, only then learning something of the unbreakable ties between them, the fact that the past bound them together. She could never know – of course not – that the future also was just such a binding influence.

And so she had learned to tolerate Koenig, and knowing the problem, for his part he kept out of the way as best he might. But in all truth their friendship grew despite Terri's obvious (though now controlled or restrained) opposition.

One more thing Terri did not know, and one Garrison never saw fit to tell her, was that Koenig was a rich man in his own right. Garrison's feelings for the German were hardly made any less by this fact, of which he had been aware for some time, that his 'gentleman's gentleman', was, like himself, a man to whom money posed little or no problem. Thomas Schroeder had seen to all of that; so that in fact Willy Koenig could leave Garrison's 'employ' whenever he wished, could go and live where and how he desired. Except of course that he had no such desire.

It was as he had explained those several years ago: he, too, sought an extension, a going forward beyond man's normal life expectancy. And where better to seek such immortality than in the presence of a man – *or of men* – he was sure would, somehow or other, breach that final and greatest barrier of all?

As for Garrison: his blindness was no longer any sort of real problem. Blind he was, yes, in that he could not see with his eyes, but his physical movements were the easy, flowing movements of a fully sighted person, so that all who encountered him for the first time were invariably sceptical of his disablement. This was due in part to certain expensive improvements in his sensor equipment, which were recent developments of the same German suppliers, in part to his own instinctive and natural independence, but mainly to the increased sensitivity – the quite *abnormal* expansion – of his four remaining senses.

Keeping pace with all of this, his interest in parapsychology had never waned, so that by now he could rightly reckon himself an expert. And it seemed only right to him that he should attribute the increased capacity of his perceptions to the gradual emergence of his ESP factors. For they *were* emerging, of that he was quite sure. It was a fact he could very easily (and regularly did) prove, often for no more reason than his own gratification or satisfaction. And their emergence was accelerating . . . except in one direction. Oddly enough that one blank area was prevision, the talent which had signalled – and disastrously so – his gift in the first place.

But since that day almost four years ago, when he had known he must go to Italy and find Terri, there had been no more prophetic dreams, no more glimpses of the future. It was as if, in that respect, the advent of Terri – his search for her, her subsequent discovery and rescue – had completely burned him out.

As for the rest of his talents: regular trips to Garrison's Retreat allowed him the full facilities of the library and ESP test-centre. These, as stated, invariably proved increasing psychic capability except in the area of prevision, the talent to gauge the future. Much to Garrison's disappointment, it appeared he was not and would never be a second Adam Schenk.

Garrison had not once taken Terri with him to the Harz; he knew well her dislike for Koenig, who must always accompany him, and her apprehension or rather uneasiness concerning his interest in metaphysics. But while both of these reasons had seemed satisfactory to her, neither one was wholly valid. The truth of the matter was that he could never go to Garrison's Retreat without remembering Vicki Maler, whose name he had not once mentioned to his wife but feared he might if Terri were ever there with him in the Harz. He could not bring himself to picture the two women together in one setting, which he knew would be bound to happen. Perhaps (he told himself) having never actually seen either one of them, they might somehow superimpose themselves upon his mind and so become one single, faceless, contradictory identity – which would be quite unthinkable.

Vicki must always remain inviolate. Another's knowledge of her would be a depletion of his own memory, like the tiny scratches on a record which come with too frequent usage, or the *hiss* that mars a tape-recording as a result of constant replaying. For this same reason, so as not to dim her spark, Garrison strictly controlled his own dwelling upon Vicki; except in the Harz, where this had proved to be an utter impossibility. For there he discovered her in every room and smelled the natural scent of her body in even the freshest sheets and pillows.

In short, Garrison – a man whose early life had taught him how to suppress even the most traumatic experiences, how to control and expel the nightmares which infest in one degree or another every last one of us – was now discovering new hangups; though as yet he was not wholly aware that they existed, or thought of them at worst as the normal process of his mind. They were for him, for the moment at least, mere sources of irritation.

Terri herself was one such source. It was not that Garrison did not love her; on the contrary, he believed that he loved her as fully as he might; it was more that he felt his love was wasted. Perhaps it had something to do with the termination implied by Schenk's horoscope:

'Girl "T". Time-scale: to eight years.'

And, 'Machine. Timescale: to eight years.'

And, 'RG/TS . . .' And of course, 'Light!' But after that, no more mention of Terri. But then again, no mention of anything.

Or perhaps his irritation sprang from the fact that she did not love him. She *made* love to him, yes, and was herself almost telepathic at sensing his needs in this respect, but . . . it was just a feeling he had.

The one other thing, the Big One, was a complete enigma. Garrison slept with Terri, lived with her, loved her (albeit with nagging reservations), but he could no more read her than his crimson eyes could read a book. And she was not any sort of book to be read *to* him. Even if she were, perhaps he would not like her story. And at those odd moments when he gave that question some thought, he knew that this was his greatest hangup. To know her – *to have known her even before he met her!* – and yet not to know her at all.

But that was the way of it. For some reason his new-found perceptions did not work with Terri. She was no sound he could define or categorize, no smell or touch on which to paint mental colours, no taste from which he might distil her essence. And perhaps that, too, was a hangup: it could be that he did not want to know what lay inside her. Perhaps he even feared to know . . .

One final thing pained Garrison: Terri's hatred for Suzy. This had been apparent right from the start. For rationalize as she might (or as Garrison might insist she do) still the idea persisted in her mind that Suzy was a creature to be feared. Even seeing the bitch's love of Garrison – seeing her almost human thoughtfulness and constant awareness of a disability others might now tend to ignore – and knowing that no thief or any other unwanted intruder could ever enter her home while Suzy was there, still Terri persisted in remembering the dog of her dream, the black dog she had so feared. Unless—

—Unless her fear had after all been for the blind man himself and not his dog.

While Garrison knew of Terri's detestation of Suzy, he was not aware of the dog's hatred for her. Nor was Terri herself, though she occasionally suspected it. The servants at the house in Sussex knew it for a certainty, as did Willy Koenig; but he had warned them from the beginning that they must say nothing of it, neither to Terri nor even to the master of the house himself.

Terri might suspect that at times she would see a strange look in Suzy's eyes, or read some unpleasant purpose into her stance, but she could never be sure. Always, at second glance, it was just Suzy, Garrison's hated, ever-watchful guardian angel; Suzy, the living memory of a frightening dream whose other details were long forgotten. Except that there had also been a powerful blind man.

As for any tidbits of food she might toss Suzy's way: the bitch would dutifully catch up whichever scrap and carry it away into some quiet, leafy corner of the gardens – and there bury it completely untouched! She wanted nothing of Terri, except perhaps . . . an end of her?

Koenig had pondered this, had worried over it. His loyalties – his very instincts – were divided on the problem. His own affection for Suzy had never faltered, nor the dog's for him, though of course the only real centre and inspiration of her world was Garrison; but after all a dog is only a dog. If Suzy posed any sort of real threat to Terri, then she should be put down at once – which would be akin to killing off part of Garrison himself! Therefore if it was to be done at all, it must appear to be 'accidental'. That would be no problem for Koenig: Suzy would simply disappear. Except—

The bitch was no ordinary animal. What was it that she knew, sensed or suspected about Terri that no one else knew, sensed or suspected? What was the source of her hatred? She had been trained to love Garrison as a God, above all others, above *any* other love. To protect, guide – to worship him – without thanks, with beatings or starvation if he so desired, to death itself. So that the adoration was not only *in* her but *was* her. And in this lay the answer. Heinz Holzer, whatever his methods, had fine-tuned and trained much more than mere emotion and devotion into the Dobermann. He had also developed her *instinct* for Garrison's protection.

And it was Suzy's *instinct* to distrust Terri. Yes, and in this way the bitch had read the future with an accuracy away and beyond anything Adam Schenk had ever achieved. But of course Willy Koenig did not know that.

In the event he did nothing, and with time he became disinclined even to worry about it. Suzy must have her reasons for her behaviour; that was enough . . .

After her father's death, Terri's Italian mother had remarried and now lived in Turin. There had been some correspondence between mother and daughter, not a lot. Terri had not forgiven her, neither for her dissolute ways nor for the death she continued to believe those ways had inspired; this despite the fact that Terri herself had inherited something of her mother's character. More than this, however, there was one other reason she could not forgive her mother, and that was for stealing from her the affections of the one man she had ever loved.

A man called Gareth Wyatt.

She had known Wyatt for six months before he met her mother, and she had been his lover for all but the first week of that time. Now Terri had had her affairs before Wyatt, and young as she was she had believed she knew something of the arts of love; but Wyatt had shown her so much more than the others that his expertise had found her utterly vulnerable. In a very short time she had become besotted with him.

As for Wyatt's purpose in seducing Terri in the first place, that had been twofold. One, his fortunes were waning and he believed her father to be a rich man. In this he was mistaken for Miller's financial affairs were already on the slide. Two, Miller's firm dealt with micro-electronics; it had seemed possible that Wyatt might make some connection here of benefit to Hans Maas in his search for better components for Psychomech.

But then, when Miller's collapse started to become self-evident, Wyatt had decided to move his attentions elsewhere. Until then he had been an occasional visitor at Terri's home on the outskirts of Winchester, but so far he had only met her father. Harry Miller, not so shrewd, perhaps, in business, could nevertheless spot an opportunist when he saw one. He had not liked Wyatt, had in any case considered him too old for Terri, had not encouraged their relationship.

Then, on what might otherwise have been Wyatt's last visit to Terri's home, he had met Maria, her mother. She had recently returned from a rather protracted stay in Italy, where (ostensibly) an obscure but loved elderly female relative had been seriously ill. Maria Miller, of course, had money in her own right, and she was no less a libertine than Wyatt himself. By now he was bored with Terri and her father's rather bleak-looking prospects, and he knew there would be no remuneration for the time and money expended upon her. Her mother on the other hand was very beautiful, mature and monied. Wyatt did not know the extent of her fortune (in fact it was not great) but he saw in her at least an opportunity to recoup his losses.

And finally Terri caught them together. This was the single grain of truth in the story she had related to Garrison; he was not destined ever to know the rest of it. He would never suspect that he had caught Terri, as it were, on the rebound from a faithless lover. But then, those three years later, with Garrison so often away and his wife so often bored . . .

Garrison had not restricted or attempted to restrict Terri's freedom. She was no bird to be kept in a cage. Since she had been groomed as something of a socialite, and since her husband's circles were continually expanding, she had become and would continue to be a socialite, with many friends and not a few admirers. This was how, following the gala performance of a stage production at the Chichester Theatre and at the opening night party, she had come to meet up once more with Wyatt the sophisticate, who by now was almost penurious. He still put on a show, but always with the knowledge that his funds were very low. Having kept a constant finger on the pulse of local affairs, he was well aware that Terri was now the wife of a rich and successful man, and that once again she had become an irresistible target.

For Terri's part, seeing him across the room amongst a crush of people and before he had spied her, her heart had given a single wild leap, and she had known at once what was missing from her life. And if anything this man – the only man she had ever truly loved, to whom she had given of herself in every possible way – had grown more attractive than ever. And at that moment Terri had known that it would take no great effort on Wyatt's part to re-acquire her as his mistress.

No fool, she had not thought herself prepared to take that chance. She had made to leave . . . and that was when he found her. Leaving the house on the outskirts of Chichester and crossing the wide gravel drive to where her car was parked, she had heard the crunch of rapid footsteps behind her and his voice calling: 'Terri! Terri, please wait!'

And turning . . . she had been trapped! As easily as that.

Which was why, when Garrison had proposed his most recent trip to the Harz, to take place during the first three weeks of February, Terri had put up no resistance whatever but had actually seemed to encourage the idea. There were friends she wanted to visit, she said, and it was time she shopped and got in early on the new spring fashions – and there were shows in London to see, which of course were of no interest to Garrison – and so on. And during his absence her affair had blossomed more wildly than ever, until she eventually became the very softest clay in Wyatt's clever hands.

Not that she allowed it to be that easy. No, for there were certain reservations and resentments in Terri forming barriers which must first be broken down. And since he had in great part created them, he alone must remove them. Prime amongst these was what she continued to see as his part in her father's decline and death, a problem Wyatt sweated over for some little time before he came up with the right answer.

Even then only a woman in love or completely besotted would have believed him. His solution was simply to lie, but in a way which especially lent itself to Terri's susceptibility, her feelings – or lack of feelings – for her mother, and the steadily widening gap between them. This alone gave credibility to his story, which was that Terri's mother, not Wyatt himself, had made all the running in their affair, and that the affair itself had been literally forced upon him. She had professed her love for him, or rather her need, which at first, along with her blatant sexuality, had repulsed him. She was after all a married woman, and the mother of his one true love at that! Seeing how her obvious lusting after him had shocked him, she had then threatened to destroy both him and Terri, break them up completely, ruin their chances beyond any possible hope of recovery. She had known he needed money for an important project – something to do with a machine, experimental psychiatry far removed from any orthodox practice – and promised him whatever financial assistance he required. He had not known that she would never be able to keep the bargain, that in any case her funds were quite insufficient.

What she required in return was . . . well, Terri could well imagine that. An affair, of course. She had had many such and usually grew bored very quickly with her lovers; doubtless it would be the same with Wyatt. Meanwhile, she would not interfere with his courting her daughter – on the contrary, she would attempt to sway Harry Miller in Wyatt's favour – and Terri would never need to know anything of it. He had believed her . . . after all, what woman would be that much of a bitch?

He should have known better, of course, but she had made it plain to him that this was the only way he could ever realize his ambition, which all along had been to marry Terri and make her his own forever. Surely Terri must know this? – that he loved her as no other woman had ever been loved? Surely she had felt it when they were together, in the perfection of their love-making, the sheer joy of their bodies coupling?

All of these lies Wyatt told, but in such a way that Terri was slowly able to assimilate and believe them, as any woman will who hears lies from the man she loves.

In a little while she had found herself admitting her own feelings, began telling him she did not love Garrison, was inviting (albeit without a single spoken word) a continuation of their love affair. And in Terri Garrison's weakness, her future, Wyatt's, Koenig's, Garrison's own and the futures of many others – indeed the future of the world itself – were clinched. It was the key piece in a fantastic jigsaw puzzle, the one piece about which all the others would fall surely and horrifically into place.

But even then Wyatt had had to push it one step further. If only Terri could leave Garrison, he said, they could be as they had been before; better, for now that she knew the 'truth' of matters they could simply live out the rest of their lives in total happiness together. As for money: what did that matter? He still had his estate, in need of some attention, true, but still a valuable property. He would sell it, buy a smaller place, bank the surplus and they could live (albeit sparingly) on the interest. He was an intelligent man; he still had a small clientele, a list of patients; he would work and provide for her. They would not starve, far from it. And there were certain projects which, with the right backing, could still make his fortune. Somehow, somewhere, he would find that backing. If only she would come away with him and be his.

In making this suggestion there was a great risk and Wyatt knew he took a chance. But – besotted as she was, still Terri was no fool. Wyatt had hoped this would be the case and breathed a silent sigh of relief when she rejected the idea of running away with him. No, she would not leave Richard Garrison, for that would be an act of the utmost folly.

For Garrison was rich. Richer than Wyatt might ever suspect. Her life as his wife was one of the sheerest luxury, even though it often left her bored, with too much time on her hands and too little to do with it. No, leaving him was out of the question, at least at this point of time. But . . . what if Wyatt's projects should prove successful? If money was all he needed, well, perhaps that could be arranged.

Her plan was this:

Richard Garrison had the golden touch. Every venture he undertook made money for him as if by magic. Now if Wyatt could interest him in this special project of his – this machine? Psychomech? – and if indeed it proved to be the winner he promised, why, then he would grow rich in his own right!

The first step would be c meeting, ostensibly accidental, between the two men. There would be no need for Garrison to know him as *the* Wyatt, not immediately, but from the very first the two should seem to have a great deal in common. For example, Garrison was especially interested in parapsychology, and so Wyatt would do well to acquaint himself with the various terms and facets of all such matters; the other side, as it were, of his own mainly orthodox psychological and psychiatric training; and so on.

So it was that in a black-sheeted bed in Wyatt's house in Hampshire, the seed of a meeting between himself and Garrison germinated and took root; and then, almost an afterthought on his part, though he did not let Terri see it, he made love to her yet again.

And in a triple-padlocked room close by, Psychomech, crouching down on its gleaming steel and plastic haunches, sat still and silent and waiting . . .

Garrison was temporarily exhausted. The trip to the Harz had been much to his satisfaction but, as usual, the extensive ESP-tests had drained him. On top of this he had missed Suzy more than usual; also, Vicki Maler's presence at Garrison's Retreat had been almost overpowering.

Vicki . . .

Once, shortly after marrying Terri, Garrison and Koenig had gone to Schloss Zonigen in the Swiss Alps. Ostensibly he was at Garrison's Retreat, but he had desired to see Vicki, if only to reassure himself that she was . . . there. It was a mistake, a nightmare, and he had vowed never to go back. Even thinking back on it was nightmarish.

. . . The tunnel with its strip-lighting, cutting like a glowing neon tube through the heart of the ice and rock; the fur boots, hooded parkas, fur-lined gauntlets; the little car on rails that sped them to Vicki's resting place; the numbered niche (2139) in the rock wall, where her body lay in frozen suspension, still riddled with the cancer which had killed her but rigid now and frozen as the emaciated shell containing it.

He had only been able to see her face, full of repose but behind which he sensed an agony – possibly his own. And the tears freezing into tiny marbles on his cheeks. And her frost-rimed tube sliding back into its niche as he turned away. The memory still haunted him . . .

This time, however, upon his return from the Harz to the house in Sussex, Terri was so obviously pleased to see him and so full of concern for his weariness that he was soon his old self again.

Of course she wanted to show off some of her new clothes. There were several parties they must attend in March and April, and one in particular at the home of Doris Quatrain, a notorious socialite friend who lived in Mayfair. This was where Garrison was to meet Gareth Wyatt, as Terri and the psychiatrist had prearranged, and this is how that meeting came about:

Willy Koenig had driven them into the city in the Mercedes, going off on his own as soon as he had delivered them to the house in Mayfair. Three large rooms had been given over to the party itself, though as usual the at present 'Miss' Quatrain's house (she had often been a 'Mrs' but was free right now) was completely open to the comings and goings, and occasional goings-on, of her guests. There was a lot of good eating, 'chic' (or to Garrison's mind 'banal') conversation, and a deal of hard drinking. He avoided the latter, securing for himself a half-bottle of mediocre Italian brandy specially provided for him by the hostess, and he and Terri found themselves seats upon a corner lounge where after a while they were joined by several of her debutantish ex-schoolgirl friends, each now grown to essentially sensual womanhood: company which only a few short years ago Garrison would have found fascinating but uncomfortable and difficult, which now affected him not at all. Or at worst merely amused him.

At once he relaxed, allowing his hyper-sensitive perceptions full range to drink in all the strangeness of these new female pseudo-colours and -textures, and after a while Terri went off to chat with Doris Quatrain herself. Fast on the heels of her departure Garrison sensed the approach of a new presence whose silhouette was tall, slim and very male. Quite uninvited, a stranger had joined him and Terri's girlfriends in their corner, and whoever he was his effect upon the women was both instant and remarkable. Their chatter momentarily died away, only to resume instantly and simultaneously, louder and even more animated than before, which Garrison could only take to signal the newcomer's imposing looks or status.

Then, sensing a hand held out in his direction, he grasped it and said: 'Garrison, Richard Garrison.'

'Oh, I know who you are of course, Mr Garrison,' the stranger's voice was deep and attractive, 'and if I may say so I admire you. And I pray you'll excuse this completely unsolicited approach, but . . . well, knowing a great deal about you, I believe we may have a lot in common.'

'Ah!' Garrison smiled. He was not absolutely sure he enjoyed the stranger's self-confidence, or for that matter his manner of approach. Perhaps he could bring him down just a little – but without being offensive. 'You know much of me and we have a deal in common? Then you can only be . . . my tax inspector?'

The ladies laughed a little but in their way sensed that their presence was now superfluous. There was something deeper here, outside their scope. They began to excuse themselves and drift away, and soon the two men were alone. 'My name is Wyatt,' said the stranger, 'and I recently became a member of the Society of Parapsychology here in London. Which is where I learned of you. They seem to

239

hold you in great esteem.'

'I've been to a couple of meetings,' Garrison answered. 'They talk a lot, drink a lot more, do very little else. Frankly they bore me, as I'm sure they'll eventually bore you. I do not intend to resume my membership.'

'You're very frank,' the newcomer laughed, 'and that's to say the least – but it's what I expected of you. And I may say that I already agree with you – about them being boring, I mean. They are, most boring. Thinkers and speakers, yes, but not doers.'

Garrison found him interesting. His voice, without being sonorous, was almost hypnotic, imparting along with his smell (his human smell, strong behind a thin cosmetic film) the image of a man of say . . . perhaps forty-eight or -nine years, but looking much younger. Slim, tall, with chestnut hair probably tinted to keep hidden the emerging grey in his well-groomed locks, this Wyatt was handsome.

His handshake, too, had seemed to agree with all of this, so that Garrison was now convinced he had a complete mental picture of the man. Physically – he guessed he would be vigorous. The depth of his voice and the strength of his handshake seemed to assure it. And if he was right, well, that would explain Wyatt's effect upon the women. Whoever and whatever he was, this man would always be devastating in female company. That was why the girls had drifted away. It had been a mutual understanding between them. To stay would have been to vie for his attention. Later, perhaps, when the booze was flowing that much faster and the veneer of decorum was fast decaying, then they might return. But meanwhile Garrison could easily check the conclusions of his heightened perceptions.

'Mr Wyatt, you realize of course that I'm quite blind.'

'Your pardon? Blind? But certainly I realize it.' The other's voice was now puzzled, mildly cautious. 'Have I said or done something to offend or—'

'No, no – nothing like that – but you said of our

colleagues at the ESP Society that they were thinkers and speakers but not doers. I am blind, but at the same time I am a doer.'

'So I've heard. That was why, chiefly, I wanted to speak to you. All my life I have been interested in psychiatry and psychology, the normal – and occasionally abnormal – mental processes, but only recently in parapsychology. It is, so to speak, the other side of the coin. And I, too, would like to be a doer.'

Something clicked in Garrison's head.

Wyatt . . . Psychiatry . . .

Connections were made but – he ignored them. Suddenly he felt inclined to show off. 'May I demonstrate the sort of thing I can do?' he asked.

'I would be delighted!' Wyatt leaned closer.

'I know nothing of you, agreed?'

'We never before met,' Wyatt nodded.

'And you agree that I am blind?' Garrison lifted his blinkers an inch or two, let the other see his eyes, heard his sharp intake of breath. 'Very well. Then let me describe you – at least your physical exterior.' And he quickly told Wyatt all that he had discerned or perceived of him. Finally, as he finished, he quite spontaneously added: 'Also, your main concern in speaking to me tonight was not with parapsychology. You attach far greater importance to our meeting than the mere discussion or demonstration of ESP ability.'

And again the sharp intake of breath.

For a split second Wyatt was off-guard, his barriers down, his mind racing in a sort of mental neutral but yet throwing out impressions which flooded into Garrison's receptive areas in a veritable torrent. A series of vivid, fleeting mental images came and went in bright flashes within the blind man's mind as he sat, apparently placid, facing the stranger. He caught at them, seized upon these chaotic fragments from Wyatt's inner being.

There was money, a good deal of it. And MME, Miller Micro-Electronics. And a picture of Wyatt himself as Garrison had so accurately described him, but successful now and smiling, however anxiously. There was Terri, too, unimportant in the great kaleidoscope of telepathic impressions. And there was something else, something that came and went so quickly that Garrison almost missed it. But it was important. So important that he grasped for it, reached after it with his mind like a man with a butterfly net after some rare species. He caught it—

—And in the next instant was reeling, his mind spinning and blurring like the colours on a roulette wheel!

Reeling, spinning . . .

Reeling astride the Machine, with Suzy's great paw upon his shoulder. The weird landscape – a landscape of unfettered mind – hurtling by, and ahead the bleached forest of brittle trees, like massed skeletal fingers clawing skywards. And beyond the forest the black lake of pitch, the black rock, the black castle – the quest!

'Mr Garrison?' the voice was worried, the hand gripping his arm full of tension. 'Mr Garrison, is there something I can—'

'No!' His voice was too high, a falsetto croak. He controlled it. 'No, I'm all right. A dizzy spell. This bloody Ligurian brandy, that's all.'

'But quite suddenly there you looked desperately ill! Your face went pale as death in a second! Something you ate, perhaps? Can I get a doctor?'

Doctor . . . Psychiatry . . . Wyatt . . .

A pattern emerging, forming, clicking into place. Garrison knew his man now, at least for what he had been – or for what he was told he had been. But . . . that was unimportant. There were greater things at stake here.

'No doctor, no,' he answered. 'I'll be fine.' He turned his silver lenses like small mirrors upon Wyatt's no doubt concerned face. No one else had seen the incident. He

242

leaned back in his seat, breathed deeply and said:

'Can you find my wife and bring her to me? I think I've had enough of this place for tonight.'

'Certainly,' the other answered. 'But are you well enough to be left on your own while I—'

'Of course!' Garrison snapped. 'I'm not sick, Wyatt! Nor am I a cripple!'

Wyatt stood, began to turn away. Garrison caught his elbow. 'Listen, I'm sorry I snarled. Contact me tomorrow. In the morning. Come to see me.'

'I beg your pardon?'

'You need money. I have plenty. Miller Micros have components you can use. I can help there, too . . .'

Wyatt's mouth fell open – but this time he caught himself. Like the valves of a great clam, his mind's edges clamped down tight upon themselves. He did not know how Garrison did it, no, but if there really was such a thing as telepathy – well, Garrison had already read his mind far too clearly.

'You're an amazing man,' he said. He nodded. 'Very well. Until tomorrow, then.'

Moments later Terri was back. She seemed a little anxious, a little annoyed. 'Richard, what on earth—?'

'We're leaving,' he brusquely cut her off. He dug into his pocket for a scrap of paper. 'Here's Willy's number. Give him a ring, Terri, and tell him we're ready.'

'What?' she gasped. 'But I've just started to enjoy myself, and—'

'And we're leaving.' He was adamant.

She pursed her lips, immediately relaxed and forced a smile, sat down beside him and took his hand. 'Richard, has something happened? It wasn't . . . *him*, was it?'

'Him?'

'Yes, that man you were speaking to. That was Gareth Wyatt.'

He nodded. 'Yes, I know that now.'

'Has he said something to upset you?' she flared up in a second, giving of her very best performance. 'About my mother? About me?'

'Your mother?' Garrison seemed distant, abstracted. 'You? Why should he mention you?'

'Then why do we have to—?'

'*Just give Koenig a ring, will you?*' he snapped.

When she was gone he sat back again, breathed deeply once more, drove all extraneous sounds from his ears and sensations from his body.

The Machine. *The* Machine. And Dr Gareth Wyatt had it. He had it, but needed financial assistance with it. Very well, he would get all the help he needed.

Coming from nowhere, chilly in Garrison's mind, like the final brief squall which terminates a sudden storm, there came a single word. He grabbed at it, savoured it. His mind spelled it out in letters of metal and plastic and electrical current:

Psychomech . . .

Chapter Thirteen

Between 10.00 and 11.00 A.M. on the following day Wyatt visited Garrison's house in Sussex and the two men talked in the study. Terri kept discreetly out of the way but Garrison secured Willy Koenig close to hand. In fact the German was out of sight behind a bookshelf partition, where he sat quietly and attempted to analyze the conversation between Garrison and his visitor. Garrison had briefed him on what to expect but still Koenig was astonished at the speed with which the blind man concluded his negotiations. It seemed that Garrison was able to grasp the principles of Wyatt's project as quickly as they could be explained to him; in fact where Wyatt occasionally faltered, Garrison was often able to supply the right phrase or key word to bring the psychiatrist back on course.

But that aside, by the time the two shook hands and Garrison showed Wyatt out of the study and to the main door of the house, several important points had been agreed and Garrison had guaranteed Wyatt his financial support and all the facilities available at MME. After Wyatt's car had driven away, then Koenig came out of hiding to sit with Garrison and silently consider all that had been said.

'Well?' Garrison asked eventually.

Koenig frowned. 'Richard, I've heard of that sort of machine before – or one very much like it.'

'Hitler's machine? The one he hoped would create supermen?'

'That's the one. Thomas told you about it, eh?'

'Yes he did. He also told me the only man who could build it was dead.'

Koenig nodded. 'Otto Krippner, yes. A warped genius.

245

Maybe he is, maybe he isn't. But this machine of Wyatt's certainly seems to bear a strong resemblance to Krippner's.' He frowned again. 'One thing strikes me as being especially odd. Wyatt understood the function of Psychomech, which of course he should if he designed it, but technically—'

'He seemed lost?'

'Exactly! Psychiatrist he may well be, but electronic engineer – never!'

'I agree,' said Garrison; and now he too frowned. 'Willy,' he said after a while, 'see what you can dig up on Dr Gareth Wyatt, will you? His recent past, I think. Put someone – a couple of someones – on to it. Actually, I know he's hiding something from me, but I don't know what it is. Although I suspect he has a weak or loose character, the actual mind of the man is tight as a vice. He's something of a paradox. Last night, when I caught him off-guard, a whole burst of telepathic mish-mash came crashing out of him. This morning – nothing! He told me just what he wanted to tell me, nothing more.'

'Krippner,' Koenig mused. He shook his crewcut head indecisively. 'Somehow . . . I still have a feeling he's in this somewhere. I mean, I know that Wyatt's not him. For one thing he's British as Yorkshire pudding and for another he's fifteen to twenty years too young. And yet . . .'

'I can't see any possible connection,' said Garrison. 'Even if Krippner were still alive, how could he possibly have got himself fixed up with Wyatt? No, we're probably heading right up a blind alley.' He paused. 'But at the same time—'

'Yes?'

'Let's play it safe. Who do we know who's big, Jewish and preferably with strong Israeli connections?'

'Are you trying to frighten me, Richard?' Koenig grinned, but in a moment he was serious again. 'We know a few such Jews. The best would be the biggest. How about Uri Angell in Golders Green? He has friends at the embassy. I take it you want to know if they're still tracking Krippner?'

Garrison's lenses stared at the German with an intensity that completely belied his blindness. He nodded. 'I've come to rely heavily on your judgement, my friend. Your natural instinct is often far more reliable than my own ESP. After all, instinct is clear and decisive, while ESP is often vague and misleading. For example: my original dream of the Machine, the black lake, castle and all. Prevision, yes – but I still haven't discovered what it was all about. You, on the other hand—'

'As Thomas Schroeder used to say,' Koenig cut in, 'I think my bad thoughts first. You call it instinct, I call it survival. Your survival, my survival. We are agreed that Wyatt probably did not build Psychomech. All right, my bad thoughts are these: if he didn't build it, who did? – and why does he pretend the machine is his invention? Or is it that he's afraid to mention the real inventor's name?'

'OK,' Garrison was convinced. 'I'll check out the Krippner angle myself. I'll do it through Uri Angell, as you suggest. He owes me several favours. Meanwhile there's something you can do. Drive up to Winchester, to Miller Micros. Get Jimmy Craig to come down and see me. I want to speak to him – at some length. You heard what I told Wyatt?'

'About sending your own man to check Psychomech over? Yes. Actually, I thought he jumped at it, grabbed at it while it was still on offer. And who better to send than Miller Micros' top engineer? But don't you see? That's just one more piece of evidence against Wyatt being Psychomech's inventor! I mean, if he built the machine, then why can't he repair it?'

'Money, he says. He built Psychomech off the top of his head, so to speak. He "understands" the machine, it's his baby – but he isn't up on micro-electronics. He can't specify what he doesn't understand. That's why he needs Jimmy

247

Craig. Time is of the essence, you see? This guy's up to his ears in debt – or so he makes out. He needs to make some money, and fast. That's something I can understand. Once you've had it, it's hard to do without.'

'No,' said Koenig, shaking his head, 'too pat. And there's something else.'

'Oh?'

'Surely you realize that this has to be *the* Gareth Wyatt? The same Dr Gareth Wyatt who was having it off with Terri's mother?'

'I know that, yes,' Garrison shrugged. 'Coincidence.'

'What?' Koenig was incredulous. 'You believe that?'

'Yes – no – what does it matter? Look, Willy, this is it! Psychomech is it!' Garrison slammed a fist into his palm. 'It's *the* Machine – my Machine! Nothing matters except I ride that Machine.'

At Garrison's last words Koenig felt the short hairs stiffen at the back of his bull neck. 'Richard, that was a dream,' he protested. 'Just a—'

'Just a dream? You're not being logical,' Garrison cut in, his voice sharp. He immediately softened. 'Look, Terri was a dream too. The bomb that blinded me was a dream. Jesus Christ, dream or no dream there's no other way, Willy! You must see that? Remember: "Machine – RG/TS – Light!" It's as simple as that.'

'But—'

'No buts, Willy. Psychomech *is* my Machine. The end of the quest. Schenk's horoscope working out to its final detail. Oh, Psychomech's the answer, no doubt about it – and I've got a ticket to ride . . .'

Over the space of that next summer and winter, Gareth Wyatt and Terri Garrison were extremely lucky. Lucky that Garrison's ESP powers were not more fully developed, that he could not read minds as well as he would like to. But in any case, he had no reason to suspect anything between them. Quite the reverse, for Terri would have nothing of Wyatt – would not even stay in the same vicinity with him – or so it seemed. They were also lucky that Koenig put himself only to the task of exploring Wyatt's past, not his present. If he had done that . . . then were they soon found out. As it was their liaison continued, however covertly, but passionate as ever. And Wyatt ensured that he kept it that way.

In fact now that he was getting the help he needed – and especially now that he had gone, as it were, on to Garrison's payroll – he had started to think of Terri as something more than merely a sprat to catch a mackerel. Where before she had been a girl, now she was a woman full-blown, and her appetite seemed great as Wyatt's own – her appetite for him, at least. For it appeared she was not a naturally licentious woman after all, just a woman in love. And actually, they made a good match. She was very beautiful, and blossoming more yet as a direct result of her affair with Wyatt; while he . . . he was not getting any younger.

As time passed he found thoughts such as these recurring ever more frequently. Disturbing thoughts for a man who previously loved only himself . . .

Meanwhile Koenig's detective work had paid off, and Garrison's Jewish contact had likewise proven fruitful. The answers had not been quick in coming, but by late October it was known to Koenig and Garrison that Wyatt's ex-gardener, Hans Maas, had been none other than Otto Krippner. Koenig had been perfectly correct in his suspicions: the ex-Nazi had quite obviously been Psychomech's architect.

Less than a year ago the Israelis had discovered a trail leading to Gareth Wyatt. Along with certain high-ranking members of British Intelligence they had gone to Wyatt's place, where finally the Nazi's spoor petered out. Exodus had obviously reached Krippner first and spirited him away. Where he was now (if he still lived) was anybody's guess. As for Wyatt: his story had seemed a little wishy-washy, inconclusive, but there had certainly been consistency in his rigid refusal to believe that his gardener had been a much-wanted Nazi. In fact he had ridiculed the whole idea. Nothing could be proved against him. His home had been searched with his approval for clues as to Krippner's present whereabouts, but nothing had been discovered. The entire investigation had been a very quiet affair, not the sort of thing to be brought to the attention of the general public.

No one had even bothered to question Wyatt about the huge machine in the upstairs room of his house; he was after all a doctor of sorts, and this was his place of practice. And in any case, who was there now to remember the Berlin Project? That had been a wartime thing, the aborted child of sick minds, obsolete now as the V2 rocket . . .

Koenig and Garrison knew better; Otto Krippner had finally built his machine in Wyatt's house; Psychomech was a reality.

And of course within a few days of meeting Wyatt for the first time, and long before all of this secondary information was to hand, Garrison himself had been to see Psychomech – which had proven as disappointing an experience as any he could have imagined. For at first Psychomech had not seemed to be the beast he remembered from his dream. No sleek Machine this, to ride over weird landscapes and feel between your legs vibrant with awful strength; not this great squatting, inert electronic monster of pumps and graphs and snaking cables and dead grey screens. But with each successive visit the feeling had grown stronger in him that this *was* the Machine, for if Adam Schenk's horoscopes were correct . . . why, then it simply had to be.

And as the months had passed swiftly by, so Jimmy Craig had commenced to work on the beast, ripping out parts which were at best obsolete – at worst downright dangerous! – and replacing them wherever possible with micro-components. And slowly Psychomech grew smaller and more powerful; and gradually the beast assumed, or seemed to assume, something of the shape Garrison believed he best remembered.

Craig was the best possible man for the job, but as he worked so he came across several major ambiguities. All of these he religiously brought to Garrison's attention in weekly written progress reports and soon Craig, too, was convinced that Wyatt was not the machine's inventor.

Garrison had at once cautioned Craig on this point. Not only was his work to be kept in strictest secrecy from the outside world, but he must on no account let Wyatt suspect his authority to be in any doubt where the machine was concerned. Craig could only shrug and agree. With the sort of money Garrison was paying him, he would have been a fool to do otherwise.

The machine was a work of genius, of that Craig was not in doubt. The more he studied its complex mechanisms and replaced its defunct parts, the more readily he could see and understand its functions. There were, however, those previously mentioned ambiguities.

As Wyatt had pondered before him, though on a different level, so Craig now pondered those apparently superfluous extensions or appendages of Psychomech, without which the machine would seem to function perfectly well in its primary capacity. Which prompted this obvious question: did these extra components constitute a secondary capacity, or were they merely part of the *real* primary? If the latter, what was that primary function? And these things, too, were reported to Garrison.

The blind man's interest and excitement had known no bounds. Craig was to carry on with his work, make no mention of any of this to Wyatt, continue replacing and improving whatever could be replaced and improved. He was not to concern himself with primary or secondary functions, merely to ensure that the machine would work as before, but on a higher plane of efficiency and with a greater safety factor.

. . . Which was when it first occurred to Garrison to ask Craig what had been wrong with Psychomech in the first place. The answer was illuminating indeed. Nothing had been wrong with the machine! It would have worked; there was even evidence to show that it had worked, several times, but with an extremely low safety margin. Wyatt had been quite right on that score: the original Psychomech would have been invaluable as an experimental model, but not as a fully tested machine for everyday use in a psychiatric clinic. And this way, of course, there were now blueprints. Craig had got everything down on paper, all of it. Why, working from his notes and diagrams, any fool could now build himself a Psychomech.

Of course!

That was what Wyatt had been after: the means – the plans, the technical data – to build more of them, to put them into commercial use, to make a killing. But that was not what Garrison wanted with Psychomech, not at this stage; for something warned him that it might be an extremely dangerous road to travel.

Which was why, in March of the following year and as the horoscope deadline grew steadily closer, when Craig's work was done and Psychomech was ready, Garrison ordered all of the electronic engineer's notes and blueprints brought to him so that he could personally burn them.

Psychomech was his and no other's. His dream, his reality. And the same day, when Wyatt came to see him and furiously protest his action, he told the psychiatrist his plan: that he intended to be the new Psychomech's first subject, that he himself would ride Psychomech down those weird corridors of the mind to whichever future awaited him. He had expected some opposition, but . . .

. . . There was none.

And all the while a spark in his brain grew brighter and

brighter, and ever and again he would see before his blind eyes those burning letters and words of Adam Schenk's horoscope:

'Machine – RG/TS – Light!'

Garrison's next two months were in the main given over to deliberation, preparation and planning, but all overshadowed by a sense of impending – *something*! An exhilaration previously unknown to him – a deathly thrill. Oh, he feared Psychomech a little now, certainly, but still he must ride. And while Jimmy Craig checked and re-checked his handiwork on the machine, dry-running the humming, crackling beast hour after hour, day after day, Garrison sat in the study of his own home not many miles away and pondered the strange trails his life had followed to bring him to this junction.

But at last Jimmy Craig completed his checks and reported that Psychomech was go, and from that moment on Garrison moved quickly indeed.

First he set the date with Wyatt (it was to begin on Sunday, 6 June), and signed a cheque to the tune of a quarter-million pounds in the psychiatrist's favour. This was partly to show good faith and bolster their original agreement, partly to insure his personal safety. His life would be in Wyatt's hands all the time he was on the machine. There would be a second quarter-million for the psychiatrist when, sound in mind and body – or, as Garrison preferred to think of it, sound in body and especially in mind – he climbed back down from Psychomech.

As for commercial implications, they would be looked into later. Such was Garrison's excitement now that he could not think beyond his actual ride. The general future would have to wait; his own immediate future could not.

And of course there was Suzy to be taken care of. Garrison had been worried about the bitch for some little time. It was as if she read the change in him, his sudden excitement, as if she knew something strange and vast was in the offing – something she feared.

This showed in her completely uncharacteristic shortness of temper, not only with Terri and Koenig but often with Garrison himself, something previously quite unthinkable. She would be particularly aggressive when Jimmy Craig called, as if she sensed that he was playing a large part in Garrison's change; and whenever Wyatt came on the scene, which mercifully was only very rarely, why then Suzy must actually be restrained! She openly detested the psychiatrist and had flown at him on three occasions, when only direct and repeated orders from Garrison himself had brought her to heel and saved the man from severe savagings. Nor was her hatred for Terri so well concealed these days, and on more that one occasion she had growled low in her throat at her mistress, baring her teeth at her.

As for her attitude towards Koenig: when he looked into her soft eyes and through them, into the soul behind them – it was as if he gazed in a mirror. He saw all of his own doubts and apprehensions reflected in their liquid depths, and he suspected that Suzy tolerated him because she sensed his empathy.

And yet it was only partly because of the strangeness of Suzy's behaviour – the irrational angers and foreign attitudes which made her dangerous – that Garrison decided to kennel her during the period of the Psychomech experiments. Wyatt had told him that these would take a few days, perhaps even a week, during which time and depending upon the initial results the blind man would spend up to five or six hours a day on the machine. Very well, since Suzy was no longer to be trusted she must be shut up for that entire week. Plainly it would not be safe to leave her alone with Terri, not with Willy Koenig away at the same time . . .

This was the first Koenig had heard of his being 'away' during the proposed experiments, and when Garrison told him he was taken completely by surprise. More than that, he was very concerned and very worried.

'Away?' he had blankly repeated Garrison's words. 'You want me to go away while you ride that damned machine? But surely I should be right there with you, if only to make sure nothing goes wrong. And—'

'No!' Garrison's tone had been sharp. 'No, you should be as far away as possible. It may not even be safe for you to be with me.'

'Not safe? I don't follow you.'

'Not safe for you, nor for Suzy. That's the other reason I'm putting her in the kennels.'

Koenig had stared hard, shaken his head and shrugged helplessly. 'You've lost me, Richard.'

'In my first dream,' Garrison had explained, 'I dreamed of a bomb. This was the result.' He lifted his blinkers and showed his blind, uniformly scarlet orbs. 'In my second dream there was another bomb – but this time it was aimed at you!'

Now Koenig had grown angry. 'But this is England, Richard, not Northern Ireland – and I'm pretty damned good at looking after myself! Also, you've said yourself that your ESP is often vague and misleading. Granted your first dream was partly prophetic, but how can you be so sure that the second wasn't simply – well, an ordinary dream, a nightmare? And anyway, didn't Suzy save you in that second dream? Didn't she drag you from the Machine just as the bomb exploded?'

'That's just it,' Garrison had answered. 'She *tried* to save me, to drag me from the Machine – but that can't be allowed to happen. I have to go on, across the lake, into the black castle. I have to find the Black Room. I have to know what's in there. Can't you see that?'

Koenig had slowly nodded. 'So the way you see it, the first dream was partly prevision while the second was pure warning?'

'Not exactly. Both of them were prevision and warning

combined. If I had heeded the first warning I wouldn't be blind now. That's why I have to heed the second warning. Look, the second bomb may be sheer symbolism, I don't know. Symbolic of some danger to you, that is. Well, I don't want you to be in any sort of danger. And not just because you're my main man. In my dream your being in danger hindered my quest. That mustn't happen. Nothing must hinder my quest. That's why I'm sending you away.'

'Mein Gott!' Koenig had exploded then, stamping to and fro in the study where they talked and astonishing Garrison with his uncharacteristic outburst. 'All this on the strength of a verfluchte dream?'

'More than a dream, Willy!' Garrison had insisted. 'Can't you see it working even now? Think! Do you remember what I said you cried out to me in that dream? "Get off the Machine, Richard," you cried. You were trying to stop my ride. So was Suzy. And sure enough, *the two of you are trying to stop it right now!*'

'But—'

'The *hell* with buts! I have to ride. I have to know. And what of my pact with your beloved Colonel?'

'Your pact?' The German's jaw had dropped. 'I had . . . forgotten!'

'Oh, no, Willy,' Garrison shook his head. 'You hadn't forgotten! It's just that the years have changed your perspective, that's all. Forgotten? Not you. Shit, you think he's already in me! That's true, isn't it? Well he isn't, and I'm not so bloody sure I want him! But don't worry, I'm not going to run out on him. At least I'll give him the chance to make it – if he's strong enough. But that's something else I have to find out.'

'The pact,' Koenig had softly repeated, nodding his head. 'Of course.'

And now, knowing he had won, Garrison relaxed. He too nodded. 'So you see, there's no other way. I ride. And you, and Suzy – the pair of you keep out of my way.'

'Yes,' the German slowly answered, 'I think I see it now.'

'Book a holiday for yourself somewhere in Germany,' Garrison had ordered then. 'The Retreat, if you like. Anywhere – but make sure you do it. I'll want to see the tickets, Willy, and I'll want to be there to see you off when you board the plane . . .'

At 10.00 A.M. on Wednesday 2 June Suzy was delivered to the kennels in Midhurst.

The journey was not a long one, little more than half an hour, but the atmosphere in the car was tangibly strained. Suzy was not happy. She whined continuously and licked Garrison's hand with a frenetic tongue.

For of course the bitch knew where she was going. She had picked it straight out of Garrison's mind, had confirmed it in Terri's controlled smugness and in Koenig's own dissatisfaction; and she did not like being sent away any more than the German liked it.

At the kennels she made a scene, yelping and snarling until Garrison was obliged to enter her into her cage. Then she was docile enough, but as soon as the steel mesh door had closed on her and her master got back into the Mercedes she set up such a howling that he must immediately dismount and command her to be still and good. And as the great silver car drove away Suzy had sat there behind a mesh of steel, her eyes softer and more moist than ever, so that anyone watching her must swear that she was crying.

'That animal', said Terri as Koenig turned on to the motorway and headed for Gatwick, 'is mad and ungovernable. The time will come, Richard, when even you will lose your authority with her.'

Garrison, now seated in the front beside Koenig, inclined his head slightly back and towards her. 'Suzy is completely sane,' he told her, his voice flat and even. 'Saner by far than any six of your so-called "socialite" friends . . . and she has

more sheer brain than any dozen of them! As for loyalty—'
and he had paused.

'Yes?' Her voice was slightly haughty, but Garrison
sensed a wary probing behind the apparently automatic
response.

'She is very loyal,' he eventually answered.

Terri sniffed but said no more, and a moment later
Koenig broke the awkward silence with: 'Sir, my plane
leaves at 12.45. I calculate a wait of at least an hour. There
really is no need for you and Mrs Garrison to put
yourselves out by seeing me on my way.'

'No trouble, Willy,' Garrison answered. 'It's just that I'll
be happier knowing you're safely aboard.'

Koenig knew what he meant: that he was to get out of
England – quite definitely out – and stay out until this thing
was over. Once aboard the plane there would be no turning
back. Like Suzy, he was being temporarily banished. Both
of them, for their own safety. For the good of Garrison's
dream-quest.

But what of your own safety, Richard? Koenig silently
asked. *What of your good?*

He lapsed into a watchful, unhappy silence, but in the
back Terri smiled smugly and congratulated herself. First
Suzy out of the way, and now Koenig. And on Sunday, just
four days away, Richard himself – for the better part of a
week!

She thought about it for a while, then let the smile slip
from her face and allowed herself an inaudible sigh. If only
it were for a year, or even longer. If only it were—

Forever . . . ?

On Thursday Garrison had business people down from the
Midlands to see him. Normally he would have had Koenig
in attendance but on this occasion handled it himself.

He felt more or less obliged to listen to them and spend
most of the day with them, however, and so had written it

off entirely to business talk and entertainment. Terri, who was not much good at the former and had her own ideas about the latter, went 'into the city' by train to see friends. In fact she did not go to London but left the train at Arundel to meet Gareth Wyatt. They spent the day at a charming, sprawling hotel in the town, whose bar was cosy and discreet and where their room was adequately intimate.

There, in the crisp, clean sheets of their bed, they made various sorts of love for many hours and to their complete satisfaction, then talked of their hopes for the future – especially the immediate future. For during the last six months their lives had changed so completely that neither one of them would ever have believed it could be like this. They were, in short, desperately in love; their resumed affair had blossomed out of all proportion and quite beyond their control.

Now, lying in Wyatt's arms while he stroked her breasts and kissed her throat, Terri had just asked him how long they would have together each day when Richard was on the machine.

'About five hours or so. He'll go on to Psychomech about 11.00 each morning and stay until 5.00. After that he'll be pretty groggy for an hour or two. He won't be coming home at all during that week. It's to be a very exacting routine for him. I expect Psychomech to drain him both emotionally and physically, even though he professes to have no hangups. It will be machine, sleep, food and drink, a little exercise, machine again, and so on.'

'What's all this about hangups?' she asked.

'That's what Psychomech is for, silly: to cure neuroses and psychoses. Richard doesn't believe he has any, but you may be sure he has. Curing them will be a great strain on him. If he's hidden them away, Psychomech will have to dig that much deeper, that's all. But afterwards—' he shrugged. 'He'll be the better man for it.'

'And while he's actually on the machine, you'll have all

that time to be with me?'

He held her close for a moment. 'Oh, yes. The process is quite automatic. I need only check the safety margins every now and then. The rest of the time will be ours.'

'And afterwards you'll be richer to the tune of half a million!' She snuggled closer to his warm, firm body.

'That's only starters,' he answered. 'If all goes well Psychomech will soon be making us a great deal more money than that. Miller Micros will build more machines, and of course I shall demand control of the patents.'

'And that's when we'll let Richard find out about us – which is when he'll divorce me.'

Wyatt pushed her gently away to arms' length and stared at her. She was so utterly lovely he knew he had to have her for his own. For the first time in his life he, too, was now truly and deeply in love. And yet he frowned.

'Is something wrong?' Her voice was suddenly full of anxiety.

'Yes,' he answered, 'something is wrong. It may not be as easy as all that, Terri. If Richard wants to fight it—'

'Fight the divorce, you mean? Then I would simply come away with you.'

'But you've told me he loves you.'

'He does, as much as he can love anyone. I'm sure of it. But I'm not necessary to him. I *am* necessary to you, and you to me.'

'Yes, I know,' he nodded patiently, 'but that wouldn't stop him from taking me for every penny I had! And then we'd be back where we started. On the other hand—' Something he had said to her a minute earlier kept repeating in his memory.

'Yes?'

'If all does *not* go well—'

She froze in his arms. 'But you said Psychomech was a hundred per cent safe!'

He tried to relax a little and smiled, but she could see that

260

his smile was forced. 'Well, it's all still very experimental, you know. I mean, how do you carry out dry-runs on a machine like Psychomech? Richard will be sort of a guinea pig. That's why I've insisted he signs an indemnity. We're doing that tomorrow, at your place.'

'God, yes, he mentioned it!' she said. 'To see you and not to be able to touch you.'

'I know,' he stroked her, '—but at least that damned dog is out of the way.'

She nodded. 'And Koenig. He's so watchful, that man.'

'Yes, but it seems the coast is pretty clear for us now.' He paused again, suddenly restless, clasping her to him so that she could not see his eyes. 'But if something were to go wrong . . . I mean, if he were actually to die on the machine—'

He felt her body stiffen once more, then slowly relax. 'I'm Richard's sole beneficiary, so far as I know,' she said, her voice very quiet. She drew back and gazed steadily at him.

'You would be an incredibly rich woman,' he told her, just as quietly.

She pulled him close, buried her head in his chest, felt him stirring against her. 'But nothing will go wrong . . . will it?' She drew him into her body, her flesh a soft vice as her hips began their gentle gyrations.

'No, of course not,' he answered, finding amazement in the fact that they had started to make love yet again, and at such a juncture. 'And don't worry about us, Terri. Things will work out. Just see if they don't . . .'

11.00 A.M. Sunday 6 June, and Garrison, clad only in a short-sleeved dressing gown, went on to the machine. As soon as consciousness slipped away and Psychomech took over, Wyatt left the room of the machine and half an hour later Terri was with him. There were only the three of them

261

in the entire house. Or rather, four of them – if Psychomech itself were included.

11.00 A.M. and in the Midhurst kennels Suzy, the great black Dobermann bitch, set up such a yelping and screaming – her screams sounding like nothing so much as those of a human being – that a keeper in a protective suit had to enter her cage and sedate her heavily. But Suzy was ever a quick learner. She would not scream again, not until it suited her purpose – and the next time she would make sure there was no sedation.

11.00 A.M. and in his hotel room in Hamburg overlooking the Reeperbahn, Willy Koenig jerked spastically on his bed and dropped his Keil cigarillo. The naked whore he was with mistook his spasm for something else and moved her hand climactically on his flesh, only pausing when there was no positive result. Then she delicately picked up his smoke by its plastic mouthpiece and placed it back between his lips, her hand returning at once to a member gone suddenly limp.

'Ist etwas los, Willy? What's wrong, mein Schatz?' she asked. 'You come without coming?'

He stared at the ceiling in silence for a moment, then looked at her. 'I didn't come, no.' He looked at his watch. 'It's 11.00 A.M. in England right now.'

'So?'

He shrugged. 'I should be there, that's all.'

'Oh, Willy!' she pouted, removing the cigar from his mouth and leaning over to replace it with her left nipple. 'But isn't it so much nicer here?'

Again he shrugged. 'Actually, I have no choice.' He forced a short, barking laugh. 'You have big sweet tits, Hannelore,' he told her. He was big again, beginning to throb. 'Sit on me.'

Happily, she complied . . .

Chapter Fourteen

12.20 A.M.

Garrison was drawn into the whorl of his own mind like a comet rushing down the throat of a black hole. Drawn backwards through years he remembered to those earlier years before memory began, years of infancy and first fear, he was suddenly a child again. But as is the way of things in dreams, he knew that he was also Richard Garrison, a man full-grown, and that his quest had commenced.

A man full-grown, yes, but clad now in a body and mind weak as those of a puling babe. A paradox and a riddle – but what sort of riddle?

As the whirling slowed and finally stopped, leaving Garrison's child mind tottery as a drunkard, he found himself deep in dreams, in a recurrent nightmare from his earliest years. He was an infant, and the room he found himself in was largely his world, with a dirty-white ceiling-sky and pink-wall horizons (his parents had wanted a girl, if they had wanted any child at all) and a gleaming square window-sun to let in the light. Except that now the window was dark for the night had come again.

The night had come – and She was not here. A child knows its mother, even a mother without love, and senses her presence or her absence. Now it was her absence, which always went hand in hand with the night. She had used to work at night to keep Garrison's father in money to drink and to spend on his women.

Garrison let out a little wail of a cry, his lips puckering in the manner of a disturbed child. He knew this dream dredged up from the murky deeps of twenty-eight years, knew and feared it. And he had every right to fear it, for at some

263

obscure point on the periphery of his mind he was still the
adult Richard Garrison and remembered Psychomech. And he
knew what Psychomech could do to this childhood dream.

It began.

The pink walls faded into dull pink shadows as a vast door
opened to let in bright electric light, hurting Garrison's eyes.
He rubbed at his eyes and turned his head away – but not
before he had seen through the bars of his crib a dark man-
silhouette framed against the brightness, from which his
father's voice had whispered:

'Shhh! We don't want to wake the little shit up. It would be
no fun with him bawling his bloody head off!'

And Garrison heard too the coarse giggle of a woman and
knew that it was not his mother's laugh. But he did not cry,
not with his father out there beyond the door and the night
outside beyond the window. He dared not cry, for if he
did . . . his father's hand was a heavy one, and She was not
here . . .

1.10 P.M.

Psychomech quietly purred and hummed, and strapped
to its padded bench Garrison's body twitched and jerked.
He moaned a little, which alone would have indicated that
Psychomech had found a vulnerable spot in his psyche, a
target.

The machine dug deeper, exciting Garrison's fear-
centres, exploding his deep-rooted, shadowy fear-dream
into a vivid full-blown shrieking nightmare . . .

The pink walls had now completely faded away into
sulphurous horizons, the dirty-white ceiling dissolving into a
leaden sky. Garrison lay naked and helpless, a man with the
strength of a baby, gazing out through the bars of his crib at
the bubbling marsh which stretched away in all directions as
far as the eye could see. He caught at the vertical bars, pulling
himself to his knees. The quicksand streamed from his thighs,

fell from his chest and forearms in splattering, stinking gobs.

He was sinking, the crib too, settling down slowly into depths of liquid filth; but in his baby's mind he did not recognize the danger and his child's eyes saw only Da-da . . . the Da-da who hated him – Da-da and his women and his booze.

There they lay, a dozen Da-das, identical upon a dozen old-fashioned identically rickety beds; and with the Da-das a dozen different slatternly women, one to each Da-da, peaky-faced and big-, loose-breasted. That had been the type he liked – like Garrison's mother herself – 'poor desperate women who were too morally weak to refuse him, or to whom the Fates had delivered blows so powerful that they had not been left with the strength to fight back. And the twelve Da-das like a dozen rutting pigs, slavering, eyes bulging, as their bodies worked frenziedly upon those of the women in as many varieties of the sex act. And where baby Garrison sank in the mire, the Da-das and the women in their beds did not sink but frothed and fornicated and laughed coarsely as they drank of each other's bodies and of the bottles which littered the marsh beside each groaning, creaking bed.

The mud bubbled as the crib sank down several more shuddering inches into it, and slime oozed half-way up Garrison's thighs. He sobbed – and at once held his breath in a frozen gasp! – but too late. They had heard.

'Look!' the slatternly women shouted, their breasts jouncing as they kneeled in their beds the better to see Garrison, pointing at him. 'Your little boy – he can see us! You left his bedroom door open . . .'

'So?' the dozen Da-das roared in unison. 'So bleedin' what? He don't know nothin', do he? I mean, he ain't goin' to tell his mother, now is he? See, he can't bleedin' talk yet!'

And the dozen sluts cackling like witches as the Da-das mounted them where they kneeled and the beds recommenced their swaying and creaking.

The real Garrison had heard and understood what was said,

but baby Garrison had heard only the shouting. He clutched at the steadily sinking bars of the crib, the mire up to his loins, and the tears rolled steadily down his man's cheeks. First the shouting, then the swinging, stinging hand on his baby flesh. That was always the way of it, it was always the same. Except . . . sometimes Ma-ma would come, and sometimes she would stop him.

'Ma-ma!' he wailed, quietly at first. But then, as the enraged Da-das sprang from their beds like a dozen drunken robots, he cried louder, and louder still: 'Ma-ma! Ma-maaaaa!'

1.30 P.M.

Wyatt slipped out of bed and put on a dressing gown. Terri lay between black sheets, her white arms and breasts showing. She stared at him through dark, anxious eyes. At first she had not been completely at ease with Richard so close, but then the idea had started to appeal to her. She remembered someone once telling her that libertines find their pleasure and excitement not so much in sin itself as in the *knowledge* that they are sinning.

But now, as he made to leave the bedroom, she felt uncomfortable once more. 'Gareth . . . will you be long?'

'Not long.' He spoke quietly, as if afraid Garrison might hear him. He too was nervous, but sure now of the course to be taken, this golden opportunity he could not afford to miss.

'Will it be . . . all right?' Again the anxiety, and of course he knew what she meant. Without ever discussing it, or only in the vaguest of terms, the two had come to a decision: that Richard Garrison must not be allowed to return from his trip. That when finally he came down from the machine it must be as a corpse.

'It will be all right, yes.'

*   *   *

. . . But in the shadow of Psychomech's bulk, Wyatt suddenly felt small and afraid.

Garrison strained and jerked upon his padded couch. Sweat streamed from the blind man's contorted face and body. A crisis? Already? As secondary systems hummed into activity, Wyatt turned to the controls.

A crisis, yes. Garrison's fear-centres had responded to the machine's electronic probing. He was now in the throes of a nightmare and Psychomech in turn was responding to his needs; was beginning to feed him raw power, the energies he needed to help him overcome his personal demons.

Wyatt reached out a hand that barely trembled. It was easier this time. Much easier than it had been with Maas-Krippner. There was the form of indemnity; and there was Terri; and there was all that money. And of course there was Psychomech itself. Wyatt hesitated no longer but quickly and deliberately set the controls to manual and turned down the three knurled knobs which controlled the feeder systems. The recently introduced humming sound declined in pitch, faded, was gone.

Garrison was stranded now, marooned in one of his own worst nightmares . . .

The Da-das sprang at him.

They sprang at the man-baby Garrison across the morass, which miraculously held them up while he continued to sink. 'Ma-ma? Ma-ma?' they cried, their identical faces dark with rage. They grasped the rim of the crib and thrust it down into quicksand, then stood over his naked, cringing, sinking figure, their hands uplifted as one. 'She's out. Out, do you hear?' and their hands came slicing down, slapping Garrison's face, his arms, back and chest.

'No, no!' cried the twelve sluts, their breasts awobble as they crouched on the rickety beds, knuckles to their mouths.

267

'Don't hit the poor wee thing! He's frightened.'

'Frightened? Frightened?' roared the Da-das. 'So he bleedin' should be, the little—' And they lifted their hands again.

The ooze was up to Garrison's waist now, and the single remaining adult spark on the rim of his mind finally saw and recognized his danger.

LEAVE HIM BE! said a Voice.

The Da-das stumbled back from the almost sunken crib, their raised arms falling limp as rags as their mouths fell open and their eyes turned up to the sky. And there, a face—

The face of the man-God Schroeder!

Garrison saw that face in the dirty sky, that awesome visage, and the baby side of him screamed in terror. But the tiny man-spark knew!

Now, while the Da-das and their women huddled on their rickety beds in fear, Schroeder's face approached, huge and awful and staring. I HAVE COME, RICHARD. NOW HONOUR OUR PACT. LET ME IN.

The upper rim of the crib was sucked gurglingly out of sight, leaving Garrison up to his chest in mire. He forced his untrained baby's mouth to speak yet again. 'N-n-no!'

THEN YOU DIE, HERE AND NOW!

'Th-th-then we both die!'

As the mud crept up to his neck and the sluts and Da-das began a weird wailing, the man-God pondered the situation. VERY WELL, he said. The slime began to lap just beneath Garrison's chin. THEN YOU MUST CALL ON THE MACHINE, RICHARD – AND QUICKLY!

The Machine!

Garrison remembered, reached out with desperate ESP fingers. He scanned, searched, saw—

Called.

'Machine!' he called with both mind and child-voice. 'Psychomech, come to me!'

The Machine came – in a loud crackling of electrical energies and a mechanical thunder – came and hovered over *the quicksand, then sank down out of sight in gulping mud that swallowed it without trace. A heart-stopping moment later ... and Garrison felt Psychomech's bulk beneath him, lifting him, thrusting up and out of the sucking slime.*

THE MACHINE IS YOURS NOW, RICHARD, *the man-God's face swiftly shrank and receded into distance,* —IF YOU CAN CONTROL IT. ONLY USE IT WELL!

Garrison sprawled across the Machine. Both he and Psychomech dripped filth as they rose up clear of the bubbling, sucking surface. 'Machine,' the ESP-endowed man-spark in his child's mind reached out once more. 'Machine, please help me. Help me!'

And Psychomech responded ...

In its room Psychomech gently purred, squatting down like a great well-satisfied cat, with Garrison a drenched mouse that quivered and sweated and played dead between powerful paws. A mouse with a mind of its own. A mouse who could not defeat and therefore must befriend the tormentor.

With his mind, Garrison stroked the beast.

Uncertainly at first, then more surely, three knurled knobs on the machine's control panel began to turn. Nothing visible touched them, no hand was near then, and yet they turned. The hum increased marginally, steadying into a rhythmic throb as the knobs came to a halt ...

Less than two dozen paces away, oblivious in their resurgent lust, Terri and Wyatt licked and teased and bit, inverted and sinuously twining, white against black where the bed covers and top sheet had been brushed aside by their love-play. As their excitement reached fever-pitch they hurriedly righted themselves and he mounted her. Moments later, spent and freely perspiring, they collapsed together. And as the oblivion receded – as the dark red roaring of their simultaneous climax faded from their minds and bodies – so the other thoughts came flooding back.

Eventually Terri asked: 'When will it be? The . . . accident, I mean.'

He lit a cigarette. 'It may have already been.'

She breathed in deeply and held it for a moment, and he felt her already racing heartbeat pick up fractionally against his own pounding chest. Then the tension went out of her and she softened against him. She reached up, took his cigarette from him and drew heavily upon it, then sighed and in a low voice said, 'While we're in here making love?'

'Yes. What better way to obliterate it, wipe it from our minds? At least for a little while . . .'

She trembled a little as the sweat of passion dried on her skin. 'He once told me that the French call orgasm the Little Death.'

'Stop it, Terri!' Wyatt's voice was harsh. 'No good being morbid about it now.'

'I wasn't being morbid.' She pulled back and stared at him, then smiled a half-smile. 'I think it's very beautiful, that moment. It's what life is all about. And it is a sort of Little Death. You said so yourself: an obliteration, a wiping clean.'

He nodded, took the cigarette from her fingers and stubbed it out, drew her back to him, thinking: *A Little Death, yes – but right now he's in there with Psychomech, and he is suffering! No Little Death for Richard Garrison, Terri my love. It's the Big One for him, the biggest one of all . . .*

3.30 P.M.

Wyatt sat on the edge of the bed and made up a fictional log of the experiment, the events leading up to Garrison's death. He meticulously falsified times, checks, bio-function levels, physical responses and brain activity readings, ticking off each entry to show no abnormality.

Obviously Garrison's heart had not been up to the experiment. The explanation would be simple as that. It would be the work of less than one hour to dummy up the machine's automatic record to agree with his log.

Behind him, wrapped in black and pale as death in her exhausted repose, Terri slept. Wyatt, too, was tired, but there was still work to be done. By now Garrison was most likely dead. Obviously dead. Without Psychomech's backup, no subject could suffer indefinitely the horrors of his own blackest nightmares. If he was not dead, however . . . then Wyatt would simply increase the degree of fear stimulation.

He shuddered. *What a hell of a way to go!* – then caught himself tight and forced the thought from his head. Too late now for pity.

Leaving Terri asleep (a troubled sleep despite her exhaustion, for she rolled this way and that) he went to the room of the machine. There, staring at Garrison upon his couch, Wyatt broke out in a cold sweat. His panic was momentary before common-sense took over. He had made a mistake, bungled it. There was no other explanation.

For while Garrison had lost a little weight in perspiration, still he was alive. Incredibly, the monitors showed all of his bodily functions to be in order and working normally. The figure on Psychomech's couch seemed relaxed, even appeared to have a grim sort of smile upon its waxen face.

Feeling goose-flesh rising on his back and arms, Wyatt stepped to the control panel. He turned up fear-stimulation, turned down the backup systems – and froze. He cursed himself for a fool. Too late now to check, but he had thought for a moment that the backup knobs were set too high. And it had seemed that Psychomech's electronic guts hummed a fraction too loudly. Impossible, for of course he himself had turned the backups down a little over two hours ago.

He shook his head and frowned. So what had gone wrong?

Somehow Psychomech had leaked aid to Garrison, obviously, else he were now dead. Very well, this time there would be no mistake; he would leave no margin for error. He turned the backup knobs all the way down until they clicked into the 'off' position.

At least it would be quick now . . .

Terri was awake. She glanced at her wrist-watch where it lay on a bedside table. 'Oh!' Her hand flew to her mouth. She saw the strained look on Wyatt's face. 'Is he . . . ?'

'No,' Wyatt answered, his throat dry. 'But it shouldn't be long.'

She propped herself up with pillows. 'Does it . . . I mean, will it—'

'Will he feel it? Is that what you're asking? Does it hurt? No,' he lied. 'It's just that he's asleep and he won't wake up again, that's all.'

'Sometimes,' her breathing quickened, 'I feel so sorry for him. But—'

'But? Are there any buts?'

'Only one: but I love you.'

'Love and murder,' he answered after a while, his mind miles away. 'Strange bedfellows.'

'Don't say that!' she gasped.

'What, murder? Well, it's true. And we're in it together. I hope you realize that, Terri – that however it goes from now on, we're in it together all the way?'

She nodded, then squeezed her eyes shut and shook her head, and finally drew back the sheet that covered her, exposing her beautiful body to him. She opened her eyes and moved voluptuously, as she knew he liked to see her move. 'I don't want to think any more,' she said. 'Thinking only hurts. I want to feel you inside me again.'

Wyatt threw off his dressing gown and got into bed with her. She reached for him, warm against his chill, and in a matter of moments all else was driven from his mind.

Sweet obliteration . . .

*　　*　　*

Garrison's ride had been easy so far.

The quicksand episode, ephemeral as the dream it was, had almost faded from his memory now. Now he remembered only the conclusion and that too was quickly, mercifully fading. Mercifully, yes, for it had not been pleasant.

Psychomech's strength had flowed into him and increased his man-Garrison awareness, driving fear from him and healing the infancy-spawned and until now long-forgotten mental lesion. Then he had known anger, and almost as a reflex action had struck back at the Da-das and their sluts – lashing out with his mind, through Psychomech.

Twelve rickety beds had gone down into the mire, carrying twelve screaming, still frantically coupling couples with them. Then there had remained only the bursting of greasy bubbles, following which even the tatty bed linen had been sucked down out of sight.

After that the infant Garrison had quickly dissolved back into dim and terrible times of infancy; and Garrison the man, not once looking back, had ridden Psychomech out of the swamplands to follow a falling sun . . .

Now the swamp lay far behind and he travelled at a leisurely pace low over a land of rolling hills and grassy plains, a land looking like nothing so much as the downs of Sussex remembered from his days as a fledgling Military Policeman. Not that he actually remembered those days, no (it seemed to him perfectly natural that he should now be here, where his real past no longer mattered or even existed for him), it was just that he felt he knew this place from some strange and dreamy former time.

But now he goaded the Machine to greater speed. The sun was sinking fast over the distant hills, and shadows and darkness crept apace. If he did not hurry they must soon overtake him, those shadows, and he had yet to find sanctuary for the night.

Sanctuary. A warm and friendly place. A place where he would not be rejected.

Rejected. The word came into and went out of Garrison's mind in a single instant. But its echo remained. Rejection. That had been a hangup, too, unrecognized until now. Rejection . . .

He was startled by the sudden chill breeze which struck at his flesh through his clothing as the sun's last ray threw the hills into silhouette. Strange that he had not noticed his clothing before; but now he saw that he wore an open-necked, long-sleeved shirt and a pair of light brown cord trousers. And his feet were clad in track-shoes. He had liked to run when he was younger. He seemed to remember that. There had been tremendous freedom in it. But—

—How does one run from rejection?

Rejection . . .

The sun had deserted him now. No, not deserted, rejected; had turned her face from him. Only her afterglow remained, a pink-purple stain on the tops of the hills. He had almost reached those hills, flogging the Machine on like a wild man, urging more speed from the metal and plastic flyer whose broad back he rode across the face of this strange world.

Yes, and this world was strange now, and ominous with shadows and cold, unstirring air. He glanced down at the terrain that hurtled beneath him, and he saw how strange and terrible it had grown.

Where there had been rolling plains of grass, now spiky ridges of white rock reared up menacingly like rows of serrated needle-teeth, threatening to snap shut on Garrison and the Machine. And long, furtive night creatures darted from shadow to shadow, showing only their burning eyes and sinuous, leathery outlines as they moved.

Garrison shuddered. If he should fall here . . . he might survive the rocks, but never those darting night scavengers.

Gratefully he hugged his body to the Machine – and yet even as he did so it seemed to him that perhaps the beast's flight was a little less speedy and its elevation somewhat lower above the jagged spires of rock. He breathed deeply of the chilly air, held his breath, concentrated all his attention upon the Machine and its flight.

And yes, its power really was waning, growing weaker along with the weakening light. Garrison's heart skipped a beat then – but in the next moment the Machine had soared across the summit of the hills, and below him in the valley—

A light!

A warm light in the darkness.

Garrison rode the Machine down into the valley, the light growing brighter and taking on shape and form. He saw now that it was not one light but many, a great domed city of lights, all friendly and gleaming and golden. This must surely be the place he sought, the place of sanctuary—

Surely . . . ?

He stood off for a moment to observe, becoming quickly fascinated with what he saw. For across the valley floor streamed hundreds of people, travellers from the four corners of this weird world; and all of them making for the gates where the great curve of the domed city's wall sank down into the valley's floor.

That domed and golden city, like a mighty beehive of metal and glass, with massive circular porthole windows looking out upon the valley, and all the people streaming through the yawning gates. And they were beautiful, privileged people, for whom the city meant food and drink and rest, sanctuary from all the terrors of the night.

The last of them entered through the gates, tail-end of a mighty caravan gladly swallowed up in a great and glorious oasis. Garrison gasped and urged the Machine forward. He had been hypnotized, spellbound, but now he too must go in through the gates before—

They closed on him!

Before he could reach them, with a great sighing of air and a massive clanging of metal against metal, they closed. They shut him out, left him to the cold and the night and the darkness.

275

The gates, the city, the beautiful people – they all rejected him!

He rode up to the gates, alongside them, hammered on them uselessly with his fists. He floated up to the windows, gazing in wild-eyed upon the people where they ate and drank and played and loved and were warm. He shook his futile fists at them. 'Why me? Why me?'

They heard him, flocked to the great circular windows, stared out at him, curiously at first. Then their curiosity turned to jeering, to harsh, uncaring laughter, and at last he saw that they were not the beautiful people he had taken them to be.

For the women all wore similar faces: those of his mother and of every girl or woman who ever rejected him in however small a way; and the men had the faces of his father, his stepfather, school teachers, Sergeants, Sergeant-majors and officers. Not that he truly recognized these faces he saw (or at best as the very vaguest of memories) but he knew that all of these people, at one time or another, had rejected him – and that now they were doing it again.

And all around him the unknown, malefic darkness, and the only light that which streamed out from the golden city's circular windows – which even now were closing one by one!

Garrison flew his now straining Machine to the last window, gazing in and crying: 'Let me in! Let me in!'

THEY WON'T, RICHARD, *the man-God Schroeder's face suddenly loomed huge and dark in a dark sky.* THEY REJECT YOU JUST AS YOU HAVE REJECTED ME. NOW YOU KNOW HOW IT FEELS. BUT IF YOU WILL ONLY LET ME IN, THEN—

'No!' Garrison snarled. 'I beat them all before and I can do it again. I beat them at their own game. The trick is to turn their own weapon against them. They reject you, so you reject them – utterly! I reject them with my mind, kill them off utterly – in my mind!'

IT WON'T WORK THIS TIME, RICHARD. YOU

MUST SEE THAT. YOU ARE BEATEN. AND YOUR MACHINE, TOO. CAN'T YOU FEEL ITS STRENGTH EBBING? YOU HAVEN'T THE TIME FOR TRICKS OR TACTICS OR MIND GAMES. JUST LOOK ABOUT YOURSELF . . .

Garrison looked all about in the darkness.

As the Machine slowly drifted towards the floor of the valley, female figures black as blots of ink flowed forward. Lamias of Loneliness, they were, their curving white fangs agleam in red-rimmed mouths. And overhead, around and about in the still cold air, scything shapes of darkness swept the night: Vampires of the Aching Void, whose talons were sharp and cold as ice-shards, whose thirst was that of the scorched desert. And behind that single window, safe in the golden city, the hostile, uncaring faces stared out as before.

LET ME IN, RICHARD!

'No! I'll beat them, I tell you!'

HOW? HOW CAN YOU HOPE TO HOLD BACK THE DARKNESS, THE LAMIAS OF LONELINESS, THE COLD OF NIGHT, THE VAMPIRES OF THE ACHING VOID? HOW, RICHARD?

'With my mind, damn you!' Garrison shouted, hardly knowing that the words were his. 'Don't you remember? After all, you showed me the way. But you've been a long time dead, man-God, and you don't know how far I've gone . . .'

THEN SHOW ME, RICHARD, SHOW ME.

Garrison threw himself flat on the broad back of the Machine, squeezed his eyes shut and concentrated. He called upon the same power which had drawn the Machine to him in the quicksand. He poured his mental strength into Psycho-mech, became one with the Machine, then desperately sought out the source of the power loss—

—And found it!

In the room of the machine a weird change came over the unconscious, dreaming, beleaguered Garrison. He stopped writing on his couch and his body grew still. His frantic pulse rapidly regulated. His face grew stern as a frown, then soft as fresh snow, then rapt in concentration. His hands curled into tight fists.

The three knurled knobs on Psychomech's control panel – the controls for the feeder systems – suddenly, simultaneously clicked into the 'on' position, then turned themselves up, and up, to the limit of their calibration – and began to glow with an incredible heat! In a very short while they melted down, the smoking plastic liquefying and fixing the knobs permanently in that position.

And as Psychomech hummed and purred with a new vitality, so Garrison relaxed upon his couch and smiled an awful smile . . .

The golden city was silent now. No sounds of revelry came floating through its massy walls; no echoes of joyous laughter; even the last window had commenced to close its shutter, but very slowly, where crowding faces gazed out upon Garrison and jostled for better viewing positions.

Garrison was fighting for his life, they knew it, and the outcome of his fight was all-important – to them as well as to him. They had rejected him, cast him out, refused him entry. And if he won his fight? What then? No, they did not want him to win.

The belly of the gently settling Machine touched the soil of the valley's floor and came to rest. Its hum faded into silence. Dim lights within its black and silvery frame flickered out. The man upon its back remained spread-eagled, as if frozen in that position. And indeed he might well have been frozen; for ice-crystals were forming on the earth and rocks, and snow had commenced to drift down from the night sky in flat flakes as big as fists. And as the shutter slowly fell on the last window and its beam of light narrowed down, so the night-things gathered; and soon the cold and darkness would reign supreme over all.

Then—

The Lamias of Loneliness, black in their inky night-rags,

white fangs gleaming, pounced upon the Machine. They fell upon it and held it down; and others of their band made to pounce upon Garrison. And descending out of the black sky and the white drifting snow, hovering on ragged membrane wings, down came those legions of the lost, those eaters of forsaken souls, the Vampires of the Aching Void; and they too settled upon Garrison where he hugged the back of the now inert Machine. And Lamias and Vampires fought to be first with him.

And while they fought—

Psychomech began stutteringly to purr and dull lights flickered into life deep within its metal and plastic mass. And as power flowed once more within the Machine, so strength returned to Garrison where he huddled to its back. He rose up, hurling the Lamias of Loneliness from him, his fists flailing like warclubs and crunching the fragile bones of the fluttering Vampires of the Aching Void.

Rejection?

Reject Richard Garrison?

Reject Psychomech?

The Machine's hum was now a roar of power. Power crackled and lashed within the beast like trapped lightning. The internal lights flashed dazzling and multi-hued, turning the Machine into a great coruscating diamond.

'Rise up!' Garrison ordered then. 'Lift me up to that window. Let them see me. Let them see how I've won!'

And Psychomech rose up, its lights a throb of colour, its power the snarling of primal beasts. And Garrison the master astride the beast's back – Garrison the Phoenix rising from the Ashes of Rejection – Garrison the Avenger!

Lamias fell like black rain amidst the white, whirling snow, shaken off as fleas from Psychomech's underbelly to crash in ruin down to the valley floor. And all the screaming, thirsty Vampires were driven back from Garrison and Psychomech, hurled headlong in a panic flight by the sheer power of the man and Machine.

'Rejection?' he cried at the white faces in the window as finally

the shutter closed on them. 'You reject me? Then damn you all! Damn every last one of you!'

I DID NOT REJECT YOU, RICHARD. *The man-God Schroeder's face was dark in darkness.* YOU REJECTED ME. BUT . . . IT IS NOT YET OVER. *And he was gone. And the snow whirled down.*

'Every last one of you!' *screamed Garrison again, and he hurled Psychomech at the dome of the golden city.*

In through that metal wall sped Psychomech as a dart through tissue paper, as a bullet through a balloon – and the result no jot less devastating. The city simply burst open, fell in egg-shell shards, crumbled like a dried-out castle of sand. And even as she collapsed, out sped Garrison and the Machine through the far wall, their exit accelerating and completing the city's destruction.

And now, speeding away towards the far dawn, it was Garrison's turn to reject. To reject and put aside every rejection he had ever suffered.

He cared not at all but curled himself up and fell into a sleep of exhaustion upon the warm, broad back of Psychomech; and the Machine glowed and purred and hummed with power as it sped him onward through the night . . .

Chapter Fifteen

6.00 P.M.

Terri had gone home now. There were the servants to think about. Silly at this stage needlessly to arouse any sort of suspicions or leave room for unnecessary, possibly harmful rumours. More than this, however, the tension at Wyatt's place had doubled and redoubled in the last couple of hours, until the atmosphere had become quite untenable for her. Also, she had seen the look on Wyatt's face when, at 5.00 P.M., after an absence of only a few minutes, he had returned to the bedroom haggard and hollow-eyed. She had not seen him looking like that before – when for once, however handsome the façade, his age had showed mercilessly through – and had experienced a thrill of alarm at the sure knowledge that something was seriously amiss.

She had guessed that her husband still lived and the 'experiment' was not proceeding as Wyatt had determined it should, but beyond that she knew nothing.

And so she had embraced him one last time and he had promised her that it *would* soon be over, and finally she had driven away and he had been left alone. Which was when he had returned to that haunted room, the room of the machine, where for some little time he had simply stood before the bulk of Psychomech and listened to its mechanical purr, staring uncomprehendingly at the control panel's melted-down knobs.

An electrical fault? Was that possible? And why – *how* – had Psychomech bypassed the backup controls? It was . . . crazy!

Wyatt felt that he, too, must be going crazy. And on top of this latest freak he now had at least two and a half hours' work

281

to do continuing his 'log' and falsifying the machine's records. Again panic struck at him, setting him trembling. What the hell was going on here? What was happening?

For the third or fourth time (he was rapidly losing track) he checked Garrison's bio-functions, the chemistry and mechanics of his life. The man's weight was down by about nine pounds in lost fluids, but apart from that . . . all else seemed normal! Everything normal! Incredible! And by now Garrison should be dead twice over . . .

Wyatt checked himself. Stupid thought, for of course a man could only die once – *but why hadn't he?* At the very least he should be a raving lunatic; and yet there he lay, apparently soundly (even comfortably) asleep! In fact he should soon be coming out of it, gradually returning to consciousness as the dream-engendering drug was lost or neutralized in his system.

Wyatt shook himself out of a state he recognized as a sort of shocked or bemused lethargy. He quickly prepared and administered a hypodermic, thus ensuring that Garrison would stay under, then returned his attention yet again to the control panel. Useless to conjecture any further upon what had happened here, and certainly useless to attempt to free the backup controls. Better by far simply to disconnect the entire system. The connections were easily uncoupled, leaving the backup as an inert and completely useless pile of machinery. Which made it utterly impossible – yes, *utterly* impossible – for Psychomech to leak any assistance to Garrison from this time forward. Wyatt barked a harsh, half-hysterical laugh. Damn it all, it should have been impossible before!

It was just after 8.30 P.M. when Wyatt finished falsifying his log. By then too he had wiped clean the machine's record of the experiment and replaced it with a clean, pre-recorded run. On several occasions he had paused in his work to go and look at Garrison where he lay. The blind man's resistance must be phenomenal.

Now, exhausted, he left the blind man to the machine's

mercy and made to return to his bedroom. On the landing he paused, then headed downstairs. He was hungry, thirsty too. He ate sandwiches cold from the fridge and drank a pint of milk. There were three unopened bottles of milk left when he was through, and enough food to hold off a siege.

He paused, frowning, with the fridge door still open. Now what had prompted him to stock up like this? After all, it wasn't as if this thing was going to take a lot of time . . . was it?

At 9.10 he wearily climbed the stairs and looked in for a moment on Garrison. The man was moaning now and straining against his padded manacles, perspiring like a fat man in a Turkish bath. Wyatt gritted his teeth and gave a vicious nod of his head. Good! If his nightmares couldn't kill him, then all of that sweating surely would. Christ, by now he should be almost dessicated! And *that* might take a little explaining away, too. Well, he would worry about that later.

In his bedroom Wyatt set the alarm for three hours, laid back his head upon his pillow and was instantly asleep. His sleep was exhausted, dreamless.

Not so Garrison's . . .

Garrison kicked the machine where it lay buried in hot, white desert sands and cursed. He did not really have the strength for cursing, but did it anyway, tiredly and automatically – and yet with the informed and vivid vocabulary of all of his Sergeant-majors rolled into one. Not that he remembered where he had learned these words, only that they seemed very appropriate.

Then, when his throat was too raw to go on cursing, he crept into Psychomech's shade and lay there panting for air. He had known days as hot as this before (where and when he couldn't have said), but then there had always been a bar close at hand where he could step out of the sun and order a cool, clean glass of Keo, or an icy can of Coca-Cola. He frowned, concentrated . . . Cyprus?

It seemed for a moment that he heard the wash of languid waves and he got to his hands and knees and peered out from the

Machine's shadow into the blistering, heat-hazed furnace of the desert. But . . . no blue Mediterranean out there. Just hot, white, dazzling sands. And mirages that hovered on the trembling far horizon.

Keo, Coca-Cola, bar, Cyprus, Mediterranean. Meaningless concepts all, and yet delicious – and agonizing – in his pseudo-memory.

Garrison was in trouble and he knew it. There was no moisture in him, no power in the Machine, no relief from the burning heat which must soon dry him down to dust and bones. He stared again at the distant mirages, frowned and narrowed his eyes.

One of the mirages seemed clearer than the rest. It was a face. The face of the man-God Schroeder.

Staring at that face in a sort of delirium, Garrison watched it expand and come speeding through the shimmering blue sky to hover over the sand, huge and seemingly omnipotent, close to where he lay beside the Machine. 'Water,' he croaked. 'Give me water, Thomas . . .'

ANYTHING, RICHARD. ONLY LET ME IN, AND I WILL GIVE YOU ANYTHING.

'Mexican stand-off,' croaked Garrison, wondering how he knew the meaning of these strange words. 'If I don't drink I die – and you stay dead. No chance for you then, Thomas.'

AND IF YOU DO DRINK?

'A chance for you. At least a chance.'

BUT YOU WILL NOT WILLINGLY ACCEPT ME?

Garrison shook his head, sending dry white sand flying. 'No.'

AND OUR PACT?

'Pact, pact, pact!' Garrison snarled, his mouth an agony where skin peeled from puffed, cracked lips. 'This is my body, my mind!'

Schroeder's face pursed its lips. His disembodied head nodded. Sadly he said: SO WE HAVE COME TO THIS. AND WHAT OF THE MACHINE? IS THERE NO HELP FOR YOU THERE?

'The beast is dead.'

NO, NOT DEAD, *Schroeder denied.* CRIPPLED. IT MAY NO LONGER FEED YOU, NO LONGER SLAKE YOUR THIRST. BUT . . . WHAT OF YOUR OWN SKILLS? EVEN A DELIRIOUS MIND MAY STILL PERFORM STRANGE AND WONDERFUL DEEDS, RICHARD. HAVE YOU FORGOTTEN?

'ESP?' the letters – the word – fell from Garrison's crumbling lips like a piece of lead. But . . . for a single instant he knew its meaning. He strove to recall it. ESP.

He remembered.

SEEK AND FIND, *said Schroeder's face, receding into blurred and shimmering distances.* SEEK AND FIND, AND USE YOUR POWERS. LIVE, RICHARD, THAT WE BOTH MAY LIVE!

ESP . . . Seek and find . . . Remote viewing . . . Telekinesis . . . Teleportation . . .

Garrison stared again at the horizon. He stared beyond it – with his mind, not his eyes. And beyond the shimmering horizon was another that did not shimmer. And it too had mirages. Or were they . . . ?

Garrison's mouth (which he had thought utterly dry) suddenly watered. One of his mind-images was the picture of the fridge. He looked inside. There was milk, food.

Telekinesis . . . Teleportation . . . To move something with the mind alone. To remove something from one place to another, instantaneously, without visible motion between . . .

Downstairs in the kitchen the catch on the door of Wyatt's fridge clicked open and the door swung silently wide. No one was there in the kitchen, no hand touched the door. The level of the milk in one of the three pint bottles suddenly decreased, falling as if rapidly sucked out through a straw; and yet no straw was there. The bottle emptied, its silver top wrinkling as it was sucked down into an impossible vacuum.

Chicken sandwiches on a plate disappeared – snatched into hyperspace – vanished bit by bit. Or bite by bite? No, for the transition was immediate and direct: the food went straight from the fridge to Garrison's stomach. It did not touch his lips.

Upstairs in his bedroom, Wyatt slept on; while, in the room of the machine, Garrison's weight suddenly increased. At the same time his temperature began to fall, from a dangerous height to a mere degree or so above his norm; and his respiration slowed from an erratic panting to a well-paced, regular rhythm. The frown of concentration slowly faded from his glistening features and he sighed.

Then, after only a few moments, his breathing grew laboured again and the look of concentration returned to his face – concentration and determination – as his tightly balled fists began to tremble as in fever. Until, in a little while, the fear-stimulation controls suddenly turned themselves down.

After that, he slept . . .

3.00 A.M.

Wyatt frenziedly worked with a screwdriver, removing the facia from Psychomech's control panel, and then the panel itself. His aspect was feverish, hag-ridden.

Shocked from sleep by the clamour of his alarms, he had stumbled into the room of the machine only to have his senses stunned by what he found there. Then, when he was more fully awake and able to accept what he saw, he had flown into a rage. As a psychiatrist, however, he had known his own symptoms and had controlled them up to a point. That is to say that he knew he was hysterical, and that in his hysteria he might well wreck Psychomech totally and beyond repair – which would of course signal the end of everything. That was not the way.

So, still bubbling with fury – a controlled fury now – he worried loose the cover of the control panel and pried within. Five minutes sufficed to satisfy him that there was no malfunction. Which in turn meant—

Someone, some unknown but very real and physical one, had somehow been in here and turned down the fear-stimulation controls, releasing Garrison from his nightmares. Someone was here, in this very house, right now. It was crazy, ridiculous, but it was the only solution.

Not only had the control panel been interfered with but Garrison had been fed. Not by Psychomech, no, for the machine's feeding was really recycling and more on the psychical than the physical side. How had he been fed? – that was anybody's guess. It should be quite impossible. There were no scraps of food in his mouth, no spilled liquids, and he must certainly have choked if it were attempted.

And yet . . . it *had been* attempted! Most certainly. And it had succeeded. Garrison's weight was up.

Which meant that there *must* be someone else in the house.

But who?

Koenig? The German manservant seemed most eligible, Wyatt had to admit. He could have gone to Germany, turned around and flown straight back. He could be here right now, looking after his master's interests as always. But if he was here, and if he knew what was going on, why didn't he just come right on out of the woodwork, free Garrison and make an accusation?

Or could it be Terri herself, half-crazy with guilt, perhaps even schizoid? Wyatt remembered thinking to himself that she was taking all of this very well. Perhaps this was her get-out, her escape route from actions she could neither control nor tolerate. No, no – a fool idea. He cursed himself for his mind's illogical processing of data. How could it possibly be Terri? She had been right here with him when things started to go wrong. And so on, chasing his thoughts in a circle – but only for a few minutes, until common-sense took over.

One sure way to check for outside interference would be,

quite simply, to search the house from top to bottom. And after that, if he found nothing and no one – which he suspected would be the case, for if there were a human adversary at work here he must be extremely clever and unlikely to let himself be discovered – then Wyatt must simply deny him access to the room of the machine, which he could do easily enough.

He searched everywhere. Up and downstairs, the cellar, the attic, all the larger cupboards. Not only was there no one there, there were no signs that anyone had been there . . .

Just after 4.00 A.M. Wyatt returned to the machine room, gave Garrison an opiate booster, turned up fear-stimulation to the full and jammed the controls firmly in that position. Then, leaving the room, he padlocked the door and pocketed the keys.

And that, he told himself, *is that! Not even Harry Houdini himself could get out of that one – or anyone else in!*

He went downstairs. Terri would be here in a little over four hours. By then everything must be under control; Garrison dead, all records completely up to date, and Wyatt's own nerves steady once more. He had work to do. But first a wash and a shave, then coffee. Lots of strong, black coffee.

By 5.15 A.M. he was drinking coffee in his study. He had not noticed the missing milk or sandwiches.

At 6.00 A.M. he felt an almost irresistible urge to check Garrison's condition, but somehow managed to fight it off. Psychomech would do the job, he was sure. And at 6.30, after a hot shower, he allowed himself to fall asleep for two hours, only waking up at Terri's insistent ringing at the doorbell.

But between times, in the room of the machine. . .

Things had started to go wrong some time ago.
Garrison had known it, had instinctively sensed it, that

draining feeling which came whenever the Machine suffered a power loss; and he had been powerless to do anything about it. It seemed that Psychomech could only help him – and conversely that he could only help the Machine – in a real crisis.

The desert had been just such a crisis; an episode which, like the others before it, had now all but passed into the limbo of lost memories. Now Garrison could only remember the food and drink (though not the actual sensation of eating and drinking), and something of the feeling of well-being which had come afterwards. Also, something of Psychomech's feeding on him: that is to say, he knew that the Machine had somehow drawn on his strength, or that he had applied his strength so as to 'make repairs' in the Machine.

After that he had climbed aboard the revitalized Machine to ride it out of the desert into a green and beautiful valley, and for some little time – though time as a real concept did not have a great deal of meaning here – he had followed a tinkling stream to where it cut a cleft through a range of high, domed hills. And as the machine had followed the stream through the great and rambling V of the deep cleft, so Garrison had once more slept upon its broad back.

And coming awake when once more the sun had fallen upon him, he had seen that they were through the pass and that the river's bed was dry and cracked in places, and that the surrounding land was weathered into strange formations here, and the the Machine moved more slowly under heavy, dark and oppressive skies.

Heavy skies, yes. They seemed to weigh on him with the weight of the Universe. They seemed almost to shut him in . . .

As a boy he had been shut in. He remembered it now, remembered how it frightened him. The cupboard under the stairs, the spiders which he had known inhabited that place, the unknown or forgotten sin (against what or whom he could not say) which had prompted his punishment. Oh, yes, he remembered it. The sin itself might be forgotten, but the darkness, the stifling closeness, the Scuttlers in the Shadows – these things he remembered . . .

Not before that time and never since, until now, had Garrison suffered claustrophobia.

Claustrophobia?

The word came and went—

—And came back.

The skies pressed down. The leaden horizon of hills pressed in. Clouds boiled up from nowhere, shutting out the sun. And the Machine's pace grew slower and slower along that cracked and crumbling river bed.

Abruptly, with shocking suddenness, Garrison's horizons narrowed down. The sky seemed to fall in on him, becoming an opaque, writhing, near-solid ceiling of compressed and leaden cloud only feet above his head. The river bed jumped upward, so that the Machine's belly slid for a moment through caked mud, dust and pebbles before all motion ceased. The banks of the river disappeared, lost behind dull walls of lead that went up to the contorted ceiling and down to the dried-out bed of the river. It was the same to front and rear.

Garrison climbed to his knees on the back of the Machine, thrust up a hand to touch the rapidly solidifying cloud-ceiling – and met with resistance. He could not force his fist through. Even as he tried again the ceiling became solid, turned to lead. Beneath the Machine the dry river bed flattened itself out, turned from a muddy brown colour to a dull silver, then to lead. Garrison was encased in a cube of lead, imprisoned in a huge lead coffin.

Claustrophobia.

A nightmare he never would have acknowledged in the real, waking world. But here in his own subconscious . . . ?

And worse by far, the cube was contracting, its walls, ceiling and floor closing in on him even as the horror of his situation gripped him in a tight fist of fear. He stared wildly all about in the dull glow which yet emanated from

Psychomech's mechanical guts. No way out .

The ceiling touched his head and pressed upon it, causing him to cringe down and goose-flesh to break out all over his body. Galvanized into action, he slid from the Machine's back, stood tremblingly beside it in the deepening gloom.

LET ME IN, RICHARD, *came the man-God's voice from somewhere outside, booming hollowly in the cube's crushing confines.* TOGETHER WE CAN BREAK OUT. THERE IS NO OTHER WAY.

And it seemed to Garrison that maybe the man-God Schroeder was right.

For a moment he succumbed to his panic, his fear. He weakened, opened his mouth . . . but the moment was past. Then—

'No!' *he denied the man-God yet again.* 'No, there has to be a way out.'

WHAT WAY, RICHARD? IF YOU ARE NOT CRUSHED YOU WILL SUFFOCATE. YOU MUST LET ME HELP YOU. AND I CAN ONLY HELP IF YOU LET ME IN.

'No!' *Garrison shook his fists at the closing walls, the lowering ceiling. No, he would not submit to the man-God. Not yet. And—*

The man-God's own words, 'Let me in,' had sparked an idea in his mind. Certainly the contracting leaden cube would crush and maim flesh and blood, but would it be able to crush the hard metal and plastic of the Machine? Even inert, Psycho-mech had massive strength. And after all, lead was a soft metal and malleable. The man-God had wanted to get inside of Garrison . . . but what if Garrison were to get inside the Machine?

He found a gap in the Machine's ribbed, flanged and riveted metal side, a space into which he might squeeze his trembling frame. With a little effort, frantically wriggling when he thought he was stuck, he forced his head and the upper part of his body into the aperture, then drew in his legs and curled himself into a tight, foetal shape. Only his right hand and arm protruded, but when he felt the contracting lead wall touch his fingers he managed somehow to draw these inside too. Then, as the last flicker of light was extinguished, he huddled down and hugged himself in the darkness, and trembled long and shudderingly.

THAT WILL NOT WORK, RICHARD, *Schroeder's voice echoed hollowly.* EVEN IF THE MACHINE IS NOT CRUSHED YOU MUST SOON RUN OUT OF AIR. IS THIS TO BE THE END? DARKNESS, SUFFOCATION, DEATH? IS THAT WHAT YOU WANT?

'*I'm not dead yet!*' *Garrison sobbed, already feeling the air growing thin in his lungs.*

The ceiling came down and the floor came up. The walls pressed in. The cube exerted its weight upon Psychomech. The Machine groaned and Garrison held what little breath he could find to hold.

And again the groan of tortured metal.

And again . . .

The cube squeezed, squeezed – to no avail! Psychomech held.

'*Air!*' *Garrison gasped.* '*Air! There's no air!*' *His lungs were on fire, sucking uselessly at the crushing darkness. He was a miner trapped in a cave-in; a submariner falling many fathoms to where the weight of the sea would crush him flat; Poe's victim of a premature burial.* '*Air, for Christ's sake! Air!*'

Teleportation . . . The ability to move something, perhaps even oneself, instantly from one place to another, without physically crossing the distance between.

'*Air!*' *Garrison screamed again. And:* '*Aaaiiirrr . . . !*'

No air . . . Suffocation . . . Crisis . . . Teleportation!

He moved!

Psychomech too, they both . . . moved!

They moved from inside to outside the cube. Gulping air, Garrison flopped out from the Machine's cold womb of metal and plastic and fell to his knees in the dust of the river's dry bed. He was just in time to see the great cube of lead crumple

*in upon itself, imploding with a whoosh, a soft tearing sound
and an almost sonic bang. Dry crusts of mud and a shower of
pebbles and dust were thrown up from the bed of the river, and
when they settled the cube was no longer there.*

*Garrison was jubilant. He laughed hoarsely and shook his
fists in the air. He had won. This time he himself had won. On
his own, without assistance. But—*

On another level, in another place, the fear-stimulation
controls on Psychomech's control panel were still jammed
wide open. And, though he was not yet aware of it, Richard
Garrison had merely moved himself from one crisis to
another . . .

8.45 A.M.

Wyatt had let Terri in and taken her up to his bedroom.
He had not yet been in to see Garrison and now steeled
himself for that task. Wyatt's sleep had gone a long way
towards replenishing him, but still he looked better than he
felt.

As for Terri: she was radiant. She had slept a deep,
satisfying, dreamless sleep; and she had known that when
morning came all would be well. For a woman scarlet with
guilt, she looked creamy cool. In Wyatt's bedroom – their
bedroom, as she liked to think of it – she turned to him and
took his hands, guiding them to her breasts. Her dark eyes
were lovely in a face full of expectation.

'It's over?'

He did not answer immediately but averted his eyes.
When finally he looked at her his face was serious. 'It
should be.'

'Should be?' Her face fell. 'You haven't been in to see him
yet?'

'I'll go now. It's just that—'

'Yes?'

'He should have been dead yesterday, yesterday evening,
last night. He should have been dead many times over. I'm

beginning to wonder if he'll ever die! And some funny things have been happening.'

She shook her head, looked bewildered, completely dispelled any last doubts Wyatt might have entertained about her own possible involvement in the strangeness. 'What do you mean?'

'Things are happening, Terri. Things I don't understand. I was starting to think someone was monkeying with the machine, but that's downright impossible. I mean, I also think that your husband has been fed – but how could he have been? And the machine itself, Psychomech, is—'

'Yes?'

'Acting up. I don't know . . .' He shook his head.

'Listen,' she said with urgency. 'Go in and see him.' She gripped his arms. 'Maybe it's all over.'

She was suddenly aware of *his* nightmare, aware of Wyatt's personal torment. Anything he displayed outwardly was for her. Possibly a little of his show was for himself, a pillar to lean on, but mainly it was for her. He had made himself totally responsible for this thing, while her part had been so small. But now . . . she was aware that if she weakened, he too might crumble. She did not know what had happened here, did not want to know, but she knew one thing: that she loved him. And she knew she must tell him so, and just exactly how she must say it.

'Gareth, I love you. No matter what, I love you. I can't help it, it's the way I am. Whatever you find . . . in there, come back to me and love me. If we can't be pure any other way, at least we can be pure that way.'

He knew what she meant and nodded. He somehow managed a smile, however wan. 'Sweet oblivion, yes. But . . . it *will* be OK, I'm sure.' He nodded again, closed the door after him . . .

The Machine was dead again and all Garrison's mental tugging and pushing, all his desperate tongue-lashing, couldn't move it. And what a place to be stuck. Below him, a slab-walled ravine going down to eternity, and before him – a viaduct. And the Machine completely inert, lying where it had come to rest upon old and rotten railway ties bearing twisted, rusty rails, the line stretching away towards the dry river valley he had left two or three miles in his wake.

He stared again at the viaduct, its arches sagging where they spanned the unknown depths. Somehow in some tiny corner of his mind, Garrison had the spark of an idea that if he could only cross this decrepit viaduct, then his strength, and that of the Machine, would be restored. The viaduct was a barrier to his quest, an obstacle placed in his way to frustrate him. Cross the viaduct, remove the obstruction, continue the quest.

Easy . . .

Garrison's overalls were ragged at the knees and elbows. He wondered about them. Overalls?

As a boy he had worn denim overalls. Yes, and there had been a derelict viaduct, too. He had always hated the crumbling brick arches of the thing, which had seemed to him ready at a moment's notice to topple disastrously. It had been like a dead and rotting old man. A corpse no one would bury. But useless and dangerous as the structure had been, for some reason the viaduct had stood there, tall and gaunt and trembling, for long years after it should have been pulled down.

And yet for all its disuse and decay, still it had served a purpose. One which had brought terror.

An initiation test, that's what the viaduct had been, means of entry into an exclusive club. The other members had been a year, two years older than Garrison's ten or eleven, and bullies all. But better to be a member of the club than a target for its constant cruelties, and Garrison, being big for his age, was invariably a prime target.

The fine details of that earlier ordeal escaped him now – except that he had been called upon to cross the viaduct, leaping the gaps in the rotting ties where sections of rusty track had long since decayed, broken free and tumbled to oblivion in the depths. It had seemed easy at first, until, as he had reached the centre of the perilous structure, the president and a couple of club members had sent an old bogie rolling upon him from the far side, rumbling and swaying as it sped by him and sent him reeling. Then, as Garrison had tripped and fallen – only saving himself from certain death by hanging on to a length of projecting, rusty rail – the old bogie had taken out yet another section of rails and ties to go plummeting into the abyss, falling hundreds of feet to crash and splinter and cartwheel down the steep wooden slope below.

Somehow Garrison had hauled himself to safety, and somehow he had completed the 'initiation test'; but after that he had wished nothing more to do with the club, and one by one he had picked off its members in bloody fist fights. And they had troubled him no more.

—Since when he had thought the incident long forgotten. And forgotten it might have stayed, but that was where he had first learned the meaning of vertigo.

Vertigo, yes, a fear he had managed to 'kill off' in his mind. Except that now—

This viaduct of dreams, this bridge of darkest nightmares
. . .

In his ragged overalls, on feet clad in a pair of worn, badly scuffed shoes with crepe rubber soles, Garrison set about making the crossing. It was evening and he must get across before the fall of night, to the other side, where a waterfall tinkled and splashed.

The viaduct's span was perhaps one hundred and fifty feet. It was of a peak-roofed, twin-walled construction with the concrete bed, wooden ties and steel rails suspended between the walls. Most of the clapboard roof was missing now, letting in the light, but in places the boards were almost intact and

296

made the way dark indeed. And the deeps below seemed bottomless.

For all the control he exerted or tried to exert upon himself, Garrison could still feel a sickness growing in the pit of his stomach and a steady increase in the wild fluctuations of his heart. Not wishing to prolong the crossing, he grew less cautious and began to take chances.

Towards the centre of the viaduct, along a section of at least one third of the structure's total length, the roof was almost entirely missing. Lengths of fallen, rotten clapboard abounded here, tumbled down and scattered all over the red rails and spongy black ties. Here, too, the masonry was damp, moss-grown and crumbly, where many of the topmost courses had fallen, mostly inward, making the way dangerous to the point of lethal. In places this choking with debris was almost in the nature of snow-bridges; where the way looks solid enough while the bridge itself is barely capable of supporting its own weight, and the reverberations of a mere shout may bring all down in a disastrous avalanche.

On two occasions as he worked his way forward inch by inch, Garrison's front-probing foot set minor masses of stone, rotten timbers and squealing track shifting, sliding, and finally thundering down dustily into the great and seemingly bottomless cavity between the walls. But the third such fall, which occurred two-thirds of the way across, was very extensive. It plunged a great section of bed and track and previously tumbled debris into the depths.

As all of this happened Garrison threw himself back the way he had come, face down on the tracks, where he clung like a limpet until the shuddering and thundering were over. Then, shakily regaining his feet and as the clouds of billowing dust settled, he saw what remained of the section just ahead. And at the sight his despair and feeling of vertigo doubled and redoubled within him.

For nothing remained of the way ahead except the sagging

rails themselves and the few ties which kept them fastened together. Why, even a tightrope walker would have difficulty crossing now!

I CAN CARRY YOU ACROSS, RICHARD! *came that familiar booming voice from the sky, its echoes causing dust and bits of rubble to trickle from ledges and crevices in the shaken wall where Garrison crouched.*

He looked up through a lattice of ravaged clapboard roofing and saw the face of the man-God, luminous in the gathering twilight. 'Oh?' *Despite his fear his voice dripped acid.* 'And at what price?'

YOU KNOW THE PRICE, RICHARD, *said the man-God, his eyes narrowing.* A PRICE I HAVE ALREADY TOLD YOU: THAT YOU LET ME COME TO YOU, THAT YOU LET ME IN.

Garrison was tempted, but—

'No!' *he answered after a moment.* 'Oh, no, man-God! I've dreamed of you before, long ago, and I remember that dream now. At the end of my quest there's a black lake with a black castle, and in that other dream you were there with me and still demanding to be let in. Well, I haven't reached the lake and the castle yet, and until I do—'

IF YOU DO! ONLY LOOK AT THE WAY AHEAD, RICHARD. IF YOU ATTEMPT THIS, YOU RISK BOTH OF OUR LIVES.

'It's a risk I have to take.'

WITH MY LIFE TOO? AND WHAT OF THE THING THAT WAITS? THE THING IN THE SHADOWS BENEATH THE WATERFALL?

'The Thing That Waits?' *Garrison's eyes turned from the face of the man-God to peer nervously across the abyss to the far side of the viaduct. Something gleamed redly in the gloom low down where the water splashed near the foot of the falls. Two red somethings, like the lamps of a train seen afar, or the warning glow of red railway lanterns.*

They were wide-spaced, seemed to peer right back at him –

and even as he gazed, with the short hairs rising at the back of his neck—

They blinked!

Whatever it was, the Thing That Waited must be huge and heavy and squat and awful. Garrison pictured again that old, careening railway bogie. Like that, yes!

But unlike the bogie, sentient – and utterly evil!

Chapter Sixteen

Wyatt came back in something approaching high spirits, at least by comparison with his recent frame of mind. 'Crisis,' he reported to Terri. 'You don't know what that means, my love, but I can tell you that it doesn't mean a crisis for us.' She was in bed. He quickly undressed and got in beside her.

She hugged him close and warmed him with her flesh. 'Then it really is going to happen?'

'Yes it is – today – at any moment.'

'And you're all prepared for it?'

'Almost. A little more tampering with the records, a couple of blown fuses to be put into the Machine, just to add a few extra complications for the "experts" who'll doubtless be called in – and that's about it. Who will ever be able to say what really happened here, eh? There are no real experts in this field, Terri. Not yet . . .' He paused, remembering Maas–Krippner. 'Not any more.'

She looked at him quizzically. 'Oh?'

'It doesn't matter.' He was warm now, responding to her hands where they stroked his back. 'Terri – God, I love you. I mean, I really love you. You know, without anything else – with everything against us – we could still make it.' He shrugged. 'I mean, I just love you.'

'Then love me.' Her voice was husky and quick with the passions he had aroused. 'For God's sake – no, since neither one of us believes, for *my* sake – love me. Fill me up, hurt me, but love me . . .'

They made love, and for the first time it was totally without pain, almost without passion. And it was pure.

The blackest jet is always the purest . . .

*   *   *

Garrison had found a way.

No tightrope walker, still he had found a way. He had picked up a six-foot length of clapboard with a stout iron bolt through one end. Now seated astride one rail, pushing the length of board before him and using it to steady himself, he inched his way forward over the abyss. The other end of the board lay across the parallel rail, spanning the gap between and holding firm where the dangling bolt projected over the rail itself. This way, so long as Garrison disposed the greater part of his weight towards the inside of the track, he could shuffle himself forward and maintain his balance without too much difficulty – but whatever he did he must not look down.

Thus he kept his eyes firmly fixed upon the slightly swaying rails ahead and on the dark, roofed-over section of fairly solid-looking track which terminated the viaduct's span. And it was as he was staring straight ahead like this and inching his way forward that he noticed the change: where before there had been the merest wisp of a breeze, now the air was still and dead – as if the world held its breath. And where before the silhouettes of great black birds had soared on high, now the darkening sky was utterly void of life. The tinkling and splashing of the waterfall now seemed subdued, hushed somehow, along with the slow scrape of wooden board along rusty rail.

Because of the obscuring effect of the looming, intact section of roofed track ahead – which he would reach in another minute or two – Garrison was no longer able to see the spot beneath the cliff where crouched the Waiting Thing; a fact for which he was half-inclined to gladness, until—

Suddenly, coming alive in an easy, instant un-shuttering of great red eyes, the roofed-in darkness ahead became one with all the world's evil. The Thing That Waited waited no longer but had come out to meet him. It sat there, squat and black and straddling the tracks, an awful silhouette in the cavernous mouth of the final section.

Garrison's eyes went wide and he froze solid, his fear

radiating from him in almost visible waves. And seeing the terror it inspired in him, the Thing eased rumblingly forward, taking firmer shape as it slowly emerged from the shadows. It was fat, bogie-like, a giant wood louse with well-oiled wheels for legs. And directly beneath its lantern eyes a ruler-straight metal mouth gaped wide as the beast itself, opening hideously and hydraulically as the creature made to spring upon Garrison's shuddering, helpless form.

He could move neither back nor forward. A shriek welled in his throat but would not emerge except as a bubbling hiss. He wobbled wildly where he sat, the board clattering against the rails to the rhythm of his palsied hands.

It lurched fully into view, wheels clattering, girder-mouth clashing, headlamp eyes glaring evilly as it sped down the incline of the sagging, groaning, abyss-spanning rails. If that awful mouth did not get Garrison the wheels surely would. He threw up his hands before his face, made a useless effort to stab at the onrushing Thing with the length of clapboard and felt it knocked from his grasp into empty space. He wobbled wildly, was aware that he toppled sideways, outwards, his rubbery legs releasing their grip on the shuddering rail. Then—

His own scream was drowned out by that of the bogie-Thing, whose voice was a squeal of brakes, a grinding of gears and a scorch of burning metal; and in the next instant the monster had gone plummeting past him into the depths. Tracks and ties and bricks and masonry too, all torn free and falling, falling . . .

Falling . . . Vertigo . . . Crisis . . .

Levitation!

To suspend one's body in empty air without physical support. To make weightless. To defy gravity as a mental exercise.

Falling, with the world whirling, Garrison squeezed his eyes tightly shut. 'Stop falling!' he told himself. 'Descend less rapidly, float, fly – but stop falling!'

The whirling sensation slowed and stopped. He opened his eyes.

The viaduct fell past him – past him! – the entire structure going down in a thundering of rubble and dust, but Garrison floated on the twilight air light as thistledown. And as the viaduct went down, so he went up.

And up too went the Machine, floating on air as he lifted it from where he had left it, drawing it to him with his mind. And Psychomech no longer bearing his weight but him bearing the weight of Psychomech. And . . . it was easy!

In mid-air he climbed on to the Machine's back, rode it free of the abyss, followed the rusted rails into deepening gloom. And even knowing that the Machine was a dead weight, knowing it for an inert useless mass, still he carried it with him. The Machine had been faithful to him in its way and now he would pay it back in kind. Besides, it had been with him in that other dream, the dream of the black lake and the black castle, and Garrison knew that these things still awaited him at the end of his quest.

He cleansed his mind of the horror so recently passed by and searched the darkening sky as he went. He looked for the man-God Schroeder but saw no sign of him now. Garrison shook a fist at the sky. 'Come all you want, man-God,' he cried, 'and may the best man win.'

Then he shivered and huddled down flat. He was cold, tired and hungry. He must find shelter and sustenance for the night.

'What?' Wyatt's eyes widened. 'No milk? But that's absurd, not possible!' He sat up straight in his black-sheeted bed and reached for a cigarette. 'Are you sure? There should be sandwiches, too, in a clear plastic box. A little curly at the edges by now, I imagine, but still perfectly edible.'

'No,' Terri denied. 'No milk, no sandwiches.' She shrugged. 'What does it matter? I can drink my coffee black and I'm not especially hungry – I ate last night. But I do think you should eat. Tell me what you'd like and I'll cook it for you. There's enough of almost everything in your fridge. Well, except for milk and sandwiches, that is—'

'I have to take a look at that fridge.' He pulled on pyjama bottoms, led the way out on to the landing with Terri close behind.

'But what's so important about it?'

He paused, turned to her. 'Listen, I told you I thought someone had been feeding him, right?'

'Yes, but—'

'Well, I don't know why and I certainly don't know how, but suddenly I have this feeling that I know *where* they're getting the food! Not how they're getting it into him, not even who they are, but—'

'But . . . it's crazy!'

'Terri,' he grated his teeth, 'I *know* it's crazy. Here—' He caught her, took padlock keys from the pocket of her dressing gown. 'Look—' He led her to the room of the machine. The door was padlocked, exactly as he had left it. 'One way in. No windows. No attic trapdoor. Only one set of keys. No way anyone can get to him. And yet – God *damn*! – he's still alive in there! I'm betting he's still alive . . .'

She clung to him. 'But you don't know that.'

He calmed himself. 'No, of course not.' He stuffed the keys back into the pocket of her gown. 'I'll go in and see him in a moment. First I have to take a look inside that fridge.'

In the kitchen he snatched at the fridge's door, glared within. The plastic sandwich container was there where he had left it – empty. The milk bottles stood empty, their silver caps sucked inwards. Wyatt drew breath sharply, began brushing his fingers repeatedly, feverishly through his hair. 'Jesus, Jesus, *Jesus*!' he said, 'I don't believe it. I've searched the place top to bottom. It can't be happening. I must be going out of my fucking—'

'Gareth!' She reached up, made as if to slap his face,

burst into tears instead and buried her own face in his chest.

For a moment he was rigid as iron against her, but then he slowly drew in air and relaxed, hugging her to him. He patted her back, quieted her. 'It's OK, it's OK.' His voice was a husky whisper. 'It must be me. Nerves. Cracking up. I'll be OK now. I can get a grip. Hell, it's a rough time for both of us. I thought I was stronger.'

'Oh, Gareth, Gareth . . .'

'Listen, you cook us up a bite to eat. I'll go and take a look. Just excuse my hysterics. Damn it all, we've no time for that, not now. And anyway, if he's still alive – well, there's one last trick I've yet to play.' He felt a trembling starting up in his arms and froze it before it could get started. Then, releasing her, he said, 'OK?'

'OK,' she nodded. She managed to smile through her tears. 'OK.'

He took the keys, left her and went back upstairs to the room of the machine. He unlocked the door, entered, and . . .

Garrison was not dead. Far from it.

He smiled in his sleep. His weight was almost back to normal; normal, too, his bio-functions. Psychomech hummed and purred as before, its fear-stimulation controls jammed wide open. Gritting his teeth, Wyatt half-snarled, half-whispered to himself: 'I don't believe it, I *don't* believe it!'

He got a grip on himself, filled a hypodermic with a dangerously high dose and administered it into Garrison's arm, then went to a wall cabinet and took out a sealed packet of sugar cubes. But these were very special cubes. He had often taken one himself – but just one at a time – or given one to a girlfriend, on those past occasions when he had wanted something different, a night's sweet tripping. Now, however, it was for Garrison. He diluted three cubes in a little water, then spooned it to the blind man drop by poisoned drop. And when all of it was gone, only then did he leave the room and padlock the door firmly shut.

'Let's see you come out of *that* one, you bastard!' he said, making his way unsteadily back to his bedroom.

12.00 Noon—

—But in Garrison's mind-world it was a night such as he had never before experienced, where time and space and the denizens of both had become completely distorted and alien. Indeed as darkness had closed in it had seemed to him that for hours without number he had simply wandered through a wonderland of benighted marvels, through grottoes of twilight mystery and shadow-cloaked beauty.

Beasts big as houses, with pulsing lantern proboscises and luminous purple eyes had floated on flimsy filament wings and in strange aerial formations across the star-strewn sky, drawn to where high over the hills aurora borealis danced in flames of such brilliance as to put all mundane colours and coruscations to shame. Silver clouds etched with ever-changing traceries of electrical fire had raced in writhing ecstasy overhead, while pallid poppies had bloomed in the light of a scarlet-cratered moon, sending up puffs of opiate perfume to make the head reel and the senses stagger. And moths big as bats had crowded in a curious cloud about man and Machine, as if puzzled by the intrusion of these visitants from outside.

From outside, yes, for of course these creatures were the dwellers of the inner Garrison; this world, however warped by Wyatt's mind-bending ministerings, was the inner Garrison. And along with the wonders of drug-induced and mechanically magnified fever came the terrors. And Psychomech's fear-stimulation controls were still jammed wide open . . .

Garrison had not completely forgotten the need for shelter.

When it came, it was in the form of a glossy pink forest of vast extent, which might almost have been some gigantic prehistoric coral reef left high and dry fifty millions of years ago, petrified and preserved to come down all the centuries intact and maze-like in its many-roomed, many-caverned *magnificence. The 'trees' of this great fossil forest were columnar and occasionally clumped, branching overhead to spread and form pink and white coral ceilings woven so close that not even a scrap of night sky showed through. The walls of the halls, passages and caves were webs of translucent coral, finely veined panels of intricately wrought organic designs with almost nacreous lustre; so that even in the outer areas of this paleogean palace Garrison might well have imagined himself in the vastly segmented whorl of some incredible and alien conch.*

Not wishing to penetrate the labyrinth too deeply – fighting the urge he now felt to explore to their full the myriad avenues and arenas of this wonder – he brought the Machine to rest before a small cave only large enough for his immediate needs. Claustrophobia was now a thing of the past, however, an elemental fear which would never bother him again.

Flopping to the sandy floor and pulling the hood of his Army parka up over his head, Garrison considered the veined organic patterns of the walls. His body seemed desperately tired while his mind, in complete contrast, was inspired by bursts of brilliant imaginings and flights of soaring fancy. Something was in his blood – some imp of the perverse in his brain – conjuring a kaleidoscope of feverish images which simply denied him sleep. Even the patterns on the pink-glowing walls took on lifelike shapes as he gazed at them; one of which—

Was that of a cat! A cat with a broken neck . . .

Long ago in another world there had been such a cat. Garrison remembered it now. It had been his pet, and when he had erred – rather, because *he had erred – the cat had been killed. And its broken neck, its death, had been his fault. His.*

Oh, yes, he remembered the loss of . . . Tiger! Tiger, little Tiger.

And the cat on the pink-hued wall was just like Tiger, and its neck at just the right angle, all twisted, and its pink tongue lolling just as Tiger's had lolled in death . . .

Garrison sat up, his flesh tingling. He sensed what was coming but was helpless to avert it.

The cat-figure on the wall suddenly expanded, exploding into three dimensions, bloating out of all proportion and assuming the shape of . . . a tiger!

A tiger knowing the agony of a twisted, broken neck – but no longer dead. A zombie-tiger, and Garrison to blame for the creature's misery.

His crime. His guilt. His punishment!

The thing sprang down from the wall and pounced upon him, its yellow eyes blazing, great jaws chomping and slavering. Garrison rolled, kicked, used the beast's own impetus to propel it out through the mouth of the cavelet and across Psychomech's inert mass. It landed scrabblingly on all fours, its head lolling awkwardly, and turned to face him. And now, in the pinkish glow of the walls, Garrison counted a dozen more of the beasts; or a dozen pairs of feral eyes at least. And all of them full of pain, hatred and revenge. They slunk as one towards him.

Trapped, he sought desperately for a way out. Teleportation? No, because even if he could find the strength to teleport, it would only suffice to remove him to some other place within this labyrinth of coral, and he knew the great cats would be waiting for him there. Levitation? Out of the question, for the cave's roof was a solid mass overhead, with nowhere a gap. But—

The tigers sprang at him. They sprang as one, their heads lolling hideously, their lethal claws unsheathed.

Garrison levitated the Machine up off the pink sandy floor and jammed it in the mouth of the cavelet, holding it there while the tigers roared their agonies and heaped their clawing, scratching, biting weight upon it. They were trying to dislodge it and so get at him, and suddenly Garrison was panic-stricken as he realized that his ESP-strength was on the ebb. He was actually straining to hold Psychomech in position. Something was weakening him and making it less easy for him to use this levitation, this skill so recently acquired.

Moreover, the totally surreal aspect of all he perceived was more sharply defined now. Which is to say that for the first time he actually felt out of place in this dimension of fever dreams. Very little of what he experienced seemed real any longer. He still knew and accepted that he lived in dreams and nightmares, yes, but he was also dimly aware that this was not his natural place. In short, he felt that he was suffering a nightmare within a nightmare, a very bad trip in a strange, strange land – which was precisely the case! The LSD in his system had worked not to increase but to define the other-worldliness of his situation. And knowing now beyond any doubt that this was an alien environment, he also knew that his chances for survival here must be small indeed.

Which was why, instinctively, while yet he retained something of his ESP-strength, he reached out with his mind and hurled an SOS into that other plane of existence, that world beyond the borders of his own psyche, that external world where once he had dwelled.

An SOS, a mental cry for help, a telepathic distress signal which someone, somewhere, somehow must hear.

Else Garrison were doomed . . .

12.10 P.M., and in her steel and concrete cage at the Mid-hurst kennels Suzy suddenly went insane. Without warning she bounded high, howling like a banshee as she commenced to crash about the interior of her cage. In a matter of moments she had turned from a quiet if pensive animal into a wild thing. Her eyes were red and bulging, her muzzle a scarlet slash bordering foaming fangs; and her screaming . . . was just that. She screamed like a human being, as she had been heard to scream once before.

In minutes her chest was heaving, her flanks lathered and dripping, and she had collapsed in a corner quivering and whimpering. She seemed spent, as if in her intense madness she had burned all of the energy out of her system – which was exactly the visual effect she had hoped to achieve.

A keeper, attracted by her fit and running to the door of her cage, spoke breathlessly into his walkie-talkie, and in a little while a padded figure came on the scene carrying a hypodermic. Suzy's behaviour last Wednesday had been noted and this relapse, while not anticipated, was not entirely unexpected. If allowed to continue she might easily do herself permanent injury, for which reason she must now be sedated. But a Dobermann pinscher is a Dobermann pinscher, not a tiny terrier or perfumed pekinese with which to take any sort of liberty.

As the bolt on the door of her cage was drawn, so Suzy's eyes flickered open; she made as if to move and then flopped down again. But when the door was opened she came out of her corner like a black bullet, shot straight between the leather-suited figure's legs and bowled him over, and was out of the cage in a moment. Then Suzy was away and running, speeding between the lines of kennels and setting all the dogs to yelping and howling.

She ran down an avenue of cages; but when keepers carrying poles with nooses appeared in a line at the far end she slowed her pace and considered the situation. Behind her – shouting, running men. In front – these keepers, experts who would trap her in a moment. She bounded on to a wheelbarrow's rim, bunched her muscles and sprang to the wire netting roof of the row of kennels. Fortunately the wire was thick and the gauge fine; it merely gave a little to her weight as she loped above the kennels and sprang to the ground on the far side.

From on high she had seen a tall wire fence curving in a semicircle around the perimeter of the kennel complex, but where the fence ended there had been a reed-fringed lake with a densely wooded area beyond. Keeping low to the ground, Suzy headed for the lake. Her sense of direction tugged her westward and the lake lay to the north. She whined as she ran, fighting the urge to turn to the west.

That way she would only come up against the tall fence. No, she must cross the lake first. Then change her course westward.

Westward, in answer to Garrison's call. Its echoes still rang in her head; that desperate cry for help, that beloved voice calling to her out of nowhere.

She would answer that call or die in the attempt . . .

Last night Willy Koenig had painted the town red. He had drunk beer and schnapps in quantities to shame the most hardened swillers and had visited all levels of establishment from 'dive' and 'bar' through 'night-club' to the most expensive bordello on the Reeperbahn. There, still drinking like some insatiable, alcohol-fuelled engine, he had finally chosen a woman for himself and at 2.30 in the morning had taken her upstairs to bed. Though he remembered little of it, he had paid for her services for the night; and this morning about 9.30 had awakened clear-headed if a little dry in the mouth, which is to say a great deal about Koenig's iron constitution.

The girl had been delighted to accept him as a client for the rest of the day, since when he had made languid love to her while stoking up on champagne, schnapps, crisp buttered rolls and honey, and coffee enlivened with liberal splashes of Asbach Uralt, the latter a habit acquired from Garrison. The stubble was still on Koenig's face and he had just decided to wash and shave when, about midday, he suddenly sat bolt upright in the huge and ornate double bed.

'*Willy!*' the voice repeated in his head. '*Willy – help!*'

Koenig's blood turned to ice and he gave a violent shudder. The voice had been real, crystal clear.

'Willy?' the girl queried, touching his shoulder and making him start.

'Be quiet!' he snapped, listening intently. There was nothing. He turned to the girl where she lay sprawled and naked on top of the covers. 'Did you hear . . . anything?'

She looked puzzled, pouted, shook her head. 'Nothing. What is there to hear? And why are you so cold? My, but you're freezing! Here, let me warm you.'

He shrugged her off, swung his legs out of bed and began to dress. 'Get me a taxi.'

'But Willy,' she protested, frowning and biting her lip, 'you said you wanted me for the day, and you haven't paid me.'

'How much was it?' he absent-mindedly asked. 'For the day . . .'

'Three hundred Deutsch Marks, Willy, but—'

He took out his wallet and she fell silent. She watched him extract and throw down three fifty Deutsch Mark notes on to the bed. 'There,' he said. 'Half a day.'

'Ah!' She took up the money, 'But that's not how we play, Willy. You *said* for the day, and so you pay for—'

'It's the way *I* play,' he told her, heading for the bathroom. 'Now be a good girl and get me a taxi.'

Under her breath the girl said, 'Shit!' She bit her lip again, hesitated for a moment, then reached behind the yellow satin headboard of the bed to press a hidden button. There had been men here before who wanted to play the game their way. Karl would convince this crewcut bull otherwise. She shuddered, hating to do it. Karl was a monster. A pity, but . . . rules are rules.

When Koenig came out of the bathroom Karl was waiting. He was much taller than Koenig, maybe seventy-five inches, with slitted eyes that glinted blue under thin, straight eyebrows. His face was angular and grey with a pale blob of a nose that looked right out of place above a twisted, sneering mouth.

Koenig's first, almost perfunctory glance took in all of these things, also the fact that Karl was of that sort which likes inflicting pain. Oh, yes, Karl was a mean one – or at least Karl *thought* he was a mean one. But Koenig liked them mean. The meaner the better.

His second glance, also deceptively perfunctory, completed the picture. Smartly if a little too sharply dressed in a black polo-neck shirt and black suit, the bouncer leaned with his back to the wall beside the room's single door. Koenig's way led through that door . . .

There was something different about Koenig, Karl decided. He eyed the bulky man up and down, noting that Koenig barely seemed to acknowledge his presence in the room. That was it: the guy was pretending he didn't exist, as if Karl were some lower species with no interest value whatsoever. Karl nodded grimly to himself. Well, he would know he was here soon enough.

'You owe the lady money,' he said at last, his voice a husky whisper. He rubbed a heavily ringed left hand on brass knuckle-dusters where they made his right fist into a club. 'I think you'd better pay her.'

Koenig zipped up his fly, moved forward. 'What's your name, son?' he asked, his manner casual, almost uncaring.

Whatever else Karl was he wasn't too bright. Koenig's question, delivered so innocently, had caught him right off balance. 'Eh?' he looked puzzled. 'My name's Karl. My job—'

'Oh, I know what you do,' said Koenig, 'but do you enjoy making love?'

'What?' Karl's jaw dropped. For the first time he became truly aware of Koenig's size, his blocky weight and the effortless strength apparent in the suddenly cat-sure flow of his movements. He was aware too that Koenig was only two paces away and moving closer. 'Do I enjoy—?'

'Get out of my way, Karl,' said Koenig very quietly, 'while you can still fuck.'

Karl's face became a vicious mask and he began a lightning movement – but Koenig was already moving. He struck Karl under the heart with his right fist. At the same time his left hand closed like a vice on the other's right wrist

313

and his left knee came up like a hammer to crunch into his groin. All of this in a single moment; and in the next, as Karl's contorted face and open mouth jerked forward, Koenig's bullet head was there to meet them. Blood and teeth flew and Karl toppled to one side, gagging. Koenig let him gently to the floor and released him, straightened up and quickly ran his fingers through the brush of his disordered crewcut. He grunted and congratulated himself. It had been almost soundless.

The girl, who had seemed paralysed until now, suddenly snatched breath.

'If you yell,' Koenig told her, his voice cold and harsh as a file on glass, 'I'll really hurt you. And for the rest of your life you'll be no good at all for gobbling.' His eyes were very hard and bright.

She let the air slowly, silently out of her lungs.

Koenig nodded. 'I'm going now. Be a good girl and don't make any more fuss. And the next time a customer wants a taxi, you get him one, eh?' He left the door standing open . . .

Help was on its way, Garrison knew it. His call was being answered. Faint echoes of other minds had touched his, bolstering him up, saying, 'Hang on, hang on, we're coming!' Other minds, yes, and one of them less – or more? – than human. A warm, loving mind, that one; a worshipful, devoted mind. Humanity? – Garrison did not care. A friend is a friend. Only that friend must be quick or all was lost.

For as Garrison sweated out the siege of tigers he knew that his strength was fast ebbing, that the bulk of the Machine was slipping from where he fought to hold it in the cave's mouth. And the tigers, as if guided by something more than merely animal instinct, continued to pile their weight upon the Machine's metal and plastic back, all the while scrabbling to find a gap and break through into Garrison's cavelet.

'Come!' he cried out with his mind into the Otherworld.

'Come quickly – come now *– if you're to save me at all . . .'*

But in sending this telepathic SOS he had further weakened himself, and the gap between the Machine's tiger-strewn back and the top of the cavelet's curved mouth visibly widened. Garrison glimpsed yellow eyes in the pink coral glow, and fangs now dripping with a saliva of anticipation. Claws like steel hooks raked at the opening and a massed growling of pain and hatred filled the cave with echoing, rumbling animal thunder . . .

Racing across country and making a beeline for Wyatt's estate, Suzy heard Garrison's second SOS and her great heart gave a wild leap. Garrison was still some miles distant from her, she knew that, but she also knew that he needed her help now.

She came to a halt, leaned her head forward and sniffed. Then she whined and her entire body quivered. Her ears, standing up straight at first, slowly lay down flat upon her head. She too lay down, flopping into the long grass and panting where she lay.

Garrison had called for her. *He* had cried out to her for help and she must answer that call now – but how? If only she could be with him, face alongside him whatever dangers he faced . . .

The link between them strengthened, bypassing the merely mundane laws of science and nature. *In her mind* Suzy sniffed him out and discovered him in his torment and terror. And *in her mind* she sped to him – flew to him on telepathic wings – to be one with him against the monsters of his id.

Her body still lay there, apparently spent, in a field of breeze-rippled summer grasses, so that any sympathetic observer might have imagined she was drowning in an ocean of green; but this was only her shell. This was her hair and skin and flesh and bones, the material Suzy. Suzy *herself* – the essential Suzy – she was somewhere else . . .

Willy Koenig was just in time to buy a ticket and board the 13.30 Britannia Airways flight for Gatwick. Aboard the plane he tried to relax but found it impossible. He calculated how long it would take to get from Gatwick to Wyatt's place. By taxi, if he bribed the driver heavily enough, maybe something less than two hours. Which meant that in less than four hours' time he would know exactly what the trouble was.

Of one thing he felt fairly certain: there *was* trouble. What else could it mean? – that voice, Garrison's mind-voice, calling to him telepathically. And thinking about it, Koenig knew why he had gone on last night's drinking binge. That too had been Garrison: Koenig had known that something was going terribly wrong, and that Richard Garrison was in the thick of it. Very well, orders or no orders he must return to England at once and find out what was amiss. And put it to rights, if that were at all possible. If anything had happened to Garrison – then let the Good Lord have mercy on whoever was responsible.

Now who would be responsible? Koenig fingered his chin and frowned long and darkly, and he sat thinking his bad thoughts from the beginning of the flight through to its end . . .

Garrison could hold on no longer. With a groan of despair he relaxed his mind-grip on the Machine; which immediately fell outwards and rolled on to its side, carrying several of the big cats with it and crushing them. The rest sprang aside and, snarling their triumph, hurled themselves at the entrance to Garrison's cave. With one final burst of ESP energy, Garrison levitated two of them and crashed them together against a pink-veined column. But as these two fell stunned, so the others were upon him.

At that very moment Garrison became aware of an extra presence here on the fringe of the fossil forest, one which blew upon him like a breath of fresh air in the heart of a burning desert. He felt a mind brush his mind, felt the warmth of a love transcending all other loves, the love of this – stranger? – for him, and was awed by the sheer raging force of the emotion.

At that moment, too, he knew that his time was up. The great cats were upon him, their teeth and claws raking him, sinking into his vital places. They were upon him, yes, but upon them . . . a great black shadow that moved and struck like dark lightning, a creature more savage yet, whose strength was love and therefore stronger by far than the vengeful hatred which motivated the zombie-tigers.

Unreal she was – certainly unsolid, ethereal – but at the same time and completely paradoxically, effective as a scythe amongst stems of ripe corn. And Garrison knew her, remembered her from that Otherworld where once he had had substance.

'Suzy!' he gasped, and the huge black ghost-dog whined worriedly, once, before snarling and snapping yet again as she hurled herself at the throat of a startled cat. And though they fought back, turning their great fangs and claws upon her, still they had little chance against this phantom hound. Her advantage was this: that where she bit they felt it, while where they clawed she was as smoke. And in the end the entire pack of them fled as one; and bounding high, their heads lolling as one head, they merged, shrank and became flat and two-dimensional, melting into a pink wall and forming a small cat-pattern trapped in the eon-frozen coral.

Only then did the ghost-dog relax and pad silently to Garrison's side, her eyes like twin golden will-o'-the-wisps in a head of black smoke. A manifestation, nothing more, but one possessed of a will and a love beyond the ken of mundane men; and where she laid her head upon Garrison's lap he felt its weight, but when he went to fondle her ears his hand passed through her as through a dusky mirror of dirty water. But he knew her strength, the strength of her devotion, and it buoyed him up.

She would be his companion on the quest, sniffing out the way for him to the end of the journey. Inspired, he stood up and stepped out of the tiny cave; and Suzy was there padding at his heels.

'Up,' he commanded the Machine; and Psychomech righted itself and floated free of the floor. Garrison climbed aboard the Machine and called Suzy up behind him. She sat there, and despite her insubstantiality he felt her paw heavy upon his shoulder; and for all that she was the ghost of a dog, still her sweet panting breath warmed his neck as they rode the Machine out of the coral complex under a night of indigo sky and jewel stars.

No longer weary, Garrison guided his massy mount towards the distant glow of dawn; and he somehow knew that the way would not be long now, and he wondered what the end of it would be . . .

4.20 P.M.

Koenig was well satisfied with the taxi driver's performance. He paid him, included a large tip, entered his master's house and questioned the servants. His original intention had been to go direct to Wyatt's place, but in the space of the last three hours he had changed his mind. What if . . . just supposing . . . how could he be *sure* that what he had experienced was real? Might it not have been conjured by his own fear for Garrison's well-being? And what now, if he went bursting in on this experiment in which Garrison had involved himself; this necessary experiment if ever Adam Schenk's forecasts were to prove themselves, if ever Thomas Schroeder were to have the chance to return, reborn in Garrison's body and mind?

The servants were not reassuring. Garrison had left the house early on Sunday morning; Mr Wyatt had collected him by car. Before leaving, the master had warned them that he would not be returning, that he might well be away for the entire week. They were not to worry but must expect

318

him when they saw him. The mistress of the house had gone out that same morning, returning in the evening, and she had gone out again this morning bright and early. She had taken her own car, the red Ford Capri. That was as much as they could tell him.

Koenig thanked them, told them that all was well and said they were not to worry. He would be taking the Mercedes out and could not say when he would be back; he, too, was to be expected when he appeared. Then he went out to the garage . . .

Koenig!

Garrison saw him there high on that jutting rock, standing square and squat atop that unscalable flat-roofed peak in the shining dawn air, a semi-solid silhouette like a burning after-image which will not remove with a blinking of the eye but seems to smoke and smoulder on the retina.

And yet the image was incomplete. Garrison recognized this scene from some previous time and knew that something was missing. A machine? Yes, a machine. Not like the Machine, no, but a machine nevertheless. A bright, silver thing. A—

—Car? Yes, an automobile. A . . . Mercedes!

Memories at once flooded Garrison's mind. Of Koenig, of the great silver Mercedes with its dual steering system. He blinked his eyes again at the figure on the high jutting rock. Koenig, alone. Koenig, like a mirage, a mind-picture.

Garrison formed an idea.

Suzy the Dobermann pinscher, however solid she felt where she hugged close behind him, was merely a ghost-dog, avatar of a creature from a separate world and life. Koenig, too. Very well, if Garrison could mind-project these images of living things – if he could dream of them, draw them to him from that Otherworld – might he not also mind-project the image of an inanimate object? Koenig was incomplete without the car, like a picture without its frame.

Garrison squeezed his eyes tight shut . . . and when next he opened them the shimmering shape of a silver Mercedes stood behind the darker silhouette of the man, who now waved and beckoned Garrison on, pointing with outstretched arm and hand.

This was what Garrison had been waiting for, this sign. Now he knew for certain that he was close to quest's end, that Koenig merely pointed the way to his ultimate objective.

Behind him now those valleys and oceans of earlier dreams, those lizard-lands of weird vegetation and tortured rock formations. Behind him, too, the cloud-capped, moon-stabbing mountains and silvery lakes of Leviathan. But ahead . . . ahead the winding mountain pass above which, impossibly perched, Koenig stood with legs wide-spread, squarely pointing the way.

The way through the pass. The way to the final confrontation.

Garrison waved his thanks to the figure on the rock and rode the Machine into the mouth of the tortuously winding pass. And behind him Koenig and the car faded slowly into shimmering distance. And beyond the pass—

Beyond the pass a forest of dead skeletal trees went down to a shore of pitch washed by a great black oily lake. And in the middle of the lake a black rock looming, and built upon it a black castle glittering like faceted coal or jet.

And somewhere in that castle a Black Room with a forbidden secret. And in the discovery of that secret the end of the quest.

The end, too, of the man who had been Richard Garrison

Chapter Seventeen

On a small wooded hill overlooking Garrison's Sussex place, Kevin Connery lay in the short grass beneath the fringing branches of a bush and gazed through binoculars at the front door of the house. His excitement made his breathing sharp, irregular. He had waited here more or less continually for three days and nights, until at long last the man he hated most in all the world had returned. Willy Koenig had entered that house just a few short minutes ago, but to Connery each one of those minutes had seemed like an hour.

Despite the fact that it was cool beneath the bush, where the springy earth was dappled by splashes of penetrating sunlight, Connery sweated. It was the hot sweat of anticipation, the sweet sweat of revenge. He mopped his brow, gingerly fingering a stipple of insect bites where they had blotched his grotesquely scarred nose and cheeks. His fingers traced the scars, ugly white river valleys on the landscape of his face, and he remembered how they got there.

He remembered his headlong flight through a plate glass window, and the delay in treatment through his natural reluctance to seek a bona-fide doctor, and the IRA 'medic' who finally stitched him up – in more ways than one – but mostly he remembered the man who tossed him through the window. Willy Koenig.

After that there had been the humiliation of his 'reduction to the ranks for gross inefficiency'; and finally, permanently scarred and hideously so, he had been advised simply to 'go away'. And that was advice he could not ignore. He had become an embarrassment; he could never pull another job, not looking the way he did. And any casual employment outside the IRA (he had always been a petty criminal) was equally unfeasible; he would be far too easily recognized. As for his needs as a man; even before his 'accident' he had been unattractive, but now—? Who would look at him now? Now he would have difficulty buying himself a whore.

And all of this had festered in his heart, producing more black pus of hatred than the yellow pus which had poisoned all one hundred and seventy of those clumsy stitches in his face. Then, a year ago, he had spotted Koenig and his blind boss at a big party in the London Hilton. By then Connery had been the head downstairs porter at the hotel and doing all right for himself, but as soon as he had seen Koenig the old sores had opened up again.

It had been a simple thing to find out about Koenig – where he lived, what he did – and only a little more difficult to keep tenuous tabs on his comings and goings. After that—

During the last twelve months Connery had used up considerable money and time and energy in putting together a far more complete file on Koenig's present life and situation than any dossier the war-crimes researchers might have constructed at the end of World War II. And over that same period he had let his hatred bleed and rot until it became gangrenous; and in the mire of his mind he had plotted his revenge, which could only be complete if it were Koenig's death.

As to how that murder would be achieved: that was easy. Connery had always had 'the knack' with explosives. After all this time he would be a little rusty, that was true, but he knew he could trust his talents this one last time. Finally his opportunity had presented itself. An Irish friend at Gatwick had reported Koenig's departure, the fact that he had returned to his homeland on an open ticket. A short visit, doubtless – for Connery now knew that Koenig rarely

·left Garrison's side for more than a week or so at the outside – but that was fine. Two or three days would be more than ample time.

And now, for the first time in Connery's life that he remembered, his luck seemed inexhaustible. Not only Koenig but Garrison, too, was absent from the house in Sussex; and the blind man's young wife much given to going off visiting; *and* the household's great dog kennelled at Midhurst! What could be simpler?

It would have to be the car, of course, that great silver Mercedes of which Koenig was the only driver except on very rare occasions. Connery had got into the garage yesterday and planted his bomb beneath the bonnet close to the dash on the driver's side, since when he had waited and watched and sweated it out.

He had been prepared to wait for several days (a good many empty bottles and cans, hastily buried in a shallow pit, and a number of full bottles and foodstuffs in a knapsack, and a rolled-up sleeping-bag close to hand beneath the bush, would readily testify to that) but it had not been necessary. Koenig was back earlier than Connery had foreseen, and only a few minutes ago he had gone into the house.

Now all that remained was for the crewcut Kraut bastard to come back—

Out!

Connery's luck was holding. It was almost as if he had willed Koenig out of the house. Moreover, the German headed straight for the garage.

'I'm not sure where you think you're going, me boyo,' Connery whispered to himself, 'but I'll bet you my last harp-backed tenpence piece you don't make it!' And his scars grew whiter still as he smiled a grim and ghastly smile . . .

Garrison had commenced to hurl himself and his Machine time and again against the Wall of Power, the invisible force-

screen emanating from the castle. A sweat of exertion already filmed his skin, and his bones felt shaken with recurrent concussions. But he knew he must go on, must break through, succeed, bring his quest to its close before—

Before those previsioned disasters came to pass. But at the same time (nightmare of frustration) he also suspected that he was already too late, a suspicion which took on flesh as he suddenly heard a splintering of bleached brittle-trees from the bone-white forest behind. It was Koenig, of course, could only be Koenig, driving the Mercedes through the forest, crashing a path through everything standing in his way.

Garrison turned his head to see, was in time to witness the Mercedes ploughing to a halt in the sticky pitch of the shore.

The German was out of the car in a moment, shouting: 'Richard, Richard – I've got to get you off the Machine. I must get you off Psychomech!'

Garrison shook his head, held up a hand as if to hold Koenig back. 'No, the Machine is mine now. I'm safe on the Machine.'

But Suzy had heard and understood their words, and she agreed with Koenig. And for the first time in her life she heeded the advice of a man other than her master, even to the extreme of going against her master's wishes. Thus she sank her teeth into Garrison's sleeve and tried to drag him from the back of the Machine. It was not to be that easy, however; he clung desperately to his metal and plastic mount, until finally Suzy's teeth tore his shirt. Off balance, yelping, she fell in a spastic thrashing of limbs to the tarry shore beside the blackly lapping lake.

Only then did the man-God Schroeder appear, that great face in the sky crying – ACCEPT ME, RICHARD! ACCEPT ME AND WIN. LET ME IN . . .

But the face was different now, full of desperation, of fear. It was an intense face, a face knowing its own weakness, the face of impending failure.

'Accept him, Richard!' Koenig cried from where he dragged

his feet in tar. 'Remember your pact—'

'No!' *Garrison screamed his answer.* 'I have won through, I myself have conquered. I don't need him – he needs me! And why should he live in me? Where was the man-God when I faced the zombie-tigers? Where was he then?'

RICHARD, I AM WEAK NOW, *and indeed the man-God's voice seemed weaker.* I AM FADING. MY FORCE IS GOING OUT OF THE WORLD, MY LIGHT IS BURNING LOW. I TRIED TO COME TO YOU IN THE CORAL CAVES BUT HAD NOT THE STRENGTH. AND HOW WOULD IT PROFIT ME? YOU WOULD NOT HAVE ACCEPTED ME. NOT THEN. NO, I HAD TO PRESERVE MY STRENGTH. BUT NOW? . . . THIS IS MY LAST CHANCE. YOU *MUST* ACCEPT ME NOW OR I AM NO MORE. AND THEN YOU WILL BE NO MORE, KOENIG WILL BE NO MORE, SUZY WILL BE NO MORE. ACCEPT ME NOW, RICHARD – PLEASE!

Garrison felt torn. He snarled his torment into the faces of Schroeder, Koenig, Suzy and turned the Machine until it once more faced the invisible wall of energy, the Power from the castle. He must make one final assault upon that barrier, break through, cross the lake and enter the castle. Then . . . the Black Room!

That was where the Horror lurked, in the Black Room, and he must banish that Horror forever.

'Richard, Richard!' *Koenig cried, his voice full of distress.* 'Please, please . . .'

Garrison suffered agonies hearing that cry. He turned his head and looked back. The silver Mercedes was sinking into the tar, going down fast, its bonnet already disappearing as black bubbles rose all about, bursting in sticky tatters.

Koenig floundered forward, his feet sinking in the black ooze but still moving fast enough to keep its hideous suction at bay; like some strange, squat insect stumbling over the scummy film on a stagnant pool, its feet trapped in tiny boots of algae.

BELIEVE ME, RICHARD, *boomed the man-God, but with a voice even less sure of itself now,* YOU DON'T WANT TO DIE. YOU *MUST* BELIEVE ME. AFTER ALL, I KNOW WHAT IT'S LIKE HERE!

And then the bomb, the burning brown-paper cube, spinning out of the sky and hovering over Willy Koenig where he struggled in tar up to his calves. 'Willy, look out!' Garrison cried. He turned his Machine upon the spinning bomb and rammed it where it flared and sputtered over Koenig's head. Even knowing that the thing must soon turn incandescent and blow him to hell, he rammed it again, knocking it away from Koenig and placing himself and the Machine between bomb and mired man.

ACCEPT ME, RICHARD! *the man-God Schroeder howled.* ACCEPT ME NOW!

Suzy, too, gave one last desperate howl as she went down into the tar, her black body disappearing into blacker deeps. For a moment only her working muzzle showed – then was gone. 'Suzy!'— and Garrison's howl was more desperate, more agonized yet.

ACCEPT ME, RICHARD, AND SUZY CAN LIVE AGAIN. INDEED, SHE IS NOT YET DEAD, NOT TRULY. THIS IS MERELY A FORECAST, A WARNING. BUT WITHOUT ME SHE *WILL* DIE AND STAY DEAD. YES, AND SO WILL I – YOU – ALL OF US!

Koenig, sucked down now and only his head showing, gurgled: 'Accept him, Richard!' The bomb flared and sputtered over his tar-spattered head.

'Damn you, man-God!' Garrison cried finally. 'Tell me the nature of this barrier.'

YOU ARE THE BARRIER, RICHARD! *the face in the sky answered at once.* IT IS YOUR LAST GREAT FEAR. IT IS THAT YOU DON'T WISH TO KNOW WHAT LIES BEYOND. IT IS THAT YOU *ALREADY* KNOW BUT WON'T ACCEPT. VERY WELL, ACCEPT *ME* INSTEAD, AND TOGETHER WE CAN COMPLETE THE QUEST.

'Promise me that!' Garrison's request was almost plaintive. 'Promise me you'll help me see beyond, help me find the answer.'

I DO PROMISE IT. I PROMISE ANYTHING.

Garrison clenched his fists, ground his teeth and rolled his eyes – then threw his arms wide. 'Very well,' he hissed, his face pale as death, foam showing white at the corners of his mouth, 'I accept you. Come into me, man-God!'

Their minds meshed, became one.

Garrison's brain felt as if it suddenly bulged in his skull.

He knew . . . things. Many things. And he knew how to discover more. How to discover . . . almost anything. Or everything!

He knew that he was still Garrison, and yet he was so much more than merely Garrison. And he knew a gnawing, greedy hunger. For life. For love. For sex, food, drink, air – for all sensual and pleasurable things. Like a man denied these things for long, long years. Like – yes, like a corpse risen up – like a man returned from death, given a new lease of life.

Life . . .

Death!

And soon Koenig would be dead, unless—

Garrison/Schroeder reached out with his mind and lifted Koenig up from the tar, setting him down again on firm ground at the edge of the brittle-tree forest. As for the sputtering, smoking bomb: he simply teleported that back to its source, returned it to its sender.

Then – almost without considering what he did, without real or conscious volition – he ate and drank, doing it quickly, almost greedily. For he was aware now of a very special urgency growing in him. And finally he drank deeply of the air, filling his lungs before once more turning his face towards the castle across the lake.

And thrusting all fears aside he sped his Machine forward, hurtling out over the sluggish black wavelets like an arrow to its target. And no screen of Power obstructed his course now,

for no power in the universe could stop him.
  Thus he hurried to quest's end . . .

As Koenig drove the Mercedes slowly down the drive, Connery rolled on to his side and took what looked like a pocket radio from his knapsack. It was in fact a small radio-control device. He jerked up the aerial, flipped a switch and a tiny red light began a steady blinking. The bomb in the car was now armed. Koenig had only thirty seconds to live.

At the end of the drive the Mercedes passed out through ornate wrought-iron gates and turned right behind a high brick wall and down an avenue of blighted elms. Connery held his binoculars to his eyes and trained them upon the spot where the car would come back into view at the end of the wall which marked the boundaries of Garrison's property. Ten seconds had gone by.

Koenig had driven half-way along the avenue of elms and was just beginning to accelerate when he felt the steering wheel twist in his hands. At first he guessed the car had gone over some unnoticed obstruction, but in the time taken for this thought to enter his head the Mercedes had already slowed to a halt. Frowning, he glanced down at the pedals. The brakes were full on – and now his frown became an astonished gape as the car's engine switched itself off!

'Verdammt!' he hissed out loud. And, 'What in the name of—?'

The short hairs at the back of his neck prickled as he felt his hands caught and gently but firmly removed from the steering wheel and pushed down into his lap.

'Richard!' he gasped.

The bonnet clanged open. Startled, Koenig jerked his head and shoulders back against the padding of his seat. As he did so he saw a small cardboard box trailing tatters of black adhesive tape rise up like a balloon from beneath the bonnet, accelerating upwards and over the wall and so out of sight.

Then, volition returning, Koenig tugged at the door release. The door refused to open, would not move a fraction of an inch – but the bonnet did! Slowly it fell, clicked shut, allowed Koenig an unobstructed view of the lane ahead. Finally, as the engine again started itself up with a throaty cough and a roar, Koenig felt his hands taken in that phantom grip and returned to the steering wheel . . .

Seven seconds to go, and Connery began to count-down. He cast a nervous glance at the second sweep of his watch and licked his lips. 'Six, five, four,' he gritted his teeth and made slits of his eyes. 'Three, two—'

Something flew in through the hanging fringe of leaves and trailing branches. Something that Connery knew just could not be. A cardboard box, it twirled like a top, suspended before his face in the quiet, sun-splashed shade of the bush.

'*One!*' Connery heard himself croak – which was the last thing he ever heard . . .

The near-distant detonation puzzled Koenig but he was given little or no time to wonder at it. The Mercedes had suddenly started forward of its own accord and its controls had been returned to him. He got a grip of himself, pushing any and all questions about the incident to the back of his mind, and drove on.

Reaching a metalled surface he picked up speed, breathing more deeply as the car responded to *his* touch and not that of some unseen other. And knowing now that his premonition had been right – that indeed Garrison had called out to him – he drove hard and fast.

As he drove he began to think his bad thoughts. Thoughts which, as always, were more instinctive than deliberate. Thoughts about Gareth Wyatt.

Yes, and about Terri Garrison, too . . .

They had made love, slept a short, exhausted sleep, and just a moment ago Wyatt had started awake from a bad dream. A nightmare which had featured (of all things!) the downstairs kitchen, particularly the fridge. The nightmare had been vivid and persistent – its images were there still in Wyatt's mind – and as he came more fully awake he took note of the contrasting quietness of the house. A contrast, yes, for the dream had been anything but quiet. He could still hear the door of the fridge clicking open and slamming shut, open and shut, repeatedly in his mind.

As the dream-echoes receded he considered again the quietness of the house. Too quiet. His flesh crept. What time was it?

Checking the time, Wyatt drew air sharply into his lungs. Garrison must surely be dead by now. Must . . .? Surely . . .? Wyatt grimly corrected himself: *should* be dead by now. He must go to the room of the machine at once. But—

—But the dream continued to bother him.

Terri came awake. 'Gareth?'

'I'm . . . just going down to the kitchen.' His voice was slurred with sleep.

She quickly got out of bed. 'I'll come with you.' Tousle-haired, pale and beautiful, she drew on a dressing gown. 'I don't want to be left alone . . . here. It's too quiet, somehow.'

'You too?' He shivered, understanding her apprehension. 'OK.'

They went downstairs, Wyatt entering the kitchen and Terri pausing in the doorway. She watched him, unable to understand his agitation. He stared all about at the familiar room and its contents, went to the fridge and opened the door. He looked inside, poked about, closed the door. Then he began to pace the floor – to and fro, to and fro – worriedly scratching at his neck. And again he paused at

330

the fridge, and after a moment clicked open the door and peered inside.

Suddenly Terri felt very much afraid. For Wyatt, for herself. She went to him and put her hand on his shoulder. He started at her touch and she snatched back her hand.

'Terri, I'm . . . sorry,' he said. His voice sounded haunted.

'Gareth—' She was filled with concern. 'What is it? I mean, if there's anything I—'

'*Look!*' he gasped. Again he was staring into the fridge, staring at his nightmare given substance. Her dark eyes followed his gaze – and widened. Her lips drew back from her teeth in an involuntary snarl of fear.

One after another, three slices of melon – slices Terri herself had cut from the fruit – disappeared before her eyes, eaten away down to the rind, snatched from the plate and invisibly devoured in a moment. The level of an orange drink in a plastic bottle declined until the bottle, in answer to Nature's insistence, crushed in upon its own sudden vacuum. Cubes of cheese on a small wooden platter vanished one by one, crumbling into thin air. Cold cuts of meat were likewise taken, bite by supernatural bite.

'Jesus Christ!' Wyatt hissed between clenched teeth. 'Jesus H Chr—' He reached a trembling hand into the fridge.

Blue tendrils of writhing, crackling fire enveloped his hand, the fridge, Wyatt himself. He was hurled back, knocked from his feet and sent skidding across the floor. The door of the fridge swung wide, slammed itself shut. The traceries of blue fire flickered out.

Terri went to Wyatt, her hands fluttering like trapped birds as she helped him to his feet. 'Gareth, are you all right? What *was* that? Did I really see—?'

'You saw,' his voice was a painful croak. 'We both saw.'

'But what does it—?'

'What does it mean? Didn't I tell you he was being fed?'

Wyatt's eyes were wild, his tone rising up the scale. 'Well, so he is – but I was wrong to think someone else was feeding him. He's doing it himself! He has powers, Terri, strange powers. And somehow – I don't know how – but I'm sure Psychomech is helping him!'

'What?' Her response was incredulous, frightened. 'The machine is *helping* him? But it was supposed to kill him!'

'God damn!' Wyatt slammed a shaky fist into the palm of his hand. 'And it *would* have killed anyone else – four or five anyone elses by now – but not your bloody husband. Not the indestructible Richard sodding Garrison esquire!'

'Powers,' she seized upon the word. 'You mean psychic powers? Yes, I'm sure he has. And you think that the machine has somehow enhanced them?'

'Yes,' he nodded, trembling, his aspect turning chalky as the anger drained out of him, was replaced with fear. 'I mean, I knew he was different, but this—'

Scared almost witless, Terri was shaking like a leaf in a gale. 'But if he's able to feed himself like this, then—'

'More than just that, Terri,' Wyatt cut her off. 'He can protect himself, too. Even fight back, yes.' He nodded, gripped her shoulders and stared deep into her eyes. 'Terri, what's going on in that room up there? I have to see, have to know.'

He released her and headed for the door.

'Gareth, wait!'

He turned back.

'Don't worry, I'll be OK.'

She followed close behind him up the stairs, and on the landing obeyed his instructions and made for the bedroom. Wyatt waited until he believed he heard the door of the bedroom close behind her, then turned towards the room of the machine . . .

The murmurs of hostile minds echoed on the fringe of Garrison/Schroeder's awareness, coming to him across unknown gulfs from the Otherworld. They signalled danger, but nothing that couldn't be handled. He put up minimal automatic defences, setting them in his multimind as an ordinary man sets an alarm clock; a trifling matter. Then he returned to a more immediate problem: namely that it seemed to be taking him an inordinately long time to cross the black lake. The black castle seemed no closer now than when he left the shore. Which, at the speed he was travelling, was plainly impossible.

Unless of course he did not actually wish to reach his objective. Unless this was simply a second barrier, erected in his own mind and just as impassable as the first. A self-imposed barrier, protecting him from that final confrontation.

The Schroeder part of him knew that in fact this was the essence of the problem, the answer to the paradox – that however much he willed the journey to its close, the Garrison part would hold back – and so, in a little while, the matter was taken out of Garrison's hands completely as Schroeder boosted and accelerated their weird flight until the Machine and its passenger fairly rocketed across the blackly lapping lake. The Garrison facet, quiescent, made no protest until, reaching the rock whereon the castle loomed, he once more took ascendance, bringing the Machine to a halt and dismounting.

Then, entering the substructure through a lower portal in the rock itself, Garrison/Schroeder found corkscrew steps leading upwards and made to climb them. But—

He paused, his foot on the first step, trembling. For while the Schroeder part knew only a keen curiosity, the Garrison facet knew stark terror. Up there in the inky blackness, in the Black Room, lurked the Horror itself; and the weight of its presence, so close now, pressed like uncounted tons on his bones until they felt like jelly. Nor would he let the Schroeder part take ascendance, for despite his desperate need to know, still his fear of the un-known denied the other's assistance. He was in the position of a man with a rotten tooth, wandering to and

333

fro outside the surgery, mortally fearing the dentist's chair.

Stalemate, unless . . .

What of Psychomech? Might he not draw upon the Machine's vast powerhouse of energy for the strength he needed to suppress his own terror? He went back out from the portal in the black rock beneath the castle and laid his hands upon the dully recumbent Machine, willing it to be whole once more and assist him in his task. And in a moment or two, as he closed his eyes and directed his will more positively, so the Machine responded.

Lights began to glow within its massy frame, and warmth issued from it in gusts like the quickening breath of a giant. And slowly but surely its hum became audible as power flowed once more in its strange plastic veins and chromium belly and loins . . .

Terri had not gone into the bedroom. She simply could not bear to be alone at this moment, in the knowledge that Richard was still alive and that his mind was somehow mobile and possibly malignant *outside* his body. She stood for a moment undecided outside the bedroom door, her hand on the doorknob. Then, fear overcoming her, she turned and ran silently back the way she had come.

She came round the corner from the landing and found Wyatt still at the door. His back was towards her but she could see what he was doing: turning the key in the third and last padlock. The other two locks lay on the carpeted floor where he had let them fall. He had not seen her, and knowing that his nerves were as badly frayed as her own, she made no sound but let him get on with what he was doing. The lock in his hand sprang free of its hasp and staple and he pushed at the door. It opened, maybe an inch, and—

The light in the room behind the door was a glaring, unbearable electric blue. It issued out through the one-inch gap as an almost solid panel, not diffusing but *striking* forth like some great flat tongue of hot metal freshly forged. Wyatt gaped, gave the door a second, almost automatic push, then angrily threw his shoulder against it. The door resisted, gave a fraction, then slammed shut and threw Wyatt across the corridor, his back flattening against the opposite wall. Though the blue light was now cut off, the door of the room still gave off a soft radiance. So did the lock in Wyatt's hand.

He dropped it – but instead of falling to the floor the padlock shot across the corridor and locked itself through hasp and staple! Then, while Wyatt and Terri stood mesmerized, the key turned white hot, melted in the lock and effectively welded it solid. The white heat cooled to a dull red, the blue radiance died away, the fused padlock swung gratingly on its staple for a moment and became still . . .

Terri drew air and gave it out in a sob. 'My God, my *God*!'

Wyatt glanced at her, not really seeing her. He forced his eyes to focus, gulped, and croaked, 'Terri, I—'

'I have to get out of here,' she cut him off, hysteria rising in her. 'Have to get out . . .' She spun on her heel, fled for the bedroom. Galvanized out of his state of shock, Wyatt followed her. She began throwing on her clothes, gibbering helplessly, unable to control the motions of her own limbs, her shuddering body.

Seeing her like that and realizing the danger if she was seen in this condition outside the house, he forced his own fears from his mind, grabbed and shook her. 'Terri!' he snapped, lifting his hand threateningly. 'Terri, get a grip of yourself. I agree, you should get out of here, and right now – but not in that state. Calm yourself down, then go. I'll finish . . . what has to be finished here.'

'Oh, Gareth!' She threw herself into his arms. 'It's all gone wrong, horribly wrong.'

'I know it,' he nodded over her shoulder, 'but we're not

through yet. Listen, you finish dressing and tidy yourself up. Then go on home. I'll give you a ring later – when it's all over.'

'Will it be over?' she asked. 'Will it ever be over?'

'Oh, yes,' he promised her. 'One way or the other.'

A few minutes later she was ready to leave and he took her downstairs. She had parked her Capri discreetly at the back of the house beneath lilac trees whose laden branches gave it good cover. At the back door she drew him close, said: 'Be careful, Gareth. I love you, you know?'

'Yes, I know. And I'll be careful.'

She opened the door, stepped out.

A low, hostile growl, rising rapidly to a snarl of hatred, sounded from the direction of the lilacs. Suzy, a black thunderbolt, her face a wrinkled black mask of hatred surrounding clashing ivory jaws, came bounding to the attack!

Terri saw, froze, was dragged back inside the house barely in time. Wyatt slammed the door on the dog and he and Terri stood in each other's arms, trembling, listening to Suzy's barking, then to her whining and frantic scratching at the door. Finally Terri freed herself and vacantly examined her torn skirt, the graze on her thigh where Suzy's teeth had sought purchase and missed, however narrowly.

'Damned dog!' Wyatt whispered. 'What's she doing here? I thought she was kennelled. And why attack you like that?'

'She was kennelled,' Terri answered. 'She must have escaped. And did you see her? She looks so – insane!'

'Crazy, yes – like everything else that's happening round here. Well, she can't cover both doors at once. Come on, we'll go to the front. Give me your car keys. If the black bitch follows us round to the front you can stay there – draw her attention – while I sneak back here, let myself out and bring your car round. OK?'

She dumbly nodded, stumbling after him through the house to the front door. In a matter of seconds Suzy had followed them, was out there pawing at the double-glazed doors, then snarling and throwing herself against the tough glass panels when she saw Terri and Wyatt where they huddled within.

'OK,' Wyatt said, but with a tremble in his voice. 'Fine. You stay here and I'll go and get your car. I'll bring it right up to the door, so you can let me straight into the house. And don't panic, she can't get in. That's good quality glass.'

'Hurry,' Terri whispered 'Please hurry!'

'I will, and if I can just get that black bastard under the wheels . . .'

While Terri stayed where she was, wringing her hands and cowering back from the door – but always letting the frenetic Suzy keep her in sight – Wyatt let himself out of the back door and into Terri's car. He drove round to the front of the house, saw Suzy where she now loped across the gravel drive towards the gardens, and aimed the car at her, putting his foot down on the accelerator.

What happened next came almost too fast for Wyatt to comprehend. It came with a roar and a rush, in the shape of Garrison's great silver Mercedes, leaping from behind a screen of tall shrubs where they bordered the garden. The Merc rammed Terri's Capri sideways-on, driving it bodily into the front wall of the house. The front half of the Capri was compressed, its windscreen buckling and flying into a thousand shards which fortunately fragmented outwards and across the bonnet. Instinctively Wyatt switched off the stuttering engine as he smelled petrol, and when the Mercedes backed off he tried his driver's door. It was buckled firmly shut.

Giving him no time to think, the Mercedes came at him again. As it picked up speed its bent bonnet began a loose flapping, like the inarticulate mouth of some great mechanical idiot. Wyatt somehow managed to scramble through the empty front window and was on all fours on the bonnet when the Merc struck. The impact tossed him clear – but not before he got a good look at the demon car's driver. Or rather, not before he had seen that the Merc *had no driver at all!*

Then Terri had the front door of the house open a crack and Wyatt was running on rubbery legs, Suzy hot on his heels, and in another moment the door was slamming shut behind him – slamming in Suzy's snarling face – and Terri was in his arms, both of them sobbing hysterically.

'The car,' she finally found space for words. 'That's Richard's car – but there's no driver!'

'I know.'

Terri took herself in hand and squeezed very hard. She stood away from Wyatt, brushed her hair back, looked squarely into his face. 'It's Richard, isn't it? He's doing all this. He has us at his mercy. We've failed.'

'It's your husband,' he nodded. 'Him and Psychomech together. Krippner put something into that machine, something I didn't know about – the little Nazi bastard!'

'Krippner?'

'Forget it. But you're right about Richard, Terri. He's controlling the dog and the car.' He gritted his teeth. 'Well, at least I can do something about the dog – and that'll be a start . . .'

She followed him through into his downstairs library. He took down a shotgun from wrought iron brackets above an antique fireplace. The stock was beautifully carved and polished. 'I bought it for its looks,' he told her, 'but it's deadly for all that. I haven't had occasion to use it yet, so now is as good a time as any.'

From a desk drawer he took cartridges, just three of them, loading the weapon with two and placing the third cartridge in his dressing gown pocket. He went back to the front of the house with Terri close behind. Through the windows they could see the Mercedes parked away down the drive facing the house. Steam coiled in wisps from its gaping bonnet. Of Suzy there was no sign – until Wyatt opened the door.

Then she came, hurtling from behind a bush, a nightmare in black that rushed upon him like some irresistible doom. Except that he had the shotgun. As she leapt for his throat so he raised the weapon and pulled one of its twin triggers.

Suzy was brought to a halt in mid-leap, stopped dead by the force of the blast. Literally dead, her head almost disintegrating and slopping back over her shoulders in scarlet tatters. Her corpse fell at Wyatt's feet. He stared at the mess for a moment, shuddering, then lifted his eyes apprehensively at the big Merc.

Then he gasped, drew back inside the house and bolted the door. And he never once took his eyes off the figure standing beside the car, the figure of Willy Koenig. Steady as a rock the squat, crewcut German stood there, staring, his body motionless but his face working and his fists clenching and unclenching where they hung at his sides.

Terri, too, had seen Koenig. She too stared at him through the double-glazed doors. 'Willy!' she whispered. 'He's come back . . .'

'Brought back,' Wyatt snarled, '—by your husband, I suppose.'

He snapped open the shotgun, popped the third cartridge into the still smoking chamber, closed the gun.

'Look!' Terri's trembling hand on his elbow straightened him up. 'He's coming!'

Koenig was walking towards the house, his face cold and impassive now, his pace measured. Only his eyes showed emotion, and they burned. If ever Wyatt had seen a man with murder in his face, Willy Koenig was that man.

'Gareth,' Terri repeated, 'he's *coming*!'

'I see him,' he answered. He drew back the bolts on the

door and opened it, then aimed the shotgun directly at Koenig. 'It's the only way now, Terri,' he said. 'Don't look . . .'

The black stone corkscrew stairs seemed to wind interminably tighter and tighter as Garrison/Schroeder rode Psychomech steeply upwards and towards that terminal turret wherein he knew the Black Room waited with its terrible secret, that Horror he had feared above all horrors.

But Psychomech had at least given him the strength he needed to face that Horror, so that now he knew only a predominant determination to be rid of the thing once and for all. His integrity – his very existence – would be impure, imperfect, indeed jeopardized if the Horror were allowed its tainting, taunting co-existence.

Jeopardy, yes, for even now he could feel the reverberations of the Horror (which must also have certain of its tentacles or acolytes in the Otherworld), telepathic murmurs which threatened once again, unknowingly warning him of imminent dangers and dooms. Dangers to his multimind here in this sinister pile of black stone, and to his physical being in—

—In the Otherworld!

And at last, as any man on the brink of waking, Garrison/Schroeder finally knew that he dreamed, that his existence was in truth a subconscious existence quite apart from his physical reality. Perhaps the Machine itself imparted this knowledge to him; or maybe it came as a result of his expanded dual mentality and his now almost fully developed ESP powers. Whichever, he knew he dreamed, and that after he disposed of the final Horror he must awaken.

But awaken to what? To all the dangers of the Otherworld? To treachery?

Treachery from whom? From which quarter?

If only he could remember more of the Otherworld . . . but he could not. What Garrison/Schroeder could do, however, was reinforce his defences. He put out mental hands, gave mental commands, and it was as if the black castle knew!

As if the castle were a living thing which feels its life ebbing, the entire structure trembled and cracks appeared in its walls. Black dust and stony debris rained down from the darkness yawning above, and a half-light filtered in through the shaken walls. And onward and upward Garrison/Schroeder rode the Machine, and the castle's quaking grew steadily worse.

Now the pile's lesser creatures took to flight, like rats fleeing a foundering ship, and their leathery shapes of darkness scuttled on the spiralling stone stairs or flitted frantically overhead. Perhaps the Horror, sensing Garrison/Schroeder's approach, might also attempt flight. He would not let that happen. Once again he extended ESP hands to set up mental barriers, sealing all escape routes. And though he acted subconsciously, still the act had its parallels in the waking world.

And at last, rising up from the great spiral stairwell, Garrison/Schroeder found himself on a great stone landing beneath a high vaulted ceiling. And on the landing a huge black door riveted his gaze, beyond which—

Beyond that door . . . a room, a riddle, and a Horror.

The end of the quest.

The Black Room . . .

Koenig saw the shotgun in Wyatt's hands, ignored it, came straight on. He was just ten paces away when Wyatt thought, *he must be stark, raving mad!* and started to take up the slack on the trigger.

At that precise moment a grey wall appeared, a dome that reached up and over the roof of the house, shutting the house in and keeping Koenig out. The German paused, came closer, touched the grey wall of the dome. It was weird, like grey solidified mist. Not warm, not cold, but hard as stone and equally impenetrable. Koenig walked its perimeter. There was no way in. It was simply a great grey blister sealing off Wyatt's house from the outside world.

Koenig shuddered and thought again of the force which had driven him, against his own will, to approach Wyatt where he had stood in the doorway cradling that shotgun. And that had been after he had witnessed Suzy's death by the same weapon in the same hands. It could only have been Garrison who had taken command of his will; but by the same token only Garrison could have created the grey dome.

Koenig nodded to himself. His life had not been in jeopardy, no. Garrison had merely used him to keep Wyatt in the house while he created a more permanent barrier, the dome. But nevertheless it had been – unnerving. To say the least!

He walked back toward the Mercedes, cold sweat drying on his back and making his shirt cling . . .

Terri and Wyatt sweated, too, but on them it was the sweat of absolute terror. They stood, mouths agape, staring at the grey wall where it loomed just beyond the open door. The wall seemed slightly translucent, letting a little light into the house but not much. It also created an overpowering sense of claustrophobia. And at all of the doors and windows it was the same story. The house had become a rat-trap, and they were the rats.

'Trapped!' Her voice was a tiny, echoing thing.

Wyatt was ashen in the dim light. 'Yes,' he croaked, 'but there might still be one way out. It's him or us now.' He reeled away towards the stairs, Terri tugging at his arm and begging:

'Oh, no! Not that, Gareth. It's murder, just murder.'

'Murder?' He turned to her. 'But it always has been. What did you think I was going to do to Koenig, Terri? What do you think *he* would have done to *us*? This has gone past right or wrong now. Now it's life or death – ours or Garrison's. Can't you see that? Can't you feel it building up? Believe me, if I don't get him, he'll sure as hell get us!'.

They were half-way up the stairs when she grabbed his arm again. 'Gareth!' Her voice was a breathless tremor of disbelief.

He turned, stumbled, sat down on the stairs. He clutched the shotgun and stared.

The grey wall had followed them, had closed in behind them, shutting off the rest of the house. The stairs went down into greyness, were lost from sight in it.

Wyatt jerked to his feet and dragged Terri scramblingly, gaspingly up to the landing. The grey wall followed, came to a halt at the head of the stairs. Terri's teeth were chattering as she hung on his neck. He dragged her almost dead weight to the door of the room of the machine. There he released her, aimed the shotgun at the single remaining fused padlock, closed his eyes and squeezed on one trigger.

The shotgun blast not only removed the padlock but slammed the door back on its hinges. Wyatt stepped inside – and staggered as if struck in the forehead! Nothing he had so far experienced could compare with this. This was utterly weird – and so frightening as to be almost unbearable.

Psychomech seemed encased in a glaring, pulsating blue fire laced with traceries of slow-flickering golden energy, like a continuous yellow lightning working in slow motion. Central upon the machine's bed, Garrison's entire body seemed to expand and contract in time with the pulsing of the alien radiance, his prone form grotesquely swollen in one moment and hideously shrivelled in the next. The whole scene – of man and machine alike – seemed to melt and flow in the pulsing light, creating an awesome stroboscopic effect which defied the eye to define any real or solid outline.

The worst thing, however, had got to be the continuous *fluctuation* of Garrison's form, that monstrous bloating and shrinking . . .

Wyatt remembered why he was there, jerked up the shotgun to his shoulder and aimed. One cartridge left. He centred the sights of the weapon on Garrison's pulsating body and pulled the trigger.

A golden web of apparently delicate energies leapt the space between Psychomech and the muzzle of the shotgun. The path of the charge was blocked. The barrels split at their ends and curled back on themselves like hot plastic, and Wyatt was snatched from his feet and hurled like a rag doll out through the open door. The door slammed shut behind him, shimmered for a moment – and where it had been the grey wall now reached from ceiling to floor!

Terri fell on Wyatt where he lay sobbing on the floor against the wall of the corridor. His back was badly bruised and his forearms singed, but apart from these superficial injuries he seemed unharmed. She helped him up, supporting him as they limped to the bedroom where they collapsed upon the bed. The grey wall followed, cocooning them in the dim room with the bed and its black sheets. It was like being underground, like being buried alive.

Wanting to scream but instead of screaming panting uncontrollably, the lovers clung, their agony of terror binding their bodies together more surely than passion, their tremors *becoming* the vibrations of passion. She felt him against her, standing erect, huge as she had rarely known him.

In the next moment they parted, stripped and fell upon one another in a frenzy.

'One last time,' she sobbed.

Last time? Yes, she was right. The last time. He could feel it. Feel it? – it was overpowering! The growing malignance, the enmity, a fearful psychic force filling the house, the room, the very air they breathed.

They made agonized love, clawing at each other, hurting one another and not caring, not even feeling . . .

* * *

The door to the Black Room.

Garrison/Schroeder's flesh tingled. He drove the Machine against the door, felt it give before Psychomech's irresistible strength. The Black Room, black as ink, with its black-sheeted bed, lay open to Garrison/Schroeder's gaze.

And upon the black bed, writhing like a nest of pallid pythons, death-white against the black—

The Garrison facet was in ascendance. He cringed, his mind shrinking down into itself, hiding, seeking solace. The man on the bed was his father, frantically copulating with one of his sluts. But could Garrison be sure? Their faces and figures seemed to be melting, changing even as he watched. Now the girl was his first true love, and the boy his best friend that had been. Or perhaps they were simply any pair of cheating lovers, caught in their act of passion by the one it would hurt the most? But no, they were not just any pair of lovers. The Garrison facet knew what he was seeing, and the knowledge was a dagger turning in his heart.

Even cringing he looked again at their white heaving flesh, then reached out a thought and slowed their frantic sexual activity. In slow motion they continued to couple – and yes, they were unmistakably his wife and her until now secret lover. They were Terri Garrison and Dr Gareth Wyatt.

Terri and Wyatt, white against black. Or black against white! Garrison's ultimate hangup: his own betrayal!

'No!' he whispered. 'No!' he shouted. 'Nonononono . . . !'

'NO!'

Crisis!

The half-suppressed Schroeder facet wanted to react but could do nothing. In another moment he would share a madman's mind.

But Psychomech – the 'repaired', complete Psychomech, the Grand Psychomech as Otto Krippner had envisaged it, the Otherworld Psychomech – was already reacting. Already delivering its surge . . .

* * *

Garrison/Schroeder came awake. He knew who he was, where he was, *what* he was. And he knew that Adam Schenk had been correct.

'Light,' he uttered the word from Schenk's horoscope. 'Let there be light!'

He opened eyes no longer scarlet but uniformly golden. And he could see. He could see more clearly than any other man or living creature before him. He saw the straps where they held him down and dissolved them. He dissolved the connections that linked him to Psychomech. He floated free of the machine's couch, his body turning through ninety degrees until his feet grazed the floor. He floated to the door and it disintegrated before him. He floated down the corridor, across the landing, and came to a halt outside Wyatt's bedroom.

And the light of his anger shone out of him, and the strength of his anger was that of an earthquake. And he was glorious in his anger. And there was a Great Power in him . . .

Wyatt came once, twice in rapid succession; Terri too, while all about the lovers the house commenced to shake and rumble. And creeping under the bedroom door from outside, a kaleidoscope of colours wove weird patterns on the carpet. Still clutching and clawing, they squirmingly adopted one of passion's oldest positions. Terri's body bucked and heaved against Wyatt's face and mouth and he tasted sweat and salt and the fruit of his own lust. Even with her mouth full of him – seeing the light from outside growing intense where it burned beneath the door – she began gurglingly to scream. She screamed in sexual frenzy, in a nightmare rictus of fear.

He came again, into her gaping mouth – came, came, came unendingly, impossibly – draining himself, destroying himself. And—

The bedroom door bulged inwards, fragmented, shattered

into a thousand flying shards and splinters.

Garrison/Schroeder stood in the riven doorway, golden-eyed, awesome – and full of anger. He could have destroyed them there and then, but something caused him to hold back. Instead he slowed them down, bringing them as he had done in his dream to slow motion where they crawled from the bed to huddle at the base of the grey wall.

No one in the whole wide world he could trust. Only Koenig.

Koenig, yes – and perhaps one other . . .

At Schloss Zonigen, a heavily muffled figure in a blue, outsize parka emblazoned with the crossed spanners of a mechanic waddled penguin-like down the vaulted, neon-lighted corridor of ice deep in the heart of the centuries-stilled glacier. His breath plumed in the air, a myriad miniature snowflakes to add their glittering layer to the frosty floor.

Reaching his objective – a stalled electric rail car, rimed white over its black and gold where it stood abandoned in a lay-by – the mechanic snapped open the battery cover and shone his torch inside, examining the bank of six large batteries. It was as he had suspected: some inefficient clown of a driver had failed to check and change the batteries. All six were dead as dodos. They wouldn't power a small boy's train set let alone the black and gold four-seater. He would have to get a service car down here and change the batteries. Or he could have the car towed back to the service bay and do it there. Christ! – as if it weren't bad enough just *being* in this God-damned morgue without actually having to *work* here!

His thought was like some demonic invocation, or so it seemed to him. For with a pneumatic hiss and a crackling of ice a cryo-unit in a nearby niche suddenly slid from its bed and stood itself on end, one-third of a ton of metal and dead, frozen contents suspended in thin air inches above the floor of the ice corridor.

'Lord—!' the mechanic gasped out loud, '— forgive me my blasphemy . . .' He fell over backwards, sliding down the bonnet of the abandoned car as the cryo-unit split its sealed seams, the two halves clanging to the floor in a cloud of cryo-vapour and ice crystals. His eyes had rolled up and his senses fled him by the time his head thumped against the floor, so that he missed what happened next. Which, for his sanity's sake, was probably just as well.

For perhaps two seconds the lumpy, black, frozen *contents* of the discarded unit remained in a hovering, standing position, suspended above the floor and issuing hissing cryo-vapours. Then, turning on end once more and speeding head-first down the tunnel, the rigid mummy-shape sought its exit.

Half-way down the tunnel a balcony looked out over a valley nestling high in the mountains, where a cable car descended towards a village of snow-covered houses, smoke from their chimneys spiralling in grey-blue streamers. The balcony's windows were of thick, triple-glazed glass – which shattered explosively as the frozen corpse of Vicki Maler crashed through them, accelerating as it sped upwards and traced a curve westward, disappearing in a moment across the farthest mountain peaks . . .

Once again Willy Koenig was witness to an impossible phenomenon, and once again he felt himself in awe of the fantastic powers his young master now wielded. For who else but Richard Garrison could be responsible for this – this blackened, plummeting, smouldering meteorite which shot out of the sky to stab like a lance, soundlessly *through* the grey dome covering Wyatt's house, leaving no hole behind it to tell of its entry?

Inside, golden-eyed, Garrison/Schroeder brought the smoking corpse to a halt in the centre of the bedroom, standing it upright an inch above the wood-splinter and glass-littered floor. Slowly he lowered the mummy until its feet touched the carpet. And—

'Be as you were before you died,' he commanded, his outstretched hand like some primordial magician's wand.

The mummy-figure coruscated, gave off lancing multi-coloured beams of light, turned incandescent-white for a single second and metamorphosed into Vicki Maler – *as she had been before she died!*

Vicki Maler tiny and ravaged. An emaciated, screaming Vicki Maler. A Vicki in agony. A Vicki full of the living cancer that killed her!

Garrison/Schroeder saw his error at once. 'Come out of her!' he commanded, his finger pointing. She collapsed in a heap on the floor, her limbs writhing, visibly shrinking smaller yet as a leprous grey mass of foaming, spawning cells *issued* from her body. She lay in a pool of heaving, living cancerous tissue. And as her screaming subsided Garrison/Schroeder's golden eyes fell upon the naked, cringing, slow-motion figures of Terri and Wyatt – and the Schroeder part knew what must be done.

Again the pointed finger, and the voice, emotionless now, more Schroeder than Garrison, saying: 'Your vitality, your energy – into her!'

They cringed down, shrank, seemed to grow old in a second – and in that same second Vicki swelled out, firmed, blossomed, grew pink and healthy where she lay amongst the living, lapping diseased slime. And before the Garrison facet could interfere: 'Now suffer as she suffered, as I have suffered, as you made Richard Garrison suffer!' And the finger, trembling a little but resolute, pointing at the cancerous mass. '*Go into them!*'

And the booming, gonging, yawning horror of their slowed down screams as the cancer flowed across the floor like some vast amoeba, splitting into two equal parts and foaming up and around their legs, their thighs and into their slowly writhing, shuddering bodies. And the two of them bloating, filling out, their eyes bulging, their mouths full of froth. And their screams choked off as they rose up, stumbled, fell, floated to the floor and lay there in the deceptively languorous contortions of certain, lingering death.

Then the Garrison facet – his common humanity – took command. 'Die!' he quickly ordered. 'Let it be finished. Be as dust.'

The grey wall went down like a light switched on, letting the sun strike through the windows once more. A summer breeze blew in across broken panes, scattering the dull powders which were all that remained of Terri Garrison and Gareth Wyatt.

Garrison/Schroeder stepped forward, lifted up the swooning, softly moaning Vicki Maler from the floor. 'Know none of this,' he commanded. 'Know only that you are mine. And let your blind eyes know the light. See, Vicki, see!'

She opened eyes golden as his own and gazed at him in confusion. Then, knowing him – knowing, too, the miracle of sight – she fell against his chest. 'Oh, Richard!' she cried. 'I had such a strange dream. But . . . I always knew you would find me again. And I knew that I would see you – really *see* you – someday, somehow . . .' She closed her eyes and snuggled close, seeming half asleep . . .

When Garrison/Schroeder left the house Koenig was waiting for him. The German gaped for a moment at the sight of Vicki Maler . . . of her, her presence, not her nakedness – gaped again at their gleaming golden eyes, but then Garrison/Schroeder caused him to understand. He reeled for a moment under the barrage of telepathically implanted knowledge from the other's supermind, then stood rock steady, a slow smile forming on his face.

'Richard,' he finally, simply said. And, 'Thomas!'

'Suzy?' Garrison/Schroeder questioned.

Koenig's smile faded. He shook his head, though that was not necessary.

Garrison/Schroeder blinked his golden eyes, searched for and found the faithful Dobermann's shattered hulk. 'Suzy,' he said, 'be as you were.' And to himself: *Come, girl, come!*

In a moment she appeared round the corner of the house, barking joyfully, bounding, throwing herself flat at his feet. He stooped and fondled her ears.

He straightened, turned to Vicki. 'Vicki, Willy is the most faithful of men. He is to be rewarded. It will be strange, but – don't be afraid. It is simply – a change.' And to Koenig: 'Are you ready, Willy?' He held out his arms.

They embraced like brothers, Koenig smiling. His clothes fell to the ground at the other's feet. No physical trace of him remained. Vicki gasped and again her man turned to her. 'I told you not to be afraid,' he said. And he made her to understand.

They walked down the drive together towards their destiny. Man and woman, hand in hand, with Suzy taking up a position to the rear. Only once did they pause, when the Koenig facet thought one of his bad thoughts. They paused – for the merest moment – and then walked on.

Garrison/Schroeder/Koenig, and Vicki, and Suzy.

And behind them in an upstairs room of the now empty house, in the room of the machine, Psychomech turned white hot and melted into slag. And the house itself crumbled, falling in upon its own foundations and puddling like lava, or a sandcastle touched by the sea. And in another moment it was as if the house had never stood there at all, and the grass closed over its scar, and the house of Wyatt was gone forever from the world of men.

And nothing was ever quite the same again . . .